OF HEARTS

AND HITMEN

Richard
Carrington

Of Hearts and Hitmen

Published in the United Kingdom by Hardline Books 2018

Copyright © Richard Carrington

www.theguyscomic.com

ISBN 978-1-78808-276-1

e: carrington_richard@hotmail.com

t: richcarty100

For Megan & Emily

1

If I don't get home before eight, I'm dead.

'Course, not as dead as the big, fat gangster stereotype snorting pasta at the corner table of Ginelli's is going to be in just a few minutes. No, I'll be dead in a metaphorical sense because Rachel's invited the Taylors over for dinner at eight and if I call in late again, she'll kill me – metaphorically speaking. The Blobfather here – well, he'll just be dead. I'm going to kill him in a very non-metaphorical way in just about, let's see…four minutes time.

That'll make it about 18:47 for the hit, back to the car for 18:54, twenty minutes to get back home give or take (depending on traffic), a quick shower then changed. I could be dressed and ready by seven thirty, just in time to rescue Rach from burning the dinner.

All I'm waiting for now is the laxatives in the mark's pasta to kick into – ah, there we go. He heads into the back, holding his big, flabby mobster gut in pain. Gives me about a minute and a half to get down off this fire escape and race round to the back alley.

See, this guy's not stupid. Even coming out for dinner, he's got a couple of bodyguards with him. He's gotta know there's a hit out on him so he's brought plenty of muscle with him but bodyguards, although they'll do a lot for money, tend to draw the line at watching their employer take a shit. So by now, the fat man should be all alone in the bathroom with half digested pasta shooting out of his ass like a semi automatic.

Now, killing somebody is all about planning ahead. Which is why earlier today I had my lunch at Ginelli's and took the opportunity to break the lock on the central cubicle window in the men's bathroom. I also bribed one of the waiters to slip laxatives into the fat man's food. Had to give him another hundred for him to smear shit all over the other two cubicles, but it was worth it – *I* certainly wasn't going to do it. The plan is that with two out of three cubicles caked in shit, fat man's going to be doubled up in the middle cubicle, exactly where I want him.

As I make my way down the alleyway at the back of the restaurant, I can already hear him grunting in relief through the open window. I climb onto a crate, quietly open the window and lean through, looking down at the sweat pouring from fat man's balding scalp. He doesn't even hear me as I slip the wire around his neck. See, I could have just put a bullet in his head but the people who're paying me want to send out a clear message and they're the ones footing the bill, so.

It only takes seven seconds, start to finish. The mark shoots up when he feels the wire and he starts to panic and struggle but a strong pull backwards using the wall for leverage and the wire slices through his fat neck like a scalpel through sausage. I'll be halfway back to the car by the time his hired thugs find him bleeding out. And if being found in the men's room of a restaurant with your pants around your ankles, your throat cut and shit running down your legs doesn't send out a pretty clear message, then I don't know what will.

So let's see; the crate I found for free at the back of the alleyway, minus ten dollars for the piano wire, the two hundred I tipped the waiter – I make that $249,790 all told. Not bad for an hour's work. Rachel's birthday's coming up so that'll come in handy. Plus I need to replace those night vision goggles that got wrecked in that firefight last month and I'm getting low on claymores too.

By the time I get home, I've already spent all the money in my head. It's lucky I took this job on really. I wasn't even going to bother what with dinner tonight, but when I found out what the fat man liked to do to little boys – well, let's just say I probably would have taken him out for free. Way I look at it, the world's a little better off tonight.

As I walk up the driveway I can already smell dinner wafting out of the kitchen window. Smells like Carbonara. Pasta - now is that ironic or not? – I can't tell any more after that goddamn Alanis Morissette song.

I head into the kitchen and Rachel's wearing the black dress I got her for Christmas. She looks incredible. There's not many women could make a pan full of pasta and an apron look sexy, but she pulls it off as effortlessly as if she's on a photo shoot. She's still got the remains of this Summer's tan on her arms and legs and I could quite happily phone Janet and Ray to cancel and just take her here on the kitchen floor but I know she's been planning tonight for weeks and I already cancelled this dinner once because of business. Well, somebody's got to put pasta in the pot, right?

I snake my arms around her waist and kiss her neck. She hasn't long been out of the shower. She still smells of that coconut oil she uses in the shower and the perfume she got from Rome.

"Glad to see you made it this time, Joe. How was work?" she purrs.

Oh, garrotted a 320 pound Italian mobster in the bathroom of a restaurant. You know, the usual.

"Yeah, fine," I lie. "The boys in the office just needed me to sign a few papers, nothing major,"

You know, it amazes me that given some of the things I do in my line of work, I never find it easy to lie to her. 'Course I know I've *got* to, but it still leaves me feeling dirty sometimes. Speaking of which.

"I'm just gonna jump in the shower before Janet and Ray get here," I tell her, taking a taste of the Carbonara sauce from the spoon. As usual, too little salt, not enough cream. I'll see if I can rescue it later when she's not looking.

The shower does me good. Always clears the head. I don't add any cold so the water's practically scalding – it sort of helps to get rid of the post-murder tingle on my skin. I'm out, dried, dressed and ready by 19: 24. Six minutes ahead of estimate. Gives me time to help out in the kitchen.

When I get back downstairs, Rach reluctantly agrees to set the table while I finish off dinner. Even though she knows I'm a way better cook than her, she still likes to seem indignant when she passes the baton over to me. Some seasoning, a little more cream, little less heat and it'll be just right.

Rach opens a bottle of wine, the pasta simmers and we're talking away when the doorbell rings. It's exactly eight o clock. I swear, Ray lives his life by his watch even more than I do – I'd bet money they've been outside for five minutes but he made them stay in the car until it was exactly eight.

Janet and Ray Taylor are good people. I've got no problem with either of them as such but I've long since worked out my tolerance level with Ray is about three hours max. He's okay over the duration of a dinner but we went away for the weekend with them two years ago and I came close to slipping a cyanide pill into his beer. Yeah, they're nice people, but they're *Rachel's* friends, you know?

Ray's part owner of The Spires golf course and golf club. Very exclusive, very expensive. Me and him have already long since established that I've got zero interest in golf but Ray doesn't seem to understand or accept that and he just can't help himself from drifting back to the subject every so often. And by every so often, I mean all the fucking time. About my only experience with golf was using a sand wedge to cave in Tony Castle's head that time. Golf's not really a manly game if you ask me what with those thin, fragile clubs. Gimme baseball any day (to watch, as well as use to cave in somebody's head).

Janet's alright. She's actually quite funny after a few glasses of wine. She seems to me like one of those women who lives under her husband's shadow though. I'll bet she's a totally different person when Ray's not around, but she probably can't see that for herself. Not that they're unhappy together or anything, they just seem to me to be sort of *existing* until a baby comes along. You ever met a couple like that, who don't think their life will be complete until they have kids? I mean, I've nothing against kids and I sure as hell want me and Rach to fill a nursery one day but there's just this sort of ticking clock over Janet's head (or should that be ovaries), you know? Still, like I say, nice people.

Rachel does the whole meet, greet, kisses on the cheek thing and takes their coats upstairs. She takes Janet with her to show her the new painting she picked up for the study which leaves me with Ray in the kitchen.

"How's it going, Joe? Been a while," he says.

"Hey, Ray. Beer or wine?"

He takes a glass of wine and I set the clock in my head to see how long before the subject of golf comes up. I carry on stirring the sauce while Ray tells me all about some movie he saw last week.

I can't help but instantly zone out as he's talking and I absent mindedly look at the guy. I notice that Ray's got one of those faces – you know like these guys who look like they *used* to be handsome? They're not any more but their faces sort of still hold onto the memory that they were good looking once.

Still, his clothes don't really help matters. Okay, I accept that the guy's crazy about golf and owns a course and all but that's another thing about the sport. Baseball caps and shirts look cool when ordinary people wear them but golfers have got this twisted fashion thing going on. Ray's wearing this knitted jumper with six colours too many on it and all in diamonds. He looks like a box of crayons threw up on him.

"Really, Joe, you should go see this movie. The CGI is amazing."

"Yeah, I might do that, Ray. I don't go to the movies half as much as I'd like these days what with work and everything," I reply, wondering what CGI is.

"How is the construction business these days?" he asks.

"Booming, Ray. Booming," I smile.

After blowing up that Russian cartel last week, I'm sure there's a joke to be made there somewhere. Rachel and Janet breeze into the kitchen smiling.

"Smells good, Joe," says Janet offering me her cheek. I give her a kiss and smell some kind of lavender bath oil and expensive but not particularly attractive perfume on her skin.

Actually, Janet's not an unattractive woman. She's got a nice smile and a decent little body but she's got the look of a woman who needs to spend way too much time to get herself looking good. She ain't got like a *natural* beauty but she has got the kind of looks that two hundred dollar bottles of moisturiser and the right kinds of clothes can get you. I'll bet that back in her day she had no problem picking guys up but they would have woken up next to a very different woman than the one they went to bed with, you know what I mean?

Ah, it sounds like I've really got it in for Janet and Ray. That's not it at all – like I say; I *do* like them as a couple, I'm just sort of speaking my mind.

Everybody moves through to the dining room and I start serving up dinner. Rachel pours wine for everybody and puts a 'Moods from the Movies' album on the stereo to increase the ambience or something. It hits me that I didn't realise until now just how much I'd actually been looking forward to tonight. It's always good for me to do something regular and normal every once in a while. The conversation doesn't get much heavier than general small talk about work, TV and current affairs. That is until Ray kicks in with a golf story after about seven and a half minutes. That's short, even for him.

Rachel slips me a sly wink and a grin – she knows exactly how I feel about Ray's scintillating golf stories.

"So this guy hasn't paid his membership fees, right?" says Ray animatedly. "And I'm talking to him about how his membership has run out …."

I zone out again.

I can see Ray's mouth moving but my ears refuse to let his stupid fucking non-story in. I mean, Jesus, he must know from everyone's face that nobody cares. Even Janet looks bored to tears as she tips mouthfuls of wine down her neck. What it must be like to live with this guy, I can't imagine. To constantly bore people at dinner with stories of *your* hobby and *your* work is really kinda selfish, I think. Like, you don't see me telling stories of strangling gangsters or punching a guy's nose through his brain. For obvious reasons though, I guess.

Ray sounds like he's wrapping his story up now. Thank God.

"...had to use his sand wedge instead," he roars.

An awkward stillness settles in. Janet's smiling politely in support of her husband but there's a weary and apologetic look in her already half drunk eyes. I can feel Rachel looking at me, hoping to catch my eye and hint to just let it go. I feel like I need to say something to him though. Like I need to tell him – even *warn* him – that the next time he's got a golf story to tell, try and put himself in his audience's shoes first to see if a) the story is actually amusing and worth listening to and b) whether or not anybody will actually *give* a shit.

It's only then that I catch Rachel's eye and she can tell what I'm thinking. Her expression speaks a thousand words, the foremost of which are 'If you say anything to Ray about his crappy story, you can forget about sex for at *least* a month.' In the interests of the evening's success and my sex life, I let it drop and just give Ray a polite smile and a half-hearted "Good story, man."

But see, as boring and as stupid as Ray's stories are – and they *are* boring and stupid – I suppose that's one of the reasons I quite like seeing him and Janet. If you looked, you couldn't find any more normal people than these two. In fact, they're *so* normal they're out and out average. They're the kinds of people that join Gyms, walk dogs and almost single handedly keep the organic fruit industry alive.

And okay, so Ray's obsessed with golf, dresses like a kids T.V. presenter on crack and couldn't tell a decent story if I put a gun to his head (which, if I'm being honest, I have toyed with the notion before now). And so what if Janet lives her life in his shadow and is about two and a half steps away from being a full blown alcoholic? They're normal and having them over for dinner and, yeah, even listening to Ray's stupid non-stories, makes me feel like I'm part of the normal world too.

I don't mean to sound all daytime soap melodramatic because I'm quite secure with what I do. Always have been. But I can't escape the fact that what I do'll never be considered normal. So hanging out with the Taylors helps immerse me in this world of normality and I quite like it.

Take today for example - Rachel's been at work all day, Janet's probably been sipping Gin for most of the afternoon and Ray had his big adventure at the golf club. And what did *I* do? Had an appointment with my arms dealer in the morning, spent the afternoon paying off a waiter to smear crap on some walls and then garrotted an Italian mobster while he was taking a shit. Now that's hardly normal in any book.

I mean, I think being a professional hitman is just about the best job in the world – the hours are great, the money's fantastic and there's all sorts of fringe benefits. And God knows I could never spend my days like Ray but it's nice to mix with normal people sometimes instead of the killers and trash I usually meet at work.

I know I've got my own construction business, but that's only ever been a smoke screen (still, business *is* up these days – it's getting so I don't know which one's the better earner). But no, my heart's always been in the hitman trade. At the end of the day, saying you're a hitman is a whole hell of a lot cooler than saying you work in construction. And I am a hitman, too – I can't stand the term 'assassin'. It's got the word ass in it. Twice.

So yeah, I think life's pretty good (as long as you ignore the fact that I'm lying to my wife every single day of our lives together by keeping this a secret from her), and who wants to be normal anyway, just another mindless drone with an asshole for a boss? Not me. I'm damn good at what I do – I'm at the top of my field, and I've got that all important thing - job satisfaction. There's not many people lucky enough to have that in their careers.

There's only two problems people in my line of work have. The first one is the fact that being paid to kill people is obviously somewhat illegal, so there's the whole 'being caught by the cops' thing to worry about. The only other thing is a conscience. Society teaches us that killing is wrong but I always seem to have had this switch in my head where it doesn't bother me. Never has so far. I'm not a psychopath or even a sociopath - I just don't happen to feel an ounce of guilt over the people I kill. And let's face it, nobody gets a contract put out on their life if they're a good guy, you know what I mean?

So, I do what I do. To those ninety nine percent of people who think being paid to kill is wrong, I say *'So fucking what? Keep your opinions to yourself or you're next.'* 'Cause I know for a fact that I keep the streets cleaner than a hundred cops do and I take care of me and Rachel at the same time.

So I keep a huge secret from my wife?

So I'll never really be normal?

So what? I'm rich, married to a beautiful woman and happy in my work, and you know what? I can live with that.

2

So the night went pretty well over all. That was the one and only time Ray mentioned golf, Janet had a little too much to drink and was laughing too hard at things that weren't that funny and Rachel got to play hostess all evening. A good night was had by all.

The Taylors have just left and I'm watching some late night TV before bed. I always need to find something to fill fifteen minutes at the end of the night because Rach takes that long to get ready. Me, I just clean my teeth, have a quick wash and I'm done. She, on the other hand, needs to go through the military procedure of removing the makeup she's spent two hours that morning applying. Ah, the mysteries of woman.

By the time I come up the stairs, she's out of the bathroom and is brushing her hair in front of the bedroom mirror. The light above the mirror shines through her night dress, revealing all her curves and I'm suddenly real glad that I didn't push Ray about his stupid story. Lying in bed, I watch her as we talk. I never let anything on and we just talk naturally, but times like this - looking at her like this - my mouth's talking but my heart's exploding with love for this smart, beautiful woman I get to call my wife.

"I'm so glad we finally managed to get tonight sorted out," she says, running the brush through her hair.

Her hair used to be a real deep brown but lately she's had these light streaks put in it and now it's a sort of rich, golden brown. Her hair's always been straight but she likes to mess with it sometimes – you know, she kinks it and tries to curl it and what not – but I like it like it is; poker straight, falling just over her shoulders. "I had a really good time. Janet and Ray are so nice, aren't they, Joe?"

"Yeah. Yeah, they are. Janet's a real firecracker when she's had a few drinks."

"I know, she's always been like that. After about her sixth glass, she really starts to loosen up," Rach smiles.

Her hair's done and she ties it up before pulling back her side of the sheets and jumping in. She snuggles up to me, lays her head on my chest and I can smell the traces of her perfume mixed with the vaguely clinical smell of her make up remover.

"By the way, Joe, thanks for not saying anything to Ray. I know how you hate his golf stories."

"Honey, between you and me, I've long since learned to zone out when Ray launches into one of his golf epics. I couldn't even tell you what this one was about, I wasn't listening." I can feel her facial muscles crease into a smile on my chest.

"I know. All the same, thanks for being diplomatic."

Rachel's hand begins to wander south and I pull her close in the darkness and when it's like this, when I want to hold her so tight I take her into me, then the lie doesn't seem that bad.

Morning after, I need to go and see Danny.

Danny's my best friend, has been ever since we were kids. We met when he moved onto our block when we were eight. He didn't know anybody then and he's always had to wear glasses so naturally, the neighbourhood kids started picking on him – they were on at him from day one, you know?

So about two weeks after they move in, Danny's sitting on his own in Station Avenue, this little park we used to hang out in when we were kids. So he's sitting there, reading a comic book, minding his own business, when Cliffie Malloy and his gang spot him. Cliffie goes over, starts baiting him for a while and when Danny doesn't bite, he gets angry, snatches his comic book off him and rips it in two. This eventually sets Danny off and he jumps up and tries to attack Cliffie. Only trouble is, Danny's only eight and Cliffie and his gang must have been about fourteen at the time. Plus Danny's always been real small, a bit weedy you know?

Anyway, Cliffie and his crew start really pounding on Danny. He's huddled on the floor, crying, and they're laughing and kicking him. Me and my friends are on the other side of the park playing baseball when we see this. I was only eight too but I couldn't help myself from walking over. All my friends were yelling at me not to get involved but I never could stand a bully. I remember I wasn't sure exactly what I was going to do because these guys were nearly twice as old and twice as big as me but I just knew that I'd got to do something.

Up until that point in my life, the only other violent act I'd committed was pushing my old man down the stairs of our house when he was drunk but something flipped inside me then. I took the baseball bat, walked over to Cliffie and his friends and beat the ever loving shit out of all four of them. I can still remember each and every swing of that bat and I can still remember the sounds they made as it broke their teeth and bones. I didn't feel an ounce of guilt or horror over what I'd done either. I just remember feeling calm and a sense of – not quite pride, just a feeling that they deserved it so they got what was coming to them.

Long story short, Cliffie and his gang never went near Danny again. In fact, I remember they tried to get *me* back about a week later but I kicked the shit out of them again – if I remember right, I left Cliffie deaf in his left ear after that one. So anyway, I walked Danny home and his face was all cut and bleeding. His parents open the door and start crying when they see him and they drag both of us in. I didn't want to go in, just drop the guy off, but they pulled me in and I told them what had happened.

Once they cleaned Danny's face up, he told his folks how I'd saved him and fought off the guys who'd been beating him. Mary and Peter – that's Danny's folks – they start fussing over me and thanking me and they made me stay for dinner. I'm only eight, what can I do?

I remember it clearly. We had these smoked ham sandwiches and after dinner, Danny took me up to his room and he had it all. All the coolest toys, all the best comic books – everything. It's not like he was rich or spoilt, it was just that I didn't have any of that stuff when I was a kid 'cause of how things were in my house. And Danny had real good taste too. All his comic books were the ones I used to read from the shelf in the drugstore.

I'm rambling here, I know. Bottom line is, we spent all that afternoon at Danny's house reading his comic books and playing with his toys. I brought Danny in to be a part of our gang around the neighbourhood and we've been best buds ever since.

You know, now that I look back on that day, that's probably what set me down the road to being a hitman. I remember all the local kids wanted to treat me like a hero for what I'd done but I never wanted the attention. I always remember though, I used to think how good it felt to really do a number on Cliffie and his gang, teach them a lesson. I've always liked seeing people pay for the shitty things they do to other people, but I've gotta be honest – I've always really liked the violence too.

Danny's what you might call my silent partner now. He's just about the cleverest guy I've ever known and where I'm sort of the brawn of the operation, Danny's definitely the brains. He runs intelligence on all my hits and he loves it. (See, as far as *we're* concerned, we're just a couple of grown ups who get paid to stop adult versions of Cliffie Malloy.) Danny's a computer genius. He knows everything there is to know about all that kind of stuff. I mean, I can plug in a microwave and I can send a text and what not, but he can do all kinds of amazing stuff. You know all this computer hacking and virtual reality, all that stuff? Danny knows it all like the back of his hand. There's not much he couldn't do given a laptop and enough time.

He's also the one that deals with all our finances, which is why I'm going over to see him this morning. Actually, Danny does pretty much everything in the business *except* the actual killing side of things. The only time I ever saw Danny hurt another person was when he smashed a bottle over this guy who was sneaking up behind me in a club – and even then, he felt terrible about it for about a month.

Still, my side of things is the dangerous part, which is why we've always split things 75 / 25 but with all the other pies he's got his fingers in, he rakes in a whole lot more than I do at the end of every month without ever leaving his chair.

Now one of the advantages of owning your own construction company is that you can build whatever you want, wherever you want.

So about six or seven years ago, me and Danny put our money into building what we like to call The Cave – it's like all those secret super hero headquarters we used to read about in the comic books when we were kids. I had my company build it and then we went about fitting it out with all sorts of cool rooms and gadgets and stuff. The whole thing cost a king's ransom but it's been worth it. Danny's got a room full of computers and junk and I swear he could probably set off a nuke from that room if he wanted to.

Me, I've built a sound proof firing range, an armoury and a gym. It's basically where we run the business from and a place where we can go to hang out. There's only the two of us ever go there and he's made sure that nobody has any records of the building even existing. He's also wired it so we don't pay any bills on electric or gas, which is just as well because all his computers and stuff could probably light up Vegas. Any people see the building, it just looks like an old, disused building from the front so nobody ever bothers us.

The entrance masquerades as an abandoned old warehouse building but there's a hidden panel on the back wall with a thumb print I.D. pad behind it. The thing scans my print and the whole back wall slides back to reveal the real front door. Once I add the code, the two foot thick steel door pushes open and I'm into the main corridor.

We've made it everything a couple of thirty year old eight year olds could ever want. There's posters from all our favourite movies on the walls and there's original versions of classic arcade games everywhere. Fourth door on the left leads to the room Danny lovingly calls The Nest. Yeah, I know- The Nest, The Cave. Just blame it on way too many super hero stories when we were growing up.

The Nest is this huge room filled to bursting with Danny's computers and machines. In the middle of the room is his main computer and a wheely chair and he likes to zip across to different terminals and different machines when he's working. On the far wall is this huge, twenty foot screen that displays everything he's working on at the time. Other than that, I don't really know where to start even describing all the junk in there. To me, it's all keyboards, switches and lights but when Danny's in there, he plays it all like a master conductor with some kind of electrical orchestra.

"Hey, Dan, what you up to?" I ask.

"Joe. Jesus, I'm glad you're here. You mustn't have heard yet." Danny looks round at me and he seems agitated – his eyes are wide and his body language is all wiry, screaming that something bad's happened.

"I've come straight here from home. Haven't heard what yet?"

Danny pushes himself away from the desk he's at and wheels his chair up to the main console. He hits a few keys and the great big main screen flickers on, shedding a blue light over everything.

"This," Danny says simply.

He pushes a button and an image appears on the screen. An image that I can feel burn itself into my long term memory. It's a picture of The Priest, but he's been butchered so badly it's only a portion of his face and his dog collar that tells me it's him.

The Priest is – *was* – a fellow hitman. He wasn't a bad sort either. In fact, we did a few jobs together some years ago. As hitmen go, he was actually a pretty stand up guy, just that he was all flipped out and thought he was a messenger from God or something. Used to wear a dog collar and leave a cross on all his hits. A bit of a fruitloop but the guy was well meaning, you know – well, for a hired killer at least. Seeing him now, like this, with the sheer white of half his skull showing and his upper body more out than in, I've gotta admit that it rattles even me.

See, here's the thing. Although I've spent over a decade killing people, there's a certain neatness to it. I mean, the aftermath isn't neat, but there's a sort of cleanness to it. Bullet to the head. Garrotte. Drowning. Thrown off a building. Yeah, it leaves a mess but these are all fairly quick ways of killing. If you want someone dead, you can do it quick and you can do it clean.

What I'm looking at here on the screen is an exercise in torture. This is someone taking their time and enjoying it. You don't turn somebody inside out and peel off half a face unless you want to make a point.

"Who did this?" I ask. "Where'd the picture come from?"

"They're FBI pictures. I was doing a routine scan of the bureau files when I came across this. They don't know who did yet it but there's more than this – there was something else they found on the scene. Hold on a sec while I punch it up."

The picture changes and there's a photo of a wall with writing on it in huge, dripping red letters. It doesn't take a genius to figure out it's not paint. The words though, they don't make any sense.

'Those who profit from the taking of life, beware - for the taking of life is left to The Prophet.'

"Okay, I give up," I concede. "What the hell is that supposed to mean?"

"No idea," Danny says. "But think about it. Do you suppose whoever did this is saying that he's going after hitmen – you know, people like us who profit from taking life?"

"I dunno, man, that seems like a bit of a stretch. Why would you turn The Priest into a human inkwell just to send a message like that? You ask me, priests and prophets and what not – it's all to do with some kind of religious shit. Maybe The Priest pissed off the catholic church or something. Those guys are *really* vicious."

"I don't think we should be making jokes about this, Joe. I think we should just watch our backs for a while."

"Relax, Dan. Do you worry like this *every* time the FBI finds a body?"

"Look, I just can't help but feel there's something more to this, you know?" he says.

"Ah, stop being such a puss and come and shoot some pool."

We head down to the games room and before I've even racked the balls, there's a nagging voice in the back of my brain that says maybe he's right.

<u>3</u>

After I've left The Cave, I head on over to The Lodge to pick up my money from last night's hit. I already owe Danny ten grand and I'll need the rest to top up my supplies. I just checked the armoury at The Cave and I'm pretty low on just about everything. I'm completely out of magazines for the berettas and I need to restock the claymores and grenades.

It's a sunny day and the ride out to Westchester is beautiful. I've got the top down on the car and some classic tunes on the radio. Life is good.

One of the people who helped get me into this job all those years ago is my agent, Stanley. He used to be a hitman himself – a pretty good one by all accounts – but he got careless on a job in the early eighties. The Russians got a hold of him before he could take down his mark. They left him alive, but just barely.

He's okay to look at in the face but trust me, you wouldn't want to see him with his shirt off. He's got a limp in his left leg which has never healed properly and he can't shoot a gun anymore – they melted all the fingers together on his shooting hand. Say what you like about the Russians but they've earned their rep as some seriously cold blooded bastards.

These days, Stanley's happy working the other side of the hitman counter. He acts as an agent - for me, primarily. He's got a few other guys on his books but I'm his main client. Although he's not out in the field anymore, in my opinion Stanley's still got the experience, the know-how and the contacts to make him the best agent there is.

See, you'd be amazed at how business-like contract killing actually is. There's no real shadowy world behind it – everything's pretty much out in the open. Truthfully, about 80 percent of our business is bad guys looking to whack other bad guys. Give or take the odd domestic contract, it's mostly gangs; the Italians, the Irish, the Russians, all trying to take each other out. They need middle men to do the job so they can avoid going to war over revenge killings and that's where us hitmen come in. Everything here at The Lodge is confidential – you can contact an agent, put out a contract on somebody and just pay them when it's done. Hell, we even take credit cards. The whole process is about as above board as it gets.

The Lodge is this big country house in the middle of Westchester. Real exclusive, real nice. It passes itself off as a men's country club but in reality, it's the working offices for us hitmen. It's pretty near holy ground actually. See, in this line of work, we all accept the dangers and the risks but at The Lodge there's no in-fighting, there's no poaching of contracts, there's no talk of lives outside the job. It's an enclosed environment where we can just work and hang out and trust me – nobody breaks the rules of The Lodge.

A lot of the other hitmen here, I quite like. Most of them think like I do – they've no love for these mob guys and are happy to take money from one to off the other, thinking they're doing society a service. Then again, there's some there who are just plain psychos. They *like* the whole killing side of things and they're dangerous guys but by and large, it's a good place to hang out - there's a bar, a pool room, even tennis courts – it's just a shame Danny never comes down here any more. He used to, but some of the guys here are a little hard core and he didn't fit in too well. In fact, he got himself into some scrapes a couple of times which has scared him off but the place is like a second home to me. Or third, if you count The Cave.

I park up and walk round to the main entrance. Larry and Pike are working the door. Now these are two guys even *I* might think twice about crossing. They look like a brick wall and a rhino got together and had kids.

"Morning, Joe. You looking for Stanley?" Pike grunts.

"Yeah, he about?"

Larry frisks me and relieves me of my gun and Pike directs me to the bar. That's another rule here – no weapons on the grounds.

I walk down towards Harvey's. That's the name of the bar here, named after Lee Harvey Oswald. Nice touch, huh?

I take the time to touch the wall on the way down. That's one of the traditions here; every one of us hitmen who's ever fallen in the field gets a small gold plaque here on the wall so he's remembered and we all just touch our hand to the wall as we pass as a sign of remembrance. It also acts as one hell of a reminder that most of us could end up on that wall ourselves if we're not careful.

As I walk in, I can tell the mood in Harvey's is quite subdued compared to how it normally is. There's a few guys playing cards, some are shooting pool and there's a baseball game on the big screen but there seems to be an air of depression about the place. I spot Stanley sitting at the bar watching the game and I sneak up behind him and jab a finger into his ribs.

"Goddamit, Joe!" he roars as he jumps out of his seat. "You're just about the only one in here who can sneak up on me like that."

"Just keeping you on your toes, Stanley. You got my money from that job on the Italian last night?"

"Yeah, yeah," he mutters. He's not playing today and I can tell by the way his bushy white eyebrows are practically meeting in the middle that he's down about something. "You want it in cash or you want me to wire it to you?"

"Cash. I've got to go see Wild Bill in a minute. Jesus, what's wrong around here? Why's everyone so down?"

Stanley's eyebrows actually meet now.

"Haven't you heard?" he mutters. "Somebody killed The Priest a couple of nights ago. FBI have got pictures – they're not pretty."

So that's it. Christ, first Danny gets all rattled by this, now Stanley.

"Yeah, I already saw them. I get that they were pretty brutal and The Priest was a good guy and all but it's nothing new that one of us gets whacked. So why's everyone so down about this?"

Stanley goes into depth about the rumours that have been flying around The Lodge. Seems by now, everybody's seen the pictures of The Priest (the FBI *really* isn't as secure an operation as you'd think) and there's rumours that this Prophet character is going to start bumping hitmen off. I can hardly believe my ears.

"For Christ's sake, Stanley. A guy gets killed and some fruitcake leaves a message that could mean *anything* and the hardened killers around this place start shitting in their pants? Man, it almost makes me embarrassed to call myself a hitman. And let's face it, The Priest was a good guy but he wasn't exactly a *tough* guy, you know – a couple of teenagers with bats could have taken him down."

"All the same, Joe, it's got people 'round here talking. Some people think it was actually one of the guys on the books here – looking to thin the field of opposition a little, see? I'd keep my eyes open if I were you, 'cause I know everyone else is doing the same."

Stanley pays me my quarter mil in cash and I fill him in on last night's job. It was just about the quickest and easiest hit I've had in ages. Nice and simple. All the same, the employers were happy with the job – being found dead on the toilet with his little Italian meatballs out on show has effectively crushed that fat guy's image on the street. In fact, they were so happy with my work that they sent an extra twenty grand as a bonus. That's Rachel's birthday all fixed up then. Plus it means I can spend a little extra at Wild Bill's.

Bill's the main arms dealer here and he works out of the poolhouse on the grounds. He's as gentle a guy as you could ever met but he'll do absolutely *anything* for a bet. I mean, if he thinks you don't believe he'll do something – doesn't matter how crazy it is, whether it's eating bugs or playing Russian roulette – he'll do it, just to prove you wrong. Most of the time he's placid but just don't dare him to do something is all. He also happens to have the single most extensive knowledge of weaponry of anyone I've ever met. From flick knives to satellite guided rockets and everything in between, Bill knows all about it. He stocks most guns and explosives in the huge basement here at the poolhouse but I reckon he could probably lay his hands on an atom bomb if you gave him enough notice.

As I enter the poolhouse, he's just wrapping up some business with another hitman I recognize but can't quite put my finger on his name. DeLane, DeLaney…something like that. I've seen him around The Lodge and I know he's got a rep but I don't think I've ever spoken to the guy. When he sees me come in, he hurriedly hands Wild Bill what looks like about twenty grand in cash and asks him to call him when it arrives, whatever *it* is.

As he leaves, he walks past me and shoots me a filthy look that sends my blood burning. Like he's wondering if *I* killed The Priest or something. Rep or no, I feel like following him out and punching his throat out through the back of his fucking neck, but rules are rules.

Wild Bill smiles when he sees me and calls me over, slapping me on the back.

"How's it going, Joe? What're you after today, huh? We've got a special on army surplus grenades. Two for the price of one. Or how about some screamer bullets? A hundred dollars for two clips."

I top up my ammo for the berettas, the claymores, take him up on a case of the grenades and order a couple of blocks of semtex. Once business is concluded, I tap Bill for a little information because if anyone knows what's happening around here it's him. Every guy here comes to Bill for their ordnance and he likes to talk so there's not much gets past him.

"All's I know, Joe, is that those pictures of The Priest have shaken a few people up, you know? That message about '*Beware The Prophet*' is getting people thinking. People are already starting to get suspicious around here 'cause most folk think it's one of our own who's done it. Kinda makes sense too when you think about it."

Jesus, now Bill too. I'm getting a little sick of this stuff already – hardened killers jumping at shadows just because one of us got nailed. I'm sorry about The Priest too but as far as I can see, the guy got sloppy and paid for it, simple as that. All this stuff with the message on the wall, I don't pay it any mind at all.

It's like I told Danny - people like The Priest tend to get mixed up in way too much weird shit and it looks like he's paid for it. Yeah, it's a tragedy and all but it sort of comes with the job. You've only got to look at all the plaques up on the wall back there to see that. It's no reason for us all to start panicking for Christ's sake.

All of a sudden, I'm sick of just being around here. I just want to get away from all these guys and all this Prophet shit. I say goodbye to Bill and make my way back to The Lodge.

Crossing the grounds, I phone in a reservation for dinner tonight at Room 15, Rachel's favourite restaurant. Personally, I find the place a little too snotty but Rach likes it and I could do with a night out, away from thinking about work. I'll surprise her with the news when she gets in.

Before I go, I take the time to drop by Harvey's. Usually I'd play a few hands or have a drink but I just say goodbye to Stanley and a few of the other guys before I leave.

This whole thing has escalated way out of hand already and I'm in a lousy mood. Danny's all in a spin, everyone here's as nervy as hell – even Stanley's spooked. Almost makes you embarrassed to call yourself a rough, tough killer.

On the way back out, I pass Pike in the hallway. He's busy screwing The Priest's shiny new plaque onto the wall.

They don't waste any time around here.

4

Rachel's wearing a black and white, all in one dress that shows just enough leg and she's got her hair wrapped up in a really intricate series of twists and curls that's taken her at least the last two hours to perfect. Me, I've put on a black suit, white shirt and a tie.

We're all dressed up and in the back of a cab on the way to Room 15. It's not my favourite place in the world to eat but they do cook a mean steak. They marinate it in these spices and what not for about a week and they cook it just right. It costs a fortune of course but it's about the best thing on their menu. Rach, on the other hand, likes to go all out whenever we eat here. She orders things I've never heard of before and her eyes light up when it arrives. She keeps trying to get me to try the stuff but I refuse to eat food I can't even pronounce.

After the day I've had, I'm just really glad to be away from things for the night. I mean, most days I love my work and The Lodge is usually a great place to hang out but today has been just a little too tense. It's good to kick back and spend some time with Rach.

The cab drops us outside the restaurant and I tip the driver. Rachel slips her arm through mine and we walk in. The guy at the door takes our jackets and our names and directs us to our table. It's a little too close to the kitchens for my liking but I only phoned to book it a few hours ago, so what the hell.

Room 15's full of all the rich people tonight and I'll bet from looking around that I'm one of the few men in here tonight with his wife rather than his mistress. It's all overpriced drinks and small food in the middle of big plates. There's a guy playing piano in the corner which is a nice touch but I think it's written into the waiters' contracts somewhere that they have to look down their noses at all the customers.

Rach orders a white wine and I order a single malt. She told me on the way over I wasn't to have a beer because this place is apparently too classy to drink beer in, which is utter bullshit because they serve beer at the bar so they must expect people to drink it. I think about pointing this unbelievably salient point out to my lovely wife but somehow I don't think she'd appreciate it and I don't want to sour the night so I let it slide.

The waiter comes over with our drinks and asks if we're ready to order. I order my steak and Rach delights in ordering a selection of small dishes, like lots of little starters instead of a main meal. That's not a bad idea actually. Means you get to have lots of different meals instead of just the one but I'm still sticking with my steak. I can already tell that when the food arrives, she'll spend more time trying to get me to try it than she will actually eating it herself.

"So how was work today, honey?" I ask.

"Oh, you know, Helen's acting up, same as usual," she replies with a sigh.

Man, that Helen really annoys me. Here we are at dinner, and I can tell she's done something to upset Rach today and it's sticking with her. (That's another good thing about being a hitman – no bosses.) Rach takes a drink of her wine before going on.

"I mean, I'm just sitting at my desk today, right? On Monday, Helen gave me this really big job to do, and it's taking up *all* my time. And you know me, Joe, I'm not saying to show off but this job would have taken any of the other girls in the office at least twice as long. So I'm working hard at it and I'm doing okay, I'm getting through it alright but it just means I haven't got time for anything else. But today, Mr Harris was up visiting the office."

"That's one of the company directors, right?" I ask.

"Yeah, he was made a director about a year and a half ago and he's really full of himself now. He likes to do spot checks without warning, to keep an eye on us."

"I bet he's the type of guy who just loves to find faults in people too. He like to look down his nose at people like all the other directors?" I ask, taking a sip of my whisky.

"That goes without saying," Rach replies. "They all look down their noses at us but the whole company would fall down around their ears without us doing most of the work for them while they sit around on their fat asses or spend the whole day playing golf."

"Hey, next time the guy comes to the office, just picture him in some of Ray's fucking goofy golfing outfits. That'll take the edge off," I smile.

Rach laughs in spite of herself.

"Somehow, I can't see Mr Harris in pringle and chinos. So anyway, this morning, just about half an hour before he gets here, I finish this job and hand it to Helen. She's all gushing about how quick I work and the quality of what I've produced. It's all *'Good work, Rachel'* and pats on the back."

"Let me guess," I interrupt. "Helen goes and gives this Mr Harris guy the work and passes it off as her own, right?"

"Right!" Rach explodes. "She's such a back stabbing, brown nosing bitch."

Nice alliteration, hon. Rachel's shoulders are slumped now – this has really gotten to her. If I didn't have a thing about hurting women, I'd go round to Helen's house and maybe pop a couple of hollow points in her legs. Wonder if she's married – maybe I could shoot her husband instead.

"And that's not all," she goes on. "Not only does Mr Harris tell the whole office what a good job Helen's doing, but he tells me to cover her work for the day so she can go and present all *my* work to the other partners. I swear, I haven't stopped all day. I didn't know whether to slap her or push the bitch out of the window."

For about ten grand, you could get both.

But I hate seeing anybody upset Rach like this and especially when it's an injustice. I can't stand to see people get away with murder – unless it's me of course. Someone needs to teach Helen a lesson. You can say what you like about what *I* do for a living, but if you ask me, people like *that* are the real villains.

Dinner arrives and Rach cheers up. I was right, and she tries to feed me some kind of meatballs in a green and brown sauce and a plate of some sort of shelled sea creature – I don't know what the hell is it so there's no way it's going in my mouth.

But times like this, listening to her talk about life in the office and her work, I wish I could talk to her about my own day without lying. I wish we could just talk about *my* job over dinner but what would I say?

'Hi Joe, how was your day?'

'Terrible. Everyone thinks there's some kind of killer hunting us so the mood in the office is low. Other than that, I just bought some magazines from Wild Bill.'

'Oh what, like GQ?'

'Um, not quite babe.'

I don't think so.

It's not all bad. I know I've got people like Danny and Stanley I can talk to, but it's not the same. See, one of the things I love most about Rachel is that she's good with people. I mean, she *knows* people. She can read a situation and figure out what the best thing to do is in seconds. It's like a sixth sense or something. Before I met Rach, I wasn't an asshole or anything but I never gave a spare thought to other people, but now she gets me thinking about how my actions affect other people and how I can treat people better by putting myself in their shoes. I don't know whether it's a woman thing or just a Rachel thing or what, but I love her for it. She can meet a person for the first time and within two minutes, she can tell a hundred percent whether that person is either genuine or a genuine asshole. Like I say, she just knows people.

So I'd love to be able to hear what she has to say about my friends and my work but all she knows about is the construction business. She's met a few of the guys from the construction office and she really likes them and she always wonders why we don't see them and their wives more often. But how do I tell her that I only own the business because it acts as a smokescreen for what I really do?

The thing about the business is that it just tends to take care of itself. I picked construction because it would give the best profits and if I'm going to own a business as a front, it might as well make some money as well. But it's low maintenance. I pay the foreman, Gerry, to run things and I can have as much or as little input as I want. He gives me monthly profit figures and that's about it. I couldn't tell you the names of five guys who work for me down there. Still, it covers me for the real business and by the time Danny's done laundering the accounts, nobody's any the wiser – not the IRS, not the government and certainly not Rachel.

The steak's really good tonight and I'm actually glad I booked in here and not just because it's Rach's favourite place. I should really ask what it is they marinate it in but sometimes, you're better off with the mystery of the dish, you know?

Another good dish they do here is the summer fruit basket. It's like this little sort of thin wafer basket, summer fruits obviously, a sauce and some vanilla essence ice cream, topped with some pointless spun sugar cage which only gets left by the side of the plate. It tastes amazing. Rach'll moan and warn me about the calories when I order it but that's only because she'll be jealous as hell sitting opposite me, watching me shovel it in. She'll order the cheese board, same as usual.

The waiter comes over and clears the plates and takes our order for dessert. I'm right about Rachel's choice. Sometimes I think the only reason she likes this place so much is because of that cheese board. See, they make a big fuss about the presentation of what's essentially a piece of wood with cheese on it. But here, it's this layered tower of boards like a wedding cake. Damn thing takes up half the table and it's covered in these tiny triangles and lumps of these rich cheeses that you just know you're not gonna find in the supermarket, you know? Then these tiny little biscuits and wafers and what not. Still, she likes it, so live and let live, right? I'm just happy with my little fruit basket (once I've taken off that damn sugar cage).

"Mm. Just try this blue one here, Joe," Rach moans in ecstasy. She tries to push this blue veined cheese my way. "It's to die for."

"Honey, no offence, but that cheese looks like my Grandma's leg so you'll forgive me if I don't. I'm just gonna stick with my little fruit basket here."

She smiles and pops the blue cheese into her mouth with another semi orgasmic sound. And now, it's time for the old McLean subtlety.

"So, uh, it's your birthday in a few weeks then?"

"And you're wondering what to get me, right?" Damn her feminine intuition. She sees straight through my cunningly deceptive ruse. I might as well go straight in for the kill.

"Well, if you want to *tell* me what you'd like, I mean it would save me from getting you something you don't really want, like last year."

Smooth, Joe. She'll never see through that one.

"Relax, you silver tongued devil. I was going to mention something anyway." She reaches across the table and holds my hand, which instantly tells me it's going to cost.

"I was wondering, you know, if it's not too expensive, if I could have…"

A pause and the head goes down and she looks up at me through her lashes. She's good. She's very good. "…a business loan."

Okay, a diamond ring the size of a house brick or a small Hawaiian island I was expecting, but this is something else entirely. Before I can even start to process this, she starts up, talking a mile a minute.

"Look, Joe, you know how unhappy I am at the office. I work my guts out day after day there and all I get for my trouble is a knife in the back. I'm just sick of it and the thought of working there even one more week is just too much. I know I don't *need* to work and you've told me I don't have to if I don't want to but I'd go crazy being around the house all day and I've always worked – I *like* to work. It's just, I'm doing work I can't stand."

She's going a bit too fast here. She's barely stopping for breath and she's excitedly animated now. Let's cut to the chase here.

"Hon, I know you're having a bad time at work at the moment, but what do you mean you want a business loan for your birthday? What, you want to start up your own company or something?"

"That's *exactly* what I want. I've never even thought about it before. I've just always been content working for other people, you know? But lately, I've been really thinking – I'd love to own and run my own bookstore."

"A bookstore?! Babe, just because you like to read books, doesn't mean you're ready to open up a store. I mean, I love burgers but you don't see me opening up a fast food joint."

She smiles but I can see by her face that she's serious about this.

"I know, but I've been thinking about this for months. I've even written up a business plan that I wanted to show you. I've thought it all through and I really think it could work. All I'd need are the premises and the opening capital."

"And that's where I come in, right? Jesus, Rach, I don't know."

That's a lie. As soon as she asked me, I knew I was going to cave. How the hell do you say no to the woman who means the world to you? Still, I think I'll just string her along a little.

"Joe, I know what I'm asking is a lot. I don't even know if we can make it happen. I know we're doing okay financially but something like this – I realise it's a hell of a lot."

Got her. She's worried because I haven't immediately said yes so she's convinced herself it's going to be a no. I could drag this on for days but I'd better put her out of her misery.

"It is a hell of a lot Rach, you're right. See, I *was* going to turn that building into apartments but, well - "

It takes a couple of seconds but then it sinks in. She raises her head to look at me, the realisation dawning in her wide, brown eyes.

"You mean - ?"

"Yep. I've just bought a disused building uptown. I *was* going to turn it into apartments but it'd be perfect for a new business like, oh I don't know, say a bookstore. Reckon we could even have it ready in time for your birthday too. All you'd need is a shitload of books."

She jumps out of her chair and flings her arms around me, tears streaming down her face. She nearly knocks her cheese board tower over to get to me and all the people in the restaurant start clapping – they must think we've just got engaged or something. Rach buries her head in my shoulder.

"Oh my God, thank you so much! I love you so much, Joe!"

"I love you too, baby."

And standing there, holding her crying tears of joy in my arms near the kitchens of Room 15, I genuinely don't think I've loved her more.

<u>5</u>

I mean, a *bookstore*. I never saw that coming. But why not? Rach can make anything a success if she puts her mind to it and she *is* wasted in her job. Besides, I don't think I've seen her this happy in a long time – she was practically glowing when she left for work. I'd love to see Helen's face when she hands her notice in.

Rach is serious though. She had a whole business plan written up with figures and overheads and everything. None of it made much sense to me but it had lots of coloured graphs and tables. I only use the computer in the study for playing online poker but who knew that all this time, Rach was up there hammering out this idea. I'm real proud of her, I've got to say.

So while she's at work probably handing her notice in as we speak, I've come down here to the offices of my smokescreen company, Magnum Construction Ltd. to see Gerry about the premises.

I called the business Magnum for a couple of reasons. I think one was that I was always a big fan of Magnum P.I. and I thought it sounded classy. Also, when you say magnum, you think of champagne too. Although if I'm honest, I think it was probably mainly because I was going through a phase of using magnum guns on my hits.

Anyway, back when I was staring it up, I hired a guy called Gerry to handle the day to day running of the company. Gerry's a stand up guy. He's invested a hell of a lot more time and effort into this business than I have. All I do is put the money in and stand back. I'm like a… I think it's called a silent partner or a sleeping partner or something? Whatever it is, I don't do the thinking or the working. Nah, Gerry's the one who's built Magnum up to what it is today.

Honestly, the business is pretty much more his than it is mine. To me, it's just a front to cover my real work but to Gerry, it's his life and we both pretty much know it. We've got this understanding where he knows he has the final say over everything and I trust him completely but I just don't want to be involved in the everyday goings on. Truth to tell, I don't often have the time and this situation suits us both just fine. Gerry's a real man's man. He must be pushing about fifty now – no, actually that's a lie because I remember his fiftieth birthday a couple of years ago. Yeah, he must be about fifty two, fifty three. Christ, where does the time go? But he's got this skin like cracked leather. I know he spends most of his time in suits these days as M.D. of the company but you can see thirty plus years of working outdoors showing in his skin. I know *black* guys who are lighter skinned than Gerry. And he's got these hands like shovels – a real workman's hands, you know? They're practically more paw than hand.

Gerry's not a big guy – he's about five and a half but he's stocky and he looks like just his bones are thicker than most guys'. His hair's gone white now but this business wouldn't be half of what it is today without him. Over the years, I've really got on with Gerry. He's even been over to our house for dinner a couple of times and Rach does this whole 'flirting with the older man' thing whenever she sees him. In all the time I've known him, he's always been solid and he never once asked me any questions about why I don't like to involve myself in the business. I've even written the guy into my will for a forty percent share of Magnum when I eventually kick it – I figure the guy deserves it.

We're up in Gerry's office and he's pouring us both an Irish coffee.

"So how've you been keeping, Joe?" he asks warmly. "We haven't seen you around since…well, I can't really *remember* when." He puts his arm fatherly on my shoulder.

"I've been good thanks, Gerry. You know - keeping on keeping on. How's your daughter? She started at college yet?"

"Uh, yeah, she graduated two months ago."

Told you I don't get around here much. Gerry just sends me the business reports every quarter so I don't even have to come down here in person.

"Oh, right," I stumble, a little embarrassed.

"Don't worry about it, Joe, it's been a while," Gerry smiles. Like I said, he's always been a stand up guy. "How's Rachel? Married life agreeing with her?"

"Well we're coming up to our fifth wedding anniversary so I must be doing something right. Actually, Rachel's why I've come down here today. See, it's her birthday in a couple of weeks and I've decided what I'm going to get her. You remember that building you emailed me about last month, the one we were going to turn into apartments?"

"Yeah, the one uptown. I was thinking we could get maybe two big apartments or two medium and one small out of it. Why, what have you got in mind?" he asks, handing me my coffee.

"Well, it's like this," I answer. "Rach hates the job she's in at the moment and I've already told her she can jack it in but she likes to work – likes to keep busy, you know? So she's come up with this idea about a bookstore and I thought, why not? Why not use the new property?"

"Jesus, Joe, who knew you were such a romantic? I wish I could get my Margaret a present like that. I'd be in her good books for the next decade."

"That's sort of the plan, Ger. So what do you think? Think we could have it ready by her birthday?" He scratches his chin, running through things in his head.

"I don't know. Let's see. Now I know the electrics in the place are all shot and the pipes are going to need replacing. The walls need plastering, lick of paint all over but it's structurally sound. Good location for a store too. Mind you, you're gonna need plenty of shelves if she wants to make it a book store. We'll have to pull a few of the guys off other jobs, but yeah, I don't see why we couldn't blitz the place and have it ready in time."

"Outstanding. So I'll leave everything in your overly capable hands and you can work your magic? You're a saint among men, Gerry."

"Hey, it's your name above the door, Joe. Why don't you have Rachel give me a call and she can tell me any ideas she's got for the place.

"Good idea, Gerry. I'll have her do that tomorrow," I reply, downing my coffee and heading for the door. "Thanks again, man. I'll be in touch soon."

"No you won't," Gerry winks at me knowingly as I walk out.

See? A stand up guy – no questions asked.

So getting the building's fine then. And if I know Gerry, he'll have it up and running *before* schedule. What we'll need now are about three stories worth of books. Hey, *stories* worth. There's a joke there somewhere. Alls I know is, that many books ain't gonna come cheap.

I'm not a big reader myself. Never have been. I don't mind reading as long as it's something good but I've got this real short attention span. Rach keeps trying to switch me on to these books but I never get past the first couple of chapters. I just find it hard to invest the time in reading a few hundred pages worth of a story.

Rach though, she's a different story. She gets through about at least a book a week. Me, I like to have something on all the time whether it's the T.V. or music or whatever, but Rach likes to escape it all. She'll sit for a couple of hours in the study in absolute silence and she'll just read and read. She doesn't just read those girly romance books either. Nah, she'll read books on philosophy or science. She's mad keen on history too, so she loves to read all about these kings and queens and past civilisations and stuff. When it comes to brains, she beats me hands down. Well, lets face it, all *I* do is *beat* people's brains in. How much smarts do you need for that?

Actually no, I'm putting myself down there. I may not have brains like Rach and I may not be some kind of super computer genius like Danny, but I've got smarts. Without trying to sound arrogant or anything, I *have* got an intelligent mind when it comes to killing. When I'm on a job, I've got this certain intelligence – like I'll know how much a guy weighs from looking at him and whether I can hold him out of a window by his feet or if he'll be too heavy. I can work out how much pressure I'll need to break somebody's neck. Like that job at Ginelli's a few nights ago. Other guys wouldn't have done it in such style or as easy as I did it. They'd have tried taking on the guy's guards as well, but to feed him laxatives and set it up so he's in exactly the right cubicle takes some kind of intelligence and forethought. So yeah, while I may not win any awards, I'm pretty clever when it comes to killing.

I'm getting off the point. How did I get here? Oh yeah, books. Yeah, setting Rach up with all those books is going to cost a bundle so I've got to head to The Lodge and see what Stanley's got. A nice, fat mafia contract should just about do it. I just hope the miserable goddamn atmosphere's picked up at that place.

As soon as I get there, I can tell it hasn't. Pike's on the door, same as usual and he looks like someone just torched his baseball card collection.

"What's up, Pike?" I ask as he goes through the regular routine of frisking me. "How're things going?" I hate that metal scanner thing they run over me. Who knows what kind of freaky rays those things throw out. They run that thing past my nuts every time I come here and I swear it could damage my sperm or something. Damn thing could leave me firing blanks.

"Not good, Joe. That Prophet guy's bagged another one. That's two now," Pike answers glumly. Pike's already got a brow line like a bookshelf but now that he's frowning, it makes him look like one of those pictures of cavemen you see. I swear, you could balance a beer on that Neanderthal brow.

"Jesus, who is it this time?" I ask.

I thought with The Priest it was just one of those things but now with two, even *I've* got to admit there may be something to this whole 'Prophet' deal.

"Jake Grey," Pike replies, letting me past him.

Let me see - Jake Grey, Jake Grey….oh yeah, I've got him. Jesus, he was about the dumbest guy I ever met. How he ever made a living at this job, I don't know. He was so useless he used to get all the left over contracts nobody wanted – all the domestic targets. If he'd have tried going after some of the mob types, he'd have gotten his spine handed to him in a second. Grey was also an even bigger pussy than The Priest. I only know him 'cause he used to play cards here with Bear and some of the other guys. As far as I'm concerned, he's no great loss to the world.

I notice his plaque's already up on the wall. They must have an engraver on twenty four hour standby or something.

Down at Harvey's, the mood's even worse than it was a few days ago. Stanley's not in his office but he's bound to be around here somewhere. I do spot a human brick wall in the corner that I recognise though. Bear.

Now in this job, it's best not to make too many friends. There's an unspoken rule that outside The

Lodge, people don't make contact with each other and their privacy's a big thing. Most guys have got families and wives but out of respect for each other, nobody ever tries to find out anything about other hitmen. Bear's an exception though and ever since we pulled that Irish job together about six years back, we've been good friends.

Turns out that while we were over there whacking those Irish, we found out we had a lot in common. We like all the same comedians, all the same films and he's a big baseball fan as well. We got along like a house on fire and we found out we worked well together too. It only took us two days to shatter that Irish drug ring and we were there a week so we spent the other five days drinking Guinness and getting paid for it.

I like to think I've got a good sense of humour but I don't tend to laugh out loud at things. I mean, I find things funny and all but I'm just not an out loud laugher. Bear though, he can make me piss myself laughing with just a facial expression.

See, the reason he's called Bear is obvious as hell the second you clap eyes on him. He's got this huge, round barrel chest and these tree trunk arms. In fact, his forearms are as big as my thighs. He's not the biggest guy I know – he's not as big as Pike on the door for example – but he is about the thickest set guy I know. Neck like a tin of paint. Plus he's covered head to foot in hair. Thick brown hair, all over him. Coming out of his ears, his nose, his neck, his back – everywhere. In fact, about the only places he hasn't got hair are his eyes and teeth but I'm sure he's working on it.

I haven't seen the guy in too long and I brace myself as I walk over for the inevitable bear hug (excuse the pun). He spots me before I reach his table and he stands up, grinning. Here it comes.

He wraps these huge, blacksmith arms around me and tries to squeeze the life out of me. Even though I was ready for it, it still knocks the breath out of my chest. I mean, I'm not a small guy and I'm stronger than most but Bear's something else. Although it's not defined in a six pack kind of way, the guy's all muscle.

"Hey hey, Joe! How's it going, you big bastard?" he grins, that wiry mess of a Z. Z. Top beard of his scratching my face all to hell.

"Good, Bear. You?" It's about all I can manage under the circumstances. Anybody else in here tried this, it'd be a knee to the nuts and a head to the nose, but I let Bear get away with things 'cause I like him so much. He eventually lets me go, slips an arm round my shoulder and leads me to the bar.

"Yeah, I've been fine Joey boy, just fine. In fact, this is my first time back here in months. I've been taking some time out of the old hitman game to pursue other interests."

"Other interests, eh? You finally made the plunge and got that sex change you always wanted?" I ask him.

Bear roars laughing and orders a couple of beers. He's a great guy, but you wouldn't want him with you on a stealth mission, know what I mean?

"No, no, Joseph. I'm happy with the frankly monstrous cock God has seen fit to gift me with. No, what I've been investing in is a bar of my own."

"Ah, good for you, Bear. Tell you the truth, I've been looking at investing in other businesses myself."

"Now's the time, man. I tell you, you want to get into the liquor business. The profits are huge and plus you can never get turfed out of your own bar."

He smiles and drains three quarters of his drink in one huge gulp.

"Yeah, I'll think about it. Say, what's the deal with Jake Grey? He was a buddy of yours wasn't he?"

"Nah, not really," Bear shrugs. " He was just about the worst card player I ever came across so me and the boys liked to let him in 'cause he was easy pickings. Jake was always kind of pathetic. Thinking about it, I don't know how he ever made it into this business. The guy had no military background and my sixteen year old niece probably would have beaten him in a fair arm wrestle. He was so bad, I heard once that he botched a job taking out some guy who'd been cheating on his wife. Jake walks up to the guy to put one between his eyes. Just before he pulls the trigger, he notices the mark was his dentist. Can you believe it? Jake gets rattled, misses and shoots the dentist's ear off. The dentist escapes and Jake had to hire one of the other guys from here to finish the job on him before he could squeal. The hit actually *cost* Jake money." Bear laughs out loud from way down deep in his belly.

"Jesus. So what happened to him then?"

"Who, the dentist or Jake?" Bear asks.

"Jake, genius. I just saw his plaque up on the wall."

"Oh, you haven't heard? I mean, I know Jake was a bit of a geek and all but I don't think even *he* deserved what happened to him. He was found last night, head down in a sewage plant. He suffocated in a big old vat of human shit. Management here got an untraceable email saying where the body was. Here, there's copies of it been handed out all over."

Bear reaches over the bar and pulls down a photo off the wall and hands it to me. You can see what I presume are Jake's feet sticking out of a sewage vat and a message written in shit on the side. *"Hitmen are shitmen to me!' Signed, The Prophet.'*

Jesus, no wonder people are spooked around here. There's no mixed messages about that.

"You hear about The Priest too?" Bear asks.

I nod, just staring at the photo.

"Well, Joey boy," Bear says grimly. "Looks like we got us a killer-killer running round!"

6

By the time I get home, I'm in a stinking mood. All this Prophet stuff is getting a little too weird and a little too heavy. On the plus side, a lot of the guys at The Lodge are going to ground after all this shit with Jake Gray, which means I got a nice juicy contract from Stanley. If this Prophet character keeps bumping people off, I could have my pick of the work. Still, I'm not so stupid that I won't be watching my back extra carefully from now on.

Rumours down at The Lodge is that it's one of us – a fellow hitman. Let's face it, we're not exactly in the phonebook and clients only deal with our agents. Kinda makes sense that people would naturally suspect the other guys from The Lodge, because who else would know, right?

Personally, I haven't got much time for playing Columbo, which is what Stanley was doing when I left him. He came into the bar and sat for a half an hour telling anybody who'd listen what his thoughts about it all were.

But, I mean, what *is* a prophet anyway? As far as I understand it, it's a guy who speaks for somebody religious – something like that anyway. Which is why when I saw The Priest I just figured it was some cult he'd gotten himself involved with but this last message leaves no question that he's targeting hitmen and bumping them off. Wonder why though?

A killer-killer. Real funny, Bear.

I can hear Rach come in downstairs. Time to put all this mystery stuff to the back of my head.

"Oh Joe, I did it. I really, really did it!" she squeals, jumping into my arms as soon as she's through the door. "I walked right into Helen's office at the end of the day and told her straight. I told her that I was sick of her stealing my work and my ideas and that she could stick her shitty little job!"

"Good for you, babe," I smile, planting a kiss on her lips. "I want you to slow down though, I've got some bad news."

She goes limp in my arms and looks up at me with those wide, brown eyes.

"Oh no, you're kidding me, right? What happened? Did the building fall through or something? Can we not afford it?"

"No, nothing like that. I saw Gerry and he said he thinks he could get the building ready by a couple of weeks. Only bad news is that he said *I* have to pick the colour scheme. I was thinking of a nice electric green with canary yellow polka dots everywhere."

She punches me on the arm but can't stop her smile.

"You idiot. My heart nearly stopped then. I thought I was going to have to go grovelling back to Helen for a second. So it's okay then? Everything's going to be alright with it?"

"Honey, all you've got to do is speak to Gerry and tell him how you want things to look. *Then* all you've got to do is go out and buy a couple of thousand books."

She pulls away and almost does a little dance in the middle of the living room, she's that excited.

"I'm going to make a success of this. You wait. It'll be the best bookstore in Manhattan. I'll have a little restaurant where people can have coffee while they read their books. And I'll have leather armchairs everywhere and I'll tell all the staff that they've got to really *talk* to the customers about books, not just serve them. People will come in for the atmosphere as much as for the books themselves. And I'll try and get writers in to sign their books and maybe open late a few nights a week and have readings and a book club. I'll make it work, Joe."

"Rach, I think anyone who believes in a project as much as you do about this will always make it a success."

That's a smooth line. So smooth that she offers to cook dinner. I was in a bad mood before and I don't really want to be put back in a bad mood again so I suggest we go *out* for dinner instead.

Rach has to put in a week's notice before she can finish work, which is great because I really don't need her under my feet for the next few days. The juicy contract I got from Stanley is gonna take some planning so I need the time.

That's always been a good thing with Rachel. Even though we're doing well financially, she's always insisted that she work. The money she earns doesn't really make a difference day to day but her working means that she's not around the house, which means I can get things done without sneaking around watching out for her.

The contract is for the head of an Asian crime syndicate. Seems he's been pissing off the Italians by muscling in on their coke operations. Doesn't bother me. This week, the Italians'll hire me to get rid of one drug pushing shitheel – next week, the Chinese'll hire me to do the same back to the Italians. The only people who win out of it are me and the normal people of this city. I can't fucking stand drugs and the scumbags who push it.

See, one of the main reasons us hitmen get so much work is because the one side doesn't want the other side to know it's them doing the killing. If the Chinese knew for an absolute fact that the Italians had put this contract out on one of theirs, there'd be retribution and all-out war and the Italians don't want that on their door so that's where I come in. A grey area with no affiliations.

Both sides have probably got a couple of hundred guys on the payroll who they could send to do the job but if the Chinese see a bunch of greaseballs with spaghetti hanging out of their mouths, they'll know who to come looking for, see what I mean? So it's better for these guys to go to an agent, pay a little bit extra for a job well done and their hands are clean. Nobody knows it was really them and there's nothing to trace it back to them either. It's all about an eye for an eye without actually having to lose an eye, see?

The other thing about all these guys is that they're all walking clichés. Seriously, there's nothing non-PC about all this. It's not racist or anything, it's just the truth. Every Italian gangster is exactly like the ones you see in the Scorcese films. Half of them are called Tony and the other half are all Bobby's or Johnny's. Not an Italian name among them. Christ, most of them have never even set foot in Italy. They're all riding on the wave of these history lectures their fathers gave to them. All pasta and bad suits.

The Irish are the same. No accents, none of them ever been to Ireland, just a bunch of badly organised idiots who've gotten to where they are by being either crazy or stupid enough to do the things the other gangs won't. All Guinness and ginger hair.

The Russians are a different bunch. They don't really have as much of a foothold here in the States but what little piece of the pie they *do* have is run smoothly and professionally. They're a mean, cold, vicious bunch. All vodka and names with too many v's and k's in them.

The Chinese and the Japanese are the biggest clichés of all. All these movies you see where all they do is talk about honour and chop their own fingers off, all that stuff? That's fucking *exactly* what they're like. You break wind in front of one of these guys and he'll accuse you of defiling his father's memory and challenge you to a sword fight. Seriously. And every one of them *does* know martial arts too, it's a cliché man. They're all samurai swords and karate and shit but they could teach the Russians a thing or two about cruelty.

So you've got all these different guys – all these gangs trying to outdo each other and bump each other off so the way's clear for them to sell drugs, kill kids and generally ruin life for normal people. All *I* do is let them pay me to pick away at each other. I'll take their money one week and shoot them in the head the next.

The mark's name is Dei Hung. Sounds like a porn star to me with a name like that. Seems old Dei's been treading on some heavy-duty Italian shoes which is what'll bring me to his door in the not too distant future. The brief says I'm to make an example of Dei Hung to the other Asian syndicates and make sure that his operation becomes a memory. Notes on Hung say he's got at least sixty to seventy people on the payroll and he holes himself up in the top three floors of a luxury apartment block. Now who says crime doesn't pay?

Well whoever it was, was talking shit because the fee for this one is half a million. Probably because of how much work is involved. See, you can't just go and blow the top few floors of a building to pieces with plastic explosives – it's too loud and too messy. No, a job like this'll need a personal touch and of course, the risk is sky high so that's why it's reflected in the price. I thought about maybe asking Bear to come in with me on this one but on a job like this, I'll need to be subtle about it and subtlety's not exactly Bear's strong point. Besides, Rach's bookstore will need all the capital it can get and half a million dollars can buy a hell of a lot more books than a two hundred and fifty grand can.

Because the Italian's want an exhibition made of Dei Hung (and they *always* want to make exhibitions of each other – the days of hiding bodies are long gone. Everyone has to send a message; it's the fashion.), I'm going to have to think of a way to get to him in that building where he'll be feeling safe. You can guarantee that any time he leaves the front door he'll be surrounded by heavies and the Italians specified no sniping. Too easy see, and they don't get their horse's-head-in-the-bed style message. So up close and personal it's got to be.

Let's see - three floors worth of Yakuza types, bound to be armed to the teeth, who knows what kind of electronic security devices up there and little old me. I think I'll need to call Danny in on a favour.

See, I'll bet that if he puts his mind to it, Danny could kill the power to that whole building. Probably the whole block if he thought about it. But if I go in and the place is totally blacked-out and I've had the amazing foresight to take night vision goggles, then guess who's going to have one hell of an advantage over the Chinese? Sounds like the beginnings of a plan.

When I get to The Cave, Danny's nowhere to be seen. I'm glad in a way too. He's bound to have heard about Jake Grey by now and he was jittery as hell last time I was here what with the pictures of The Priest. I really don't need Danny to be going through one of his anxiety episodes right now.

See, because Danny spends so much time wrapped up in his computer stuff, it sometimes makes him a bit of a recluse. Of course *he* doesn't see it that way but anyone who'd rather spend six hours straight, flirting in some chat room with what's probably a sixty year old guy pretending to be a confused twenty one year old blonde rather than actually going out and conversing with real people, is a little socially challenged if you ask me.

Dan's always been a bit shy, a bit geeky, and he was always into computers in a big way but these days, with the Internet and all, he can spend a week buried in these e mails and websites and shit. Me, I've never even sent an email before 'cause what's wrong with picking up the phone and calling someone? I prefer to do all my dealings face to face. That way you can see if someone's lying to you - and you can break their jaw if they are. I couldn't break someone's jaw *virtually* now could I?

Dan's also one of these conspiracy freaks. Everything from aliens to the Kennedy assassination, he loves it. Spends hours researching it and trying to hack into government files for these supposed black ops secrets and documents. He spent two months once trying to persuade me to break into Area 51.
So with Dan being the way he is, this Prophet stuff is going to really push his buttons. He'll totally obsess

over it and nothing else will matter to him but finding out who it is. Still, if anybody can do that, it's Danny. I spend an hour working out in the gym, then shower and watch the game on T.V. until Danny eventually comes back.

He walks into the room loaded with brown grocery bags and just by the look on his face I can tell that wherever he's been, he's been looking over his shoulder every step of the way.

"Don't tell me. You've heard about Jake Grey right?" I ask, already knowing the answer.

"You're damn right I have. Jesus, Joe. Drowned in a big vat of shit! What kind of a way to go out is that, even for someone like Jake? Even *you* have to admit there's something going on now. The Prophet's out there, man!"

"What's in the bags?" I ask, tactfully ignoring his conspiracy theories.

"Supplies. I'm going to ground for a while, staying here where it's safe. I'm not going out there where some nut job can tear off my face or drown me in shit, no way. I've got enough food here for a couple of weeks at least. Let some other poor joker end up as a plaque on The Lodge wall."

"Oh, come on Dan. Alright, I admit there does seem to be something behind these murders but let's face it – we're hitmen. We *tend* to make enemies. We're all killers ourselves and we take our chances out there. The Prophet could be anybody at all, right?"

I follow Danny through to the kitchen and he starts packing his supplies away into the cupboards.

"Yeah, but you think the same way I do. You think it's another hitman, right? Someone from The Lodge?" he says.

"Okay, I admit I think it's a fellow hitman but that's only because I don't have any better ideas - but I just can't work out the motives. Both messages this Prophet has left have said that he hates hitmen, so why would a hitman be doing this? It doesn't make sense, you know? Besides, I've got better things to worry about just because Jake and The Priest couldn't look after themselves."

"That's easy for you to say, Joe. You're tough as nails," he says, gesturing wildly now. "You could probably take out any one of the guys down there but not all of us are quite as bullet-proof as you are, man."

Danny motions me to follow him into The Nest. He settles himself down at a keyboard and the huge centre screen flickers into life, reflecting blue off his glasses.

"So with all of that in mind," he says, tapping away at the keys "I've compiled a list of suspects."

With an overly dramatic stab of a key, five faces flicker onto the screen - three of which, I have to admit, were on my list of suspects too.

The first is Spider; the slyest, creepiest, most slimy bastard I've ever met. He's got this shaved head with cobweb tattoos all over it. He's also just about the skinniest, wiriest guy you could meet. He never mixes with anyone down at The Lodge and he keeps himself to himself most of the time. He's certainly got no friends there and only ever turns up to see his agent. Man, I wouldn't trust that guy for a second but I do know he's good at what he does– if it's a quiet, low key hit you want, then Spider's your man. Personally, I think the guy's an assassin, not a hitman, and assassins are a cowardly and sneaky bunch – Spider would probably go down with one punch in a fist fight but that's not how he operates. He melts into the shadows and you never hear him coming. Yeah, he was high on my list just for the reason that he stands out the most and he's a miserable son of a bitch.

Next to him is a picture of a guy called Johnny Turk. Now Johnny wasn't on my list, simply because I think he's just too stupid to pull something like this off. He's this big ex-mafia bruiser. Something bad happened between him and his crime family a while back. I'm not sure what, but I do know that Johnny's been left with a face like a meat feast pizza and no Italian gangster with any self respect would even look at the guy. Because of all this, Johnny's a little unhinged to say the least. He's got nothing to lose in life and he acts with the kind of crazy recklessness of - well, of someone with nothing left to lose. He's a dangerous character to be around.

The next piece of shit on the list is Lincoln. Now Lincoln was first on *my* list of suspects, for the main fact that he's a walking scumbag. He's the guy who'll take all the contracts that everyone else turns down. Families, women, children – Lincoln doesn't care, it's all the same to him. I'm sure most people, if they knew, would frown at what we do for a living, but there's still this whole 'honour among thieves' thing with most of us. I've killed hundreds of people in my time, but I've never killed anyone who a) didn't deserve it, or b) was either a woman or under the age of twenty one. You've got to have something that separates you from the evil scumbags and Lincoln ain't got that in my opinion.

Only thing is, he's one of the toughest hitmen on the books. A lot of the guys have got gimmicks or are good in one field but weak in others. Like Spider's weak but he's clever, or like Bear who's strong as a bull but he's a slow mover. Lincoln's one of these well rounded guys – strong but not bulky, fast but not slight, and he's mean as hell. If I thought there was one guy from The Lodge who could potentially take me, I'd have to begrudgingly say it was him. That said, I'd have to be having a bad day and he knows it too. He tries to intimidate some of the guys, tries to muscle in on their contracts, but he knows better than to try that shit with me. Something like killing the competition off would be just the kind of thing he'd do too.

Danny's spot on, because the fourth face is my number two suspect - this DeLaney character I saw coming from Bill's a few days ago. He's high on my list because nobody knows anything about him really. Every man there's got his secrets, myself included, but there's usually something to go on, like perhaps information on someone's training background or even an anecdote about a hit gone wrong, you know – anything. But with this DeLaney, he's a blank slate. Plus I don't like the look he gave me when I walked into Bill's. Never trust an unknown quantity.

The last one on the screen is someone I'd have never thought of. It's the one and only woman on the books, a deadly little hellcat called Widow. She's actually on Stanley's books so I guess that makes us stable mates. For whatever reason, she's decided she wants to become a hitwoman and she's doing damn well out of it, simply because when a contract comes through to take out a woman, there's really only her and Lincoln will take it, so she's sort of cornered the market.

She uses these dark, smoky Mediterranean looks of hers to entice the men before slipping them some lethal cocktail or other. Poisons and a quick knife in the back's her style. I doubt if she's ever held a gun in her life, but she gets results all the same. She mixes with the guys even less than Spider does, but I guess I can understand why when I think of some of the warped characters that hang around Harvey's.

"Gotta say, Dan, if it came to it, I'd agree with your choices here. Only why Johnny Turk and the Widow?" I ask.

"I was thinking, Johnny's just crazy enough that he'd do something like this just for kicks. The Widow though, do you think maybe she's got some grudge against guys like The Priest and Jake? Like maybe they tried it on with her or something, I don't know."

"Dan, if she was to kill every guy who made a pass at her, The Lodge would be pretty near empty, you know what I mean?" I answer.

"Yeah, I guess, but she just stands out to me. It could be that she's just one of these man haters you hear about," he says.

"I don't think so for a second to be honest with you, but it's good that you're at least thinking about it. My money's on Lincoln though. That guy's just pure bad news."

"Yeah, but he's no problem for you though is he, Joe?" Dan says. Nice to hear he's got some confidence in his old buddy.

"No, but it'd be a piece of cake for someone like him to take out Priest and Grey, you know?"

"Oh man, I tell you Joe, I'm not surfacing until this Prophet's been found out and taken care of, whoever it is," Dan says. He's clearly rattled by all this.

"Between you and me," I say, turning away from the monitor. "I think I'm gonna start spending a little *more* time at The Lodge and keeping my eyes and ears open. Meanwhile, I need to ask a favour. You think if you tried, you could cut the power to a whole apartment building?"

Danny looks up at me as if I've just asked the dumbest question in the world.

"Joe, I could probably switch off a lamp in the oval office from in here," he answers.

Perfect.

7

I've worked out the details of the plan with Danny and I'm pretty happy with it on the whole.

I'm going to break in by parachuting onto the roof because as Dei Hung owns the top three floors of the building, it makes more sense than trying to fight my way up from the ground. Only problem with that is if they see me coming, I'm a sitting duck in the air so I'll have to look into his rooftop security.

See, when you know you're dealing with about fifty plus in numbers, you can't just barrel in somewhere and start shooting. I could take around fifteen or twenty guys down if I'm lucky but it only takes a few more than that before somebody gets a lucky bullet in. I'm good but even I can't beat the law of averages. So on a job like this it's always best to whittle down the numbers before they even know you're coming.

With that in mind, once I'm in the building I'll rig up a canister of ambitoxin… no, wait, ambitoxic-hydro-something-a-cide that Danny's managed to get his hands on. I can't remember the name of the stuff exactly right, I just know it's some kind of fast acting nerve gas. Plan is to rig it into the ventilation systems and pump it into the top three floors at the same time as Danny kills the lights to the whole building.

If everything goes right, Hung's men'll be trying to get the lights back on while the gas fills the place. Anyone who doesn't get hit by the gas will be floundering blind which is when I make my move with the night vision goggles and the berettas. Danny's pretty confident he can get at least partial control of the building's electronics depending on the level of Hung's defences so everything should be cool.

Timing is critical on a job as complicated as this. The plan only works in theory and there's a million and one different variables that could come into play – the big trick is being able to adapt quickly. But if you've got a plan and a time frame then stick to it. I've got to know the exact time Danny's going to hit the lights so I can act accordingly. After your weapons, a reliable watch is the most important piece of equipment on a hit.

We settle on Wednesday night for the hit because our intelligence says that Hung takes piano lessons that night (if you can believe that) so we know he'll be in the building. Plus it gives us time to rent out a chopper. I can't remember the last time I took on a job quite as big as this and I've gotta admit, I'm really looking forward to it.

In the days running up to Wednesday night, life is slow and easy. One of the days, me and Rach spend picking out furniture and a colour scheme for the book store. Things are running okay down there and Gerry and his guys are making good headway. Another day, I even found the time to relax and I went to the movies on my own, saw one of the best action flicks I've seen in years and promised myself I'd see at least one new movie a month from now on. Just life as usual, you know?

So wouldn't you know it, come a couple of hours before I'm due to meet Kenny (The Lodge's private pilot-for-hire) on Wednesday night, who should come knocking at the door in floods of tears and damn near hysterical but Janet. Of course, Rach takes her in and sits her down where Janet proceeds to cry her way through a whole box of tissues. I very kindly offer to make myself scarce but Janet insists I stay and listen to what she has to say.

"I want you both to hear this," she blubs. "I want you both to know exactly how big a piece of shit Ray is."

Oh man, I can see where this is going. A hundred bucks tells you he's been cheating on her. Unless maybe he's hit her in which case I'll cancel Hung and go over there and kick the shit out of Ray myself.

"Ray's…he's…oh God, I can't believe it. He's been having an affair with some little slut who works at the golf club," Janet mumbles, sobbing into Rachel's shoulder.

"Are you sure, Janet?" Rach asks, stroking the quivering woman in her arms. "You and Ray are so great together, what would make him do something like this?"

I feel like saying *'Because he's a guy, he's got a dick and for some men that's all it takes'* but I demonstrate remarkable restraint and manage to stop myself.

"Look, I'm just going to go and leave you two to it. You don't need me hanging around here," I offer, ever generous to a fault.

"Oh Joe, I'm so sorry to come here and lay this on you. I just…I didn't know where else to go." Janet sobs and a big old snot bubble forms on her left nostril which has got to be the least attractive thing I've ever seen.

Rachel flashes me a dirty look.

"Hold on a second, Janet. Let me go and fix you a strong drink," Rach says. She lets go of Janet who crumples into the corner of the sofa, sobbing. Rach grabs me by the elbow and pulls me through to the kitchen.

"I can't *believe* you, Joe," she smoulders. She always looks so sexy when she's angry. "Janet's in there crying because her husband's cheated on her and all you can do is stand there making her feel bad for taking up your precious time."

"I know, I'm sorry," I say, holding my hands up. "But what can I do? Listen, you two open up a bottle of wine and talk it out. That's what Janet needs right now is to just open up and let it all out and she won't want me hanging around. Besides, I've got a card game set up for tonight so you'll have the house to yourself all night."

"A card game?!" Rachel explodes into a really loud whisper. "Joe, this is our friends' marriage here and you want to go and play cards?! Forget it, pal. You want to know what you can do? You can go round to Ray's and you can talk to him face to face and find out what the hell he thinks he's doing, that's what you can do."

I want to turn to her and say *'I can't go round to Ray's because I'm late for my meet with my pilot – I should be parachuting onto the roof of a gangster's building in half an hour'* but obviously I can't. Besides, she doesn't often get this steely, determined look in her eye but she's got it now and I know better than to argue.

Looks like I need to reform my plans.

By the time I get to the airfield, Kenny's just stubbing out his last cigarette on the floor and about to leave. I park up and make my apologies but he's cool about it. Kenny's a real interesting guy. He's got a dry sense of humour and he used to be a pilot back in 'Nam and I listen intently to his old war stories as he starts the chopper's rotors.

Stanley set me up with the guy 'cause apparently he's the best flyboy on The Lodge's books and he handles the bird like a dream. We take into the night sky and head back into the city. All the lights twinkle far below us and it's a pretty stunning sight. I've been in a helicopter plenty of times but never over Manhattan at night and I decide to book me and Rach a flight at some point 'cause it's pretty magical and romantic up here.

"We're coming up on the building, man," Kenny says. "I'm just going to circle round once more to get some height."

"Cool," I answer and start to get myself set up. Because I know there's going to be a boatload of guys in there, even with the gas I'm not taking any chances so I've got the berettas and a whole shitload of grenades. I wrap them in holsters over the Kevlar jacket and make my way into the back of the chopper. The gas canister gets strapped to my leg and the nozzle thing goes on my other. I buckle up the parachute onto my back and finally, the finishing touch to my master plan, I put on my headset and hook it up to my phone. All set and good to go.

Kenny takes the chopper higher and higher until even the buildings seem small, then he swings the chopper round.

"This is as high as we can safely go," Kenny shouts out. "We'll be over the building in about thirty seconds so get ready to go."

I make my way to the door and slide it open. Ice cold wind rushes in to meet me and I lean out, looking for my target.

"Okay," shouts Kenny. "This is you. Don't forget, you're aiming for the one with the helipad on the roof."

"Got it," I shout back, spying Hung's building far below. "Thanks Kenny, you're a diamond."

"No problem, man," he replies. "Be careful down there and good luck."

I smile back at him, salute the guy then jump out into the cold night sky. The freezing wind hits me as Kenny's chopper gets smaller and the ground gets bigger. As soon as I'm safely away from the helicopter, I pull my chute open because I'm not high enough for a leisurely sky dive – I just need to hit the roof unseen.

If Hung has got any kind of roof security whatsoever I'm screwed. I'll be dead before I even hit the ground but it's a cloudy night and the moon's pretty well covered so you'd have to be looking for me to see me if you know what I mean. As I descend, I press the 'dial' button on my headset and launch phase two of what I like to call 'Operation: Two Birds.'

The dial tone rings out twice before Ray answers.

"Janet, is that you?" he practically shouts in panic.

"No it's not, asshole. Did you really expect it to be?" I answer back. I have to shout over the rushing wind.

"Joe? Joe, is that you?" Ray says. "I can barely hear you."

"Yeah, I'm at the construction site," I shout back. "I'm halfway up a crane so that's why there's a wind blowing on the line."

"Oh, okay," he buys it. "I guess you know about me and Janet then, huh? Have you seen her?"

"Seen her? She's crying her fucking eyes out on my couch, you idiot!" I yell at him. I know, not really subtle but then I'm not a relationship counsellor.

"Oh Jesus, man," he blubs. "I know I'm an asshole. I know I am but you should see this girl, Joe. She's twenty three years old and she's got the body of a swimwear model."

"So you telling me you're leaving Janet then?" I ask, banking the chute to the left to stay on target for Hung's building as the big white 'H' of the helipad comes into view on the rooftop.

"No, I…no, I don't want to leave Janet, I absolutely don't. I just- it's just I couldn't help myself, you know?"

"No I don't fucking know, Ray," I answer. "Because I've never cheated on my wife. I understand having urges 'cause you're a guy and we all have them but you're thinking with your dick right now man, not your head."

"I know I am, Joe," he says and he actually starts crying down the phone. "Look, I don't want Janet to leave me. Please, will you just – please, can't you tell her that it's not true and she's got it all confused. She'd believe it if you told her, Joe."

"What did you just say?" I growl.

"Jesus, the wind is terrible on this line, Joe," Ray answers. "I said, can't you just lie to her and…"

"I heard what you fucking said, Ray!" I explode. "And if you ever ask me to lie for you again, especially over something like this, I'm going to take your golf clubs and beat you to a fucking pulp, okay?"

I know my reaction might seem a little hypocritical here but fuck it.

"You need to face this shit storm you've created like a man, Ray," I yell at him. I'm practically on top of Hung's building now and the coast seems clear – no roofguard but all the same, I really need to stop shouting now.

"Listen," I tell Ray. "I've got to go now but take some time out to think about this. Janet's staying at ours tonight but if you want to win her back, you're going to have to prove it to her."

"God, you're right, Joe. I'm going to…"

I hit the button on the headset to cut Ray off because a) I'm coming to land on the roof and I need to concentrate and b) the guy was getting on my fucking nerves. That shit'll have to wait until tomorrow now because I need to get my business head on. At least Rach'll be happy I spoke to him.

I'm pleased as hell to have not been spotted dropping out of the sky and the rooftop is empty. No guards or even a trace of anybody which means Hung must be pretty confident up here in his ivory tower and I'm suddenly real glad I didn't try and enter from the ground floor up.

I check my watch and there's only two minutes and change until Dan is going to hit the lights so even though I'm bang on time, I've gotta work fast here. I race over to the roof ventilator and feed the nozzle and hose down the shaft. Dan managed to get the blueprints for the building and assures me that the vents are going to take the gas straight to the first five floors so apologies to the folks on the two floors underneath Hung who are going to wake up with apocalypse sized hangovers tomorrow. I attach the hose to the gas canister and push the red button that starts pumping the shit out. By the time I've done that I recheck my watch just in time to count the last minute down until Danny hits the lights.

Right on cue, any and all lights on the building immediately wink out leaving it in total blackout. I give the gas another thirty seconds, then it's go time. I put on the gas mask and night vision goggles, kick open the roof doors and head down into the building.

Going down the steel steps from the roof, there's a couple of guys lying unconscious at the bottom. I pop a couple of rounds into them just to make sure they don't wake up and sneak in behind me.

Moving into the top floor, there's bodies lying everywhere on all these plush Chinese couches that are scattered about. Good thing about the gas is that it's odourless so they wouldn't have even known it was being pumped in which means they've dropped where they were sat.

I can hear noises up ahead so not everybody was taken out by the gas. I can see torchlight flashing and even though they're speaking in Chinese I can tell they're panicked. Now that the surprise is up and they know they're under attack, I don't need to be stealthy anymore.

I pop my head quickly around the door and back in case a flashlight hits me. There's eight of them, guns in one hand and torches in the other. Won't be long before they get themselves organised so I flip the pins on a couple of grenades and toss them into the room. These guys are trained because their shouting tells me that even though it's dark, they know what's just happened. If the lights were on maybe they'd see where the grenades had landed and act but in the darkness they react too late. After the explosion, I slide into the room – six dead, so I put the two injured goons out of their misery and move on into the building.

I can see they've got it nice up here. It's all big open rooms and huge Chinese vases and oriental statues. Actually, thinking about it, these top floors'll be empty by the morning and their owner will be dead – I might give Gerry a call and see if we can put in an offer to buy them perhaps.

A few more rooms full of dead bodies then the stairs then I'm on the middle floor. According to intelligence, Hung's personal rooms are on this floor and I make my way towards his offices. Everything seems quiet and there's not as many bodies here. I'm starting to get a bad feeling.

I kick open these big oriental double doors and inside it's bad.

Hung's living quarters are basically this huge, open plan room with pillars and very little furniture and he's standing there by his piano surrounded by about twenty, maybe twenty five guards. The whole fucking room's lit up by candles and I stand out like an idiot. Everybody turns to look at me and suddenly it's like the last reel of The Wild Bunch.

I manage to dive back out of the way just in time as a million bullets fill the air. The sound's deafening but the walls are solid and not plasterboard so I can actually hide behind them, all of which means I've got about three seconds before they come and get me. As if on cue, I hear a voice – I assume it's Hung's – shouting orders. I don't speak Chinese but I can guess it's something along the lines of '*bring me that guy's balls in a sweet and sour sauce!*'

All the windows in the room have been smashed so some clever bastard had the bright idea to shoot out the glass and ventilate the place. And trust me to pick a mob boss who's got a thing for goddamn candles! All the advantages the gas and darkness gave me are lost but at least I've got some grenades with me – the ultimate equalizer.

As soon as the shooting stops, I fling my last four grenades in the room which should even things up a little. I use the blast and the smoke as a diversion to get me into the room but there's nothing left for it now but to get in there and start blasting.

I roll low and keep to the floor – see, nine out of ten guys will hold their guns straight out in front of them and shoot at head or at least chest level so if you go in low then you're cutting down the odds of getting hit by at least half.

The grenades have taken out about twelve of these guys but it's still fifteen plus against me. Make that thirteen as I get two in the head before ducking behind a pillar.

In a fire fight like this when you're totally outnumbered, there's a few things that are vitally important. First thing is, you can't let yourself panic. If you stop and actually think realistically about what's happening – the fact that you could get your head blown off any second; no more life, no more Rachel, no more anything – you're gonna freeze and that's just about the worst thing that could happen. You've got to keep your mind clear, concentrate on the job but not let the enormity of what's happening get to you.

Which brings me to the second point, and this is only a personal thing – most guys I know don't do this but to keep my head clear I find that if I play a song in my head and listen to that then instinct takes over and in my opinion, you can't discount the effectiveness of instinct. Right now, I've got Bowie's 'Heroes' playing for some reason. Doesn't matter what the song is, just so long as there's something for the front of your brain to occupy itself while the back part takes over if you see what I mean. It's not always easy what with all the noise and the chaos going on around you but it always helps me settle into my groove.

There's a million other things too – make every shot count, keep moving, use your environment, keep count of your shots (which isn't easy when you use two guns but it does come with practice) and think fast – but sometimes, keeping your fingers crossed and saying a prayer can be important too.

But even doing all this, nobody's indestructible, least of all me. I've managed to whittle twenty five goons down to roughly single figures but through the guy getting lucky rather than me getting sloppy, one of them manages to wing me. Luckily it's a clean exit through my left arm but it still hurts like the devil. With a cry of pain, I slump up against a pillar and return the favour with a shot between the guy's eyes.

You know in the movies when the hero gets shot in the arm but just keeps on fighting anyway? Forget it. You get winged and you ain't lifting that arm to fire back, end of story. Fortunately, I'm a much better shot with my right hand anyway but how the hell am I going to explain a bullet hole in my arm to Rach? I guess that's something to figure out if I get out of here alive. Man, my arm hurts.

There's only a handful left now and they're surrounding Hung by the piano. The remaining goons fire their guns at me but I keep moving and weaving and they keep missing. *I* don't though. And that's another skill. Most guys can hit a target eight times out of ten if they're standing still but you try shooting something when you're running about you'll be lucky if you can hit your target once out of ten shots when you're moving. But it's like anything – it comes with practice.

Five become three, become two, become one, become dead. And all of a sudden, it's quiet but for the sound of Dei Hung sobbing under his piano. He's a small guy and crying like a schoolgirl doesn't exactly make him seem like some big, tough ganglord. I grab his ankle and drag him out but he holds onto the piano leg.

"You...you are not human," he whimpers.

"*I'm* not human? You're the one sells crack to kids, motherfucker," I answer.

"Please...please, whoever you are, I have money. Please don't kill me. I can pay you. Please."

Seems Hung speaks English just fine.

But that's another rule of the hitman – the mark will *always* try and offer you more money not to kill him. Always. Hung's obviously loaded but it's never worth it to break a contract and it's never worth the hassle to get greedy and try for more. Just take out the mark and collect the money for the hit, nice and simple and black and white. Besides which, Hung deals drugs to kids, is a known mass murderer and general all round scumbag so he deserves what's coming – you can't buy your way out of karma when it comes knocking.

The Italians are paying for the whole '*message to be sent*' thing so I can't just shoot Hung and get out of here but the clue's in the name, right? With a name like that it's just obvious how he's got to go which is why I came prepared with a rope.

I crack him over the head with my gun butt to loosen him up a little then drag him out from under the piano. I tie one end of the rope to the piano leg, quickly make a noose, slip it around his neck then walk him to the shattered window.

"Do you believe in reincarnation, Mr Hung?" I ask him.

"Y…yes, oh God, yes, I do," he sobs.

"Good. Well in the next life, try not to come back as a drug pushing asshole."

With that, I push him out of the window and he screams for a full second and a half.

That should please the Italians. Cops'll find him hanging halfway down a building and the newspapers will have a field day with a headline that'll write itself. All I've got to do now is get out of the building before the cops get here.

The hard part is going to come later when I try to explain to my wife how I got shot in the arm.

I think I'd rather face another building full of Chinese gangsters.

8

I manage to get out of the building without anybody seeing and can already hear the cop cars coming in the distance. All in all, clipped wing aside, I'm delighted with how that went. Okay, so it wasn't perfect and I could have done things quieter but all the variables were accounted for and the job got done, which is the important part.

So that's a half million, minus a little to Danny for his help with the lights and the ventilation and then Kenny's fee on top. Should still be plenty to get Rachel's business well up and running. That much money'll buy a hell of a lot of books and the way I see it, it's something good coming out of the death of someone bad. I'm not really one for karma and all that stuff but I do like a sort of symmetry to things like this.

There's just two things bothering me now. First is what's happening with Janet and Ray. When I phoned, I wanted Ray to deny it – say there'd been some kind of a mistake and he wasn't cheating on her, but he came clean which throws a spanner in the works. See, I don't want Janet and Ray to break up. Janet is to Rachel like Danny is to me - they've known each other since forever. And although Ray can be an asshole, it's nice to have such normal friends and I'd rather they didn't split up. Also, from a purely selfish point of view, I could really do without having my wife be Janet's agony aunt for the next year.

Second thing bothering me is the pain in my arm. I haven't been shot for three years and it hurts like hell. I've wrapped it up as best I can so it won't bleed on the car but it'll need to be looked at before I go home because I can't keep Rach from seeing it forever.

Every year, each hitman on the books at The Lodge have to pay their membership fees. These fees ain't cheap by any means – we're talking seven figures here – but what you get for that money is access to a bunch of handy little enterprises scattered throughout the city which range from garages with untraceable cars available for those tricky emergency getaways, the use of guys like Kenny, weapons and munitions dumps and also 'off the books' surgeons.

There's one a couple of blocks from here which is where I'm headed right now. These guys aren't some back alley sawbones with rusty scalpels. They're qualified professional surgeons who just happen to have come to realise there's a hell of a lot more money in working for The Lodge than there is for a hospital. These guys are on call to people like us twenty four hours a day and best of all, there's no questions asked.

I phone Stanley up and tell him what's happened.

"Stanley, it's Joe."

"Hey, Joe. Jesus, that was quick, you done already?" he asks.

"Yeah, I got done about ten minutes ago. The cops were just getting there when I left."

"Ever the professional, eh? So how'd it go? You make an example of Hung like the Italian's wanted?"

"Yeah, I left him hanging out of a window on the forty ninth floor. There were a couple of glitches along the way but the job's done now. Anyway listen, the thing is I've been winged. Could you do me a favour and phone ahead to the surgery on Twelfth Street, just let them know I'm on my way? Should be about seven, eight minutes."

"Sure Joe, no problem. You alright?"

"Yeah, it went straight through. Few stitches and I'll be good as new."

"Okay, I'll let them know you're coming," he says. "Good job tonight, Joe. You just get yourself fixed up and I'll let the Italians know so they can send the money through as soon as possible. I'll see you soon."

"Thanks Stanley, I'll see you soon."

I've gotta say, Stanley's just about the best agent there is working down at The Lodge. He always says he puts quality over quantity, which I suppose is true – as arrogant as it sounds, he's got *me* on his books for a start. I don't want to sound too arrogant here but I don't bother with the small time contracts like some people. Stanley looks after the few people on his books (quality not quantity) and he's a reliable contact because he knows the job inside out, being an ex hitman himself. He's an all round good guy to have in your corner.

I arrive at a respectable looking building on Twelfth and push the intercom. The buzzer sounds and I'm let straight in. A tall guy in a white doctor's coat meets me at the door and leads me to a clinically white room.

"You must be one of Stanley's clients. A bullet wound to the arm is it?" he asks. He's got a kindly face. He was probably a doctor for normal people for years before this.

"Yeah, but it's gone straight through, doc. Hopefully, it shouldn't be too big of a job," I reply, hoping that it isn't. I've got to get back to Rachel soon.

"Let's have a look, shall we?"

I take off my shirt and he looks at the bleeding hole in my arm. "You've done a good job of tying this up –

you haven't lost much blood. It's a fairly smooth exit so we'll clean it up and stitch it, okay?"

"You're the boss, doc, only can we make it sooner rather than later please?"

He understands and gets to work straight away. The sharp pain has gone now and has been replaced by the dull throbbing pain and the doctor gives me an injection of pain killer before he starts sewing. As he works, he starts making small talk to try and distract me from the pain.

"You know, you're the second one I've had in here tonight but you're luckier than the other one. He practically knocked down the door about an hour ago in a real state. How he managed to make it here I don't know. He's suffered terrible burns – his clothes had been melted onto his flesh and it's a wonder he could move at all, let alone make it here. I doubt if he'll make it through the night, poor guy. Still, I guess it's part of the risks in a job like yours."

"Hey, you think I could see who it is after we've finished here?" I ask. I don't know who it is but I know that if it was me dying, I'd want to see a friendly face. Least I can do is try and make the guys last few hours a little easier, you know?

The doc wraps up and he's done a superb job. The stitch work is immaculate – small and tight. Hopefully, it'll be enough to fool Rach until it heals properly.

He takes me through to a room down the corridor and inside is a bed with what looks more like beef jerky than a man lying on it. He's hooked up to a drip which presumably contains about a gallon of painkiller. There's no hair on the guy's head and his skin is charred, all blackened and burnt. I'm amazed the body's not still smoking. I walk over to get a closer look but I can't make out who it is.

His eyelids pop open and these cloudy, gummy eyes look up at me.

"Joe…is that you? It's me…Frankie," the beef jerky wheezes and a cloud of smoke practically escapes his lips.

Frankie. Who's a Frankie at The Lodge? Oh wait, I know.

"Frankie Slater? Jesus, what happened to you, man?"

"It was…The Prophet. He set me up. I was…given a loc…location for a hit and when I got there…there was a note from The Prophet. It said…the building was gonna blow. I…bolted out of there but the…the blast got me. How's it look, Joe? Be…honest."

Be honest? How do you tell a guy he looks like Kentucky Fried Hitman and he'll be lucky to make it through the next hour.

"Well you'll never make the cover of Cute Hitmen Monthly or anything Frankie, but I think you'll pull through."

It's a lie and we both know it. Frankie looks up at me as if to thank me for lying to him. Christ, I'm becoming a more professional liar than I am a hitman these days.

"So what…what are you doing here, Joe?" he asks, closing his eyes.

"I got shot in the arm about an hour ago by some lucky Chinese fucker and the doc's just been stitching me up."

"Tell me about it. How'd it…how'd it go?" You can tell it's taking everything Frankie's got just to talk.

His eyes are shut and his breathing's slow and I'd give him about half an hour before he's gone.

I start telling him about my night. He smiles weakly as I tell him about trying to talk to Ray at the same time as I'm jumping out of a helicopter. I run him through the operation – the gas, the lights, the shootout – and by the time I get to the end of the story, I know he's dead.

Poor bastard. He's another one I never really got to know. Must have only spoken to the guy a dozen times in my life and looking at him now, all burnt and dead, makes me kind of wish I'd made more of an effort to get to know him at The Lodge.

By the time I get home, Rach and Janet are still up talking. When I think of everything that's happened to me in the last three and a half hours and these two are *still* sitting talking? Still, I suppose Janet's got a lot to talk about.

They both look at me as I walk in. Janet looks more composed than the last time I saw her and Rach looks at me as if I'm going to say I've sorted the whole thing out. I wait until Janet's not looking and nod towards the kitchen. Rachel follows me in where Janet can't hear.

"Well? What did Ray have to say for himself? Tell me Janet's got this wrong and he's not cheating on her," Rach says.

"Look, I spoke to Ray and he admitted everything. He told me he's been having an affair with the girl from the golf club for the last few months. The slimy bastard even asked me to lie for him. Can you believe that?"

"Oh Joe, this is terrible." Rach says, putting her head in her hands. "All this time I hoped Janet had got things wrong, but now? God, I can't believe Ray could do this to her."

"Just goes to show, you think you know somebody. Still, I think he genuinely realises he's been an asshole and wants to get her back," I offer, trying to give some ray of hope (no pun intended).

To be honest, as much as I like Ray and Janet, I couldn't care less about either of them much at the moment. I just want Janet gone. I'm tired, the painkiller's wearing off and my arm is starting to throb with pain and I'm thoroughly depressed about what just happened to Frankie Slater and this whole Prophet affair.

"So, how did Ray look when you confronted him about it? Did he look sheepish or what?" Rach asks.

"*Look*? How did he *look*? Uh, he…well, he looked, you know," I stumble unconvincingly. The question throws me and Rach instantly knows I haven't actually been over to see Ray. She gets that sexy angry look on her face but now it's a whole lot more angry than sexy.

"You've been to that card game! You haven't been over to Ray's at all, have you?" she growls, just about keeping her voice down because Janet's still in the living room.

"Honey, just because I didn't *see* Ray, doesn't mean we didn't have a good, long talk over the phone," I offer by way of an excuse.

"For Christ's sake, Joe, you play cards all the time and the one time our friends really need us, you just phone through and try and sort this mess out in a few minutes. I can't believe you. You're so selfish!" she yells and punches me on the arm – right on the bullet wound - before storming out of the kitchen.

White pain fills my body and it's all I can do to control myself so she can't tell there's a goddam hole in my arm. She's my wife and I love her but I could easily shoot *her* in the arm right now, just to see how she likes it.

You know, some days it's just not worth getting out of bed. I risk my life and get shot in the arm just to get money together for *her* new business and try and help a friend out at the same time, and just because I don't go round in person, that makes *me* selfish. Man, sometimes I wish I could just tell Rachel about my job and maybe then she'd cut me some frigging slack!

She comes back in, grabs a fresh bottle of wine from the rack, flashes me a filthy look and storms back into the living room. I can guess that her and Janet will be staying up into the early hours talking about how terrible men are and how they'd all be better off without them, so I drag myself upstairs and into the bathroom. I get ready then flop into bed, thankful for the small mercy that Rach is still downstairs so I won't have to explain the bandage on my shoulder to her.

When I wake up in the morning, Rachel's not there and her side of the bed hasn't been slept in. Obviously, I'm still in the dog house.

I jump into the shower and let the boiling water wake me up. My arm is still aching but it's not the worst bullet wound I've ever had by a long shot. Long shot. There's a joke there somewhere.

I get dressed and head downstairs and the living room looks like a bomb site. There's plates full of junk food littered about and more wine bottles than there should be when you consider there was only two of them. They're guaranteed killer hangovers this morning from the looks of things.

I start clearing up and Rachel wanders down the stairs, her hair a mess and her eyes barely open. She's in her dressing gown and her hand is pressed to her forehead in the universal gesture of 'I think my brain is about to burst its way out of my skull'.

"Joe, do you have to make so much noise?" she asks.

"Sorry, baby, I'm just clearing up your mess from last night. How are you feeling?" I ask, with not much sympathy if I'm being honest.

"Lousy. I think I may well be dead by this afternoon." From the look of her, she could be right.

"Well, I've got no sympathy for you. If you want to drink yourselves stupid and moan about the many failings of men, you deserve the hangover from hell. Where's Janet?"

"She's upstairs in one of the spare rooms." Rach mumbles, looking more than a little sheepish as well as sickly pale.

"Right, well, I've got to go out. I'll see you when I get back," I tell her.

"Hang on a second, Joe," she says and comes at me, wrapping her arms around my neck. She stinks of booze and looks like hell but I still melt and all my anger at her slips away. "Look, before you go, I just want to say – I'm sorry if I got at you last night. And also, I just want you to know that I feel so lucky to have you. Talking to Janet last night and seeing the problems *they're* having made me realise how good we are together and how lucky I am to have one of the good guys."

I pull her close and kiss her hair as she buries herself into my neck.

"It's okay, babe, just so long as you *realise* how lucky you are," I smile.

"Alright, don't milk it," she laughs.

"I mean it," I go on. "Guys like me don't come along too often you know."

I kiss her again and sit her down at the kitchen table.

"Sit down kiddo and I'll fix you a little hangover cure before I go. Looks like you'll need some kind of a lift."

"Thanks, Joe. I feel like absolute death."

She picks up the paper and reads the front page while I mix together some orange juice, Tabasco sauce and stomach salts.

"Hey, speaking of death, look at this." she says. "How terrible. '*Local businessman Mr. Dei Hung was found last night hanging from the window of his penthouse suite. Hung, forty three, is believed to have some connections with the Chinese Triad crime syndicate and his murder is thought by police to be a gangland murder.*' Christ Joe, what kind of world is this we live in, huh?"

"Good question, hon, good question," I answer honestly.

"I mean, what kind of person could hang someone out of a window?"

"I don't know," I say, handing her the drink "But doesn't it say there that the guy was a known gangster so he probably did something to deserve it. He probably dealt drugs to kids or something. You ask me, he probably deserved it."

"I don't know about that, Joe. Listen to this though. It says here that he was surrounded by bodyguards and the police found at least fifty two bodies. They think that a large group of people broke in through the roof and shot the place up but no killers were found."

Large group of people. Shows what the cops know when it was just little old me. Still, making the front pages should make the Italians happy – I should get a nice little bonus for this.

"Let's face it, Rach, nobody who needs over fifty bodyguards is a good guy, you know? And what's that saying – 'Those who live by the sword, die by the sword'. Sounds to me like this guy had it coming to him," I offer up.

"But this is modern day America we live in, Joe. There's a process to things like this – everybody deserves a trial, everybody should be allowed their day in court. That's how things work. When people start taking the law into their own hands, that's when chaos starts to creep into our lives and the system breaks down."

I want to tell her not to be so naive. I want to tell her that the world isn't that black and white. I want to tell her that the law isn't big enough or powerful enough to deal with people like Hung, but *I* am.

I want to tell her that *I* did it and exactly *why* I did it and justify myself… but I end up telling her that Janet can stay as long as she likes and that I'll be back later in time for dinner instead.

I'm such a coward sometimes.

9

I leave Rach behind to nurse her wounded head and her even more wounded best friend and make my way over to The Lodge. Again, I'm not looking forward to going and that's really starting to piss me off 'cause it's usually a cool place to hang out.

Time was, going to The Lodge was a good thing. You were guaranteed a few laughs and as relaxed an atmosphere as you can get in a room full of professional killers. Nowadays though, everyone's running scared from this Prophet guy and it's starting to get on my nerves.

I mean, Danny's locked himself away, half the people on the books are staying away from The Lodge and even Stanley's starting to pull away a little. Jesus, I just hope Bear's there today, I could use a few laughs.

So that's three people now The Prophet's killed; Priest, Grey and now Frankie Slater. I wonder why he's doing it – if it even *is* a he? And I wonder why those guys in particular? And I wonder who's next?

I'm determined now that I'm going to get some answers at The Lodge too, one way or another.

As I pull into the driveway, a silver Beemer streaks past me and I have to swerve out of the way. Behind the wheel is Lincoln, shades on and a big grin on his face. Son of a bitch nearly crashed into me and from the look on his face, I'd swear it was on purpose. One day, me and him are going to have serious words – as in, I'm just looking for any excuse to kick the shit out of the cocky bastard.

I park up and my bad mood has turned to anger now. I'm sick of everything being up in the air in my life all of a sudden. There's Rach leaving work and starting up this new business, there's this whole mess with Janet and Ray and then this bullshit with the Prophet. I mean, what the hell is going on around here? It's time to start getting proactive instead of just sitting back and letting all these things wash over me. Starting with the mood around here.

I throw the doors open to Harvey's and stand dramatically framed in the doorway. The smoke from the bar swirls around me and out through the open doors which adds to the impact of the scene. I feel like Alan Ladd in *Shane.*

"Alright guys," I announce in a no bullshit tone "It's time we all had a meeting about what's going on around here lately. I for one am sick and fucking tired of this Prophet character literally getting away with murder. I watched Frankie Slater die in front of my eyes last night and some time soon, it could just as easily be any one of you in here. Now I'm calling a meeting out on the tennis courts in ten minutes so drink your drinks, meet me out there and we'll sort this shit out."

Short and sweet. That ought to get their attention.

I storm back out without even waiting to see what people's reactions are. See, I've got a rep around here as being just about the meanest guy in the place and people respect me. I don't mean to sound arrogant or anything, it's just the way it is. I'm not the boss by any means but a lot of people look up to me here as some kind of pack leader or something so I know people will turn up.

I walk out to the tennis courts fifteen minutes later (it's good to build the tension) and everybody's there, even Pike and Larry from the door. Everyone's deathly quiet and they're all looking at me as I walk out onto the courts.

"Alright, I don't know about any of you guys, but I think it's about time we got something sorted out around here," I growl, looking people square in the eyes. "Because I think that three men down is more than enough and this shit has got to stop. Now personally, I think that this Prophet character is a hitman himself so that puts just about every man here as a suspect."

"Yeah, you included Joe," shouts a voice from the back. It's Spider. That's typical of him and his sneaky fucking ways.

"Of course it does Spider, of course it does. Now you're thinking. That said, I ever hear about you accusing me of being an assassin out loud again, I'll save the Prophet a job and tear your fucking head off myself, understood?" I answer subtly.

Spider looks suitably scared, bows his head and nervously slinks back into the crowd. That should do it

– it's always good to make an example of someone early on.

"Okay, now that we've established *I'm* not The Prophet, I want people to start thinking about who *is*. I want people to start thinking about this logically. Who's got a motive to be bumping us off, unless it's one of us looking to thin down his opposition?"

Stanley steps forward and offers his view of things.

"Joe's right, we can't trust each other for a second. Jesus, The Prophet's probably stood here right now. We're all killers here so take a look at the guy stood next to you and tell me if you couldn't see him sticking a knife in your back."

"So what are we supposed to do then, just wait and hope we're not next on his list?" says a voice from the crowd.

"No, you could act like a man and accept it," I bark back angrily. "Jesus, you're all meant to be hardened killers. Every day we take our lives into our hands on every job we pull and all of a sudden, some ghost has got you all shitting in your pants. I'm almost embarrassed to call myself a hitman here."

A voice pipes up from somewhere in the middle of the crowd.

"So what then, Joe? What are we supposed to do?"

"You could grow a pair of balls for a start," I reply tactfully. "Everywhere you go, you take double care and you pay double attention to everything, and not just when you're working either. We're on the receiving end of what we do to others now – it looks like there's contracts on each and every one of us and guys like The Priest and Frankie Slater have already had *their* dose of instant karma. The main thing I want is for people to start sharing information. Any leads anybody has should be shared so we can find out who this idiot is and shut him down sooner rather than later."

"I have a lead," says this soft, low voice. The Widow steps to the front and the eyes of every guy fix onto her like laser sights. She's got a shake in her walk that lets you know she knows *exactly* how sexy she is and her black dress does nothing but accentuate her curves. If I'm being honest, if it wasn't for the fact that I'm married, even *I'd* go for her.

"The hit that Frankie Slater took on last night told him to go to a disused building which promptly blew up as soon as he entered. One of you brave, strong men should go and investigate the rubble and try to find the explosives," she says with obvious sarcasm.

"And why would we want to do that?" asks Pike.

"Because the remains of the device could give us any one of a hundred clues as to the identity of the killer," Widow replies, and she's right.

"I'll do it," says this big, dumb Frankenstein voice. Johnny Turk has his hand up like he's back in school and he's got this stupid grin plastered across his burnt face. "This is just like something from Murder She Wrote. I'll go down and see what blew up the building, only I'll have to bring it back here and someone else can examine it, okay?" he says.

"Good man, Johnny," I tell him encouragingly. "Good to see not everyone around here has lost his balls," I say, eyeing the others. "Alright, let's see what Johnny comes back with and for Christ's sake - can we at least start having some fun around here again?"

The crowd starts to drift back to Harvey's and people are mumbling in small groups and eyeing each other warily. Thankfully, Bear's there and he makes his way towards me, slapping a massive paw on my back and flashing me a smile from somewhere deep in his beard.

"Quite a display there, Joey boy. A rousing speech for the troops. You should think about starting up a hitman's union or something," he says with a grin.

"Screw you, Bear," I answer. "I'm just tired of people around here walking about with black clouds over their heads is all. Bunch of miserable bastards."

"Yeah, I know what you mean. Place hasn't been the same lately. All the boys aren't even into playing cards anymore – they can't trust each other at the best of times but lately, everyone's looking at each other like *they're* The Prophet."

"They should be, Bear, they should be. I'd put money on it that whoever The Prophet is, he's just been stood in front of us listening to that whole speech. I'm glad too – let the bastard know his card's marked, maybe he'll make a mistake."

"Yeah, the sooner the better too," Bear says. "I know business is booming for those of us who haven't been scared away yet but I miss how things used to be. I just want things back to normal around here."

"Look, Bear," I say, turning and looking the guy square in the eyes "You're the only guy around here who even comes close to being what I'd call a friend. So just, you know, keep your eyes open, okay? I don't want you dying on me."

Bear just looks at me.

"This isn't going to turn into a gay thing is it?" he asks.

"Fuck you."

"That's what I'm worried about," he laughs, putting his arm around my shoulders again.

All the way home, all I can think about is Rach. I just want to open a bottle of wine, run a bath and jump in it together. Just lie in the bubbles and the hot water the two of us and let the world just wash off us. But I know that Janet will still be there with all her problems.

I asked Bear if he wanted to go for a drink but he said he had some business to take care of this afternoon. I would go over to The Cave and hang out with Danny for a little while but I know he'll be panicking and running around in circles after hearing about Slater. Jesus, there's just nowhere clean in my life at the moment.

When I get in, there's a note on the table saying that Rach and Janet have gone out shopping and will be back later. Great, so I've got the afternoon on my own. Fine, I can handle that.

I eventually pass the afternoon by going to the movies and it really perks me up. I even bypassed the action films which is what I'd normally go for and decided to watch a comedy instead. I never usually go in for comedies but this one was genuinely funny. The theatre was pretty near empty and I found myself laughing out loud at some scenes. That's it – I've got to promise to make time to go to the movies at least once every couple of weeks. Time was, I used to go all the while but I don't have the time any more but I've really enjoyed just sitting in the dark on my own and investing an hour and a half in a good movie.

Maybe I could get into the movies or something. I don't mean acting or anything but maybe I could finance a movie or get involved in the producing side of things. Yeah, I could really see myself on a movie set. A guy I knew from The Lodge quit the game a couple of years back now and got himself a job in L.A. as like a gun fight co-ordinator or some such. You know, where the director paid him to set up the gun fights in the movie to make them look genuine and realistic. Hell, nobody knows better than me how a gun fight works. Or maybe I could be like a fight co-ordinator for some of these big Hollywood action movie stars. I could see me and Rach walking down the red carpet to some movie premiere and mixing with the cream of *Hollywood. 'Oh, what's that Mr. Scorcese? Of course, I'd love to choreograph your next movie.'*

Hey, it could happen.

It's dark by the time I get back home and Rach has ordered Chinese. She's sat on her own in front of a plate of noodles and Kung Po beef with her chopsticks. She's had the damn things for months now and she can never get a decent mouthful on them but she insists on using them still, saying it feels more authentic. Me, I just dig in with a fork but each to their own, right?

"Hey kiddo, where's Janet?"

"Oh, she's staying at her mother's house tonight," she answers as the noodles slide off her sticks. "She spoke to Ray earlier and he asked her to go home and talk about it but she's not ready just yet. I got you your favourite, it's in the kitchen."

I thank her, go through, put the food on a plate, get myself a drink and a *fork* and join her back at the dining table and I'm sure in all that time, the food on her plate hasn't gone down at all and she hasn't managed a decent mouthful.

"So what, you think that's it for those two?" I ask, taking a big forkful and instantly catching up with her in terms of food consumption.

"I really hope not," she says, pushing her food around the plate with her sticks. "I mean, I hate Ray for what he's done and he's a bastard for doing it to her but they're so good together, you know? It'd be a shame. I just hope they can patch things up but it's still early yet."

"Couple like them, look for all the world like they're gonna grow old together? And Ray goes and does something like this. Just goes to show, you never know," I tell her.

"Hey, Joe. You'd never, you know…you'd never mess around on *me* would you?" Rach asks, noodles flopping over her chopsticks again.

"Jesus, honey, that you would even ask that. No, I know it's easy to say but there's not a woman I've ever met could make me do that to you. But I tell you, in all honesty, I think every guy, no matter how happily married he is, will always at least *look*. It's a man thing. But it's also a hell of a good feeling to look around and know that there's genuinely nobody out there better than what you've already got at home and that's obviously where Ray's fallen down."

"We're okay, aren't we Joe?" she asks and it's not rhetorical.

"This whole thing has really shaken you up, hasn't it?"

"Well yeah, it just gets you to looking at your own marriage and wondering," she answers.

I push my plate away, lift her out of her chair and sit her on my lap and lose myself in her bright, brown eyes.

"Honey, I love you more now than I did when we first met," I tell her. "That's just about as clichéd a line as they come, but it's also true. I'm not a single person any more. You're half of me now and I just don't work without you. It's that simple. In fact, I think you can probably feel how much I love you right now."

She smiles a content, lazy smile and reaches her hand down between our legs.

"Tell me you'll never lie to me, Joe," she whispers softly into my ear.

She might as well be asking me for the moon.

The sad part is that without pausing or even skipping a beat I reply; "I'll always be honest with you, babe. I promise."

I'm such a fucking liar.

<u>10</u>

So a week's gone by and in all that time, Gerry and the boys at Magnum have been working like stink and have got Rachel's bookstore close to being up and running. There's electricity now and the guys have sorted all the plumbing out, fixed shelving into place, have plastered the walls and painted it all to Rach's specifications throughout. Gerry rang about nine thirty this morning and told us we could go down and check out the finished product. He also said it was one of the best jobs they'd ever pulled so it must be something.

All the way over in the car, Rach has done nothing but grin and practically bounce up and down in her seat. I don't think I've ever seen her this excited since our wedding day and I think I've underestimated just how unhappy she'd been at work all these years.

"Oh Joe, this is just the best thing in the world," she grins. "I always dreamed of running a bookstore but to actually *own* one – I can't believe this is happening. Oh God, I hope the building is okay."

"Relax Rach, Gerry said they've done a great job. It'll be fine. From what he was saying over the phone, you could be open for business by the weekend."

"God, it's so sudden. When Gerry started, I thought it would take months to complete. I don't know if I'm ready in myself for all this."

"That's what happens when you sleep with the boss of a construction company – things happen for you. And don't worry, you'll be fine. We'll get everything set up and you can open to the public whenever you feel like it."

"Oh Joe, imagine it. You could drop in to see me out of the blue and the store would be full of people buying books and reading and talking about the latest authors, and you'd ask one of the workers at the register where I was and they'd say I was out back and you'd come straight through and I'd be sitting there looking at the finances and the book orders and we'd just tell people to take care of things while we just went out for some lunch."

She's practically vibrating in the seat now and I can't help but laugh.

"Okay Rach, calm down. It's gonna be exactly how you want it to be," I smile.

We park the car up and walk over to the building. It's in a real nice area uptown. There's plenty of stores and businesses around but it's not one of those crowded and cramped areas. Looking about, you can practically *smell* the money up here and as far as New York City goes, this is one of the safer, upmarket areas. Hopefully, it'll be just about the ideal location. We round the corner and the both of us stop in our tracks. Staring back at us is this huge, classy looking sign reading *'Rachel's Corner'* above a pristine and modern building. There's a bright new glass front that's empty at the moment but even I can visualise some impressive window display. There's still a few of the guys from Magnum hanging around just clearing up when Gerry walks out of the front door giving orders.

Rachel bursts into tears, runs over to him and flings her arms around his neck. She tries to say something but can't. Gerry smiles that warm, fatherly smile and pats her on the back.

"You're welcome, Rachel," he says "But wait'll you see inside. It'll knock you off your feet."

I walk over, separate my blubbering wife from him and shake his hand.

"Hey, Gerry. The place is looking damn good."

"Magnum Construction doesn't do bad work, Joe, you know that. Especially not when it's for the boss' lovely wife," he smiles.

This sends Rachel into floods of tears again and she grips hold of me as we walk in.

As soon as I walk in, I instantly feel like I don't pay these guys enough.

It's incredible. They've knocked down all the walls and it's now just this huge open space with all these originally designed shelves scattered throughout the middle of the floor. All along the walls are lines and lines of empty shelves and littered throughout are plush leather sofas still in the protective wrapping. I've got to say, it's pretty breathtaking. God only knows what it's cost me but it's worth it to see the smile on Rachel's face.

Once she can see properly through the tears, she goes running from wall to wall and everywhere in between, and every new thing her eye meets gets an 'Oh my God!' She really is like a kid in a candy store. She makes me follow her around everywhere while she tells me in great detail what she's got planned for just that particular section of shelf or her ideas for what could go on that particular two inch square piece of floor space. Meanwhile, I'm just grinning and listening to the energy in her voice.

Later, once everything has settled down, me and Rach take a trip over to the supplier's warehouse. Basically, it's this bunch of large, open warehouses literally stacked floor to ceiling with books – I mean, everywhere you look and in every direction, there's just books. I've got this weird, irresistible urge to just start a little fire by accident and see the whole lot burn up but that's quite a worrying little impulse. Probably just some kind of a regression to my teenage years or something.

Rach meets with the head supplier, who actually *looks* like a librarian and the two go running off between corridors of books while Rach points things out and he writes it all up on a pad. Me, I'm just left there like a spare part surrounded by all these books. An hour and a half later and a fleet of trucks takes off, packed with pallets full of books for the store. Strikes me that although I'm doing this for Rachel's sake and it's costing me the earth, I hope it makes a profit. I mean, I know that something like ninety percent of all new businesses fold in the first two years but I'd hate for it to not be a success for Rach. I'm sure it will though because she'll put her heart and her soul into it. You know, maybe that's what I should do. I should write like a book or something. Yeah, imagine that. Rach could sell it in the store and I could do a guest signing one day.

Ah, who'm I kidding? If I haven't got the patience to *read* a book, I damn sure haven't got enough to write one. And what the hell would I write about anyway? It's not like I could write an autobiography or anything. *'How I Became a Hired Killer' by Joe McLean.* Not exactly a coffee table book, you know? More I think on it, Hollywood's really starting to appeal to me. I could set up shop there and work in the movies, training these soft, pampered actors how to be action movie stars. I mean, I've never seen a Hollywood movie yet with a totally realistic shootout. But no, New York's home. We've got the house, we've each got a business now, we've got friends here and I'm established at The Lodge. We've got it pretty good all things considering. Rach wouldn't leave for L.A. now anyway, not with the business about to start up.

Speaking of which, I haven't seen her for a while. She'll be lost in these corridors of books somewhere. Just then, the phone rings and it's Ray.

"Hey, Joe, it's Ray," he says sheepishly. "Look, I don't suppose Rachel's there is she?"

"Uh, yeah, she's about somewhere. She's looking at books right now, we're down at the suppliers. What's up?" I ask.

"Ah Jesus, Joe. I've really done it this time. I've really screwed things up," he says in this pathetic, shaky voice.

"Slow down, Ray. What's happened? What've you done?" I ask, almost positive I can guess.

"Oh, Jesus. You know how I've been seeing that girl from the club?"

"Ray, let's call a spade a spade here, okay? You've been screwing a young girl behind your wife's back."

A pause.

"Yeah. Yeah, okay, but me and Janet have been talking, you know? She's living at her mother's place right now but we've been talking about giving things another shot. I think she was going to take me back."

Here it comes. I can guess the rest.

"So anyway, I agreed never to see Tanya from the club ever again but I figured I owed her an explanation so I asked her round to the house. I mean, Janet's not there anymore so I thought it was safe, you know? Anyway, I was just saying my last goodbye to Tanya…"

"Let me guess," I interrupt. "You were saying goodbye with your dick."

"Ah Christ, Joe, it's all over. Janet came back to talk things through and found Tanya's underwear on the floor," he says, starting to sob. "She's never going to take me back now. But I was going to finish it with Tanya, I honestly was."

"But you just couldn't resist a last little taste though, huh? So what do you want from me? You want me to take your side here or something, tell you that I think it's okay what you've done? Fuck you Ray, I think you're an idiot. You let a classy, good looking woman like Janet get away just so you can feel young again with some airhead kid."

Honesty – always the best policy.

Rachel's back and she hears everything I'm saying down the phone and she just stands there watching me in shock, her eyes wide.

"God, I know. I know. I deserve that Joe, I know I do. But I'm serious. I'm finished with Tanya and I really want Janet back. Please Joe, I need you to help me – I need you to get Rachel to tell Janet the underwear's hers or something, I don't know."

Another pause, this time from me.

"Ray, I'm about to hang up this phone," I reply in a quiet voice. "But if you ever ask me that again, I swear I'll punch your nose out through the back of your fucking head."

I snap the phone shut and Rachel practically jumps on me, quickly asking me what that was all about. I tell her and she shakes her head disgustedly and calls Ray a name which almost makes even me blush. She's in a bad mood now which completely takes the shine off the fact that she's just ordered several libraries worth of books. I really could kill Ray at the moment and when I say that, it's usually not just a figure of speech. He's wrecked his marriage, wrecked our friendship and now he wants me to try and get Rach to smooth things over for him. Jesus, why has he had to go and screw things up so badly?

Rach is quiet for the whole drive home. We get into the house and I head for the kitchen to fix us both a drink when she stops me with her hand on my arm.

"You'd never cheat on me would you, Joe?" she asks.

"Jesus, honey, no. God, that you'd even think that." I answer, holding her by the shoulders. "I thought we established that last night."

"I know, it's just that, well, I bet Janet never even saw it coming. A few weeks ago, she thought her marriage was fine and her and Ray were happy, you know? Then the next thing she knows is, her husband's been living a lie with her and sleeping with a girl ten years younger. I mean, how do things get like that?"

I lead her to the couch and sit her down.

"Honey, I know Janet's a friend, but she mustn't have been giving Ray something, you know? I mean,

I'm not defending him for a second. After this afternoon, I could quite happily choke the guy but there must have been problems there for Ray to look elsewhere. All guys look at other women – it's in our nature, but for somebody to actually do something about it isn't just a moment of weakness. There's got to be something missing at home. And there's more to it than just sex too. Ray must have been missing affection from Janet, or maybe they just weren't connecting anymore. All I know is that Ray must feel he's missing *something* to make him look elsewhere and that's not the same with me. I've got everything I want right here with you. I love you physically, I love you as a person, I love the way you love me and I love how we work better together than we ever would apart. Trust me, Rach, you give me no reason to ever look somewhere else."

Rach wraps her arms tightly around my neck.

"Oh, you'd better not look anywhere else, mister," she says. "We're business partners now."

"Well hey, listen, I'm only saying that's true for *now*. I'm not guaranteeing things'll be the same five years from now. You've gotta keep working at it babe, keep me interested, you know?" I tease.

"Oh, I think I can manage that," she smiles, slowly peeling her top off. "Just promise me one thing, Joe," she says, in between kissing my neck. "Just promise you'll never lie to me."

"I promise," I reply without even skipping a beat.

She pulls my shirt over my head and sees the bullet wound on my arm for the first time, recoiling in shock. I can't believe I totally fucking forgot about it!

"Oh my God, what happened to your arm?" she says, her hand over her mouth.

Now what was it I just promised her?

"It's nothing, babe, honest. It's my own stupid fault really. I was trying to fix a nail gun down at the site just the other day and the damn thing went off in my hand. It's nothing major really, I didn't want to bother you with it."

Christ, see how easy it slips off the tongue. The promise didn't even last ten seconds.

"Are you sure?" she asks, reaching out to touch it. "It looks pretty nasty to me."

"It's fine, hon, honestly. The doctor said I was lucky. Just one of the hazards of the job, you know? Don't worry about it."

"And you kept it to yourself because you didn't want to bother me with it. You really are some kind of man, Joe McLean," she smiles wickedly.

"Yeah? C'mere and I'll show you just how much of a man I really am," I growl, dragging her towards me.

And for the rest of that night, I don't think about Ray, I don't think about Janet, I don't think about The Prophet and I don't think about anything other than losing myself in my wife.

11

A week goes by in a flurry of activity. In that time, I pull back from goings on at The Lodge. I even pull myself back from Danny for a while and just concentrate on helping Rach get the place ready for the grand opening this Saturday.

Actually, it's been nice. We've spent some real quality time together at the store putting the finishing touches to the place and her enthusiasm for the whole thing is totally infectious. I never knew that stacking books on shelves could be so relaxing and therapeutic.

The store looks absolutely amazing too, if I say so myself. It's part book store, part art gallery, part coffee house and all classy. Really, I'm sure that people will find the actual buying of any books almost second to the actual experience of just wandering around the place.

We had some fun holding interviews this morning though. Out of thirty nine applicants we had a stoner student, perhaps the fattest guy I've ever seen in my life and a woman who spoke so quietly I'm sure there was only dogs could hear most of what she was saying. Anyway, outside of all the fruit loops, we hired four girls and three guys and took on a real nice woman called Sarah to be acting manager 'cause although it's Rachel's baby and she has final say over everything, she admits she doesn't really know much about the day to day running of a business.
Sarah used to run a bookstore for one of these big chains so she's got the experience and she said herself she'd never seen a bookstore in her life like this one. She was so excited about it that her and Rach hit it off on the spot. In fact they're both downstairs now, going over final preparations for the opening while yours truly is stuck up here like an idiot, loading books onto the shelves for the sci-fi and fantasy section. Ah, the glamorous life I lead.

You know, all those years ago when I first decided to set up Magnum Construction as a front business, all I really had to do was just come up with the money, find a guy like Gerry who knew what he was doing, tell him how I wanted the business to run and just step back and let him get on with things. Easy. But me and Rach have been really hands on here. Okay, we got the place set up and we bought a boatload of stock but it's the little things that have been throwing us. Things like getting hold of cash registers, receipt rolls, computer systems, uniforms for the employees – little things that you'd never think could cause so many problems.

But the absolute worst thing has been setting up the coffee shop on the first floor. Jesus, that has been an absolute nightmare from start to finish. First off, we bought these fancy coffee machines. The ones that can't just make a regular cup of coffee – no, it has to have a foot and a half of foam and a cappuccino this and a fucking latte that and some chocolate powder sprinkled on the top. I suppose that's what the customers'll want so that's what we've got, but the damn machines are so temperamental that I can see someone's hand getting burnt off.

Then we had to worry about getting the health and safety guys to look around because we'd be serving food and drink to the public. *Then* we had to have more checks done to make sure the building is structurally sound even though my own construction company had only just finished renovating the entire building. All in all, this whole thing has cost way more than I thought it was going to.

Don't get me wrong, I don't begrudge Rach a dime of it but it has cost one hell of a lot more than I budgeted for. Still, that said, it *is* a business venture and it could be that, hopefully, it'll start making some money once it opens.

Speaking of which, Rach is unbelievably nervous about the grand opening. We've got press people coming, we'll be giving out free coffee and cookies at the door and Rach has even managed to get some famous writer in to do a book signing. I've never heard of the woman myself, but for what she's charging just to sit down and sign copies of her own book (which she's gonna be making money on by selling anyway), I think I may be in the wrong business.

All the pressure has been getting to Rach and that, mixed with her excitement, means that she hasn't been sleeping the last couple of nights. And because *she* hasn't been sleeping, guess who *else* hasn't been either. Not that I'm really complaining too much because she has come up with some very interesting ways of working off her nervous energy in the middle of the night. It's just that I could really do with not being stood here at six o' clock Saturday morning, trying to show one of the employees – a long haired, vacant eyed student called Scott – how to use the cappuccino machine. We're throwing the doors open at nine, which gives Scotty here just over three hours to learn how to pour coffee. Personally, I don't think he'll make it.

So we're nearly there. One of the first things Sarah did when she started in her role as manager was to cover the marketing. We've placed ads in newspapers and magazines and we've posted flyers all over the city with money off coupons attached. We've even put ads out on the radio so I'm hoping there'll be plenty of people turn up. All in all, I'm hoping that 'Rachel's Corner' is going to open with a bang and become the premiere bookstore in New York - both for Rach's sake and my own pocket.

08:59.

Everything seems to have fallen into place just in time. Shelves are stacked, employees smiling – Scott's even managed to work out which end the hot water comes out by now. The press are outside along with about two hundred book lovers. Rach goes out to them and effortlessly delivers the opening speech she's been writing all week and then, with the cut of the ribbon and the pop of champagne bottles and camera flashes, 'Rachel's Corner' is finally open for business.

The crowd flows into the store like mercury and I'm suddenly overwhelmed with how protective I'm feeling. The book displays I've spent all week perfecting go from a display to a pile within minutes. I see shoppers picking up books and creasing the spines and bending the covers back and I want to go over and break their fingers, let them know that I've spent a fortune stocking these shelves so they'd better be careful with the fucking merchandise. It's stupid, I know, because the whole point is for them to come in, look around and buy the stuff but I can't help feeling watchful.

09:37.

I finally get to see Rachel. Christ, if she's been glowing all week she could light the Vegas strip now. It's like when you're a kid and you get all excited in the run up to Christmas morning and you're looking forward to that new bike you asked for, but it doesn't compare to the excitement of actually *getting* the bike and riding on it, you know?

"Joe, this is incredible," she beams. "It's everything I thought it was going to be. Everyone's just been going crazy about the place, they love it."

"Just remember, kiddo, it's all down to you," I answer. "This has been your project from the start. If it's a success, it's only because you made it one."

"Now don't be so modest, husband o' mine," she says, slipping her hand in mine and leading me up to the coffee shop. "You had more than your share to play in this little success story."

Over her shoulder, I can see a young kid folding the cover back on a book.

If I see one more person manhandle another book I'm going to turn this place into a fucking bloodbath, I swear it.

11:45.

"Hey Scott, how's things going up here?"

He jumps when he sees me coming and he clumsily tries to hide his left hand, which is a decidedly bright and scalded red.

"Oh, uh, fine Mr McLean," he stammers. "Everything's fine here, things are going really well."

"That's great Scott. Keep up the good work, okay?"

"I will, Mr McLean."

"Oh, and Larry?"

"Yes, Mr McLean?"

"Why don't you go put some ice on that hand? It'll help soothe the pain."

"Yes, Mr McLean," Larry replies, his face turning as red as his hand.

God it's good to be the boss. Sounds funny someone calling me Mr McLean though. The usual response in the movies is to smile and say "Oh don't call me that, Mr McLean was my father." But when your father was actually *Mr-White-Trash-Waste-Of-Oxygen-Wife-Beating-Piece-Of-Shit*, then being called Mr McLean sounds pretty good to me.

Now see, this is real normality. Being someone's boss, running a legit business, dealing with the public. It's clean and it's refreshing, you know? This week has been really relaxing to me in a funny kind of way. There's a different kind of pressure in trying to get a bookstore to open on time than there is trying to whack Chinese gangsters.

16:47 and the day's nearly done.

All in all, I think it's been a real success. We've had press coverage, the public reactions have been overwhelmingly positive and the cash registers have been ringing all day. Rachel and Sarah are in the back office right now sorting through the books and the days takings, and the employees are winding things down out front.

I can already see this place becoming a success in its own right rather than just being something to keep Rach interested. So what with this *and* Magnum, I'm becoming quite the little business tycoon.

I wander upstairs to the coffee shop and order a normal, black coffee – no froth, no powder, no marshmallows, no fuss. Scott serves me and he's just about managed the whole hot water/coffee relationship by this point. I perch myself on one of the stools and watch him as he struggles to clean up and close things down. By now there's no more customers around wanting drinks and I can tell he's unbelievably glad about that fact.

"So how was your first day with us, Scott?" I ask, taking a sip of my drink.

"Good, Mr McLean. We've been real busy," he says, sweeping his hair out of his eyes for about the fiftieth time this minute. If I had hair that got in my eyes as much as his does I'd get it cut, you know, but I guess that's just me.

"Good to hear. What's been the big seller of the day?"

"Uh, probably the blueberry muffins. People seemed to like them a lot," he says, spraying the tables and wiping them down with a dischcloth.

"Say, can I ask you something Scott?"

"Sure, Mr McLean," he answers, looking up at me vacantly.

"Do you ever feel like you're missing something in your life?" I ask.

"Yeah. Yeah, I do," he says earnestly, putting his cloth down.

"And what's that Scott?"

"DeForest Kelsey's autograph."

Okay, gotta admit, I didn't see that one coming.

"Who the hell's DeForest Kelsey?" I ask.

"He played Bones in the original Star Trek. You see, I've got everybody else in the cast's autograph and I just need his to get the whole of the original Enterprise crew."

Scott looks wistfully into the distance for a couple of seconds and then turns back to cleaning the tables. I wonder if it's against union regulations to shoot your employees on the first day?

17:04 and the last paying customer has finally left.

Rach shuts and bolts the doors and calls all the employees for a meet. I watch her over the balcony from upstairs as she gives everybody a speech praising them for a great opening day before opening a few

bottles of champagne. The staff cheer her, then break off to talk to each other, drinks in hand. I can see Rach scanning around looking for me but I've pulled back up here out of the way to give her her moment.
After a while, I eventually go down and mingle and Rach slides over to me.

"Where've you been the last few hours?" she smoulders.

"Just giving you your moment in the sun, baby," I say, gratefully taking the glass of champagne she hands to me.

"What a day though, huh?" she says. "I still can't believe it's really happened. It all seems like a dream or something, like I'm going to wake up tomorrow and find out that it's *not* real and I've got to go back to work for Helen."

I wrap my arm around her waist and pull her close.

"As corny as this is going to sound - and it *is* going to sound *really* corny – but sometimes people's dreams do come true," I tell her.

She looks into my eyes dreamily.

"Jesus Joe, that *is* corny."

I pretend to be annoyed and pull away but she playfully pulls me back.

"I'm sorry, hon," she smiles "That's was a really nice thing to say and not at all like something you've read from the inside of a greeting card. Tell you what though…" she leans into my ear "…the words haven't been invented to describe what I'm going to do to you tonight."

01:34, Sunday morning.

She was right – I can't find the words for some of the things we've just done. I'm fairly sure some of them are only legal in certain Eastern European countries. Man, after nearly five year's marriage, she can still surprise and amaze me.

She leans over me to grab a glass of well-earned water from the bedside table and the moonlight from outside filters through the curtains and frames her beautiful body, a film of sweat glistening all over her. This heaving, firm, smooth, perfect body lying next to me. Neither of us can talk for a minute, we're so exhausted. We just lie next to each other, not touching. The whole room is filled with heat and it smells of sweat and sex.

After a minute, she quietly snuggles into my chest and I wrap myself around her.

"Joe?" she whispers.

"Yeah?"

"Thank you," she says softly.

"What?" I laugh. "Thank you for what?"

"Just…just, thank you."

And then she silently goes to sleep on my chest. Man, have I gotta be husband of the year or what?

<u>12</u>

I like to think I'm just like most guys. You know, I like to watch sports on T.V. with a beer, I think that John Wayne is the greatest actor there's ever been, I give to charity every month and I try to be a good husband. But sometimes, that last one can really cost.

I'm going to talk money here for a second. Now I've said before that I don't begrudge a dime of what I've spent on 'Rachel's Corner' but the whole thing has put a bigger dent in the old finances than I thought.

Don't get me wrong, being a hitman is a really profitable way to make a living but there's certain overheads to it the same as there are for any business. For example the fees for membership at The Lodge are pretty steep, you've got to constantly update your armoury and ammunition and then there's the cut for your agent and any other outside help you might call in on a job but being a hitman still brings in more than enough money to pay for me and Rachel's frankly lavish lifestyle, get the bills paid and still have enough left over.

On top of that, Magnum Construction will always turn a profit so there's that too. Usually, if we're talking a monthly take home salary, I make more than we could ever realistically spend but now, what with the bookstore and everything, the pot has taken a bit of a hit. See, although the building was bought by Magnum and it was mine to give to Rachel, we'd still bought it hoping to turn it into apartments, so I'm down on the cost of the building itself and whatever profit we'd have made. And a piece of real estate that size doesn't come cheap in Manhattan, even if it *did* need work on it.

And that's another point. I'm down on the cost of labour for the Magnum crew. Usually they're working on something that'll make its money back but this was a private job for me as the boss, so I'm out the cost of all their paycheques on top of whatever money they'd have brought in if they'd been working on a normal job. I know I got well paid for the Hung job, but that only really covered the costs of buying all the stock and accessories for the store.

I'm confident that Rachel's Corner will turn a profit eventually but because it's only just up and running we won't see any return for quite a while yet. Plus I've pulled back from The Lodge and been spending time on the new business so I haven't taken any contracts since the Hung job, which means that for the last few weeks there's been no money coming in, only a ton of it going out.

Now I'm not saying we're anywhere close to being broke because we're not, it's just that I'm the type of guy who likes to be secure and know that we've got plenty saved away and in my profession, the reality is that you risk being killed on every hit you make so I want to know that if that ever happens, Rachel has got enough money to live on comfortably for the rest of her life without having to sell the house or the new bookstore.

Which is what brings me here to The Lodge looking for work. Also, if I'm being totally honest, even though it's been nice involving myself in something like the bookstore, I still haven't forgotten about this 'Prophet' character running around out there and I told myself I'd do more to root the fucker out than I have been doing so coming in today can kill two birds with one stone.

As soon as I step foot in Harvey's, Stanley comes straight over from the bar and flashes me a big, fatherly smile. From underneath his bushy white eyebrows, his eyes are sparkling, which either means he's got a really good job for me or he got laid last night.

"Hey, Joe," he smiles. "Where you been, man? I've got a really good job for you."

Figures.

"I was hoping you would, Stanley. What is it?" I ask, letting him lead me to the bar.

"I'll show you in a minute. Let's just go get a beer and we can talk huh?"

Something's wrong here. Stanley *always* puts business before the pleasantries. He's angling for something here. I wonder what.

"So, uh, where've you been lately?" he asks. "We haven't seen you around here for quite a while pal." Jesus, that didn't take long. Subtle as a house brick to the temple.

"*We* haven't seen me around for a while? Who's we, Stanley?" I ask.

"Well, you know, I meant me meaning just me. I mean…" He's stumbling now and blushing slightly, and he knows he's given something away. "Ah Jeez Joe, you might as well find out from me - people have been talking around here. They've noticed that in these last couple of weeks since you haven't been here that even though nobody's seen or heard from Johnny Turk either, the Prophet killings have stopped and people are – well, you know, people are making some kind of a connection."

"What, just because I haven't been around for a few weeks, people are accusing me of being some fucking loony killer. Gimme names Stanley, I want names," I tell him, anger slowly burning its way up from my stomach to my head.

I'm fucking furious now. Christ, I give myself a nice couple of weeks break to spend with my wife and I only did that because the atmosphere around here was too fucking gloomy. Now, five minutes through the door, I find out these morons have been running me down behind my back. It takes a long time to build up a reputation in this business and I won't have anybody trying to damage that rep.

Stanley starts back pedalling a little when he sees how angry I am.

"Well, it's not like it's been just one guy Joe," he says.

"That's okay, but one guy is all I want."

"Joe, calm down, remember management rules about any fighting around here," he says, putting his hand on my arm.

Fuck management rules. I notice now that all the eyes in the place are on me and have been ever since I walked in. Alright, time to put the rumours to rest.

"Okay, you sorry bunch of fucks, which one of you has got the balls to admit you've been talking shit about me behind my back?"

A loud quiet settles over the bar and all eyes are turned away. None of them can even look at me. "And just for the fucking record, this is why I haven't been around the last few weeks. Last time I was here, you were all crying into your beers about The Prophet and everyone was too busy filling their pants with shit to have a decent time around here. And now you all think it's *me* has been bumping hitmen off? You fucking idiots. I'll tell you something though, if I *was* The Prophet, most of you wouldn't be sat in here today."

"Is that so?" comes a low voice from behind me.

I turn round and see DeLaney standing there like it's a scene from a Clint Eastwood western. He's wearing a three quarter length duster jacket and his long hair is covering the one side of his face. He looks like he belongs in an 80s rock band.

"Finally," I say, turning to face him. "Somebody around here with some balls. It's just a shame they're dangling from underneath that big dick on your head." DeLaney seethes visibly as the room erupts in muffled giggles. He grinds his teeth, and a big, purple vein appears on his neck. Fitting, really.

"You've got a pretty smart mouth there," DeLaney growls. "But don't you think it's a coincidence that there's been no more killings since you've been gone?"

"No more a coincidence than if the men's room still smells of shit and *you* haven't been around for a couple of weeks, know what I mean?" I answer.

The vein on DeLaney's neck gets even bigger and I can hear a few more sniggers from the 'audience'. He walks slowly and dramatically towards me and tries to square up to me, which totally doesn't work because he's a good three inches shorter than me.

"You know, I don't think you're anywhere near as tough as people say you are," he says, loud enough so that everyone can hear him. "Lodge rules say no fighting on the grounds, but you just watch your back man, you hear me?"

"Why, you're not The Prophet are you?" I ask him.

There's out and out laughter now from the guys watching and a look flashes over DeLaney's face, like he doesn't care about the management, he wants to go for it right now. The look fades quickly though and he replaces it with a calm front. He winks at me and smiles before walking away, like that's supposed to intimidate me. What a maroon.

I call over to George, the bartender.

"George, give these guys a drink on me, show them there's no hard feelings. I know they didn't really mean to talk about me behind my back."

Everybody gets up and goes to the bar for their free drink and with that, everything's back to normal and my reputation's back intact.

Stanley sits me down in his back office. All the agents have their own working offices at The Lodge and most agents keep theirs plush and clean. Stanley's, on the other hand, looks like that crazy thing from the Looney Tunes cartoon has been through here. Remember the furry thing, never spoke? Just span around chasing after Bugs and blowing raspberries all the time. The Tansanian Devil or something. Okay, so it's a shit simile but you get the idea – papers everywhere, fast food cartons and beer cans all over the place. You can't even *see* the carpet. Now Stanley may not be the most presentable guy and I doubt very much if he even *owns* a suit but he is, for my money (quite a lot of my money actually), the best agent there is here.

Somewhere, in all the chaos of his office, I know that Stanley knows exactly where everything is. In all this mess he's running the smoothest, most efficient operation in this whole place – the trick is for him to not *look* like he is.

He clears some old McDonalds cartons from a leather chair at his desk and offers me a seat. I tell him I'd rather stand because I don't want my ass to be stinking of Fillet-O'-Fish. I sit on the edge of his desk while he sits down in his chair and sorts through all the folders on his desk.

"That was pretty ballsy, Joe," he says, pulling a red file from the middle of the pile. "That DeLaney's a dangerous character."

"Ah, I'm not worried about him," I reply, picking up a folder from the top.

Stanley snatches it out of my hand disapprovingly and puts it back.

"Maybe you should be, Joey boy, maybe you should be. You're not bullet proof you know, even though you think you are sometimes. He's got a real rep as a stone cold killer."

"So has everybody here," I reply honestly.

"Don't be smart, you know that I wouldn't even mention it if he didn't have a real *solid* rep, you know? The guy's good Joe, real good. You should be careful."

"You finished, mother?" I smile.

"Fuck you. You want to make enemies with psychos, you go ahead," he says, pretending to be angry at me.

"Ah relax, you old goat. I think it's precious that you look out for me," I laugh, rubbing his balding head.

He slaps my hand away angrily. "You want to pull back a hand like mine, you carry on boy. I'm not so old that I can't still handle cocky punks like you, you know."

"Alright, enough with the young student/old sensei shit. What've you got for me?" I ask

His eyes sparkle again, the same way they do every time he gets a juicy contract through.

"You ever hear of a guy called Jean-Claude Nouvelle?" Stanley asks.

"Who, the kick boxer from the movies?" I answer.

"Naw, you dummy. Nouvelle. Jean-Claude Nouvelle. He runs the equivalent of the French mafia, an outfit calling themselves 'Les Huntres'."

Stanley opens the file and hands me a photo of a guy in his mid thirties with slicked back hair and a power suit, all powdered and perfumed – got eurotrash stamped all over him.

"You're kidding me, right Stanley? The French mafia? I mean, the French can barely get themselves an army together, never mind having themselves any organised crime. This is a joke right?"

"No joke, Joey boy. Read the file," Stanley says. "Nouvelle's got his froggie fingers in pies all over Europe, from drugs to arms. He's a real up and comer, one to watch – at least he would be if hadn't tried to get in on a piece of the American pie and pissed the wrong people off. Get this – the Italians *and* the

Russians are clubbing together on this one, offering a cool million for somebody to dismantle Nouvelle's entire operation."

Stanley's still got that gleam in his eye, probably thinking about his commission on a job this big. Still, I've gotta admit, a million dollars would sure come in handy right now. It'd go a long way to refilling the old coffers.

"Okay, Stanley," I reply, after about three seconds thinking time. "Let's do it. Let uz kick uz some French derriere. I weel teach zis horse flesh chewing, garlic smelling, war fearing fool a lesson."

"Glad you think it's so funny Joe," says Stanley. "'Cause you've gotta go to Paris to do the job. Nouvelle's gotten wind the Italian's and the Russians aren't happy with him so he's lying low at home right now. You'll have to go to France to get to him."

Now, the old McLean mind goes to work. Although I'm not too keen on going to France on my own, I *could* combine it with a romantic break for me and Rach. Yeah, not only do I earn a million bucks, I also earn huge points on the old *husband-o-meter*. That's settled it then.

"Not a problem, Stanley my man. Besides, it's been far too long since I ate a plate of disgusting food and got looked down on. France sounds like just the ticket," I tell him.

Stanley grins, reaching into his drawer and pulling out a flight ticket. "That's good 'cause I already took the liberty of getting you yours."

It's no problem to get a second ticket to Paris for Rach and she's not surprisingly more than keen to go, leaving the book store to Sarah to look after while we're gone. I told her I decided to book us a romantic break just so we could unwind and relax together after the pressures of the last few months, and what woman wouldn't want to go to the capital of romance?

I'm actually looking forward to it myself because it feels like too long since we had a real holiday together. The only problem I'll have is getting the job done on Nouvelle without Rach knowing what I'm doing, but I've already taken steps to see to that. Although by now, after all this with the book store and now a romantic break to Paris, I could probably confess everything and shoot Nouvelle in front of Rach over a plate of frog's legs and she'd be okay with it, that's how high up in the good husband ratings I am at the moment.

Rach is outside the airport right now, phoning Sarah and checking that the store hasn't burnt down in the twenty minutes since she last rang, which leaves me in the airport terminal bar to pay around four times over the odds for a beer and a glass of wine.

"I can't believe we're actually going to Paris," says Rach as she comes back, puts her phone down on the table and drinks her wine.

"Yeah, it should be good as long as we can avoid actually making contact with any French people," I reply.

She laughs, nearly snorting wine out of her nose, then her face slowly morphs into a more serious one.

"Joe?" she asks, looking at me with one eyebrow raised. "I know you never like to talk about money, but are you sure we can afford all this? I mean, what with the book store and all."

I hold her hand across the table and smile reassuringly.

"Baby, we wouldn't be going if we couldn't afford it. We're fine, really."

At least, we will be when I get the mil for the frenchie.

Once we're on the plane, after a talk about Rachel's plans for the future of the Corner, she finally leans her head back and goes to sleep. While she's out, I reach into my hand luggage and pull out the folder with Stanley's intel on the mark. I haven't really had a good look through and I'm not too sure what's actually waiting for me in Paris.

There's photos of Nouvelle and pictures of his gang in the folder. From the information here, he's quite a big noise in France. Powerful and rich. Still, who ever heard of French mobsters? The field of opposition can't be that great, you know what I mean? Stanley's got intel on where Nouvelle hangs out too – the Moulin Rouge district. Hey, even *I've* heard of that. Can-Can dancers, windmills, prostitutes, stuff like that. Stanley's also given me the name and address of a contact of his in the city where I can pick up guns, ammo and whatever else I'm going to need. See, say what you like about Stanley. Call him grumpy. Call him rude. Call him a smelly old midget with eyebrows like two dead sheep - he still comes up with the goods.

I settle back and try watching the in-flight movie but fall asleep myself before the credits even finish rolling.

13

You know, credit where it's due, the French have got one hell of a nice city here. You can really see why they call Paris the city of love. It's totally got this whole romantic, European vibe going on. All gothic style buildings, street vendors and atmosphere. Everything just reeks of class and style.

Still, having a beautiful city doesn't stop the French from being a bunch of snot nosed jerks. All of them strutting about, eating onions and feeling superior to the rest of the world. Not that I'm generalising of course.

The flight got us into Paris late last night, so we just about had time to drop our bags at the hotel and head out for a drink. We ended up in some little wine bar off the beaten track with these cosy little brick alcoves and wine bottles with long candles burning in them. Just about as far away from the meat market cocktail bars in Manhattan as you can get.

Now, after a late night and a continental breakfast (which basically means the hotel chef is too lazy to make bacon and eggs so they just wheel out these French breads and croissants and shit), me and Rach are heading over to The Louvre.

Rach, being the classy dame she is, wants to go and see the original painting of the Mona Lisa. Even *I* know this painting – ugly chick, smug grin on her face.

No wonder it's hanging up in France.

Rach leads me all around the huge gallery, her head spinning this way and that like she's Linda Blair or something. She's all '*Look at this sculpture, Joe*' and '*Ooh, isn't this a great example of Baroque painting*' and other such intellectual sentences. Me, I'm just planning in advance how the hell I'm going to whack a French mob boss in the middle of a city I don't even know.

Eventually, we end up in front of the Mona Lisa and boy, is she a let down. The painting is fucking *tiny*. It's supposed to be the most expensive painting in the world, so expensive people can't even put a price tag on it. This tiny little painting of a miserable old witch who can't even be bothered to smile properly is meant to be priceless. You ask me, old man DaVinci should've given Lisa a good screwing, then maybe she'd have given him a real smile.

As Rach keeps talking, telling me all about the 'enigmatic ambiguity of her smile' or something, all *I* can think about is what kind of security they've got around here and whether or not I could lift the painting. Obviously it's only hypothetical thinking – I'm not just going to try and steal the goddam Mona Lisa with ten seconds notice and my wife by my side – but it doesn't look too tough to me. Couple of smoke grenades, maybe throw one of these chattering

Japanese tourists towards the painting, see what security measures he sets off. If I was on my own, I'd probably give it a try. Ah well.

We eventually leave the throng of Japanese cameras in front of Mona and head to the gallery café. Rach seems totally overwhelmed by all the sculptures and paintings she's seen but if I'm being honest, I'm pretty well bored by now. To me, looking at a painting only takes a handful of seconds, a minute tops. By that time, you know – I get it. But for Rach (and everybody else here apparently), it seems you've got to spend at least a quarter of an hour without moving, usually with your chin in your hand, staring at the painting in question, and every now and then nodding to yourself as if you just figured out something real important. I don't know, what with my whole 'not being a big reader' thing and now with not being an art lover, I must seem like a real Philistine.

Over coffee, I get a message through on my phone. Earlier this morning while Rach was in the shower, I sent a text message to Stanley's weapons contact here in France. I sent an order through to this guy and wired him the money so this is probably just him getting back in touch to tell me where I can pick up the stuff.

"So who's sending you messages out here in France?" she asks. It's an innocent question – she's not prying or anything, but I can't really tell her it's a French arms dealer, telling me to pick up guns and ammunition in the back room of a brothel near the Moulin Rouge.

"It's just Danny, babe. Letting me know he's met the girl of his dreams."

"What'll you give her? Two weeks?" laughs Rach.

"Knowing Danny, I wouldn't give her 'till this time tomorrow."

Jesus, the ease of a practiced liar.

The rest of the day is perfect. Apart from it being about three thousand degrees below zero and we have to stop and buy scarves, hats and gloves in some over priced store. We spend the afternoon walking the streets, our arms wrapped around each other like a couple of teenage lovers, like on the cover of that Dylan album. In a way, it just makes what I'll have to do later all the more difficult.

Back at the hotel, Rach jumps in for a hot shower (another one, I know) before we change for dinner and head out for the night and I take the opportunity to order a bottle of champagne from room service. Now I'm not only doing this because I'm an incurable romantic, but it's also the ideal way of slipping the Mickey Finn I had the incredible foresight to bring with me into Rach's glass. As soon as she drinks this, she'll be out like a light all night. It makes me a bastard, I know, but if you think about it – I'm only doing this so I can pay for the amazingly expensive book store I bought her so the karma comes full circle. The scales are balanced as far as I'm concerned, you know?

I drop the tablet into Rachel's glass and sigh as I watch it dissolve in the fizzy bubbles. I've always hated champagne. All those bubbles and shit. Whoever said you had to have champagne for any celebration has to have come up with the greatest marketing strategy of all time, otherwise I bet nobody'd even drink the stuff.

Rach emerges from the shower in a haze of steam, like a rock singer on stage. She's got a towel wrapped around her middle and her skin's glistening. She looks amazing, which doesn't help.

"Ooh, champagne," she says, eyes wide.

"Well, we're on a romantic getaway here, right?" I say, handing her a glass. "Why not?"

"I like the way you think," she says, pressing herself up against me. "Cheers," she says, and downs the drink in one.

Yeah, '*cheers*' baby.

While she busies herself putting on her make up and dolling herself up, I jump into the shower myself 'cause all of a sudden I feel a little dirty. I don't add any cold and let the scalding hot water try and wash the metaphorical dirt away. It doesn't work and I leave the shower feeling dirtier than when I went in.

Rach is sitting in front of the mirror, going through that procedure of brushing her hair (which I'm sure could be trimmed down by at least twenty minutes if she only realised that she always settles on the first style she put it in). She doesn't look particularly well already, which makes me feel like shit.

"Joe, we've got to eat soon," she says. "I'm getting real bad hunger pains."

"No problem," I answer, towelling myself off. "Maybe we should eat in the hotel restaurant, save going out far if you're that hungry."

"Yeah, would you mind? Only I've got to try and get rid of this stomach ache," she says.

"Course I wouldn't mind," I answer.

Yeah, course I wouldn't mind, 'cause it's easier to get you back to bed when that tablet gets to work and knocks you out in about half an hour. I'm such a prick.

By the time we make it down to the hotel restaurant, Rach looks even worse. The particular sedative I slipped into her drink is a strong little number, designed to give the 'victim' a real dose of the cramps as a side effect, before kicking in on a two hour timed release and knocking the mark out for a good ten hours. I must have used it on twenty, maybe even thirty marks in the past, and I can't believe I'm using it now on my wife.

I order a glass of beer (which the waiter frowns at because it's not Le-fucking-Vino) and Rach just asks for water. I have the steak because even though I know we won't actually be eating it, I don't want Rach to suspect anything if I just order a salad or something, you know? She orders the same, hoping that it'll shift her cramps. The snotty waiter leaves us alone and as I talk, Rachel's eyes start batting. She won't last much longer.

"Joe, I don't know what's wrong with me, I feel lousy. I…I feel like I'm going to fall asleep any minute," she sighs.

"You know, you don't look too good either. Maybe it's just the flight catching up with you, making you tired. Or maybe it was the lunch we had earlier making you feel sick."

"Yeah, maybe it is jet lag. I just can't seem to keep my eyes open," she says.

I move around the table and put her arm around my neck, lifting her out of her chair.

"Come on, baby, let's get you upstairs to bed."

"But Joe, what about dinner? What about tonight?" she mumbles, though her eyes are closed now.

I don't even bother with a reply because she goes limp in my arms and I can tell she's out for the count. A herd of elephants with epilepsy couldn't wake her up now.

I scoop her up into my arms and take her back up the stairs to our room, undress her and put her to bed. She looks so cute lying there but she'll stay here sleeping soundly and safely until the morning, which leaves me free now to take care of the business side of this trip.

I duck out of the hotel without anybody seeing me. I don't want some nosy porter to see me 'cause the next thing you know, me and Rach will be down at breakfast tomorrow and he'll be all '*Ah, mon sewer Mc Lean. Did you enjoy zee sights of gay Paree last night?*' Nah, I want Rach to think I spent the night in the room with her, watching T.V. or something.

Hopping into a cab, as soon as I tell him where I'm going, the cabbie just nods and smiles like he understands. Like it's all '*Zeese crazy Americans, coming over 'ere to visit our world renowned brothels'.* Man, these French are just getting right under my skin the longer I stay here. I spend the whole journey trying to break down the language barrier and convince this smug, garlic eating asshole that I'm happily married and I'm going to a brothel in the Moulin Rouge district for business and nothing else. Not that that'd be easy even if the guy *did* speak English, but all I get out of him is that smug grin.

When he drops me off, I climb out, pay him and for the first time in about ten years, I don't tip.

Looking around here, it's clear what kind of area of Paris this is. There's dark alleys everywhere, right next door to big, wide, busy streets filled with people, noise and neon lights. Hookers sit in windows looking out and trying to entice you in by leering at you and smoking a cigarette but the soft, red lights still highlight their yellowing teeth and moustaches. Christ, don't the French believe in dental hygiene or something?

The name of my whorehouse is The Peacock, which is ironic 'cause I bet that's what most French guys have got. Stanley's contact's text message said I was to walk up to the front desk and introduce myself as Monsieur Washington. It's all very clever – just like James Bond (I don't fucking think). Ah well, as long as I get the stuff I've ordered. Of course, thanks to those silly little airport regulations about flying with twin berettas and hand grenades, I've had to come empty handed and order the equipment over here, but man, the dollar is strong here. For what I paid this guy for two unmarked guns, ten clips, ten grenades, a silencer and a couple of knives, I would have gotten change from a dinner at Room 15.

I'm on my guard as I push open the door of The Peacock. Just because he's Stanley's contract, doesn't mean I'm not going to be watching my back. He's already been paid and the goods should be here and there's no reason for us to meet face to face but all the same, I'm in alien territory here with no weapons just yet, so.

There's a thick haze of smoke that hangs heavy in the place. Perhaps the single ugliest hooker I've ever seen comes up to me and says something in French that I don't understand but I get the meaning clear enough. Jesus, I wouldn't sleep with her if *she* was paying. She's got skin that's so bad it looks like a novel's been written on her face in Braille and her tits sit either side of her belly button. As a hooker, she must be in a mountain of debt. Low standards, man, you know?

I ignore the hag and walk straight up to the desk where - and if you'd told me ten seconds ago I wouldn't have believed you - but there's a woman behind the counter who's even *uglier* than the hag on the door. What is this place, a whorehouse for masochists?

"Hola Senorita," I say "My name is Mr. Washington."

The small slit on her face that is her mouth opens wide to reveal the scariest thing I've seen for a long time. Man, even The Priest looked better than her, and half his face was missing. Her teeth look like the keys of a piano that's been smashed with a sledge hammer and there's gaps in between them so big that I'm sure she could floss with a tow rope.

"Ah, monsieur Washington," she grins, and I shudder hard. "I have been expecting you. Follow me, s'il vous plait."

She pushes through a plastic bead doorway and I follow after her. She leads me down a narrow corridor and I can hear the varied noises of rutting Frenchmen behind the doors. She stops, turns and flashes me that broken grin of hers and opens a door at the end of the corridor.

I step into the dingy room and it's bare except for a dirty looking bed, a bedside table and, romantically, a box of tissues. The only other thing of note in the room is a large suitcase sitting on the bed. My goods I presume.

Freaky French prostitute lady leaves me alone in the room and closes the door behind me. I go over to the bed, open the suitcase and inside is my order and a note. First things first, I inspect the goods and they're solid. Nice guns, well oiled - good knives, nice weight. The note is just thanking me for the business and asking me to send Stanley the guy's regards, whoever the hell he is.

I slam in a couple of magazines, check the sights on the berettas, strap on the knives, grenades and extra clips, slip my coat back on to hide this mini arsenal and walk right out past the hags and back into the cold Paris night.

Time to get my groove on.

14

Paris. The witching hour. The handsome,
strong and exceptionally well endowed hitman walks
the streets of the city, drawing the admiring glances of
the mainly hideously unattractive French women. 'No
fucking chance, madamoiselle' the hitman muses to
himself. He strides purposefully...

Ah, to hell with it. I'd never make one of those
Bogart types who narrates the story in those old black
and white movies.

It's not raining, thankfully but it is unbelievably
cold. Feels like the sun's decided not to give French
people any heat during the day – probably because
they're French - so by night, they have to sit in
freezing cold conditions, trying in vain to warm
themselves by the light of a single candle in a wine
bottle and the heat of their own acrid breaths.

Man, I have *got* to get over this hatred of the
French. I've only ever been to France once before
when I was a much younger hitman and got collared
by the mark. Him and his French buddies spent three
days torturing me and I guess I might have developed
a slight intolerance for every French person alive.

Now that I'm locked and loaded, I make my way
through the streets towards Nouvelle's club. My intel
strongly suggests he'll hole himself up there where he
feels safest because he knows the Russians and Italians
are out to get him. It's just on the outskirts of the

Moulin Rouge area but just close enough to the centre that I don't have to get a cab out there.

I haven't really thought ahead enough to have come up with a plan of action so when the club comes into view I have to make things up as I go along, which is usually when I do some of my best work.

The club is pretty non-descript from the outside. It's a big, warehouse sized building that stands apart from any other buildings around the area, which is just as well 'cause I'll be making a lot of noise pretty soon. There's a crowd of young kids queuing up outside to get in and the girls are all wearing a lot less clothing than you'd expect would be healthy in this cold. Jesus, when did I get old?

I join the back of the queue and try to zone out of all the high pitched French squeaking all around me because I can see obstacle number one coming up. The doormen. Now I don't speak a word of the lingo but I'd ordinarily be able to talk my way into a club using the universal language of dollar but I think it'd take one hell of a kick back for these guys to let me in once they pat me down and discover the arsenal.

I wait until I'm about five people from the front of the line before 'accidentally' tripping some kid over and pushing him into the guy in front. The guy in front turns around, pushes the kid back saying something in French that I don't understand but the meaning's pretty clear. Now the trick here is to keep people moving without them knowing it's you doing all the moving. It's an old trick I used to use as a kid to get me into clubs. See, most queues are pretty tightly packed and all it takes is a little shove in the right place to set off guys who've been drinking for five hours already. What you need to do is stay right in the middle of it all and keep the action going with a well placed push or a trip. Pretty soon, you'll have made your very own little mini riot.

Within seconds, I've got seven guys trying to punch each other's heads off while I keep the momentum and flow going with an elbow to the nose here and there. Because I've started it at the front of the queue, the coolers are on it straight away and trying to break it all up, which leaves the door open for the discerning, gun and grenade wearing customer to slip through unnoticed, leaving all the chaos behind. Simple. It's an old one but a gold one.

Once I'm in the club, I try my best to mingle in with the crowd which is easier said than done because I stand out like an American in a trench coat surrounded by skinny little French twenty one year olds.

Luckily, it's dark in here and the lights on the dance floor are low and muted yellows and oranges. The music is this euro-pop bullshit which keeps the dance floor filled and which'll hopefully make my job a lot easier.

Only thing is, I can't see any back rooms or VIP areas where Nouvelle might hang out. Guess I'm just going to have to flush him out. Flush - hey, I just had a brainwave.

With all the people out in the club, if this thing turns into the last twenty minutes of The Wild Bunch, somebody's liable to get hurt. Somebody innocent that is. So not only have I got to draw Nouvelle out from whatever seedy little back room he's in but I've also got to clear the club, so here I am in the gents' bathroom – and yes, I have got something better up my sleeve to clear the club out with other than just laying down a really smelly shit.

First, I need to clear the bathroom of people. I easily achieve this by flashing a beretta under their noses and scowling. Obviously, what with them being French, the two guys taking a leak don't take much persuading and bolt it out of there like someone just asked them to join in a World War or something.

The next step is to set the cover for what's going to come. I lock myself in one of the cubicles and cover it with as much toilet paper as I can find. Then I flip open my lighter, set fire to the bottom of the pile of toilet paper and quickly hightail it over the top of the locked cubicle.

Once I'm back out in the club, I move far away from the restroom and walk casually towards the dance floor. Now it's time to follow the mobster rule book number one - whenever you want to stay hidden, always post the biggest, ugliest guys you can find outside of your door.

Towards the back of the dance floor there's a staircase leading up and there's two of the biggest uglies you've ever seen at the bottom. Man, these two would give Larry and Pike a run for their money in the thick-necked-thug stakes and you can just bet that they're standing guard over these stairs for a reason.

I put on my best dumb American tourist expression and try my luck with Laurel and Hardy.

"Excuse moi, but I ain't from 'round these here parts," I smile stupidly.

One of them, the size of a goddam rhino, puts his fat hand on my shoulder, says something in French and squeezes just hard enough to let me know that he's not interested in anything I've got to say. I can already think of about fifteen ways to remove his hand, at least two of which would leave him in something other than a coma.

Rhino lets me ramble on for about five seconds before using his fat fucking ham hands to turn me round and walk me back into the club. I let him, and as soon as we start walking, he sees a kid running out of the restrooms in the distance being followed by a thick plume of smoke. Already, there's something of a riot on the dance floor as everyone turns to look at the smoking bathroom.

Rhino instantly forgets all about the stupid American, letting me go as he shouts to the other guy and the two of them push their way through the dancers to get to the bathroom to try and put out the fire.

I stride up the now unguarded stairs, taking them two at a time. I don't know what's waiting for me at the top but it's guaranteed Nouvelle will have cameras trained on me right now. Sure enough, three guys in ill fitting suits burst out of the doors at the top of the staircase and start shouting at me in French. No point in any subtlety now.

The first guy coming down the stairs, when he sees I'm not backing away, aims a kick at my head. I duck it easily and grab his leg by the ankle, using the momentum of his kick to lift him through the air and throw him down the steps like a straw doll. The second guy reaches into his jacket for a gun but I grab him by his lapels and slam him into the wall, too quick for him to put his hands out to stop himself. His face smashes unhindered into the brickwork and he's out of the fight.

It's always harder fighting uphill but luckily, these guys ain't great fighters. See that's the thing with guns – they're the great equalizer. Anyone with a pistol in his hand is on equal footing to anyone else, you know. But the art of hand to hand combat is badly ignored by today's criminal underclass. They just rely on guns, and that's all.

To prove my point, the third guy has managed to pull his piece. Only thing is, he's shitting himself after seeing what I did to his buddies and it's that, along with how fast I turn out of his way, that makes him miss his shot even on this narrow staircase. The bullet misses by a good ten, twelve inches and smashes into the wall by my left shoulder. Before he even has a chance to squeeze the trigger again, I'm up the stairs and on him, snapping his neck with practised ease.

That's another thing when it comes to fighting. You can have all the skill in the world and be able to throw a punch like Ali and a kick like Bruce Lee, but unless you get the *chance* to, it's not going to do you any good. What you've absolutely got to be, above all else, is fast. Greased lightning fast. You've got to be moving on instinct – moving against your opponent before he has a chance to even think what you're doing. Speed will win out on strength every time, trust me.

Through the doors at the top, everything turns from plain, dark nightclub to plush, carpeted corridors and I know I'm on the right track. Even if Nouvelle hasn't seen anything on the security cameras, that gunshot will let him know I'm coming. No point in worrying about surprise now, so I ditch the jacket and pull the twin berettas.

The Stones' '*Satisfaction*' starts playing in my head.

There's doors all along the red carpeted corridor but I move past them, my instincts telling me that they're either counting rooms or a little somewhere for the staff to take the local hookers.

The corridor ends in a T-junction. I spin the pins on a couple of the grenades and throw them around both sides, just to be on the safe side. When the smoke clears, I'm glad I did because although there's nothing to the left, there's a couple of freshly smoking bodies down the right hand side. A little ambush no doubt. So, right turn it is – if that's where the goons are, then that's where the boss'll be.

The right hand corridor opens up into a plush reception looking area with a big, wooden desk, a fish tank and a leather couch. Just past the desk are a set of double doors and double doors usually means big room. And big room usually means lots of people. Which, in this case, means lots of people with lots of guns.

I toss a couple of grenades at the door then duck behind the wall back into the corridor. At least with the doors off their hinges, I can see what I'm dealing with inside. I swing my head around for a split second once the smoke has cleared and I can see tables and couches pushed over inside the room. They couldn't make it more obvious they're hiding behind them if they tried.

Not a bad plan really. They see some guy tearing his way through their club so they hole up in the one room, throw together some makeshift barriers and wait. If this was a normal gunfight, me with my two guns and them with however many there are of them, I'd already be halfway back down those stairs and out of the club. Still, bet they're wondering if making barricades from furniture was such a good idea now they know I've got a few grenades.

I holster up and spin the pins on all the grenades I have left and leisurely toss them underarm into the room, making sure they fly over their precious little barricades. Man, am I glad I ordered so many pineapples. They fill the room with noise, smoke and metal, leaving me to mop up the pieces.

(Incidentally, if you're thinking that there's not much skill involved in all this and that any idiot could walk in and start throwing grenades around, well be my guest and try it. See how far you get. There's an art to using grenades in a firefight without blowing yourself to pieces thank you very much).

I draw the guns again and step warily into the open room. More bodies litter the floor but I can hear a few groans which means there's someone still kicking in here. I toss a desk aside and there's three bodies behind it, only one of which is making any kind of noise. Looks like his two buddies took the brunt of it but this guy's still cut up pretty bad. I grab him by his hair and hoist him up. He winces and gurgles blood. I lean into his face and say one word.

"Nouvelle."

The guy, his eyes wide with pain and terror, starts talking in French so I head butt him sharply on the nose and say one more word.

"English."

Now that the language barrier has been broken down, the guy tells me that Nouvelle escaped out of the back of the club when he saw me coming. Shit. If I'm too late and Nouvelle goes to ground here in France, I've got no chance of ever finding him.

I race out the back of the room and into another plush corridor. Gotta try and catch Nouvelle up now, wherever he is. The corridor ends in a staircase leading back down to the club which I almost run down before I notice a metal door in the side of the wall. Thing that makes me stop to notice it is the fresh muddy footprints leading out of it.

On a hunch, I kick the metal door open and fresh air rushes in. The door leads to a fire escape that looks down over the twinkling lights of the city but in the alley below, I can see Nouvelle and two flunkies jump off the last six feet of the ladders and head for a waiting car. Nouvelle looks just like his photo – wiry little bastard in a tailored suit.

If I tried to chase them down the fire escape, they'd be gone by the time I reached the bottom. Got to do it from here. I lean over the top of the metal balcony and aim a shot at Nouvelle which just misses him but hits one of his flunkies in the foot. It's a pitch black night and visibility's poor down in that alley so I'm lucky to have hit anything at all.

By now, Nouvelle's made it to his car and they'll be gone within seconds. I've got no grenades left and no way of getting down to ground level…unless.

This is the back of the club and there's a couple of dumpsters pushed towards the far wall. One of them's filled with glass bottles of beer and wine but the other one's filled high with boxes and garbage. I can't believe I'm going to do this but if I think about it too much, Nouvelle will get away. So.

With a deep breath, I climb onto the edge of the escape and throw myself off and the Paris night rushes up to meet me. God, I hope I don't hit the dumpster with the bottles. Go limp, Joe, go limp.

The flight down takes about three seconds and I hit the dumpster with the boxes sweetly, pulling my hands into my side at the last minute or I'm sure the impact would have smashed every bone in them. Can't fucking believe I've just made that. I've just jumped thirty five feet into a fucking dumpster. I feel like Colt Seavers from The Fall Guy.

In the three seconds it took me to get from roof to floor, Nouvelle's started the engine and screeches off down the alley. Without even taking the time to get out of the dumpster, I quickly stand up and fire both guns at the car. Now this is much easier – I can see exactly what I'm aiming at here. The back wind shield shatters and I know I've clipped driver and passenger at least once. The car swerves into the alley wall and grinds to a halt in a shower of sparks.

Climbing out of the dumpster, I slowly make my way down the alley towards the car. When I get there, I can see the driver's dead, his head slumped forward on the wheel. In the passenger side (which is on the wrong side of the car incidentally – goddamn French design) Jean Claude Nouvelle is sitting there, blood running from a cut on his forehead and a little pistol held in his hand, but his arm is hanging limply in his lap. He knows he's helpless as I walk up to the car window and he also knows his time has come. Still, it doesn't stop him trying the usual.

"Please, m'sieu," he pleads. "Please, I will give you anything. Please, you do not 'ave to do this."

"You'll give me anything, huh?" I ask, lowering my gun from his temple and scratching my chin with it contemplatively.

"Oui, m'sieu. Anything!" he begs.

"Okay. I want you to give me your word that you'll never eat another horse as long as you live," I answer with a smile.

"Wh…what?!" he stutters.

"I knew you couldn't do it," I say, replacing the barrel at his temple.

And with the squeeze of an index finger, the McClean coffers are replenished to the tune of a million dollars.

I disappear into the night just as the local police and fire teams start arriving on the scene. All the clubbers are still outside watching the building burning down and hopefully the authorities will be busy out front for a while before they check this little scene of carnage in the back alley.

I make my way back down towards the Moulin Rouge and even this early in the morning the streets are filled with drinkers and curb crawlers. I ditch what's left of the arsenal down one of the city's many sewers and flag down a cab back to the hotel in the main part of Paris.

The hotel lobby's quiet but I still make sure that no porters notice me make my way back upstairs. I slip the card key into the door and creep into the room –I know Rachel will still be out like a light after what she took and even though I could potentially plug in an electric guitar and start rocking out to some Hendrix, I still tip toe around. She's lying in bed in exactly the same position she was when I left here a couple of hours ago. I jump in the shower to wash the smell of garbage off me and to clear my head after the hit, then I climb into bed next to my heavily drugged wife and sleep as soundly as a goddamn baby.

15

I wake up early the next morning and Rachel's still sound asleep next to me. If it wasn't for the fact that I can totally justify why I did what I did last night, I'd feel pretty guilty right now because I know that she's going to wake up feeling lousy. The drug that I slipped her last night had to be heavy duty enough to keep her out all night because I couldn't have taken the chance of her waking up and seeing me gone so because of that, the after effects are going to hit her pretty hard.

Still, this time tomorrow her headache will be gone but we'll still be a million dollars better off.

You see how you've got to try and justify things sometimes?

I'm going to wake her in just a second but first I'd better order some breakfast and juice for her. I'm sure she won't feel like eating anything when she wakes up but it's the best thing for her to get her back in shape.

"Rach?" I gently shake her by the shoulder and she moans lowly.

Her eyes slowly bat open and I help her to sit up. She looks around the room confused, apparently forgetting that we're in Paris but she suddenly adjusts. I stroke her hair and ask her if she's okay.

"I think so. It's just my head feels like it's packed with cotton wool. I can't believe I slept the whole night through. Oh Joe, I'm so sorry. You went to all the trouble to take us on a romantic break and I just fall asleep all night."

Her apologising to me. The one thing that makes me feel even lousier than I already do.

"Honey, don't worry about it, okay? So you had a little jet lag and a headache, so what? We're here another night. Just so long as you feel okay now."

Wow, I'm such a caring, loving husband huh?

Breakfast arrives at the door and although she doesn't want to, I manage to get Rach to eat some toast and have a glass of orange juice. I run her a bath and she manages to get out of bed but she's still groggy. It's early afternoon by the time her head's cleared and we leave the room and head into Paris even though she's still not 100%. I'm determined to make it up to her today and make the rest of this break as perfect as possible.

I make a hell of a good start as we head back to that big, long road of ridiculously over priced shops with that big archway at the end of it. I ask the driver to take us to the best jewellers in the whole of Paris and this is where he drops us.

All of a sudden, Rach forgets her headache as she looks in all these cabinets full of jewellery and rings and necklaces, all brilliantly lit by what look like million watt light bulbs. The store assistant starts off by being your typical snotty French woman, (making sure both me and Rach are *fully* aware of how annoyed she is by us for asking her to actually get the stuff out of the cabinets) but she soon changes when she hears me tell Rach that she can have anything in the whole store she wants. Then she can't do enough for us and she suddenly starts getting animated and showing us as many things as she can.

Rach gets giddy and asks me if I'm sure we can afford it. I just made a million dollars last night so the least I can do is to buy her a little something to say sorry for drugging her last night.

After a half hour of trying on everything in the store, she finally settles on a diamond necklace that costs a stupid amount of those Euros but roughly translates to about $30,000.

It's a small price to pay to ease my guilt.

Outside the store, Rach links arms with me and we walk up towards the big archway and it seems like her headache has worn off completely. It's still absolutely freezing cold and we're both wrapped up against the wind. The necklace has made us both feel better to be honest, so now we can enjoy what's left of this holiday.

We head towards the Eiffel Tower because that's the one thing we haven't seen yet. You can pretty much see the tower from anywhere in Paris, even if it's just off in the hazy distance and credit where it's due, the closer you get to it, the more impressive it seems.

Don't get me wrong, it's no Empire State or Statue of Liberty or anything but it'll do.

On the way towards it, we stop off at a street vendors cart and buy a big French hot dog and a cup of mulled wine which tastes like hot mouthwash and I end up throwing mine in the garbage. Our feet are hurting by the time we get close to the tower but we're laughing and having a good time so the freezing cold doesn't seem so bad, you know?

We arrive at this big open plaza where there's people milling about and everybody just feels small next to this great, big metal tower. I've gotta admit, it is one hell of an impressive sight. There's steps running up the whole of the inside of the metal framework but it's way too cold for us to screw around with that so we queue up to take the elevator right to the top.

We queue in the cold for twenty minutes, just talking and laughing, and we just about reach the front when Lady Luck goes and takes a great big steaming shit, right on my head.

Walking past the line of people is Rhino – the doorman from Nouvelle's club last night along with the other guy from the staircase and another, smaller guy I've never seen before in a suit. Of all the fucking odds, this muscle headed idiot just happens to look up at that exact moment and sees me standing in line. There's this time frozen instant where we both lock eyes and the realization of where he's seen me before dawns on him. His eyes go wide and I shake my head at him slowly, as if to warn him not to fuck with me.

This gesture stops him for about two seconds then, acting on some misguided sense of loyalty to his dead boss or whatever fucking reason, he shouts at his buddies, points to me and they start muscling their way through the queue to get to me.

Shit. This is just about worst case sce-fucking-nario.

Rachel's stood next to me and luckily she's got her back to Rhino and his buddies so she can't see what's happening. I've got about twenty seconds before they get here because the people in line don't stand a chance against guys this big and they're all just getting shoved aside like bowling pins. I can deal with these guys easily enough, that's not what's worrying me. What's worrying me is Rach either getting hurt or seeing me kick the holy living shit out of these guys – then how do I explain that one?

Luckily, before I can even think of a plan, the elevator   arrives on the ground and the guy in charge starts ushering people on and I bundle Rach in. Rhino and his buddies are about two thirds of the way through the queue and I'm waiting for the elevator to start and take us up the tower where I can think of what to do, when this party of withered old wasps in the elevator with us start fishing around in their bags for cash to pay the guy. Jesus, I haven't got time for this shit.

I fish a bundle of Euros out of my pocket and shove them in the elevator guy's hand.

"Here pal, will this pay for everybody to go up?" I ask quickly.

"Oui, monsieur," the guy says smiling and starts the elevator up. Thankfully, we start to make our way up the middle of the tower just as Rhino gets to the front of the queue, pointing at me and shouting. I wave at him, smiling the cockiest smile I can manage and they start chasing after me up the stairs. The fat fucking idiots'll never catch up by foot and at least now I've got some time to think.

"Who are those guys?" Rach asks, confused. "They seemed to think they knew you."

"No idea, hon. Maybe they thought I was a movie star or something."

"You're not a movie star are you, dear?" asks one of the ancient old women stood next to us. "Only paying for us all like you just did is the kind of thing generous movie stars do. I was thinking that maybe you were Cary Grant or somebody."

Great. American tourists. Senile, toothless, shrivelled American tourists.

"Lady, Cary Grant died years ago. And how old do you think I am exactly?" I say with remarkable restraint considering the circumstances.

"So you're not Cary Grant then?" asks a white haired, hunchbacked crone.

"No, I'm *not* Cary fucking Grant!" I snap.

"Are you sure?" she says.

Rach has to put her hand over her mouth next to me to keep from laughing. Her shoulders are shaking and she's crying which is just cruel really because she knows I've got this natural allergy towards old people. Especially fucking senile ones.

The elevator ride only lasts a minute but it's the worst minute of my life. Instead of looking out at the view, I spend the time thinking about the three guys who are running up the tower to try and kill me and at the same time I'm busy denying I'm any one of a number of dead actors these old bags think I am. Rach doesn't get to see the view either 'cause her eyes are streaming with tears of laughter.

The elevator comes to a stop on the huge middle section of the tower and we have to get out. I usher Rach away from the old women as fast as I can and I can still hear them behind us – "You're not James Stewart are you?"

Once we're away, Rach leans up against the railings and struggles to catch her breath, she's been laughing that hard. Glad to see she found the funny side of that.

"Oh Jesus, Joe, that had to be the funniest thing I've ever seen in my life. Oh, those old women were so cute. Do you think we could take one home with us?" she laughs.

"Yeah, sure. When customs ask if we've got anything to declare, I'll just tell 'em we've got a four foot, bearded and senile old witch who's still living in nineteen fifty eight in our luggage."

Rach can't breathe, she's laughing so hard. Now there's people everywhere on this middle level, all looking out at the views over the city and waiting to get the elevator all the way to the top. The good thing is that because it's so cold, everybody's getting the elevator up and nobody's using the stairs – except the goons of course. That means that if I can slip away from Rach for five minutes, I can deal with them on the stairs without worrying about anybody seeing us.

"Hey Rach, come and take a look at this."

Wiping the tears from her face, she comes over and we both look out on these gardens below and all the buildings between us and the horizon. Very impressive but I'm having trouble relaxing enough to appreciate it, you know?

"I'm just going around the other side to get a look," I tell her.

"Okay, I'm going to stay here a little while and I'll meet you 'round there," she says and I know she'll start laughing again as soon as I'm gone.

Doesn't matter, as long as I've got a few minutes to myself to deal with things. The platform ain't all that big but it's big enough that we could conceivably miss bumping into each other for a few minutes.

As soon as I'm out of Rach's sight, I head for the stairwell and fly down them. I've got no weapons on me because I dumped them all last night – the last thing I expected was to need them today – so whatever happens, I just hope Rhino and his pals aren't packing. I lean over to look down the metal framework and I can see them, red faced, still banging up the steel steps. Jesus, they must have really loved their boss. Hiding behind a girder, I wait until I can hear the idiots thundering upwards and I quickly spring out and punch the first one clean on the jaw before he has any idea what's happening. He's out cold before he even hits the floor. Rhino, who's coming up close on his friend's heels, stumbles into the now unconscious body and hits the deck hard. The third guy, the one in the suit I don't recognise, stops himself in time and stands there shocked, just looking at me and panting for breath.

I move towards the poor guy and he panics, swinging a clumsy punch at my head. I block the punch with my forearm and counter with a backhand to his nose. His nose spreads out over his face and before he knows what's happened I reach down, grab his feet and toss him over the side of the railings. He screams all the way down.

Rhino's on his feet now and he shouts something as he sees his buddy go bungee jumping without a rope. Yelling, he charges at me with his arms outstretched. Once again, speed counts as I side step his attack and slam a well aimed punch into his kidney's as he thunders past. He's already out of breath from running up all those stairs and this knocks any air he had left in his lungs right out of him. I don't care how big a guy you are, you get a punch in the kidney like that, you'll be as breathless as a skinny guy.

He leans up against the railings doubled up in pain. Before he can recover, I slam my knee into his face and he still doesn't go down. He's a tough one, I'll give him that. Doesn't matter though 'cause one way or another, he's going down. Once I slam his head off a girder a couple of six times, he's out like a light and he's so heavy it takes all my strength to lift him up and tip him over the railings. I watch him as he plummets down to the ground like a stone, his jacket flapping comically as he heads down. I lift the third guy up by his jacket and decide I might as well throw him over the side too so there's no evidence and the French cops'll maybe think the three of them jumped together. I run back up the stairs as quickly as I can considering I think I've put my goddamn back out lifting those fat fucks and just as I reach the middle level, somebody looks down and sees these three red splotches on the ground with ant sized people crowded around them, and starts screaming. Everybody teems over to the one side to take a look at what's happening on the floor and it becomes obvious what all the red is.

"Oh Maude, don't look," says one of the old women from the elevator. "It looks like somebody's jumped off. I think they're dead."

You *think* they're dead, lady? You think? There's nothing left of them but a bloody red stain, you stupid old crone.

Rach comes rushing up to me and puts her hands up to my face.

"Joe, where the hell have you been?" she asks in a panic. She must have thought that one of those stains was me.

"Uh…" I stammer, unable to think of anything.

"These people must have jumped off the tower and I just saw you come up from the staircase," she sobs, her eyes wide in horror.

"Oh yeah, it was horrible. I just saw these three guys down on the stairwell and they looked like they were about to jump over the side, so I ran down to try and talk them out of it," I say, pretending to be all shocked.

"Well, what happened?" she asks.

"I don't speak French," I reply with a straight face.

Once it becomes clear what's happened, we all get ushered back down to ground level by the guys who work on the tower and while we're waiting to get back down, Rach tries to persuade me to talk to the French authorities and tell them what I saw. I tell her that I didn't see anything of any note really, just these three guys who I assume were all lovers or something, holding hands and then jumping off and that there's really no need to tell the French cops because all they'll do is detain us for statements and we'll end up missing our flight. She eventually agrees to this and when we get back down, we're quickly ushered away from the three red blots which are already cordoned off and asked to stay around and wait for the police to arrive but we slip away quietly when nobody's watching.

All over the plaza, people are walking or running towards the tower to see what all the fuss is about so I put my arm around Rach and guide her the opposite way through the crowds 'cause she's still in shock over what's just happened. We walk away and the cold streets suddenly fill with the noise and lights of ambulances and police cars.

All of a sudden, I'm sick and fucking tired of France.

I just want to get back home.

16

I've never in my life felt so glad to be back home.

The last night in Paris, we pretty much just stayed around the hotel. Rach wasn't feeling too good what with the after effects of the drugs and seeing the three 'suicides', so she was pretty subdued as we called time on our bittersweet romantic break.

We arrive home in the early afternoon and unpack our bags. I know Rach is glad to be back too. It's not that she didn't have a good time out there but what with everything, she's as glad to be back in the good old U.S.of A. as I am.

We unpack our suitcases and after a quick coffee, she says she wants to head over to Rachel's Corner to check out how things have been going since she's been away. I tell her that I'm going to Magnum to talk to Gerry and see how business is holding up. Actually, I've got no intention of going to see Gerry. I figure it's been too long since I spent any quality time with Danny so I put off going to see Stanley to collect my million and drive over to The Cave.

I place my hand over the scanner and the secret panel slides open. Man, it doesn't matter how many times I come here, the secret panel *never* stops being cool! I tried to persuade Danny to let us install a couple of poles like in that old Batman T.V. show but he said it was too camp. I don't see what was so camp about a grown man and a teenage boy running around in tights and masks.

Danny's voice comes over the speakers as I walk down the corridor.

"Hey Joe, good to see you man, it's been a while. I'm down in The Nest."

He's right though – it has been a while. I've been so busy the last few weeks what with Rachel's Corner and now Paris that I haven't spent any quality time with Dan for a long time. Maybe we could go bowling tonight, grab a few beers.

The Nest's all lit up with the computer screens and panels and who knows what else and Danny's sat at his desk at the main console.

"Hey fucknose, how've you been?" I ask.

"I'm good, dickface. You?" he answers.

Ah, male bonding. You've gotta love it.

"Yeah, good. Me and Rach just got back from Paris a few hours ago. Mixed a little business with pleasure while we were out there."

"Oh, hey, the Nouvelle contract – that was you who took it? How'd it go?" Danny asks.

"Not too bad – had to burn a nightclub down and jump three stories into a dumpster, you know – the usual. Had a little trouble when the guy's lackeys spotted me and Rach up the fucking Eiffel Tower."

"Jesus, what did you do?" Danny asks.

"Kicked the shit out of them and threw them over the side."

Danny laughs out loud and starts tapping away at his keyboard. I think because he's such a non-physical guy he's always sort of lived vicariously through my exploits in the field, you know? He loves to hear all the stories of what happens when I'm out on a contract. Gives him a buzz.

A few seconds later, he taps a button and calls the front page of a French newspaper up on the huge screen. Of course, it's all in French and we've already established I don't speak a word so Danny translates the headline out loud.

" Here we go - '*Triple Suicide From Eiffel Tower*'," he laughs. "Oh man, this is priceless, listen to this.

'*Yesterday, three men fell from the Eiffel Tower to their deaths. The unidentified men were seen pushing through queues for the famous attraction before running past tour guides without paying. Minutes later, having desperately made their way up the world famous steps, the three men are presumed to have jumped from hundreds of feet high in what appears to have been a multiple suicide bid. Local police suspect the men may have been on drugs.*' And that was you huh?"

"What can I say, it was an eventful holiday," I shrug.

Danny's laughing and it's good to see. He's seemed to have been under a cloud lately, what with worrying himself about The Prophet – now *there's* something I haven't thought about for a while. I think (as patronising as it would sound if I told him) but I think the guy needs a good woman, you know? Not one of these top heavy blondes who are just hanging around with him because of his money but a real, caring loving woman like Rach. ('Course, it would be a bonus if she was top heavy as well…)

We make our way down towards the lounge and I collapse on the couch while Danny goes and gets us both a beer from out of the fridge. Man, it's only now that I've sat down that I realise exactly how tired I am. I'm determined to do as little as humanly possible for the next couple of days. I crack the beer and goddamn if it doesn't feel great to taste real American beer again instead of that warm and watery French shit.

"So what's been happening lately, Dan? I feel like I'm out of the loop here."

He seems relaxed as he starts to tell me all about the latest girl he's been screwing. Apparently she was a little kinky and she liked to film them at it and she got off on people watching her do it over the internet so Danny, technical wizard that he is, hacked into the Interpol mainframe and jammed their computers with a full twenty minutes of them humping like teenagers. He says she came like a demon and his snow white ass is probably number one on their most wanted list. He can barely tell me the story for laughing and it's real good to see him back to how he used to be.

"So there's been no sign of this Prophet fucker then?" I ask, hoping that everything's back to normal around here again. Big mistake. Danny's face drops.

"Yeah, you wouldn't have heard if you've been away," he says, his smile vanishing completely. "The latest one to go is Chuck Reeve, you know – the redneck?"

I can't picture the guy. I don't think I know anybody called Chuck. Danny describes him to me – a skinny fellah with a real bad haircut, broken teeth and a thing for knives.

"Oh wait, yeah I know him. Some wiry little Texan fool. The Widow laid him out with one punch last year," I say.

"That's him. You know, that makes him the fifth victim now - this is all getting too much, Joe. It's just too much," Danny says and his face drops again. "What if we're next?"

"Look, Dan, just relax. You're safe as hell here in The Cave. Besides, everyone he's killed so far have been field operatives. He hasn't gone for any intelligence guys like you yet. And I can look after myself, you know? It's these guys that can't who need to watch their backs."

I pause and let what I've just said sink in.

"Hey Dan, maybe that's it. Maybe that's a pattern, you know?"

"What is?" he asks.

"Think about it. All the guys The Prophet has killed so far – Priest, Frankie, Jake Grey – and now Chuck Reeve. What's the one thing that links them all together?"

"I don't know. What?" he asks

"They were all pussies!" I yell, animatedly, spilling my beer. "See what I'm getting at? Of all the people from The Lodge - and you're looking at experienced, trained and hardened killers here – the only ones who've been killed so far are the weakest, most useless pussies on the books, you know? The Priest was just an untrained guy with a God fixation, Frankie Slater wasn't exactly what you'd call a tough guy and as for Jake Grey, well I think even Rach could have taken him out blindfolded. See? All the victims have been easy targets."

"So what does that tell us?" Danny asks. You know, for someone as intelligent as he is, he can be pretty slow on the uptake.

"It tells us that The Prophet is a pussy himself! We know he's got a thing about killing hitmen but all the ones he's done so far have been easy. He's not going for people like me or Lincoln or DeLaney – guys who can handle themselves. No, he's going for the weakest of us which has gotta mean that he's weak himself."

"Jesus Joe, you're right. That *is* a link. Besides, it's all we've got to go on," Danny agrees.

"So our list of possible suspects – DeLaney, Lincoln and the others – they're all tough guys, so maybe they're *not* The Prophet after all. Maybe we should be looking at some of the third-raters at The Lodge instead."

Danny pauses to let this theory sink in before he says anything.

"You know, I think we could be on to something here," he says finally with a grin.

We spend the afternoon shooting pool, drinking beer and talking about every single guy on the books at The Lodge, discussing motives, methods and just generally trying to play Columbo. An hour later, we're still no further on to figuring who's behind the murders but we've got a few good ideas.

I've gotta say though, it feels great to spend some quality time with Danny again. You know when you've got a buddy who you've known since like forever and it doesn't matter what's going on in your life because you've been through so much together, and whenever you hang out it's like putting on an old, familiar and comfortable pair of shoes? That's Danny.

Turns out he's been seeing that girl for a month now, which is practically a long term relationship by his standards. Dan usually dumps them after a week or so because he's bored, so this new girl lasting four weeks is something of a miracle. He says it's been way too long since he saw Rach and he wants us both to meet this new girl so we arrange for the four of us to go out for dinner next week. Nice to be getting back to how things used to be around here.

No sooner does that thought pass through my mind than my phone starts ringing in my pocket. It's Stanley.

"Joe, that you?" he says with a tone of worry in his voice that tells me this isn't going to be good news.

"Yeah, it's me. What's up?"

"Joe, I think you'd better come down here," he says.

"Why, what's happened?" I ask.

"It's Bear – he…he's dead," Stanley says quietly.

It's a miracle no cop cars are after me as I tear up the highway towards The Lodge at 120 miles an hour. Even if a cop *did* come after me, the way I'm feeling right now, I'd probably shoot the fucker off the road. Goddamn it, I can't fucking believe this shit! Of all the useless fucking pricks that have died lately it'd be hard to shed a tear for any of them, you know? But not Bear. Bear was a buddy, a real stand up guy. Like I say, in this game you don't really ever trust anybody but when you happen to come across some diamond in the rough who'll get your back with no worries, you hold onto a guy like that like he was gold dust. Bear was a pure guy – there was no smoke and mirrors with him. He was all surface, what you see was what you got. He looked like a big, hairy, beer drinking redneck – and that's exactly what he was. God-fucking-dammit, I can't believe this has happened. So much for my fucking theory about The Prophet only going after the pussies at The Lodge. Bear was about as tough as they come.

I remember once, he was trying to open a can of beer and he snapped the ring pull off with those heavy hands of his, so he just rips the top of the can off with his bare hands. Took him about five seconds. Whatever's happened to him, it must've taken a fucking army to take him down.

Stanley wouldn't say over the phone what had happened, just that he figured I'd better get down there because he knew me and Bear were tight.
I thunder the car through the gates of The Lodge and drive up the path, screeching to a halt in front of the main doors. Lodge rules say nobody's allowed to park up front but right at this moment, I could give two shits.

Pike comes over to me as soon as I step out of the car. He's got a vaguely apologetic look on his face – a look which says *'I'm sorry Joe, I know what this is all about but I'm still gonna have to do my job.'*

"Pike, don't fucking start on me okay?" I say, walking towards him.

"Joe, please, you can't park there. You're gonna have to calm down before I can let you in, okay."

As I reach him, Pike blocks my way. The guy's like a literal brick wall, only made of meat and bone instead of brick. I stare up at him and he's a good head and shoulders taller than me, but the look in my eyes makes us the same height. Pike can't meet my eyes for too long and he looks away but when I go to walk past, he grabs my shoulder in a steel vice.

"Joe, I've gotta search you for any weapons," he says firmly.

"Let me save you the trouble. I've got two guns in shoulder holsters and a knife tucked in my boot. Now I've always liked you Pike – don't make me hurt you," I say without turning around.

Pike's grip on my shoulder goes loose for a fraction of a second, but then he tightens it and says. "Sorry Joe, I've got a job to do."

Quicker than he can make a move I kick backwards, my foot smashing into his knee. Screaming in pain, he lets go of my shoulder but he's still on his feet. It'll take more than that to put Pike down as big as he is, and I couldn't bring myself to kick him that hard because I genuinely like the guy and don't want to do any permanent damage. That said, the way I'm feeling right now I could do with taking my anger out on someone.

Pike makes a lunge at me but I weave through his lumbering charge like a boxer and come up under his outstretched arms with an uppercut to his jaw. This staggers him but he still doesn't drop. He's got a look like an injured puppy, like he's upset at me for not letting him grab me. I know Pike doesn't want to fight me any more than I want to fight him but he should have just let me in then.

There's not many things more dangerous than a big guy who's also fast, but Pike isn't one of those – he's just big. If he ever got hold of me in his hands, I'm pretty sure he'd crush the fight right out of me but I'm just too fast for him. I can telegraph every move he makes and I move just out of his reach with every pass and land another punch to his jaw for his troubles. There's no point in trying to punch a guy like Pike in the stomach to wind him, he probably wouldn't even feel it. No, I've got to knock him out cold and as he comes at me again, groggy now, that's exactly what I do. My fifth uppercut lands square and sweet on his jaw and he's out cold before he hits the floor. My hand feels bruised and I'm sorry to have taken it out on Pike of all people, but I feel a little better for venting.

As I approach the doors, Larry's standing there, blocking the way. I flash him the same *'Don't fuck with me'* look and he thinks for a while, weighing up the options of doing his job or getting his ass handed to him by me. It takes a few seconds for him to think as he looks into my eyes and he finally decides, flashing me a sad and understanding smile of sympathy as he lets me go and walks past to see to Pike.

Down in Harvey's bar, all the loud and animated conversations suddenly quieten down as I enter. Half of them turn to look at me, the other half turn away and suddenly become interested in the backs of their hands. Pricks.

I stride through the bar, not looking at any of them and right into Stanley's office out back. Stanley's sat behind his desk, his eyes invisible behind his tightly furrowed brows. He's obviously been waiting for me because there's two glasses of whisky in front of him.

"What the fuck happened?" I say, and there's thunder in my voice.

Stanley looks up sadly and offers me one of the glasses of whiskey.

"Here kid, have a drink. You…you ain't gonna like this," he says lowly.

"Fuck the drink," I growl. "What happened to Bear?"

Stanley throws his whiskey back in one go, sits down and pours himself another, bigger drink. He takes a breath and starts talking.

"The cops found him at some bar this morning," he says, unable to meet my eyes either. "He'd been poisoned. The Lodge's source at the precinct house told us when they found him he'd practically choked up a lung."

"Poisoned?! A guy like Bear and he goes out like that?" I shout. I'm fucking furious now and I slam my fist down on Stanley's desk, knocking his drink over.

"Look, that's not even the worst of it," Stanley continues. "There was a note attached to the body. It was signed 'The Prophet.'"

The world turns red. I explode and take my rage out on a filing cabinet, roaring in anger and slamming the thing to the floor with a crash. Stanley leaps out of his chair and tries to hold me back.

"Joe, calm the fuck down!" he shouts. "Come on, man. Get it together."

I breathe and let the anger go and slowly replace it with a burning hate.

Before now, all this murder mystery, this 'killer-killer', this Prophet stuff – it was all just a lot of bullshit to me. Sure, it had people rattled but I thought it was just someone trying to settle a score or something. But now it's gone too far. You want to take out people like The Priest 'cause they've pissed off the wrong guy or something, that's one thing. But when you kill one of the only men in this fucking world I call a friend, then I take that personally and from now on, finding out who this Prophet fucker is just became priority one. Then I'm going to feed him his own liver. Me and Stanley head back out into the bar and I get us both a drink. A couple of hours later, people start to drift away and everybody's watching everybody else as they do. Can't say I blame them really. I watch each and every one of these tough, hardened men go and not a one of them can lift their heads to look at me as they leave.

It's late night now. Rach must be wondering where I am and I'm dog tired. Everything that happened in Paris, the flight back and this afternoon's drama has left me feeling like I could sleep for a week.
Before I leave for home, me and Stanley go back into his office to settle up for the Paris hit. I watch as he wires my account the million dollars and I tell him all about what happened with Nouvelle. He laughs out loud when I tell him about the incident at the Eiffel Tower.

"So what are you going to do now then, kid?" he asks

"How do you mean?"

"Well, I mean, are you going to disappear for a while like last time. 'Cause if you are, I want you to know that I'll back you up against those trash talking mother fuckers like Lincoln and DeLaney," he says. I smile warmly at him.

"Thanks, pops," I laugh "But I'm going nowhere. In fact, after tonight, I think I'll be spending more time around here than ever before. I'm going to find out who The Prophet is and break his fucking neck."

"Good for you. Anything you need, you just let me know," Stanley says with a serious nod.

I return the nod, and turn for the door. Just as I turn the handle, Stanley calls me back and asks me if I'd be interested in another job seeing as how I'll be around more. I almost turn it down but I decide to take it on, thinking it'll be a little diversion.

Oh, it'll be a diversion alright.

When Stanley hands me the picture of the mark, I can't believe my eyes. I can barely take in what I'm looking at and when I see who the client is, my eyes practically bug out.

The mark in the photo is Ray.

I flick through the folder and, wouldn't you know it but the one who's put the hit out on him is none other than his loving wife, Janet! Jesus, I knew she was mad with him but I never thought she'd ever have the balls to have the poor guy whacked. I'm kinda impressed though, tell the truth. Impressed and shocked.

And what the hell am I gonna do now? I can't whack Ray, much as his golf stories annoy me. Man, it's a good job nobody else here has picked up the contract 'cause if it was anyone other than me, old Ray'd be dead by the morning. I'm going to need some time to think about this.

Christ, as if I need any more complications in my life. That just about puts the nail in the coffin of what's probably been the longest day I've ever had.

On my way out, I see a guy on his knees starting to screw a brand new golden plaque to the wall. It's got Bear's name on it.

I flip out and grab the guy by his collars, slamming him into the wall and looking straight into his eyes. He starts shitting himself, wondering what he's done wrong.

"You leave it a week before you put that plaque up, you understand? You leave it a week," I snarl.

He nods, telling me over and over that he understands and I believe him. It's too soon to put that up – let's have some time to mourn the fucking guy for God's sake.

Larry and Pike are on the door as I walk out and Pike looks a little the worse for wear, his jaw all bruised and swollen. Neither of them makes a move as I leave.

"Hey, Pike?" I say, looking back. Pike looks up at me. "No hard feelings huh?"

"Shuh Dyoe, nuh huhd fuhlings."

17

It's late by the time I make it back home. Right now about all I want is a cold beer, a hot shower and to hold my good lady wife, 'cause after what's happened today I just want to lose myself in Rach. In the course of one day, I've flown across continents, lost one of my best friends and picked up the weirdest fucking contract I think I've ever taken on.

As soon as I walk through the door, all my hopes of a quiet night disappear.

The T.V.'s on and Rach and Janet are sprawled out on the couches, surrounded by a sea of chips, popcorn and alcohol. Unbelievable. This is absolutely unbe-fucking-lievable. Man, she's got a nerve.

She puts out a contract to kill her husband and now she's sitting here in my house and using my wife as a goddamn alibi. She wants some faceless hitman to bump her husband off because he's cheating on her. What is this, a Raymond Chandler novel or something? Christ, I can't remember the last time I took on a domestic contract (and for a pissy little twenty grand too!) and when I do, it just so happens it's on one of our closest friends. Well this won't stand, Janet. This won't stand at all.

Rach sees me come in and she knows me well enough that she can read the expression on my face.

"Hi Joe," she says, not wanting to alert Janet that she thinks anything's wrong. "How's your day been?"

"Not bad, hon," I lie, pecking her on the cheek. "Hey, Janet. Long time no see. How've you been?"

Janet smiles warmly at me and her eyes are slightly glazed from the drink.

"Oh, I'm good Joe, thanks for asking. How was Paris?"

Man, she doesn't let on a thing. For all she knows, the guy she's paid to kill her husband is choking Ray to death right now and she's here making small talk with me. Unbelievable. What she doesn't know is that she's actually sitting on the *couch* of the guy she's hired.

I'm not in the mood for dancing around to Janet's tune here, so I cut her off flat.

"Yeah, it was real good thanks. Say, how's Ray doing? What's happening with you guys, I'm just *dying* to know. It's *killing* me to see if you guys're gonna get back together."

Janet visibly blanches. As fast as the colour drains from her cheeks though, it's quickly replaced with a deep flush of red. Rach glares at me to warn me that I'm being insensitive but I don't give a shit right now. My ever so subtle use of words pass Rachel by but they hit Janet like a left hook. If only Rach knew poor, down trodden Janet's little secret.

"I…I haven't seen Ray for days now. We're…well, we're…" she stutters.

"It's okay Janet, you don't have to answer that," interrupts Rach, leaping to her poor friend's defence. "Joe, show a little sensitivity here, huh?" She frowns angrily at me, which would usually make me back off but I feel like shouting out in a rage.

I want to tell Rach that I'm a hired killer and that Janet here has unwittingly hired me to bump off her hubby. I tell you something though – of everyone at The Lodge who could have picked up the contract, it's just dumb fucking luck that it was me, otherwise Ray would probably be lying in a ditch right now with a hole in his head and Janet would be guilty of murder.

See, hiring someone to kill someone else means that you're just as guilty of murder as if you'd shot the guy yourself. All you're doing is paying for a middle man. It's like hiring a gun and paying for someone to aim at the person of your choice. Me, I'm just the bullct.

But obviously, I'm not about to kill Ray. He may be a pain in the ass at times and he deserves a fall after what he's done to Janet but I can't believe she'd want him dead. Just goes to show - you think you know some people.

As much as I'd like to goad Janet some more, I can't run the risk of her even suspecting I know she's taken a hit out on Ray so I've got to back off a little now. Even so, I can't believe how she's just sitting here calmly.

Janet, sensing the tension, excuses herself and leaves for the bathroom. As soon as she's out of earshot, Rach comes at me with both barrels.

"Jesus Joe, what the hell were you thinking? What's gotten into you?" she says angrily.

"Hey, I'm just trying to find out what the hell's going on with those two. I'm sick of us being in the middle of their shit."

"Show a little sensitivity though, will you? The latest is that Janet moved back in but Ray's still screwing around with that little tramp from the club. Janet's totally cut up about it."

Hell, Ray could have been cut up too if someone else had gotten the hit on him. Which still leaves me with the problem – if I don't complete the contract, someone else will eventually and as pissed as I am at him, I don't want to see Ray dead. And I really don't think Janet does either, she's just paid for the hit because she's so angry at him. So what to do?

"I'm going to see Ray," I say.

"What? What for?" Rachel asks.

"Because it's about time somebody sorted these two out. If he's screwing around again, then maybe I need to have a talk with him."

"But it's so late, can't you go see him in the morning?" Rach asks, and she already knows the answer from the look on my face.

"No, you stay here and keep Janet company. I'm gonna see what Ray's got to say for himself."

I'm tired, frustrated and angry. And I've had about enough of this shit between Ray and Janet. I'm not just going to sit back and watch our friends' relationship crash and burn in front of my eyes. Not when I can do something about it. Christ, how'd they get to the point where one can cheat and the other can order her husband's death. I mean, I know I've lied to Rach every single day we've been together but looking at these two, it makes our marriage seem perfect.

As I drive over to Ray's house, I get to thinking about how weird all this is. Back when I was starting out, I admit I took on a couple of domestic contracts. Ten grand to bump off a cheating husband here and there – easy money. I didn't take on many though because it's not my style. I don't mind being paid to bump off a drug dealer or a killer but I don't really agree with killing a guy just for thinking with his dick. Still, it's how a lot of guys learn the ropes before taking on the big contracts. But in all the domestic jobs I've ever taken on, I never once thought about trying to fix the couple's problems and try and get them back together. First time for everything I guess. I make it over to Ray's house in record time. I'm not even sure if he'll be there if him and Janet have split, but there's a light on. They live in a big house out in the suburbs and it's not too overlooked which is a good thing. I should be okay anyway for what I've got planned because it's late night by now.

I park the car around back of the house and easily work my way around the security systems. In fact, last time we were here, I remember telling Ray his security needed updating but he clearly didn't listen. Couple of motion sensors and a camera aren't going to keep anybody out, least of all me. In the false bottom of the trunk of the car there's a couple of guns, a Kevlar vest and some other stuff for emergencies and luckily, there's also a ski mask. As I reach the house, I put the mask on because if Ray suspects it's me breaking into his house, my cover's blown – then I really *would* have to kill him.

I slip the lock of the back door easily and creep into the darkened kitchen. There were no night vision goggles in the trunk but it's just as well I know the layout of the house so I can make my way around without crashing into everything. I can't hear any voices, but the light was on in the study at the front so I silently move up the stairs.

Weirdly, just when I'm slipping into 'hired killer' mode, I see a photo on the wall of the four of us in New Orleans taken a couple of years ago and it reminds me why I'm here.

I hear a tapping from the study – the noise of a keyboard being hit. Without making a sound, I peer around the door of the study and see Ray sitting there in front of his computer screen. He's dressed in shorts and a vest and he's humming a tune to himself, completely oblivious to what's about to happen to him.

I clear my throat on purpose and Ray spins around in his chair. My marks don't usually hear me coming but when he sees me, all the colour drains from his face and he jumps out of his chair and backs himself into the corner.

"What…what…what the?" Ray stammers like a little girl.

Obviously, I can't say anything because Ray'd recognize my voice. Instead, I make my way across the floor of the study and clench my fists which tells Ray all he needs to know. He's shaking visibly and as I reach him, he takes the most pathetic swing I've ever seen. I mean, I don't even have to move to avoid it, that's how wide it is. I return the favour with a well aimed punch to his jaw which makes him collapse limply to the floor like he's got no bones in his body.

Man, that felt good. Even though I'm here to help the guy out, I owe him that punch from that time he asked me to lie for him. I mean, me – a liar. Whatever next?

Because it's so dark and so early in the morning now, I don't worry too much about wrapping the unconscious Ray in a carpet and throwing him in the trunk of the car, old school Mafia style. Nobody notices though as we pull away and I'm beginning to think my plan might actually work here.

I drive over to The Cave, park up round back and unload Ray. I drag him in, still wrapped in the carpet and still unconscious. The one time I actually need him, Danny's not here which is a shame because I could really use his help with my idea but I'll manage. Besides, I'm just glad he's ventured out of here in the first place – maybe he's finally gotten over his fear. I unroll Ray from the carpet, pour his limp body into a chair and tie him to it with handcuffs, one pair on his hands, another keeping his ankles tied together. I put the ski mask over his head the wrong way around so he can't see but I roll it up enough so he can breathe. Man, when he wakes up, he's going to shit himself so bad. He'll probably scream the place down but everywhere's sound proofed so he can scream as much as he likes. He's in for a long night.

A long night on his own too, because I'm going back home to my wife.

By the time I get back, Rach is fast asleep. I'm tempted to wake her, just to talk to her, but that's a little selfish so I climb into bed next to her as quietly as I can. I'll worry about Ray and Janet in the morning. By now, I imagine *she's* drunk a bottle and a half of Gin and *he's* screamed himself hoarse but they brought this shit on themselves. Okay, so my own marriage is based on a lie but the difference is we love each other and I'd never cheat on Rach. And I'm sure as hell she'd never order my death. As my eyes close, all the anger and frustration of the day leaves me and I just feel lucky.

Lucky I'm still alive, unlike Bear.

Lucky I don't hate my partner enough to have them killed, unlike Janet.

And lucky I'm not tied to a chair with a ski mask over my head and wondering if I'm ever going to see the morning, unlike Ray.

Man, I feel like I could sleep for a week. I'm so tired. Can feel myself slipping into nice, warm, hassle free sleep.

Damn, I'll miss you Bear…I'll really miss you…

Morning, and I'm woken up by one of the most wonderful sights in the world. My beautiful wife in practically see through nightwear holding a tray of bacon sandwiches and coffee. After a day like yesterday, I needed a deep sleep and I feel a little drowsy but the sight of Rach soon perks me up.

"Hey, sleepy head," she smiles. "I would have let you lie in a little longer but it'll be practically dark again soon."

"Huh?" I mutter, propping myself up onto my elbows. "What time is it?"

"It's one in the afternoon," she says.

Shit!

Ray.

I hadn't planned on sleeping so late today. He's been on his own for over twelve hours. The guy must be a nervous wreck by now, not to mention starved. I should really head over to the Cave and go see to him. I should. I really should…

…but I never could resist a bacon sandwich.

It's gone two by the time I make it out of the house. Rachel's gone over to the bookstore for the rest of the afternoon but before she went, we had a little talk about Janet. Rach asked me why I was so rude last night and what I spoke to Ray about and I made some junk up but I *did* get around to asking where Janet's staying. For the last few days, she's been staying at her parent's apartment near the park. I know where that is because we were invited there for a party a few years back for her parents' anniversary. The only problem will be getting to Janet without anybody seeing.

I drive over to the affluent area of uptown where Janet's parents live in what they oh so modestly call apartments. These things are so big that you could probably fit twenty or so normal sized apartments in them. You know - all high ceilings, big glass windows and views across the park. I think I remember Ray telling me once that they'd made their money in boxes. You imagine that, making millions of dollars out of cardboard boxes? I think Janet's grandfather was some kind of big noise in the box industry. Man, how do you become big in boxes anyway? Makes what I do seem almost normal.

Janet's parents' apartment building is a big, elaborately built brownstone tower almost opposite Central Park called the Werner building. Even giving the size of it, I'd guess there's probably only a dozen or so apartments inside. I'm betting there's a reception on ground floor too with a stupidly dressed and over paid bell boy waiting in the lobby. Man, I wouldn't live in the city if you paid me.

Assuming Janet's even there right now, the trick is going to be to get her out, get her unconscious and get her into the trunk. Lucky for me, I've got something up my sleeve. See, *she* doesn't know who she's hired to kill Ray. In all likelihood, she'll be here at her parents' because she doesn't know when the deed will be done either so being here all day with them will act as her alibi so when she gets a call from a mysterious person saying he needs to meet her and that something's gone wrong with the contract, she'll have no choice but to go along with it. Perfect.

I slide one of Danny's voice scramblers over the mouthpiece of my phone and try to stop from smiling as I phone Janet's mobile.

"Hello?" Janet says when she answers, in a voice filled with sunshine. She's probably expecting a call from the cops any time soon to tell her that her husband's been murdered so she's trying to sound as normal and cheery as she can.

"Hello, Mrs Taylor. This is your employee calling," I say.

My voice will be scrambled to sound all deep and creepy and electric so she'll never know it's me and there's a good fifteen second pause as she lets it settle in.

Eventually she speaks, her voice sounding almost the opposite of what it just was.

"Is…is the job done?" she whispers.

"There's been a complication, Mrs Taylor. I'm going to need to see you. In person. Today."

"Today? But…but…what kind of complication?" she stutters.

"I'm going to need to see you. In person. Today. I'll meet you in the alley behind Werner," I reply.

Another pause, this time even longer than the last as Janet realises this mysterious killer she's hired knows exactly where she is. We're talking thirty second pause here.

"How do you…how do you know where I am?" she asks, her voice quaking.

"I'll meet you in the alley behind Werner. Make it quick."

As soon as I've hung up, I can't help but start laughing.

The good thing about a building this size is that it casts one hell of a shadow. The alley round back is more of a serving entrance and delivery point rather than an actual functioning entrance. The kinds of people who live in a joint like this have probably never even been back here. It's shadowed and secluded, even in the middle of the afternoon, which is perfect.

I park the car just around the corner and hide myself in the alley behind a dumpster. Janet appears in the sunshine at the end of the alleyeway and makes her way into the shadows. She's shaking visibly and her face is a picture – she looks like she's just taken a big bite out of a dog shit sandwich.

"H...hello?" she whispers nervously.

She's looking all around her, practically turning around in circles looking for someone. She doesn't even see the dart come flying from behind the dumpster and hit her in the neck. She's out before she even hits the floor.

As cliché as the old blow dart is, you can't argue with its effectiveness. Remember all those old Tarzan films where the local guys – usually running around in tiger skin loin cloths and bone necklaces – would sneak up on the lord of the jungle and put him down with a quick dart in the back. Cheesy, I know, but something about it must've stuck with me as a kid 'cause now I use them all the time.

I pluck the feathered dart out of Janet's neck, throw it in the dumpster and hoist her up over my shoulder. I peer around the corner to check the coast's clear, pop the trunk and bundle Janet inside. There's no point even binding her because with the amount of poison on that dart, she's not waking up for hours yet.

So that's two little flies in my web.

Time to get to work.

18

I remember back in grade school, Mrs McGregor told us this story about King Solomon. Apparently this guy was super intelligent. He could solve any problem and back in Jerusalem or wherever the hell it was, if anybody had a problem, this Solomon was the guy to go to.

I just remember this one story about two women who both thought that a baby was theirs and they wanted Solomon to sort out whose the baby really was. Old King Solomon says to cut the baby in half and they can have a half each. I always remember asking Mrs McGregor if that wasn't going to be really unfair on the woman who ended up with just the kid's legs and she told me off for being stupid and made me stand in the corner. But anyway, King Solomon orders this baby cut in half and the one woman couldn't care less but the other woman cries out and Solomon says that she's the real mother because she gives a shit what happens to the kid. That's the story as best as I remember it anyway.

Long story short, that's kind of the inspiration for what I've got planned for Ray and Janet. See, if nothing gets done soon, he'll carry on playing around and she'll just go ahead and put another contract out on him. So what I've got planned is pretty much a last chance for both of them.

It takes me a while to get to The Cave because by this time it's rush hour, everybody's leaving work and the streets are crammed with yellow cabs. All this means is that Ray's got even longer to wait on his own. Thinking about it, I hope Danny doesn't just turn up because It'll shock the shit out of him to see some guy blindfolded and tied to a chair in the lounge because I've never let my work intrude on the privacy of The Cave before now.

I park the car in the underground garage, shut the doors and unload Janet from the trunk. Looking down at her, it suddenly strikes me that this is *Janet*. The same Janet who threw up in my shoe last Christmas. The same Janet who brings burnt apple pie nearly every time we have them over for dinner. The same Janet who ordered her husband's murder. Man, this is weird.

She'll still be out for another couple of hours yet so I leave her on a couch and crack open a beer from the fridge before heading down the brightly lit corridor to the lounge. On the way, I stop by the utility room where we've got all our gadgets stored. There's some great stuff in here, real James Bond stuff.

Most of it's Danny's to be honest, because I don't really go in for anything other than guns and knives, you know? But some of this gear has come in real handy in the past. Things like electronic eyes, remote controlled sirens and flashes – spy junk like that. What I'm after is the hand held voice scrambler. As long as I speak into that, neither Ray nor Janet will have a clue it's me.

I take a swig of my beer and open the door to the lounge. Ray's still tied to the chair, the ski mask over his face and his head snaps up as soon as he hears me come in.

"Who's that? Who's there?" he asks, his voice trembling.

"Mr Taylor, listen carefully to me," I speak seriously into the scrambler and it comes out sounding like Darth Vader on crack. "If you want to stay alive you will keep your mouth shut and only answer yes or no to the following questions. The first question is, do you understand?"

Ray pauses, fighting the urge to ask a million and one questions. Eventually, a sense of self preservation wins out over a sense of curiosity and he answers "Yes".

"Good. I'm sure you have many questions but your survival depends on you asking none of them, only answering mine quickly and honestly. Now, is your full name Raymond Taylor?"

Pause.

"No," Ray answers.

No?! What the fuck does he mean, no?

"Then what is it?" I ask, genuinely curious now. No answer. Oh I get it, Ray's thinking he can only answer yes or no.

"You may answer that question," I say.

"My...my full name is Raymond Augustus Taylor," Ray answers.

I have to take the scrambler away from my mouth and bite my knuckles to keep from laughing. Augustus?! Jesus, that's the funniest fucking thing I've ever heard. Oh man, how have I never known that? Augustus! That's hilarious.

"Are you scared, Raymond Augustus?" I ask, hoping he doesn't pick up on the tremble that's in my voice because I'm trying so hard not to laugh.

"Yes," he answers.

"I am a professional hitman, Raymond Augustus, and I have been hired to kill you. Do you believe me?"

"Yes," he answers in a trembling whisper.

"Good. Tell me, Raymond Augustus, do you think you know who hired me to kill you?" I ask.

"Yes."

"Who?"

"It was probably…it was probably my wife," he says and his head hangs. I almost feel sorry for the guy. Poor Augustus.

"Why would she hire you? What did you do? What brings me to your door, Raymond Augustus?"

"I…I cheated on her," he answers.

"Am I to assume then that you do not love your wife?"

"I don't know," Ray answers in a broken whisper.

"Then think upon it further. I will return with something that will help you decide in a moment."

Oh I'm really getting into the drama here. As I walk out of the room, Ray babbles some incoherent bullshit which I ignore because I'm too busy stifling my laughter.

Augustus – boy, that's priceless.

I leave Ray to keep on shitting himself for a few minutes while I head back to the utility room and pick up the video camera. Danny's got a collection of all sorts of surveillance equipment in here and I pick up the nearest camera and tripod. When I go back into the room to set it up, Ray doesn't make a sound other than a few mousy squeaks. I point the lens over his shoulder to catch all the forthcoming action but aim the mic at him so as I can catch everything he says, which is where this plan will hopefully work.

Next phase is to bring Janet in. I haul her off the couch, bind her hands together with tape and lift her through to Ray's room and unceremoniously drop her unconscious body in front of him. Ray's head is moving left to right as he tries to figure what's going on. Now, fingers crossed, is where it all comes good.

"Tell me, Raymond Augustus, have you decided? Do you love your wife?" I say into the scrambler.

"What? I…I…"

"Allow me to help you make up your mind," I growl.

I set the video camera running, move to stand behind Ray then whip the ski mask off his head and put it on myself in one quick movement. I could probably take as long as I like because Ray's been in darkness for so long now it'll take his eyes a while to adjust but it's probably best not to take chances.

I walk in front of Ray and the camera and stand over Janet's body. I draw a beretta from my belt and point it at her head then bring the scrambler up to my mouth with the other hand.

"You are correct, Raymond Augustus. It *was* your wife who put a contract out on you. Your infidelity has forced her hand but now I give to you the opportunity to turn the tables."

Ray's eyes eventually adjust and he sees some lunatic in a ski mask with a gun pointed at his unconscious wife's head and this gets reflected in his facial expression. It's priceless. Absolutely priceless.

"Yes, it was your wife who hired me. Yes, it was your wife who ordered your death because of your infidelity. But I don't care about any of that shit so I have a new game to play. I have one bullet in this gun, Raymond Augustus. I will let you decide who receives it – you, or your wife."

Now here's where I'm hanging everything. Either Ray realises Janet's ordered his death and he thinks *'screw her'* and asks me to kill her, in which case we're back to square one and there's nothing else I can do for them. *Or*, he realises he really does love Janet and he'd die for her. All depends on how much he *really* loves her.

There's a tense moment in the room as Ray weighs his options.

A really tense moment

Really fucking tense.

"Me," Ray says finally, his chin touching his chest. "Kill me. Just…just leave her alone."

Perfect.

He really *does* love her.

"An interesting choice Raymond Augustus." I walk over to Ray and he closes his eyes tight, expecting to be shot in the head. I feel bad for putting him through this but the guy's gone up about a million steps in my estimations. Anyone who'll give up his own life to save a wife who's ordered him dead has got to be a real man. Good for you, Ray. Who knew you had a set of balls with anything on them other than Dunlop?

"Listen to me very carefully Raymond. You are not going to die and neither is your wife. That is, as long as you continue to follow my instructions, are we clear?"

"Yes," Ray whispers, his eyes still closed.

"Now listen very carefully," I tell him. "I am going to gag and blindfold you, then I am going to wake your wife and offer her the exact same choice I just gave you. If you make any movement that even suggests you are conscious, you will both die. All I want you to do is hang your head, close your eyes, listen very closely and hope your wife loves you as much as you clearly love her."

He hangs his head and keeps his eyes closed. It's crunch time now.

See, Ray being willing to take a bullet for his wife is great – it means he really does love her and hopefully all this has made him see that and he'll quit playing around behind her back. But *now*, I'm going to wake Janet and offer her the same deal only this time around it's more risky because she's already willing to have him killed so no way is she going to take a bullet for him, right? Guess we'll see.

I put a hand around Janet's neck, lift her head off the floor and run a bottle of smelling salts under her nose. On the third waft, she shoots bolt upright wincing at the smell then her head spins left to right as she tries to take in her surroundings. I squeeze the back of her neck just hard enough to let her know who's in charge here. I drag her to the back wall and prop her up against it and she screams as she looks up and sees Ray tied to a chair in the middle of the room. To his credit he doesn't make a move but then again, abject terror will do that to a man.

Again, I speak into the voice scrambler so she can't recognise me. Luckily she's unable to even look at me which helps keep her from even recognising my eyes.

"Listen to me very carefully, Mrs Taylor. You know who I am – I'm your employee. You have paid me twenty thousand dollars to kill the man in that chair and as a bonus to you as a first time buyer, I have brought you here to watch."

Yeah, I know I'm laying it on a bit thick here but what the hell. Considering the circumstances, a little melodrama ain't going to hurt.

Janet's making a lot of whimpering noises. She's not actually forming any words, just little bubbling noises as she stares at Ray and starts shaking.

"Wait a minute….just…just wait a minute, please," she whimpers. "I've changed my mind. I…I don't want you to kill him. Please."

"It is too late for that, Mrs Taylor. I am a professional and I always honour my contracts."

"But, but wait. I'm the one who's paying you anyway. Please, I'll double what I paid you if…if you don't kill him," she stutters.

"Unfortunately, if I don't honour this contract it will be bad for my reputation," I say. This is looking pretty positive here – she's realised already she doesn't really want Ray dead.

"I won't tell anybody, I swear. I won't tell a single person, I swear on my life!" Janet begs.

"You swear on your life? Very well, I will hold you to that, Mrs Taylor." I lift the beretta in my right hand and put it to Ray's temple. "There is one bullet left in this gun and I *will* kill somebody tonight as I have been hired to do. Now as you are my employer, I give to you the opportunity to barter your own life to cancel the contract."

I can see by her face that she understands me but she's too much in shock to speak.

"Your choice, Mrs Taylor. You or your husband."
She pauses.

I feel bad for putting them through this but it's the only way. I can only imagine what Ray must be thinking right now. To his credit, he does as I told him and he doesn't move a muscle – either that or he's genuinely fainted. I pull the hammer back on the beretta for effect and to force her decision. Ray stiffens but Janet doesn't notice, she's so busy making the biggest decision of her life. Maybe even what she thinks is the *last* decision of her life.

Janet's eyes eventually break and she starts crying. I'm talking big, sloppy tears here. Understandable really. Hopefully, this whole thing is coming to an end now because even *I'm* starting to feel the emotional strain here.

"Please don't kill him. Please…just don't kill him," Janet sobs.

"I don't understand, Mrs Taylor. I thought you paid me to kill him. Why the change of heart?"

"Because I still love him, that's why!" Janet shouts her answer at me in rage and frustration. Ballsy woman. Like Ray, she's just gone way up in my estimations.

I tap Ray on the back of his head with the end of my gun.

"Wake up, Augustus. Your life is saved."

Ray lifts his head and looks up at his wife, still kneeling on the floor in front of him, expecting to be shot in her head any minute. She's crying, then Ray starts crying – shit, even *I* feel like crying. After all the years I've known these two I've only ever seen them as a lush and a golfing freak but my eyes have well and truly been opened to the kind of people they really are and I'm impressed.

"Listen carefully to me, both of you," I speak into the scrambler. "Although it may not feel like it right now, you are both incredibly lucky. For one thing, if you had hired somebody else to kill your husband, he would be dead now. You are lucky that it was me who took the contract as I have recently seen the error of my ways and am no longer interested in killing for money. Instead, as this is the last contract I will ever take, I have decided to act as counsellor rather than executioner. You are extremely lucky in other ways – you both have each other. Although there is infidelity in your relationship and a thirst for revenge, when it came to it you were both willing to sacrifice your own lives to save that of the other. You are both truly blessed. I only hope you now realise that."

Beautiful speech, Joe – nearly brought a tear to my own eye there.

It works on Romeo and Juliet though. Janet, still crying those big dopey tears and with her hands tied behind her back, crawls along the floor to Ray's chair and throws herself on his feet. Still tied to the chair and crying as well, Ray tries to lean down to kiss her but he can't reach down and she can't reach up. It's one third comical, one third pathetic looking and one third romantic.

As they both – *writhe* I suppose is the best description – as they both writhe at each other, pleading how sorry they are and that they love each other, I have to clear my throat just to remind them I'm still there because it looks like they've forgotten all about the masked man in the corner with the gun.

They both turn to look up at me, hope and fear and love and confusion in their eyes.

"Does this mean…?" starts Ray.

"Yes. You will both live. Hopefully I have shown you the errors of your ways and you can now see the love that you still have for each other and can begin your relationship anew." Anew? Heh, where did that come from? Man, am I laying it on thick or what?

They both assure me one hundred percent that they have and they will and how thankful they are. And I believe them. I toss them the tape from the camera that's caught all this footage so they can see what the other was willing to do for them.

You know, I could have stumbled across a whole new area of marriage counselling here. The Joe McLean kidnap-then-scare-the-shit-out-of-them-and-threaten-their-lives technique. It'll work every time.

I cut Janet's bonds and she leaps to her feet and hugs Ray, smothering him in kisses. While she does that I remove the cuffs from his hands and feet and they're both up then, holding each other and sucking each others' faces off. Excuse me, I'm sure. Sorry to be in the way.

With a prod of my gun in his back, I remind Ray who's still boss around here.

"Stay here and I will return shortly."

They barely hear me, they're so busy. Jesus, the nerve of some people.

I go out to the utility room and can't help but smile like an idiot to myself. That worked out better than I ever thought it would. Now there's no chance that Ray'll cheat again 'cause a) he just found out he really loves Janet and b) if he does think about it, he'll be so scared that she'll order him killed that not even the best looking woman in the world would tempt him. Nice and healthy huh?

I pick up a couple of heavy duty army canvas sacks and return to the lounge. Surprise surprise, they're still necking like teenagers. I lift the voice scrambler and talk into it.

"Your ordeal is nearly over. To protect this location, you will both climb into these sacks and I will return you to your homes. I assure you, you will both be safe but should you ever mention what has happened here to anybody, then I will return to your home and come out of retirement for one last kill, do you understand?"

It's clear that they do as they both nod furiously and clamber into the sacks. I pull them tight over their terrified heads, run the rope through the loops tight and drag them out to the car.

I mean, how bizarre is this? I'm dressed in a ski mask dragging my two friends in sacks and bundling them into the trunk of my car like they're a couple of cats ready for drowning.

It's dark by now and I decide it's too far to their house so I drive them out to the docklands where there'll be no prying eyes. It's up to them to make their own way home. I'm not running a goddamn taxi service here as well as marriage guidance. I park up in the shadows of the buildings, pop the trunk, bundle tweedle-dumb and tweedle-dumber out onto the sidewalk then grab a loose piece of the sack and cut a hole in it. Without saying a word, I get back in and drive off. It'll take Ray a minute or two to tear his way out of the sack and by that time, I'll be long gone. Man, it was a long day but I think that's been a job well done with those two. I'll tell Stanley the contract's finished and hopefully, Janet and Ray's marriage'll be stronger than ever. I feel pretty good about myself right now.

I'm keeping the twenty grand though.

<u>19</u>

You know, as arrogant as this is going to sound, I think I'm a pretty good person. If there was every any bad karma in being a hitman (and personally, I don't think there *is*) but if there was, then I think my scales would balance out with all the good things I do for other people. Recently, I've bought a business for my wife and taken her to Paris, rid France of a class-A scumbag and saved the marriage of my friends. Okay, you might argue there's a dark edge to all those things but as long as people don't know the truth, the good deeds still stand right?

As well as this, I'm about to start avenging my friend's murder and saving the whole hitman community from itself by finding this Prophet fuck and strapping a grenade to his forehead.

So with all that, I figure I'm due some down time. I'm feeling just a little burned out here. Not physically, not even mentally, just – as new-age as this sounds and I can't believe I'm going to say it – but emotionally. No, fuck it, I'm a modern guy. I can admit to being a little emotionally strung out with everything that's been going on and if that means I take some time out, then so what?

Now that the dust has settled after Paris and the whole Ray and Janet thing, I've got a chance to catch my breath and unwind.

Which leads me to being here in a darkened movie theatre on my own, stuffing my face full of popcorn and nachos. The curtains go back and I sit through a half hour of trailers. There's a couple of romantic comedies, a comedy about two guys who get mistaken for astronauts, a western of all things (I didn't think they made those any more) and a handful of brainless action films. The screen is lit up bright by orange explosions, muscle men in vests outrunning the obligatory fireball, car chases and love scenes. The surround sound system in the theatre erupts with the sound of gun shots and the explosions and that voice over guy with the deep voice comes over the images saying stuff like 'A cop on the edge' or 'Once, they were friends – now, they are sworn enemies.' I know deep down that they're all shit and the plots of most of these films couldn't fill a napkin but a big part of me still loves the movies. Have done ever since I was a kid.

Now I'm not going to go all weepy and talk about just exactly how bad my childhood was and how fucked up it's left me, but whenever I needed to escape as a kid, the movies was it. Get me out of this shit for a couple of hours and let me sit in the dark and lose myself in someone else's story – that's how I used to think. My love of the movies still stands today and maybe that's why I became a hitman. Trying to be

Clint Eastwood, the mysterious stranger who cleans out the bad guys. Maybe.

Anyway, the movie plays for two and a half hours and it was pretty good. The special effects were absolutely unbelievable though. I mean, I really couldn't believe what I was seeing. I don't know if it's just me getting old or whatever but as incredible as the effects were they sort of detracted from the story. The performances were okay and all but the film just seemed a little soulless. Good way to spend a couple of hours though.

After the movies I head for *The Rib Shack*, a cheap and cheerful little place that's hidden away behind all these big department stores. Thinking about it, I usually eat pretty well with Rachel these days. She cooks healthy balanced meals and when we eat out, it's always at good restaurants. But here, sitting in front of a plate of steaming barbeque ribs, buffalo wings and chilli, it feels good to be eating junk for a change, just like I used to. It all tastes so good it almost feels like a guilty pleasure.

I had thought about ringing Danny and asking him along on my little day trip of luxury here but I know we'd have started talking about The Prophet and I'm not ready for that just yet. That can wait until tomorrow because today's all about doing things for me.

It's mid afternoon now – about the time the bars start filling up with the jobless and the alcoholics of this city. My kind of people.

I pick the nearest bar with a pool table and go in. It's a fake Irish bar, all low lighting with shamrocks and old Guinness posters everywhere. I'll bet there's not a single bar in Ireland that looks anything remotely like this place.

There's hardly anybody in the bar and I order a tap beer then settle down to watch a baseball game on the big screen T.V. In the back of the bar there's a small games area with a dart board, games machine and a pool table and the cigarette smoke hangs heavy in the dim light. There's four guys hanging around in there shooting pool and I pick up my beer and walk in.

"Hey guys, this a free table?" I ask.

They look at me, all scowls and attitude. They're all about my age, all tattoos and hairy shoulders. I can tell they don't want me in there but I'm an unknown quantity and they can tell I'm not some geek they can tell to get lost.

"Sure, why not? Challenger pays though," one of them says.

"No problem," I tell them as I drop a coin into the table and set up the balls. We flip a coin to decide who breaks and I win, slamming the white into the pack and potting three balls from the get go. The guys frown at each other, obviously suspecting me for some kind of hustler. Now I'm not here looking for a fight. Sure, ten years ago I would have been here baiting these guys until they took a swing and then I'd have beaten the shit out of them but these days, genuinely all I'm looking for is a game.

I beat the first guy easily and offer them a rematch. There's a moment where they're not sure whether to just walk away, stay and try to beat me at pool or just stay and try and beat me. They decide on the second option and the guy with the shaved head feeds the table and sets the balls for the second game.

This guy's a better player than his friend and he's up on me at one point but I eventually take the game, potting the last six balls in a row. This upsets them and they gather round me, trying to intimidate me.

"Guys, come on, please. I'm not here trying to hustle you. I just want to play," I say, hoping they'll listen.

They don't.

"Well maybe we don't want to play with you, buddy," the shaved headed guy says, squaring up to me.

"Why, because you lost?" I say. "Look, I'm not after any trouble but I'm not about to let you try and intimidate me off this table. All I want is to play a few games of pool, okay? I'll even buy you fellas a round of drinks, what do you say?"

"I say fuck you, man," he says creatively.

Jeez, and here I am trying to be nice on my day off. Why is it that violence always follows me? I genuinely didn't come in here looking for this.

They circle me and try to intimidate me, hoping I'll shit myself and walk away.
I never could stand bullies.

Unfortunately for these idiots, they're trying to pick a fight with a guy with a pool cue in his hand. Not that I'd need a cue to trash these guys, but it's pretty stupid of them anyway. I slam the heavy end of the cue into the bald guy's foot and he yelps in pain. I bring the tip up hard just under his jaw and I feel it pierce the flesh and force its way into his mouth. He goes down hard.

The one guy tries to take a swing but I whirl the cue up and swing it round hard into the side of his face. Teeth and blood spray into the air. The other two guys back off a little which is a mistake 'cause by doing that they're giving me the room to move.

I whirl the cue above my head so that they can't rush me, then feint high and when the third guy, some biker looking fool, blocks high I bring the cue around into his midsection, knocking the breath right out him. Within ten seconds, there's three guys on the floor – one holding his jaw, the other holding his stomach and the other unconscious. The fourth guy, a bearded trucker type, takes a look at me and comes up with the most sensible idea he's probably ever had and he bolts it out of the bar.

By now, the bartender has pulled a pump action from under the bar and is pointing it at my head. Or at least as close to my head as he can manage because he's shaking so much. If I was to move quickly he'd miss his shot but I put my hands up where he can see them and try to talk him down instead.

"Look man, I didn't come here for this. There was four of them and they brought it to me, okay?"

The bartender - a sharp featured, ratty little guy - is sweating and shaking now, the shotgun wobbling in mid air.

"Just – just don't you start anything," he says.

"Got no intention to," I say calmly. "I'm just going to walk out of here nice and easy and leave you to either call the cops or throw those guys out."

I make my way towards the door keeping my hands in clear view and he follows me with the barrel of the shotgun all the way but he's not going to do anything. I open the door and turn back to smile at the bartender.

"Top o' the morning to ye," I grin, then head out into the crisp New York night.

All in all, today's been the most fun I've had for a long while.

<u>20</u>

The morning after and Rach has already left for work by the time I get up and that's fine. After everything that's been going on around here lately, I feel like I've been taking too much on for other people, you know? I feel like I've been spreading myself too thin. Yesterday really helped clear my head a little and I'm determined to spend some more quality time with myself in the future. Feels like there hasn't been room for any down time in too long, I've been so wrapped up in other people's lives and problems, but new day, new start.

Which brings me to the last problem that needs sorting and the one that's just gone on for too long now - The Prophet.

I admit that before, when only the bottom feeders at The Lodge were getting scrubbed, I couldn't give a shit. But now this mystery soon-to-be-dead-man's taken out Bear, well – as unbelievably clichéd as it sounds – now it's personal.

This fucker's killed the only guy in my life who could make me laugh beer out of my nose, has turned my best friend into a recluse and is screwing up my entire professional community. And now that I've seen to the needs of most of the people in my personal life, it's time to turn my attentions to the needs of my colleagues in my professional life – and if I'm not wiping The Prophet's brains off my boot by the end of the week, then I'm hanging up my guns.

The first thing I need is to snap Danny out of this spineless funk he's in. If I'm ever going to find out who this 'killer-killer' is, then I'm going to need his technological know how. All we've done so far is put together a list of suspects and now we need to step it up a gear. We need to get proactive and if that means Danny has to run tabs on every man and woman at The Lodge, then that's what we'll do. One way or another, this Prophet nonsense ends soon 'cause I've got an awful lot of guilt, frustration and rage that needs channelling.

I drive the long way to The Cave. Traffic's heavy but I don't mind because it's a sunny day, I've got the top down and the Stones on the radio. Besides which, it gives me time to think.

Now, I admit I haven't really taken this whole thing seriously but, I mean, it's tough to when you're dealing with a guy who calls himself The Prophet. And let's face it, like I said before, guys in our line of work have got to sort of expect shit like this. At first I thought it was some wise guy out for revenge. *Then* I thought it was some pissant shlub from The Lodge, looking to thin out the competition in the minor leagues.

But now, after Bear, I don't know what to think. I can't see a motive for these killings. I can't see a link between the victims and I can't think of any primary suspects other than *every* fucker on the books. Maybe this is why I never became a detective. Priest, Grey and those other monkeys I could give a shit about but why would he have gone after Bear? Besides the grizzly old bastard being the most jovial and friendly guy in the world he was as tough as hell. My theory on The Prophet's previous M.O. suggested that he was targeting the weaker guys so why go for Bear now? It just doesn't make sense. Can't think of anyone who would have a grudge against him either. I don't know who the hell The Prophet is yet but I do know that I owe it to Bear to make sure he was the last one the fucker nails.

I weave the car in and out of the mid morning traffic. Seems to me like I'm the only *real* car in a sea of yellow cabs and it takes me a good twenty three minutes to get down to the rough part of town but it feels like coming home.

The Cave hasn't really been the sanctuary it's supposed to be lately. Instead of going there and it being my fortress of solitude, I've been tending not to go at all because Danny's hiding out there, jumping at his own shadow.

The blast door slides open and I'm instantly reminded that it was only a couple of days ago that I was dragging Janet through here. Weird. Dan's definitely here though – I can smell his aftershave. It takes an aftershave that's real expensive to smell this cheap, you know?

And that's the thing about Dan. We've known each other pretty much all our lives and we both got into this business at the same time. I mean, I wouldn't have made it as far up the hitman ladder as I have on just two guns and a ridiculously handsome face so it was Dan's computer know how, his gadgets and his smart financing that's helped us get where we are. But where the success and the money have changed my life – I've got the car, the house, the business, the lifestyle – Danny's stayed pretty much the same as he was at thirtteen and I love him for that because he's a constant in my life. A constant reminder of who we both are and where we came from. A reminder of those simple days when I'd beat any jock half to death who even looked sideways at him and he'd strap a video camera to a radio controlled airplane and send it into the girls' locker room. Good times.

Sure, he's got more money than Scrooge McDuck and he can afford to buy all the latest tech and can wine and dine women who wouldn't ordinarily go near him, but his general outlook's still the same. He's never happier than when he's knee deep in computers, trying to solve some puzzle or something.

I remember this one time, he had a bet running with a guy that he could set off the sprinkler system in the White House within a week.

Dan managed to soak the oval office within three days.

"Hey Dan, it's me," I call out. Well of course it's me, who else would it be? "Where are you, dicknose?"

No answer.

Suddenly, I hear a mechanical, whirring noise behind me and practically draw my gun.

Turning, I see a little radio controlled kid's car turning round the corner of the games room. What the hell is Danny up to with this?

"Hey, Joe. Stick 'em up," comes a tinny, electronic voice from the car.

"What's up with this, Dan? You gonna mug me with a toy truck?"

"I warned you," goes the voice and with that, the hood of the car pulls back smoothly and a gun barrel pops up, aimed right at me.

"Knock it off, Dan, I'm not in the mood," I say, moving out of the line of fire of the car's gun, but the thing swivels to keep a bead on me. I move the other way and the gun moves with me.

"Seriously, Danny, knock it off," I growl. I move my way past the car so that the gun can't swivel but the fucking thing starts reversing so that it can keep me in its sights. The hell with this.

I pull the beretta from its shoulder holster and fire a couple of rounds into the car, smashing it to pieces.

"Fuck's sake, Joe, what'd you do that for?!" Danny whines, coming sprinting into the corridor out of the door that leads to his Nest, the remote control still in his hand.

"What did you expect me to do, Dan? You know I can't stand to have a gun pointed at me, even by a goddamn toy car," I answer, holstering the gun.

He drops to the floor, holding the remains of the car like it's a beloved dog that's been run down.

"It wasn't a toy, man, that was a prototype 'Guard-car'. That thing's taken me all week to make. It had a three mile range, motion sensitive guidance system, a twelve round…"

"Yeah, well now it's got one hell of a body scratch. What the hell were you thinking pointing that thing at me, man?"

"I was just testing it out, checking that the tracking worked okay. It did though, didn't it huh? I got it down. Just imagine a whole load of these cars patrolling outside this place if The Prophet comes calling. Or maybe I could sell them in stores. You know how insanely protective and gun loving us Americans are - they'd go nuts over something like this. I could mass manufacture these babies and make a fortune!"

"Slow down," I smile, helping Dan up from the floor and leading him down the corridor to the bar. "Firstly, this place is secure enough as is – stop worrying. Second, don't you think America's screwed up enough as it is without you putting killer cars into every home. Besides which, you'd have to work on that name 'cause 'Guard-car' sucks."

"So to what do I owe the honour, man?" he asks. "I haven't seen you here in an age. What, is Rach keeping you under lock and key?"

"I'm surprised you've seen *anything* here lately, Dan," I reply, pulling off the cap on a bottle of beer.

"What's that supposed to mean?" Danny asks, but his eyes are looking straight down at the ice he's clinking on the side of his glass. He knows what I'm getting at.

"What I mean is, when the hell was the last time you left this place? Look at you. You've been locked away in here, probably jumping at shadows even though *you* built the security system. You're spending all your time wrapped in paranoia, building these little cars with guns in them, scared all shitless of this idiot Prophet who, by the way, I guarantee I'm going to kill. As well as that, and no offence man, but you smell like a goddamn bum here."

Okay Joe, maybe a *little* harsh but what the hell. I've gotta try and snap the guy out of it somehow. Dan's head hangs even lower so his chin touches his chest. I'm striking a nerve here.

"Come on, Joe. The Prophet's sent ripples through the whole community and I know for a fact I'm not the only one who's gone to ground. As I've said before, not everyone's as invincible as you," he says with a wobble in his throat.

"Yeah, that's right, I *am* invincible. I'm the toughest son of a bitch you know and you know some tough, evil, vicious fuckers. I'm the guy who you've seen punch a man's jaw clean off. I'm the man who took out the whole New York chapter of the Jigsaw gang on his own – in under an hour. I'm the man who's taken care of you your whole life and I'm also the man who, if you help me, is going to force feed the Prophet his own ball bag."

Dan laughs despite himself.

"I know, Joe, it's just I can't help feeling like this is some sort of karma for guys like us. Someone like Grey? They're not really good guys, you know? I mean, even Bear…"

"Hey, that's bullshit Dan and you know it. Bear, me, you, we've always known the reality of what we do and it's always been about more than just the money. We do good work and we get rid of some real scumbags along the way. Granted, a guy like Grey was always in the job just for the money but fuck him. Yeah, maybe he got what was coming to him but Bear didn't. No way. Bear was different, same way me and you are. And that's why we're going to put The Prophet to sleep. I just need your help to put me and him in the same room."

Danny looks up, a crooked and resigned smile on his stubbly mug.

"Okay," he says. "What's the plan?"

<u>21</u>

In The Nest, all I can smell is Tacos and Pizza and I know that Danny's barely been out of *here* the last few weeks, never mind The Cave. There's a couple of extra monitors in here than there was last time and he's pulled one of the leather couches in.

"Jesus, Dan, what have you been sleeping in here now or what?" I ask, nodding towards the couch. He looks sheepish again.

"Well, yeah, I mean... yeah, I have but only because I've been working so hard lately," he says.

"What on, making the world's smelliest room? It stinks in here, man."

"Yeah, well," he mutters.

"Look, if we can find out who The Prophet is, I can take the fucker out and you can come out from behind the couch – literally."

Dan sits down in his wheely chair, tapping away absent mindedly on his keyboard while all sorts of numbers and junk flash up on the screens.

"How we going to do that then Joe, huh? The guy's a shadow. Nobody has even a slight idea about who he is and what he looks like," Dan says.

"Assuming it's a he," I reply. "Don't forget, The Widow's on our list of suspects. I mean come on Dan, you said it yourself weeks ago. Chances are it's *somebody* from The Lodge. We've just got to find out who."

"So what do we do?" asks Dan, the realisation of what I'm about to ask slowly dawning on him. He knows damn well what we do.

"We hack into The Lodge and we run Watchers on every fucker there – that's what we do," I tell him.

"Oh, of course," Dan mumbles, going white. "Why didn't *I* think of that? 'Cause I thought we were going to do something *dangerous*."

See, the thing is with Danny, he's a good guy. He'll do what he can for people, you know? For me though, he's always done everything he can and more. In some cases, he's worked absolute miracles for me. But the other thing with Dan is that, underneath everything, deep down – the guy's a coward.

Now me, it feels like my whole life has been about making sure I was always that step above the other guy. Someone beat the shit out of me? I learnt, I got better and I came back harder. But with Dan, he'd always back right off. Always. And it's not just a physical thing. I mean, he's always been small and skinny but the guy just hates conflict of any kind. You lock him in The Nest and tie him to a computer, the guy's like a goddamn tornado. Put him in the real world, he'll back away from a high schooler with an attitude.

So now the poor guy's turned an odd shade of grey. He's sitting on the couch with his head in his hands, trying to think of a way around what I'm asking. Sorry Dan, it's the only way.

"Jesus, Joe, think what you're asking," he whines. "There's Lodges all over the world, but none bigger than the ones here in America. There's Lodges all over America, but none bigger than ours in New York. I mean we're talking literally – *literally* – the biggest, most dangerous Lodge in the world man. You don't just hack into somewhere like that. You just don't piss people like these off."

Man's got a point.

Still, what's life without a little risk?

"I know all that, Dan, but think about it. If the N.Y. Lodge is the best, and I'm the meanest bastard at the N.Y. Lodge, then what's the worry?" I reply.

"Don't, man. Don't try and laugh this off. We've both been on the books for years and in all that time, we've never screwed with the house once. Not once. *Nobody* has – you just don't do it and you know that as well as I do."

"Well that's not *exactly* true," I reply, knowing full well that what I'm about to say won't especially help matters but my mouth gets the better of me. "Remember Eddie Carlson?"

Danny jumps up, waving his arms animatedly.

"Do I remember Eddie Carlson? Jesus, how could I forget? How could any of us? The only guy since Prohibition days to try and fuck The Lodge and what happens to him? They drag him out of his house, beat the guy to within an inch, kidnap him *and* his wife then offer *her* a million dollars to shoot Eddie in the face."

"She didn't have to take the money though did she?" I tell him.

"But then they killed her anyway, just 'cause her last name was Carlson as well! One thing we said when we started there, Joe. One thing we agreed on – hell, that *everyone* agrees on - is that we wouldn't end up like Eddie fucking Carlson."

"Look, Dan, we're not doing The Lodge any real harm are we? We'd just be sort of '*using their facilities*' for a while. And if it leads us to The Prophet then I can rip the guy's spine out and we can hang it above the door."

Dan pauses and looks straight at me, pretty much for the first time since I came in.

"Bear's death has really gotten to you, hasn't it?" he asks.

"Yeah. Yeah, it really has. That and the fact that you've turned into fucking Anne Frank all of a sudden."

Dan blushes and the nerve is hit again.

"Come on, Dan, all this is bullshit. Since when did me and you roll over on anything? With the both of us on this, we'll be sipping cognac out of The Prophet's skull by the weekend."

His head drops again and I know I've got him.

Now, running a Watcher on a guy isn't a particularly easy thing to do. It involves hacking into computer systems, manipulating data and all sorts of other nerdy know-how to track and trace somebody's every step. But it's not impossible either, and for Danny it'd be a snap.

The reason you *don't* put a Watcher on somebody is pretty simple though. It's breaking one of the four golden rules of The Lodge, and that's not something you'd ever do lightly.

Okay – history lesson.

There've been Lodges pretty much ever since there's been people willing to hire other people to do their dirty work for them. I think they started in England in the 1600s but the idea of a place where you can gather all the cut-throats in one place just sort of makes sense. Okay, there's no dental and no pensions scheme but there's always a steady flow of work if you're good at your job. Hell, even if you're not, you can make a decent living just being willing to strangle some old dame for insurance or whatever.

These days, there's hardly any such thing as an independent any more. You've either got an agent and you're on the books at a Lodge or you're struggling, you know? It's all business.

Anyway, these places have been doing this for a long time and like Dan says; The Lodge here in New York is one of the most dangerous in the world, so you do not screw with them in any way, shape or form. Every Lodge, as far as I know, insists on four golden rules.

First rule – you pay. You pay your medicals, you pay your agent and you pay the house. No exceptions, no instalments, no excuses. You just pay.

Second – every man's entitled to his privacy. You go to The Lodge, you're there as an employee, nothing else. They won't tolerate targeting guys families and their home lives or anything like that. You want to team up on a gig or get friendly like me and Bear did? That's up to you. But as soon as you pull away from the end of The Lodge driveway, you become invisible. Anyone breaks this rule, see the subheading entitled *Eddie-Carlson-the-fucking-idiot-who-tried-to-break-rule-number-two-and-whose-kneecaps-are-in-a-glass-case-over-the-urinals-as-a-message-to-other-people-who-might-possibly-entertain-the-idea-of-breaking-this-rule-as-well*.

Third – no muscling of any kind. This means you don't try and muscle in on anyone else's contracts and you get by on your rep alone. You certainly don't throw your weight around The Lodge. Now admittedly, I've been known to stretch this little rule to breaking point in my time, but I always reign it in so that I don't quite get to rule number four, which is simple;

You don't try and fuck the house.

Ever.

Or else.

See The Lodge is, for all intents and purposes (apart from the nature of the employment opportunities of course) a legitimate business and it's run that way. You build yourself a rep, get yourself a good agent, follow rule one and two and there's no problem in getting more work than you can handle. But if you ever get a little too big for your boots, a la Eddie Carlson, you'll get yourself fired in the most permanent way you can imagine.

So I guess Danny's got every right to be feeling nervous here 'cause I'm planning on breaking rule two *and* four by having Dan hack The Lodge's files, find out where everyone lives and what contracts they've got and run tabs on them. Simple right?

And if it's not, well - goodbye kneecaps.

But the way I see it, I'm left with little choice here. I'm not a dumb guy but that said I'm a killer not a detective so I don't stand a chance in hell of working out who The Prophet is by myself, even though I could make a few guesses. Plus I also think the faceless, shadowy management who run The Lodge could and *should* be doing stuff like this themselves to send a message out and stop the whole hitman community from self destructing. Bunch of assholes.

Besides which, there's no chance of them ever finding out it's us running Watchers 'cause Danny's a ghost when it comes to computers. He just needs a little confidence boost, that's all…

"Come on, Dan. Stop being such a pussy," I tell him.

"Pussy nothing, Joe, this is practically suicide by computer," Dan says.

"Ah, grow some balls will you?"

"I've got balls man, I just don't want them pickled in a glass case is all," he replies, although he doesn't stop tapping away at the keyboard. I know damn well he's getting off on pitting his nerdy wits against the computer geeks The Lodge has got working for them. My computer know how is pretty much frozen at buying vinyl records and shit from ebay but as Danny taps away, the screen gets filled with all these ones and zeroes which don't mean a thing to me but I can tell something good's happening because his eyes have got that glazed over, hungry look in them.

"Look, Joe, just so you know, I *can* do this. I don't *want* to, but I can. The security systems in place at The Lodge are way advanced and they've got defences against pretty much any type of virus, even symbiotic ones. They're fully defended against apple cores, tornadoes, African blues, X-700s *and* 750s…"

"Whoa, whoa, whoa. Turn the nerd down a little pal. I didn't understand a word you just said," I tell him.

Danny smiles and his fingers speed up a little at the same time.

"Jesus, Joe, what did you, stop still the day Pacman was released? You're like a caveman, man. Just trust me, The Lodge is well stacked so like I say, this is going to take me a while 'cause I know what you're thinking," he laughs.

"And what's that?" I ask.

"You're thinking that computer manipulation is just like Richard Pryor in Superman 3, same as you always do," he laughs.

"Okay, my four eyed sidekick, point taken. Just do whatever you need to do. You just tell me what our usual suspects are up to, I'll track them and find out which one's The Prophet. Then I'll kill them slowly over say three, maybe four weeks, then you can come out of here into the daylight, get a proper goddamn shower and we can get as drunk as our livers will let us. Deal?"

Danny smiles resignedly.

"Deal."

By the time I get home, I'm feeling so good that something's finally happening about The Prophet that I decide to cook dinner.

We tend to eat out most of the time these days and then the rest of the time, Rach'll do the honours. That usually means either she'll phone through for take out or she'll make her infamous lasagne - a dish which couldn't taste any *less* like lasagne if it was a cheeseburger.

But, feeling good like I do, I buy the groceries on the way home and start making a chilli. Not exactly high class cuisine I know, but there's plenty of it and it's hot.

Rach comes in from work just as I put the rice on to boil and sweet mercy on a motorbike – look who she's got with her. It's only our good, good friends and blissfully happily married couple, Janet and Ray.

"Hey hubby, look who's come for dinner," Rach calls out.

Great. Wonderful. I really need this.

"Oh, hey guys. Come on in. You're just in time for chilli," I shout down, in my best *'Oh-isn't-it-great-that-you-two-freaky-cheating-on-your-wife-and-willing-to-pay-someone-to-kill-your-own-husband-mother-fuckers-are-here-in-my-house-expecting-food-and-drink'* voice. Now admittedly, it's a voice I've never used before but it comes to me surprisingly naturally.

Nah, actually this is the first time I've seen Janet and Ray since that whole thing the other night and it's actually good to see them so I've got to pretend that things are fine and that I *didn't* kidnap and threaten to kill them just a few days ago.

Cue small talk, the obligatory golf story from Ray, a whole 'Oh I wish I could get *Ray* to cook once in a while' schtick from Janet, a whole 'I can't believe he's cooking *myself*, he hardly ever does it' thing from Rach, and before you know it, we're sitting down to eat.

I've made a huge bowl of rice, a massive bowl of steaming chilli, a whole mess of salad and a side dish of garlic bread. Again, not too fancy but it works.

Now no sooner have we started in on dinner, than Janet and Ray start playing around as if they were teenagers. They're playing footsie under the table, feeding each other from their plates and generally making goo goo eyes at each other. I swear, if I hadn't made the food myself I'd probably throw it up.

I guess what this means is that things are back on an even keel for the two of them. But that said, there's suddenly a part of me that – seeing them all over each other like a couple of virgins on prom night – makes me wish I'd just shot the pair of them when they were in those sacks.

Ah, I'm just being overly cynical. Really though, I think it's great. Looking at them, I feel as if I've actually achieved something here. Like as if what I did the other night has actually worked and these two morons have realised they actually love each other. It's sweet really. And that was probably – no, *definitely* – the only time in my career where I've spoken at a problem rather than shot it and look at the results. Maybe there is something in my whole 'shock therapy' marriage counselling. I might have to patent the idea.

"So me and Janet just booked a romantic get away," says Ray, practically glowing and wearing the world's mightiest shit eating grin. "Italy. Luxury five star hotel with *two* eighteen hole golf courses would you believe?"

"Two courses, huh?" I answer, faking an interest. "Bet you can't wait eh, Janet?"

"Oh, I'm sure we'll find other things to play as well as golf," Janet smiles, flashing Ray her most sultry and lascivious smile.

Aaaand I think I just threw up in my mouth.

"I'll…I'll just go and rustle up some dessert. Shall we go through?" asks Rach. Thank God for my wife. She knows how to diffuse an embarrassing situation, only now it leaves just the three of us heading into the lounge and I feel like a third frigging wheel here.

I mean, what is with public displays of affection? Don't get me wrong, I think it's great that they're back together and we can have normal things like this where they come over for dinner but why the hell do they need to drool over each other like they're a couple of kids in a Bon Jovi song?

Now, I love the bones of Rach. She's an ex model for Christ's sake, with a killer body and the world's greatest smell. We have electric – and I mean *electric* sex - and sometimes when I look at her, sure, the temptation's there to rip her clothes off and just go for it but I wouldn't do it in public. I hate these people who feel the need to show the world their relationship's so strong and they're so in love with each other that they couldn't *possibly* walk round town without stuffing their hand in the ass pocket of each other's jeans. I mean, give me a break. Nine times out of ten, you ask me, those people are hiding the fact that they're about a whisper away from hiring a guy like me, you know?

But above all that, I think it's just plain lack of manners. I mean, here we all are now in the lounge, I'm fixing a drink and Ray's got his hand practically in Janet's bra – like I'm not even here! Like I can't see you getting to second base on my fucking couch.

"Jesus you guys, do you want to go up to the guest room or something and I'll bring you up your drinks in twenty minutes?" I say, unable to hold it back any more.

They laugh innocently and break apart just long enough for me to hand them their glasses.

"Sorry, Joe," Janet says, taking a sip of her drink. "I don't know what's come over me."

"I will...later," Ray whispers in her ear, loud enough for me to hear.

And *that* is the *final* fucking straw!

"Alright, that's enough! No more! You two have got to knock this shit off for the love of all that's holy," I shout, slamming down my drink just as Rach comes in with a tray with four long flutes with some kind of green and brown ice cream in them.

"Joe!" she says, her eyebrows forming a perfect V. "What the hell's gotten into you?!"

"Raymeo and Juliet over here, acting like love's young dream," I reply.

"Hey, Joe, sorry if we've been a little full on tonight," says Ray, holding his hands up like he's guilty. "We're just…we've just sort of had our relationship reaffirmed in a way and it's left us both – I don't know…"

"As horny as hell?" I offer helpfully.

"Joe!" Rach cuts in, the V brow getting even deeper.

"It's all right, Rachel," Janet simpers. "Joe's right. We feel like we did when we first started dating. It's great."

"Good for you, but do you have to ram it down *our* throats by ramming your tongues down each others?" I ask.

Wow. Look at that. Just when I thought it couldn't get any deeper, Rach's V brow gets so furrowed, it turns into a W.

"I apologise for my husband's unbelievable lack of decorum," says Rach, handing out the ice cream flutes with grace. "I think it's just great that you guys are back together again."

Man, if I knew what decorum meant, I'm pretty positive I'd be pissed off.

"Yeah, relax you crazy kids, I'm just pulling your chain," I say, forcing a smile. "It's great you're making a go of things and not trying to *kill* each other anymore."

Sorry. Couldn't resist.

Janet chokes on her dessert, practically spraying ice cream out of her nose. Ray goes white and red in equal measures. Remind me to *definitely* play poker with this guy in the future.

"What, what...ah, what do you mean?" he mumbles.

"Ah, you know, getting on together. Not fighting, at each other's throats anymore."

"Oh. Hah. Yeah, yeah, it's all good," Ray says with the world's worst poker face.

They both get up to leave. Now whatever could have made them want to go now that we're having such a nice time I wonder?

"Uh, we'd better be heading off actually," Janet says while Ray quickly bolts down his ice cream. "Ray's got a big business meeting in the morning."

"Oh no, stay," Rach says. "Come on, we were having such a nice evening and we've only just had dessert. Ignore Joe, he's just an insensitive brute with no manners."

"That's me guys, I'm just a brute. C'mon, let's open another bottle of wine and get tanked," I offer.

Ray and Janet sit back down but this time, there's actually enough room for a sheet of paper in between them. Man, I can see me having some fun with these two guilty consciences in future.

The rest of the night is spent having wonderfully normal and boring conversation. Janet, taking a leaf out of Rachel's book, reveals she's decided to invest in a store with a friend of hers, selling overpriced ladies clothes. The two of them discuss running businesses for a good half hour. Ray politely asks questions about the construction business so it makes it fair when he inevitably gets back to golfing.

All in all, it feels like things are back to normal here.

By the time they leave in a cab, it's early in the morning. We managed to get through four bottles of wine between us and a round of shots and what started as a little impromptu dinner turned into a pretty good drinking session. Janet, as ever, is a hundred times better company when she's drunk and she actually started doing a strip tease on the bonnet of the cab.

"Wow, I can't believe we had so much to drink," Rach says, waving them off and closing the door behind her. "It's nearly two in the morning and I've got to open the book store tomorrow."

"Ah, don't worry. We've got hired minions to do that kind of stuff for us," I say, wrapping my arms around her from behind and pressing myself into the small of her back so she knows what I mean.

"Why, Mr McLean, is that a golf club in your pocket or are you just glad to see me?"

"Why don't you reach behind and find out?" I say, my hands finding their way under her top.

She purrs warmly as her own hands find what they're looking for.

"Oh my, somebody's feeling frisky tonight. Has all that stuff with Ray and Janet got you feeling all hot?" she asks, rubbing me teasingly.

"Honey, the thought of those two going at it is just about enough to make me disappear in your hand."

"And we wouldn't want that now, would we?" she says, playfully squeezing me.

I pull all her clothes over her head in one swift move, spin her around and pull the rest of her clothes off as she frees me. Grabbing her gently, I hoist her up and push her against the wall. She gasps breathlessly as I lower her slowly onto me. She wraps her legs around my waist and we just stay there like that for a second, inside each other.

"I love you, Joe," she whispers in my ear.

"I love you too, baby."

By the time we get to bed, it's after four.

Life is good.

22

Rach gets up at eight, phones to say she isn't coming in to the bookstore until later on today and then comes straight back to bed. By the time we get up for real, it's not morning any more.

I make eggs, coffee and juice and we eat breakfast with the papers. We make love again. We take a shower together. We make love again. Once we're dressed, she heads out to put in the last couple of hours in at the store.

In fact, this is one of the only times since the book store opened that Rach hasn't been there to open up.

She's absolutely loving the business and thinks it's the best thing she's ever done in her life (apart from the whole marriage thing of course) and credit where it's due, she's making it work. The books (excuse the pun) have come in and the figures are good.

So far, the place is making an average profit of just over 40%. Now I know it's still early days and a lot of new businesses do well in the first six months and then fold, but I think 'Rachel's Corner' has got legs. In a day and age where everything's electronic and downloadable, who knew there was money in good old fashioned paper books?

Once Rach has gone, I spend the afternoon relaxing at the house. I make myself a sandwich and pop open a can of beer from the refrigerator. There's an old black and white Jimmy Stewart film on the T.V. that passes an hour and a half nicely. By the time four o' clock hits I'm pretty bored so I decide to take a drive down to Magnum to see Gerry. It's been weeks since I checked in and I've got nothing better to do, so. When I get there, Lisa, Gerry's secretary, smiles widely as soon as she sees me. She's had a crush on me for years and flirts outrageously with me whenever I'm down here. Still, who could resist the rich, mysterious and elusive boss eh?

"Mr McLean, what an unexpected pleasure," she says, arching her back and sticking her chest out. "It's so nice to see you. You just don't come to the offices often enough these days,"

Lisa must be in her mid-thirties now and she's got that whole sexy, secretarial thing going on. You know, trouser suits and low cut blouses. Her hair is long, straight and jet black and her legs go all the way up to the top, you know? I don't know how good she is at her job but I don't blame Gerry for hiring her. The construction guys must go nuts for her if they ever come in here and she's just the type to appreciate all the attention from a bunch of hairy, sweaty guys.

"Hey, Lisa," I smile as I walk towards the back office. "Gerry around?"

"Yeah, he's in the office. You know though, Mr McLean, any time you want to take me out on a business lunch, that's okay with me. I'd love to hear your inside take on the business and what new erections you have coming up."

Wow. Not *too* subtle.

"Sorry, kiddo," I smile, opening the door. "Business before pleasure."

Inside, Gerry is busy sorting through a mound of paper. Rather him than me. Which is why I hired him of course.

"Jesus, Ger, you got a regular man eater out there." Gerry looks up and he beams widely.

"Yeah, you would say that. She's been working for me five years and hasn't so much as even laughed at one of my jokes," he smiles.

"You ever think that's because your jokes aren't funny?" I offer.

"Could be, Joe. Could be. So what brings you down here so late in the day? In fact, what brings you down here at all? It's been weeks since I saw you last."

"Honestly? Just checking in. You and the boys did a great job on Rachel's bookstore but I know it took a lot of the firm's focus away from other jobs – actual paying jobs – and I just wanted to check that the business isn't hurting."

Gerry smiles, lights a stogie the size of a baby's arm and takes a bottle of bourbon from the safe, pouring us both a large shot.

"You kidding, Joey? Things've never been better 'round here. Rach's store just added to the portfolio is all. We're the sixth biggest construction company in Manhattan. Might even be fifth by the end of the year. Don't you worry yourself over the business kid, it's in safe hands."

"I know. Ger. The safest. I guess if I'm really being honest, I came here looking to maybe get away somewhere normal for a change."

"Normal?!" Gerry explodes laughing. "Normal? Are you kidding me? Just this morning I had to shout at one of the guys for eating a trowel full of sand on a bet. It's just about as far away from normal here as you can get."

"Yeah, good point. It just seems that there's a lot of crazy shit going on in my life at the moment is all and I feel like I needed a breather, you know?" Oh man, I'm always like this around Gerry – the guy's like a kindly uncle to me and I always feel like spilling my guts like a redneck on Springer.

"Listen, Joe," he says. "We've known each other a while now right? And in all that time, I've never asked what you do or what's going on in your life. I figure that's your business. But whatever's got you feeling like you need to get away from it all and come here of all places, then you gotta deal with it head on."

"I'm trying to, man, but the thing that needs dealing with won't present itself," I say, taking a swig of the bourbon.

"Well then maybe *you* need to present yourself to *it*," Gerry answers.

Holy shit, the man's a genius. Of course!

"Gerry," I smile, standing up and throwing my arms around him and slapping him on the back. "I think you just solved my problem."

"Glad I could help," he wheezes.

Man, if this plan works, I'm going to give Gerry a big fat pay rise. What's that old kid's saying? If the mountain won't come to Mohammed, then the mountain'll go to him or something like that. Whatever the saying is, it means that instead of running myself and Danny into the ground looking for The Prophet, we let him come looking for me. Perfect.

See, about all we know about The Prophet is that he (or maybe she, who the hell knows?) hates hitmen and is going around killing as many of them as he can for whatever fucking reason. The other thing we know is that so far, he's only really bumped off the *punks* from The Lodge – the guys who would let a girl scout get the drop on them. The only one time this asshole has set his sights on a real tough guy was Bear, which doesn't fit his previous M.O. but at least shows he's willing to bat outside of his league.

Now if he's upping his game, which Bear's death suggests he might be, then he'll flip if he finds out that the best hitman around – yours truly, if you'll forgive the ever so slight arrogance – is weak and easy prey.

If, like I'm absolutely convinced is the case, The Prophet is working out of The Lodge, then all I've got to do is get the information convincingly leaked out that I'm lying somewhere broken and battered and hopefully it'll be too sweet a target to pass up. Then when the fucker turns up, I fire a couple of hollow points through his face and then head to Disneyland.

And I know just the right guy to help lay the bait.

"No way, Joe, no fucking way! No way!" Stanley says, refusing to look me in the eye and busying himself with some flotsam from the paper tsunami on his office desk. "I've got a reputation to uphold here."

"Maybe as a poker cheat and closet homosexual but that's about all," I reply. "Look, all I'm asking you to do here is leak a little bit of false information, not whack a priest or anything."

Funny – Priest getting whacked was how all this started.

Stanley scoops up some files and unconvincingly pretends to put them in order.

"Joe, you know I love you man, you're like a son to me but you don't know how things are around here 'cause you haven't been here. But trust me, I'm telling you, anyone who gets found doing anything suspicious here lately – and leaking some bullshit story about you knocking on death's door would definitely come into that 'suspicious' category by the way – gets a message from on high in no uncertain terms that their time at The Lodge is over, you know what I'm saying here? The Prophet has got the whole community on edge like nothing I've seen since the '60s."

"Man, that's exactly why I'm *asking* you," I reply. "You get the message out, The Prophet comes for me, I kill him dead and things go back to how they were around here. That's why the plan works, see?"

"It ain't that simple though Joe," Stanley says. "The thing is..." He stops his fake secretarial bit and seems to steel himself for something. He rubs his good hand over the stubbly white whiskers on his chin, trying to muffle what he says next. "See, the thing is that, well – everyone here is totally convinced that *you're* The Prophet."

Stanley winces, expecting me to go ape and start throwing furniture around the room but I'm too taken aback to even lose my temper.

"Which dead man started *that* rumour?" I ask.

"It wasn't really one guy as such Joe, it's just that that's the general concensus lately. I mean, think about it – since The Prophet came on the scene, you haven't been around here anywhere near as much as you used to."

"I thought I explained that," I answer, still keeping control of myself even though I can feel my blood starting to simmer. "I told every one of the jerk offs here that until they grew fucking backbones and stopped being such pussies that I wasn't going to have anything to do with the place. And as I recall, the reason I even said that was because plenty of guys weren't showing up here themselves."

Stanley puts his hands up, trying to calm me down. He knows me well enough to know that I'm close to the red here.

"Hey, *I* know that," he says. "But think about it, this is the world's biggest back handed compliment, you see? They're only accusing you of being The Prophet because you're the only one *tough* enough to be."

"Get your nose out of my asshole, Stanley, it ain't going to work. We both know that Bear aside, my grandma could have taken out the rest of the jokers on his hit list. Nah, someone's gone out of their way to make out it's me, so who'd gain something from trying to muddy my rep?"

"I dunno, kid. That's the thing with being top of the tree – there's always someone climbing up behind you, ready to pull you down. I should know after all."

Man, Lodge rules aside, I feel like going out into that bar and breaking people's bones until they tell me who started that little rumour but I can't. If my plan is going to work, then everybody needs to see me leaving here as normal. Any kind of extreme actions from me are going to make whichever one of them's The Prophet suspect something's too easy about me lying somewhere injured. No, I've got to go out of here with my usual swagger as if everything's normal.

"Okay, Stanley," I say. "I'm through with all this shit. If I haven't got The Prophet's dead fucking body hanging above the bar out there by the end of the week, I'm hanging up my guns. Now don't even fucking pretend that I don't make up at *least* seventy percent of your income as an agent so I'm asking you to just please leak the story about me and we can be done with this whole 'killer killer' shit."

Stanley pauses but not for long.

"Alright, you pushy bastard, I'll do it. But if I get in any shit over this you're off my Christmas card list."

On my way out of The Lodge, I make sure to have a drink and shoot some pool with some of the guys, being my usual cool and suave self.

The plan is that tomorrow night, Stanley gets word out around The Lodge that he just got a call from me and that a hit went bad and I'm holed up in an old warehouse by the river, all shot up and broken. Then he lets it be known that that's where I'll be for the next few days healing up and I want him at some point to drop me off some supplies. Then hopefully, the thought of me lying all weak and wounded will draw The Prophet to me 'cause he won't be able to resist such an easy target. All I've got to do is go there, sit and wait with a newspaper in one hand and a beretta in the other.

As I park up in the underground garage back home, I'm glad to at least have a plan of action. Now I know that The Prophet might not even take the bait but it feels good to be doing something proactive about the whole situation. I really feel like ordering a pizza tonight too – a Mexicano with double jalapenos and chilli powder should just about do it. I just hope Rach hasn't cooked something and a plateful of mystery food is waiting for me in the oven.

Inside, all the lights are on and I call out for Rach but there's no answer. At this time of night, I think I can guess where she'll be.

I creep upstairs and into the bathroom and there she is, lying in the bath tub up to her neck in bubbles.

She's covered the place in candles, has opened a bottle of white wine, is listening to music through headphones and has slices of cucumber over her eyes. I never understood the whole cucumber over the eyes deal, you know? I mean, why not just take a shower with a lemon up your ass?

I come up behind her and put both hands on her shoulders. She screams loud enough to wake the dead and jumps practically clean out of the water.

"Jesus fucking Christ!" she yelps, sending the cucumber and her phone flying across the room. "You asshole, you nearly made my heart explode!"

"Sorry hon, couldn't resist it," I smile. "You having fun?"

"I was until *you* came in like Norman goddamn Bates."

"That was a shower in Psycho, not a bath," I correct her.

"I don't want to get into a whole pop culture trivia quiz here you idiot, I'm just trying to…"

"You know, you look incredible wearing nothing but soap suds and a scowl," I say with my best smile.

She scowls some more, stops, sighs, then smiles.

"Get in here, you lunk head."

Now, with a six pack in an ice bucket by the side, I've joined Rach in the bath. She's leaning back against me and I'm massaging her shoulders as she purrs contentedly.

"So where have you been all day?" she asks.

Now this is just one of the great things about Rachel. When she asks, she's genuinely asking where I've been and what I've been doing – there's no hint of suspicion at all, just genuine interest. I imagine a couple like Janet and Ray, when they ask each other, there's a hint of mistrust, you know? With Rach though, she's just asking.

"The usual, just down at work," I answer honestly. "Listen hon, about work. I know it's real late notice and all, but I've got to go to Chicago for a couple of days. Me and Gerry have got a few properties we need to go and look over."

Listen to me – from honesty to lies in one sentence.

"Really?" Rach says. "Is it one of those trips where I can come along, leave you to it and hit the shops all day?"

"Nah, not really. It'll be a quick and boring trip. No nice business lunches, just me and Gerry tapping walls and looking for cracks," I tell her.

"Not to worry anyway," she says. "Having you out of the way gives me the perfect excuse to have everyone from the store over for a party. Only in the interests of employer/employee relationships you understand."

"Oh, I understand alright. The workforce that plays together, stays together. And if, in the process, you get to play hostess all night, then so much the better right?"

"Well bless my soul, that never even crossed my mind," she smiles.

"Yeah, sure."

Okay, that's that. By now, Stanley should have gotten word around about the warehouse and hopefully our target's taken the bait. Only one loose end to see to – my trusty and ever cowardly sidekick.

After our bath, Rach wraps up in her dressing gown and heads back downstairs with the rest of her wine while I phone Danny. I want to see if he's dug up anything so far and he'll need to know about my plan over the next few days.

The phone rings out for way too long but I know Danny's too scared to leave The Cave so I let it ring until he eventually picks up.

"Finally, man. What were you doing, whacking off?" I ask him.

"Yeah, I just had to wipe up at the end there. Actually, asshole, I was just looking through some files I hacked from The Lodge which, by the way, was a hell of a lot harder than I thought it was going to be. I've hardly slept for the last two days."

"Ah, stop complaining, you've been having the time of your life, you know you have." I can practically hear the thrill in his voice. Man, he's like the king of the nerds or something but I love the guy.

"Well okay, even though it's been tough, I did come up against a really tricky fifth generation ice wall in the system which I could only bypass by implanting a sixteen cell viral replicanth…"

I don't understand the next twenty two seconds of our conversation.

"You're doing it again buddy. Turn down the geek and just let me know what you found out will you?"

"Okay, sure, sorry," he says. "Long story short, for those of us still stuck in the fucking eighties, I've managed to run Watchers and hack into the files and records of most – about eighty percent - of the agents, so I can see who put The Prophet's victims on what jobs on the day they were killed and who else knew they'd be there. If The Prophet *is* someone on the books, then maybe it's an inside job and he's working with an agent, otherwise who else would know where Priest, Grey and the rest would have been, you know?"

"Shit man, you could be right." The idea never dawned on me that the killer would need to know where his victims were going to be. It's not exactly as though hitmen are easy to find and who else would know but an agent? You fucking idiot Joe. But I can feel it now – the noose is getting tighter 'round the bastard's neck. "So what's the next move then?" I ask.

"You've just got to give me time," Danny answers. "I need to hack the other twenty percent of the agents, then triangulate the data to come up with a list of suspects that would have known what the killer knew. So what's happening your end?"

I explain my warehouse plan to Dan and he laughs, calling me a – and I quote - *'an unimaginative, stone age luddite.'*

Maybe if I knew what the hell that meant, I might be angry.

<u>23</u>

Twenty million dollars for a movie. Twenty million. And people think what I charge for smashing a guy's elbows and kneecaps to powder is extortionate.

I mean I love movies, don't get me wrong. But twenty mil? Just for reading out lines from a script? Crazy. There's no way any actor, I don't care how good they are, can possibly justify that much money for what's basically spending your day playing make believe. Not when nurses and firemen are struggling just to get by.

Now sportsmen getting paid well I understand but even they're starting to take it too far. Okay, you earn a fortune for playing in something like a pool tournament, I can see how you've played your best and beaten all the others so you deserve a pretty sweet pot at the end. But when these ball players are earning more in a week than the most helpful waitress in the world could earn in fifty years worth of tips, it makes you think that something's not right here.

At least being a hitman, you're *doing* something to earn such big paychecks. Alright, on one level, people are paying so much because you could easily just turn around and say 'The price too steep for you? Fine. *You* shoot your cheating husband in the face then, be my guest.' But in our job, from the big hits to the small and everything in between, you're always putting your neck on the block so the money has to reflect the danger. But twenty mil for acting? That's bullshit.

Reason I'm thinking about actor's wages is that I'm sitting here hidden in a back room in the warehouse by the river reading through a stack of movie magazines, just waiting for The Prophet to take the bait so as I can behead the guy and go home.

I've set the place up with a mattress in the far corner, with a yours truly sized mannequin tucked under the sheets. There's a lamp about arms reach from the dummy so you can see enough to know there's a body laying there but not enough so you can make out too much detail. I've left one of those little metal kidney shaped bowls surgeons use with a couple of spent shells in it and enough blood splashed around the place to make it look like I'm pretty done in. It won't all hold up to close inspection but under these dark conditions, it's good enough that someone'll believe what they're seeing is real.

Rach thinks I'm in Chicago right now so I'm going to dig in here for a couple of days and wait. I've got the magazines, plenty of junk food and beer and a personal stereo too. I've even got a book I picked up from 'Rachel's Corner' about a baseball player who keeps getting dropped from the team so he goes around killing the other ball players so as he can make the cut. I'm actually looking forward to reading that one.

All in all, I'm going to treat the next couple of days like a relaxing break. And should The Prophet wander in looking for me then so much the better. In fact, I might be having such a good time that even if I do kill him, I might stay here for a couple of days extra anyway.

Man, I'm bored.

Really bored.

And I've only really been here for what…Jesus, only an hour and a half. I realise that the limit of my attention span is about twenty three minutes tops. I'm bored of reading the magazines. And the book was weird too. I must have read like the first thirty or so pages and all I got was how this pro baseball player had been beaten black and blue by his folks when he was a kid. Join the fucking club pal. Who wants to read that?

I only made it through one album on the personal stereo too. Springsteen's 'Born to Run.' A stone cold classic. Love every track. But see, Rachel's fed exactly one thousand three hundred and fourteen different songs into the ipod. After The Boss, I started turning the little wheel thing looking for another song and it just blew my mind exactly how much is in there. I mean, most of it's her songs in there anyway – Celine Dion, Mariah Carey, shit like that – and I just got bored of looking for a decent tune in there. Great idea having a personal stereo with thousands of songs in it but a bad idea having one filled with shit, you know?

So I'm bored.

Man, when The Prophet eventually turns up, I'm going to take it slow with him. Start with blowing his ankles away then I might get creative with him.

You know, I once read about these Asian guys who do the meditation. All the sitting cross legged and burning oils and humming and shit. See, what these guys do is they sit in absolute silence for days on end just thinking. No food, no water, no sports on the T.V. Just thinking. Nothing else.

Supposedly, what happens is, these guys eventually enter a trance like state and they can achieve inner purity or something. Just by cutting off all noise and thinking about shit.

I close my eyes and try it but within three minutes, the thought of Rachel in a white silk teddy and a beer in one hand and the T.V. remote in the other pops into my head and ruins my whole frigging karma.

This is no good. There's no way I'll ever be able to stay in here for the next two days. Not without losing my mind anyway. Still, I suppose I might be bored now but I'm even more bored with listening to everyone around me talking about The Prophet all the while so I guess maybe I'll stick it out.

You know, I've never seen *anything* get into the hitman community like this.

I get there's been no killings for a while now but people are still jumping at shadows like little girls. Embarrassing is what it is. I can't wait to kill the guy and be done with it. Get things back to normal.

I manage another two hours and twelve minutes of absolute boredom before the phone rings. If The Prophet was sneaking up on the place, he'd have heard the damn thing a mile away. Forgot to switch it to silent like a rookie.

Turns out the phone call makes all that irrelevant anyway.

"Joe, it's Dan," he says in that excited voice he usually saves for talking about software. "I've done it. I've only gone and fucking done it! I know who it is." At last. The fucker's mine.

"Brilliant, Dan, I knew you'd do it. So who is it? Who *is* the dead man? Don't tell me – it's that prick DeLaney. Please tell me it's him. I've been looking for an excuse to shoot that guy."

"Joe, it's…it's not DeLaney. It's somebody else," he says hesitatingly.

"Don't tell me it's The Widow. I don't think Bear could have handled getting killed by a woman," I tell him.

"It's not The Widow, man. Will you just listen a second. I finally managed to hack into the rest of the network files. I just got through running the data files and I've got the evidence. Absolutely stone cold evidence – I…I know who The Prophet is"

"Well come on, Columbo, who is it?" I ask, feeling like a kid about to open his presents on Christmas morning.

"It's – it's Stanley," he says.

Shit.

24

"How?" I ask.

That's the first thing that comes into my head. Not why, but how. I'm so fucking stunned right now that that's all I can think to say.

"How what, Joe?" Danny answers. "How did he do it or how did he…"

"No," I stop him. Suddenly my voice is like gravel and nails. "How do you know it's Stanley? If I'm going to tear the guy's fucking head off with my bare hands, I need to be sure it's him."

Danny takes a breath. He knows I'm not taking this easy. I've known Stanley pretty much ever since I turned pro and although our relationship isn't quite father and son or anything, he's the closest thing to Mickey from the Rocky movies that I've got and the thought of killing him isn't an easy one.

"You know how I've been cross referencing agents' records, looking for patterns? Well it turns out the only agent not to lose someone from their stable is Stanley," Dan says.

"So what?" I growl. "That doesn't mean a thing. I'm in the guy's stable. Just because I'm not dead, doesn't mean it's him."

"Wait a second man," he says. "I know this isn't easy for you to hear, but there's more, just let me finish. I think Stanley's been slowly bumping off rival agents' men so as he can get more business for himself and he's fabricated this whole Prophet persona so people aren't going to look closer to home, you know?"

"Hold on here just a minute," I stop him. "This isn't an episode of Scooby fucking Doo here Dan, this is some pretty serious shit you're throwing around. You'd better have something a little more solid to go on than some hunch."

"Joe, just listen man," Danny says, and I can tell by his voice he's about to dish up some real evidence, much as I wish he wasn't going to. "This would also explain why The Prophet's victims weren't such tough guys. With Stanley's bad leg and withered hand, there's no way he was ever going to take out someone like DeLaney or you. Hell, the only reason he managed to take out Bear was because Bear saw him as a friend and let the guy near him."

Danny pauses, waiting for a reaction from me. I don't say anything though – I'm just trying to weigh things out in my head here.

"Okay, so there's that," he carries on. "But that's not even the real evidence. You ready for this? I was scanning the web for information about Bear's death and I came across this guy's blog and he..."

"Wait a minute, what the fuck is a blog?" I ask. I'm having enough trouble taking all this in without Danny going into nerd speak on me.

"Jesus Joe, join the fucking Twenty First Century will you?" Dan practically squeals. "A fucking blog is where a guy will put up like a daily diary entry on the web. Anyway, this guy, Steven Broker, he's a second rate writer. Had a book published about ten years ago that sold like, fifty copies. So this guy, this Steve Broker, seems he's been buddying up to Bear over the last few months. He's been going to Bear's bar and it seems that now Bear was thinking about retiring, the big lummox wanted to write a book about his life as a professional hitman. Now we both know that Bear, rest his soul, could only just about spell his own name, so when he sees a writer coming into his bar he thinks he'll get him to ghost write it."

"Anyway, long story short," he continues. "Broker puts in one of his blogs that he was with Bear the night he was murdered. Says he saw him leaving with, and I quote – '*some old guy with a white moustache, a limp and a fucked up hand.*' How Broker never made it as a writer with such eloquent descriptions as that I'll never know, but nevertheless, it all points to Stanley right? So then this gets me thinking – why not try and hack into the setup at Bear's bar. Can't think why I didn't try this sooner, right? Takes me just under ten minutes and I'm in. I can manually control his security systems so I call up all CCTV footage from the night Bear died. And who's there on screen, slipping poison in his drink when his back's turned, plain as day? Stanley. We always said from the start man, that The Prophet was an insider at The Lodge. We just never thought how *much* of an insider!"

He stops again, waiting for me to say something.

"So that's it. It's Stanley! Surely you don't believe it *isn't* now?" he asks.

I pause.

"No. No I don't."

Dammit. Damn this whole fucking situation to hell. Why'd you have to do it Stanley? I know you've always cared about the money above everything else but Christ, you could have just undercut the other agents. You didn't have to start fucking killing the competition.

Just before I hung up with Danny, he asked me what I was going to do. As I drive the car down the country roads to The Lodge, I'm still not sure. I've pretty much headed here on autopilot since I left the warehouse.

Which is another thing. No fucking *wonder* my masterplan didn't work out. The only guy I revealed the plan to and it turns out *he*'s been The fucking Prophet all along! He must have been laughing his ass off when I came to him to help set the trap.

Man, but you know if Stanley had just rubbed the other guys out, I would have still played this differently. I could have maybe told him I knew and got him to stop the killing. Maybe I'd have just let the management know and let them deal with it.

But why'd he have to go and kill Bear? If he'd just known the guy was thinking of retiring he'd have left him alone. And to use their friendship to get close to him to do the job makes me feel sick.

But you did kill him, Stanley. You knew he was one of my best friends and you killed him anyway and that's why you've left me no choice.

You've got to die.

By the time The Lodge's grounds come into view, I've made a monumental life decision – Stanley is going to be the last person I ever kill.

I've had it with the whole hitman thing after this. Fuck Stanley. Fuck The Lodge, its rules and everyone there. Fuck the whole fucking thing. Who needs it? I'm going in, I'm killing Stanley then I'm retiring.

But first, I'm going to need a plan. I can't make a scene here because of Lodge rules. Second, I'm hoping I won't need to because Stanley doesn't know *I* know it's him. As far as he's concerned, I'm still lying in wait at the warehouse like an idiot, so I've got the element of surprise. Third, for what he did to Bear, I want to hear him explain himself to my face and I want to look him in the eyes just before I make them pop out of his skull. I suppose I owe it to the miserable old bastard to make it quick and painless but I'm so angry that it's been him all along that I'm not sure how I'll play it.

Larry and Pike smile when they see me coming.

"Hey Joe, what's happening?" Larry asks.

I'll miss these two. I hope if anything goes sour in there I don't have to do anything I'll regret.

"Nothing much guys. Same old same old, you know? How about you?"

"Wife left me again. That's the fifth time in two months. She'll be back in a day or two though. Wish she'd just do it for real one day," Pike says as he pats me down.

I'm not carrying 'cause I knew they'd have to frisk me on the door but I also know that Stanley keeps a couple of loaded guns in his office drawers. I'm killing him with my bare hands but if I need to, I'll take them from his desk if anything goes wrong.

"Say, I thought you were supposed to be dying or something," Larry says. "Stanley's been telling everyone how a job went sour and you got all shot up."

Yeah, I'll just bet he has.

"Nah, I'm fine boys. Mixed messages, that's all."

I walk in and head to the bar and on my way, I see Bear's plaque on the wall and my blood starts to boil. The way I feel right now, I could burn this whole place down to the ground with everyone in it.

Down in Harvey's, the place is practically empty. In fact, the whole *place* is like a ghost town. What's going on around here?

"Hey George, you seen Stanley around?" I ask.

George looks up from his paper.

"Seen Stanley? I've hardly seen *anyone* for the last hour," he says.

"Yeah, what's with that? Where is everyone?" I ask.

"Take a look at the tables," George replies, going back to his paper.

I never noticed before but looking at the tables in the bar, they're strewn with little fliers. I pick one up, turn it over and my life turns to shit.

My throat dries and tightens.

My stomach goes cold and white and I nearly throw up.

The flier's for a one million dollar hit in big black letters.

And underneath is a picture of Rachel.

<u>25</u>

Fuckfuckfuckfuckfuckfuckmotherfuck!

Oh Jesus, please let me get to her in time! Please, just please let me – where the fuck are the bikes!!? A million cars clogging up these piece of shit roads and not one mother fucking bike! Not – there! There's one.

I screech from seventy to zero in front of the bike. I cause a four car pile up behind me but who gives a fuck. I jump out, leave the car behind, drag the guy off his bike and tear away towards the store.

Pleasepleasepleasepleaseplease. Oh fucking please. I'm panicking. I never fucking panic. My heart's pounding in my chest here. Forgot to grab the guy's fucking helmet so at the speed I'm tearing through the streets my eyes are watering and I can barely fucking see. Fuck you Stanley, you dead piece of shit. I can't fucking believe you did this.

A million dollar bounty means every asshole from The Lodge is probably trying to find Rachel as we speak. George said the fliers only went out an hour ago but it won't take them long to find her.

Oh God, if she's dead, I'll kill every last one of them. I'll fucking blow that place – oh shit! Joe, you dumb fuck. I don't have any weapons on me! Not even a fucking knife. I'll just have to – get the fuck out of the way you prick! Memorise the number plate of that car. I swear, if anything happens I'm going to track that driver down and run that car over his fucking skull.

Not far now. Two blocks. Two blocks, that's all.

Hold on baby, I'm coming.

Finally, mercifully, as I weave the bike through traffic, Rachel's Corner eventually comes into view. Please let me be the first one here. If any other hitman's got here and even looked at Rachel funny, I'll dedicate the rest of my life to making him suffer. Calm. Calm. Got to keep calm here. There's no screaming from inside so maybe I'm the first one here. I ditch the bike by the side of the road and quickly open the doors to the store. Everything looks fine – there's customers milling around and it's pretty quiet. One of the kids on the cash register sees me come in.

"Oh hello, Mr McLean. Are you looking for Mrs McLean?" the kid asks.

"Yeah, she around?"

"Sure, she's upstairs in the back office," the kid answers. "Is everything alright sir, you look a little worried."

"No, everything's just fine," I lie.

Damn. Don't want Rach to know anything's wrong. At least she's okay though. Thank God I got here first. I just need to get her out of here and somewhere safe now. Don't worry. Figure something out later. Just need to get Rach, then a weapon and then the fuck out of town.

I take the stairs three at a time, desperate just to get to her. And there she is! She's just talking to a customer but then she moves to the side and…

My heart freezes in my throat as I see the little bald head with the cobweb tattoos. The guy she's talking to is Spider. That sneaky, slimy little walking corpse is talking to my wife. Dead. He's fucking dead. No time to be clever.

"Pete! Long time no see!" I say, all smiles and teeth as I cover the space between us as quickly as possible and wrap my hand around Spider's neck and squeeze. I squeeze on the nerve endings between his neck and shoulder and my grip means Spider couldn't even move right now, let alone talk.

"Joe? What are you doing here?" Rachel asks, shocked but smiling. "I thought you were meant to be in Chicago. Who's this?"

"Hey babe, this is Pete, an old friend of mine from back in Brooklyn," I say, still smiling and still holding tight of the now rigid Spider. "Let me just catch up with him and I'll meet you in the back in a second."

I drag Spider away from her but make it look as though we're walking away with my hand around his shoulder.

"*Joe!*" Rach shouts behind me but then storms off indignantly into the back office. Thank God.

I push Spider behind a stack of books and let go of his neck and he falls against the shelves gasping for breath, his bony little hand reaching up and rubbing his throat.

"Jesus, Joe," he croaks looking up at me. He wants to get mad but he knows I'd fucking kill him. I still might. "What the fuck?! First come first served, you know? Who says you get dibs on the million dollar bitch, huh?"

I slap him hard across the face and he hits the deck, blood sputtering from his mouth. I grab him by his collar and pull him back up, pinning him to the shelves of the Non-fiction section.

"That's my fucking wife you slimy little prick," I growl and a look of fear spreads across his face.

"Oh Jesus Joe, I…I didn't fucking know. I'm…I'm sorry, you know?" he mumbles through his thick and bloody lip.

"Shut the fuck up, Spider, and I just might not break your worthless neck right here and now. You got a weapon on you?"

"Yeah, yeah, I got a gun in my belt here," he says.

I reach round his back and take the snub nosed six shooter that's tucked into his trousers. Typical. Hasn't even got a real man's fucking gun. I jam the barrel under his chin and lean in close.

"Listen, Spider, you know me," I whisper dangerously. "You know what I can do but today's your mother fucking birthday alright? I'm going to forget that you're here at my wife's place of work with the intentions of killing her. I'm also going to forget that you're a waste of fucking oxygen and that I should just shoot you in the fucking face right now. You're going to forget all about the million dollars, slither back to The Lodge and give everyone a message. You tell them from me that if any one of them even fucking *thinks* about coming near my wife I'll kill them, their friends *and* their fucking families. And you tell Stanley. You tell him that I know now and that I'm coming for him. You tell him that. Now get the fuck out of here and if I ever see you again I'll take a mother fucking wood plane to your chest and slice strips off you until I reach your heart, you understand?"

His eyes tell me he understands.

He crawls away without looking back and I head into the back to get Rachel. She's stood, leaning against her desk, arms crossed and a look like thunder on her face.

"Joe, do you have any idea how rude that was? Why couldn't you have just introduced me to that guy? What are you, ashamed of me or something?" she says angrily.

"Oh, I'm sorry honey, I didn't think. That was just an old friend I haven't seen in years, nobody important," I tell her, just relieved to see her alive.

" Okay, fine but all you had to do was introduce me, you know? That was really embarrassing, Joe."

You've got to love her. She's got no idea she was minutes away from being killed and that there's a million dollar bounty on her head. All she's worried about is me not introducing her to some guy she never even met. God, I don't know what I'd do if I lost her. She turns around and starts writing in a book on her desk, her pen scribbling furiously – she's trying to let me know she's upset. She'll be a hell of a lot more than upset if I can't get her out of here right now.

"Honey, let me make it up to you, okay?" I say, putting my arm on her shoulder. "Let me take you out for dinner. Just drop everything and we'll go right now, huh?"

"I can't just up and leave because you've *finally* got time for me. I'm working," she pouts.

Jesus honey, let it go will you?

I'm standing there trying to think of something I can say to make her come with me when the office door opens and in walks Eddie the Fish, one of the biggest fucking bottom feeders from The Lodge. Somehow, after Spider, *he's* the first prick to find where Rachel works and he's here to collect the million.

The Fish sees Rachel, smiles greedily and reaches into his coat for his piece figuring he's home free but suddenly he sees me standing in the corner of the office and he freezes. I give him a look that says *'Get the fuck out of here, Eddie, this one's mine'* but all he can see are dollar signs and the stupid son of a bitch goes for his gun.

Before he can draw it, I whip Spider's six shooter from round my back and with one perfect shot right in the middle of Eddie's forehead, I send my entire life straight to hell.

26

Time freezes.
The red mist that used to be part of Eddie's head hangs in the air.
His skull runs down the office door.
Rachel goes white.
My stomach turns.
Everything's fucked.

The moment's forever shattered as Rach starts screaming her lungs out. I run over to her and grab in a tight grip, forcing her head to look at me not the body.
"Rach! Rach, listen to me! I need you to listen to me baby!"

She starts shaking uncontrollably then bends over and pukes all over my boots. When she's finished, I pull her to her feet and make her look me in the eye again.

"Honey, listen. I know you've got about a million and one fucking things going through your head right now but we're in trouble okay? That guy was here to kill you and I think there's more on the way. We need to get away from here right now, okay? I'll explain everything later, I promise, but for now we've just got to move alright?"

"Whuh…huh…whh," she replies. Fuck, I think she's going into shock.

Before I can do anything, almost mercifully, a little red dot appears on Rachel's temple and I move quicker than I ever have before. I push her over and land on top of her a split second before the bullet rips through the glass window and I'm reminded just how much I fucking hate snipers.

Staying clear of the window, I push Rach up against the far wall of the office and brush the hair from her face. She looks at me with empty eyes and a blank expression like she can't even fucking *begin* to process the last minute and a half.

"Babe, we can make it out of here but you're going to have to snap out of it and hold on. Just hold on. You've got to listen to me carefully now and do everything I tell you to do okay? Don't think about anything, just do what I tell you and it'll all be fine, I promise."

The sniper switches to rapid fire and sprays the room but doesn't hit anything except the desk and window. The noise terrifies Rach and she screams, burying her face in my chest and trembling in my arms. I stroke her hair and lift her head to look up at me at the same time. She's crying now and her eyes are asking me questions I'm so fucking ashamed to answer.

"Rach, I love you. I've always loved you and no matter what happens from here on in, I need you to remember that. But right now, I need you to just trust me 'cause we need to move."

"Mrs McLean? Mrs McLean, is everything alright? I thought I heard some crashing noises and what sounded like a ..." Scott, king of the cappucinos, arrives at the door and stops dead as he takes in the carnage. It's the first time I've ever seen *any* kind of an expression on his normally vacuous face.

Arm around my wife, I usher her along the wall, out of the door and past the gawking Scott. He doesn't even look up from Eddie's body.

"Scott, I'll give you a hundred grand bonus in your next paycheck if you get rid of that body," I call back to him as I race for the stairs down to the book store.

Halfway down, I hear Scott's monotone voice from upstairs.

"Cool."

Okay, I've got to stay calm here. If I let myself think about what's happening here, I'll start fucking up and I can't afford to do that. Got to detach myself from the situation and think with a level head.

Forget the fact my wife just saw me blow a guy's face off. Forget the fact that the lie I've been keeping from her since the day we met has just been shattered forever. Forget the fact there's a million dollar contract out on her head. Forget the fact there's God knows how many professional killers out there trying to get to her. Forget the fact I've only got a fucking snub nose with five shots left in it. Forget all that and what's going to happen in the future – just keep clear and make sure there *is* a future to worry about.

Sure.

Piece of cake.

First things first, I know there's at least one asshole out there. Whoever it is has probably dropped the sniper rifle and is running across the street right now to finish the job hand to hand. I've got to create a diversion somehow and there's a store full of book buying people down here who'll do nicely.

With one arm still wrapped around Rach, I use my free elbow to smash the fire alarm on the staircase and the store erupts with the noise. The customers and the store workers look around for a few seconds then slowly head down towards the main doors and I don't think, by the speed they're all moving, that any one of them thinks for a second that there's a real fire and this is anything more than a drill. I've got to get us out of the store quick and I need people moving quicker so I fire a shot in the air.

Although the gunshot sends customers panicking and screaming towards the exits a damn sight faster now, I didn't want to have to do it because that means I've only got four shots left. When she hears the gunshot, Rach tightens into a whimpering knot and clings onto my waist. As long as she's holding onto me I'm hoping we can use all this chaos to slip out of the front door in the crowd and unseen by whatever hitman's out there but as I move Rach towards the door, I see a broad figure pushing his way against the tide of panicked people and making his way into the store. Our eyes meet and, above the crowds of screaming civilians, we share an unspoken moment of recognition and hatred.

Lincoln.

As soon as he spots me and with Rachel in my arms, he pulls a nine mil (a *real* fucking gun) and is about to take his shot but his arm gets knocked upwards by the sea of people and he yells in frustration. Now I could either empty my gun and hope that from this distance one of my four remaining shots hit him or I can use his situation to my advantage and get Rachel out of harms way and save my shots.

If I was here on my own, I'd probably take my shots but I can't think like that with Rachel in danger. Besides which, there's a chance I could hit an innocent customer so for once I retreat instead of attacking. I drag Rach back up to the next level and out onto the floor. I can't risk going any further up because the stairs are too open so I race to the other end of the floor and hide her down between the shelves of books. The fire alarm is still ringing loudly which is good because it will cover our sounds from Lincoln, who I'm sure has hit the stairs by now.

"Joe, what the hell is happening?" Rach asks, having finally found her voice. She's hanging onto my arm, her nails digging into my flesh through fear and there's a look of sheer terror in her eyes.

"No time to explain honey, we gotta be quiet. The guy making his way up the stairs is a stone cold killer and I've got to go out there and stop him. I need you to stay put and not make a sound, okay? Everything is going to be fine – promise."

We share a silent look at each other and my heart breaks as I touch her cheek and disappear in between the shelves of books, putting as much distance between me and her as I can.

"Lincoln?" I call out hoping to draw him away from Rach. "I know there's a big price on the woman's head but I'm asking you once, real nice, to walk away from this one, man."

Nothing. He doesn't want to give away his position. I'm sure he's made it onto the floor by now and he's got to have a rough idea where I am and sure enough, he answers me conclusively as I look up and see a little round, shiny, black stinger bomb come sailing my way through the air.

Bastard brought bombs.

I pull a display of books crashing to the floor and hide behind them, seconds before the stinger hits the floor a few feet away and explodes in fire and noise. Luckily, Stinger bombs are only meant for small jobs and are more noise than explosion but the concussion still rattles me even behind the books. I sprint across the floor before he can draw a bead on me and I hear a couple more explosions behind me. I look back and see thick grey smoke starting to billow up – the fucking asshole's started a fire in a goddamn book store!

"Hey Joe, come on out and we'll ice the million dollar bitch together huh? What do you say old pal?" he shouts - the cocky prick.

Man, if it would have been anyone else but Lincoln. He may be a king size piece of shit but he's as tough as hell. Always knew we'd have it out between us one day but why now?

"Last chance, Lincoln. Walk the fuck away now and I guarantee you never see me again," I yell to him. "I'll even give you the million myself."

There's a pause but I know it's not because he's thinking about it – he'll be moving through the aisles looking for me. Man, I can't believe I'm hiding here with a fucking snub nosed pistol! If we get out of here, I'll use this fucking thing to pistol whip Spider to within an inch of his life.

"Hey, Joe," he shouts from somewhere to the left of me. "You know what I think? I think you know the bitch otherwise why else would she still be alive, right? She your sister or something? Your woman? Doesn't much matter anyway Joey, 'cause I think you're trying to draw me away from her. Maybe I'll just double back a little here and see what I can see."

Clever fucker.

I've got no choice so I break position and stand up hoping against hope I'm quicker than he is. I see a quick flash of movement to my left and move just as the bullets scream past my head. I empty all four of mine in a desperate effort but he's as quick as I am and not one of my shots hit him.

I'm out. No bullets, no knives, not even a fucking set of keys I could gouge his eyes out with. Ah fuck it, if I lose Rach my life's over anyway. Let's do it.

I throw the gun at Lincoln and he dodges it with a grin but as I run at him, I grab books off the shelves as I pass and manically toss them at him like a crazy man flinging his own shit around a padded cell. My plan works and he can't draw a bead because he has to shield his face from the barrage of hardbacks aimed at his head.

He fires a couple of shots off but they miss by a mile and this dumb, crazy move gets me in close and I slam my fist into his stomach. This knocks the air out of him and he doubles over but doesn't let go of his gun.

He brings his arm around in an arc and – man, he's fast – connects the barrel of his gun with my temple. He cuts the skin and I feel blood trickle down my face. That's about all I feel though, the amount of adrenaline pumping through me.

I leave my ribs open and Lincoln falls for it. He lands a beauty of a rabbit punch to my kidneys which just about downs me but that I knew it was coming and roll with it. My plan works though and letting him get his free shot in with his left means I can get to his right hand – the one with the gun in it. Before he can swing again, I manage to sink my teeth into the fleshy part of his hand just above the thumb and tear a good, bite sized chunk out, blood and meat filling my mouth. Lincoln roars in pain but drops the gun which is what I wanted all along. Least now it's a level field – hand to hand, 'cept I've got more hand than him now.

The pain maddens him and he elbows me in the face and grabs me around the neck, lifting me up and charging me into the wall. How strong *is* this fucker anyway?

He head butts me real hard, right on my nose, before I can even think. My eyes fill with tears and I bring my knee up in desperation and with every last bit of luck in the world, I manage to bring it up square into his balls. Now I don't believe in God or anything but I feel like I need to say thank you to *someone* after that.

Lincoln doubles over and I land a sweet right hook to his jaw and he hits the canvas. Now I could stay here and try and finish it but there's no time because the place is full of thick black smoke by now and I've just got to get us out of here. I take the time to kick Lincoln in the face one last time then pull a whole shelving unit full of books down on top of his ass. Mother fucker's lucky I don't have the time to spend settling this with him.

"Rach?" I holler out. The building's really going up and I can barely see a thing.

"Joe?" she calls back meekly from exactly where I left her behind the shelves. The fact she stayed put where I told her to even though the whole place is going up in flames around her is a good sign. Shows she can follow orders. We might just get out of here in one piece.

As I round the corner, I see her sitting huddled on the floor, her knees brought up to her chin and she's shaking hard.

"Joe? What's happening? Oh my God, what happened to you?" she says as she looks up at me with those big baby seal eyes. My face must look a little pulped.

"I'm fine baby, it's nothing. Come on, we've got to get out of here now, the fire'll be on us in seconds," I answer noncommittally, lifting her to her feet but keeping her bent low under the smoke.

We head for the stairs and have to go up because the fire's spread down the stairs and the ground floor already. Man, the store is screwed. A fire this size in a store full of books? There could be a hundred firefighters outside right now and they'd have no chance of stopping this place burning to the ground in the next ten minutes. At least I'm insured.

With the smoke following close behind us, I drag Rach up past her office and up to the attic floor. The whole upper story is used for storage – boxes of books, files, papers and business stuff – but that's where the fire escape door is to the roof. On my way past the office though, something dawns on me.

"Rach honey, head on up and wait for me on the roof okay? I'll be right up." I yell to her.

She hits the stairs without saying a word. I think she's on autopilot by now.

I go back and open the office door, Eddie the Fish's skull still decorating it. In the far corner of the office is Scott, hunched over and trying pathetically to wrap Eddie's body up in the carpet.

"Scott, what the fuck are you doing?!" I ask incredulously.

"I'm trying to earn my bonus, Mr McLean," he answers, looking at me like *I'm* the fucking stupid one of the two of us.

"Scott, do you even *see* the black smoke out there? Did you not hear gunshots and fucking explosions from downstairs? You didn't think to get the hell out of here?"

He thinks hard for a second.

"I thought it was some kind of health and safety staff training or something," he says.

Either this kid uses an obscene amount of drugs or he really is as dumb as his vacant, mouth breathing face would have us believe.

"And the headless fucking body at your feet, Scott? That doesn't bother you either, no?"

He thinks hard for another second.

"I really need that hundred grand bonus, Mr McLean," he answers sheepishly.

I pause and think hard for a second now.

"Scott, listen to me very carefully. The store is on fire right now and we need to get up to the roof. If you do anything other than follow me up there in the most reverential silence you can manage, I'm going to drag you up onto the roof anyway and then I'm going to throw you over the side. Understand?"

He opens his mouth like he's about to say something then some primal survival instinct of his kicks in, he closes his mouth and nods silently.

I kick open the fire door and me and Scott crash out onto the roof. The fresh air fills my lungs and Rach comes running over to me.

"Joe, what are we going to do? The whole building is on fire. We're going to die," she says hysterically.
"Nobody's going to die here, hon, we just need to be a little creative is all," I tell her, trying to be as reassuring as I can.

"Maybe we could find a fire hose, wrap it around our waists and sort of abseil down the building," Larry suggests in a tone astonishingly devoid of irony.
I turn to look at him.

"You saw that in a film once didn't you, Scotty?" I ask.

"Yes sir," he mutters, his eyes looking ashamedly at the floor.

I scan the roof quickly and there's no options. The FDNY wouldn't be able to get us off this rooftop in time and I'd sooner not answer any of their questions anyway. Only one thing for it.

"Alright, there's only one way off this roof and that's to jump," I tell them both.

"No way, Mr McLean," Scott says. "We're at least ten floors up and there's nothing but sidewalk down there. I'd rather take my chances abseiling."

"I'm not talking about jumping over the side Scott, you fucking moron. We've got to jump to the next building over."

The building to the left of us is about fifteen storeys high but luckily, the neighbouring building to the right hand side stands a good two floors lower than us. With a good run up, there's no reason why we couldn't make it. Only thing is, there's a pretty sizeable gap between the buildings and if we fall short, it's like Scott so rightly says – there's nothing but sidewalk down there.

Thick black smoke follows out of the fire door and starts engulfing the roof. Why'd she have to open a goddamn bookstore? Why couldn't she have opened an asbestos store or something.

"Look, if we stay here a minute longer, we're going to choke to death. Scotty boy, you go first. Take a good run up and jump like your life depended on it. The natural angle should take you across."

"*Should*?" he says, displaying the first real emotion I've ever really seen in him.

"Just do it, Scott, before the smoke gets too thick."

He backs away from the edge, clear to the other side of the roof. With as steely a look as his little stoner eyes can manage, he finally psyches himself up and charges across the roof, yelling as he goes. I fight the urge to trip him up and over the edge just for yucks.

Credit where it's due, Scott hits the edge and springs himself up and over, his arms flailing in the air. He sails down and over the gap, arms flapping all the way like a cartoon until he just about hits the lip of the other building and crashes like a rag doll onto the hard asphalt roof.

"Jesus ,Scott, are you okay?" I shout down and over.

He takes a while to move but I eventually hear him make a little whimper.

"Uh…Uh think uh broke muh jaw," he mumbles across. "Und muh leg."

"Never mind that, Scottster, that jump was awesome. That was at least a nine point eight," I yell back.

"Thunks," he mumbles over, flashing a broken grin and a thumbs up.

Rach comes up behind me and starts manically shaking me by the elbow.

"Joe, there's – there's fire coming out onto the roof and the smoke is everywhere. I…I can't make that jump, Joe," she says, trembling.

Thing is, she's right. Scott only just about made it so there's no way Rach can jump that far and I can't throw her across. Only one thing for it.

"Rach, honey, you still trusting me?" I ask.

"Always," she replies

Man, she's unbelievable. If we ever get off this roof she's going to throw this moment back in my face but first things first.

"Okay, I need you to stand here, close your eyes and keep them closed no matter what, alright?" I say, leading her to stand right on the edge of the rooftop. She lets me position her on the lip of the rooftop and closes her eyes. I kiss her softly on her forehead and back up clear to the other side of the roof.

The thick smoke stings my eyes and I can see the raging flames are already making the rooftop melt and bubble beside me. God I hope this works.

My heart racing, I sprint across the length of the rooftop as fast as I can, building up as much speed as possible. I try and tell myself that this is just like high school football only with my wife instead of a pigskin.

I thunder ever closer to Rach – who's still standing there with her eyes closed firmly shut – and without breaking my stride, I wrap my right arm around her waist and throw us both over the side.

Rach screams and I grunt in pain as we sail through the air making Scott's earlier attempt look positively fucking balletic. The ground reaches up for us but the momentum I built up carries us across the gulf.
Just when it looks like we're going to hit the roof hard, Scott pops his head up like a gopher and me and Rach crash into him like a fucking missile.

We hit and hit hard. Rach goes sprawling out of my arms and screams out loud as she scrapes her forearm all along the rooftop. I feel my ankle twist but thankfully, Scott takes the brunt of things. In fact, I think we may have killed him. The poor kid just played crash mat to two adults jumping off a burning roof. There's a story to tell his grandkids if he ever makes it.

"Christ, I can't believe we made it. Just unbelievable," I say as I slowly get to my feet. "Man, Scotty, you alive?"

Out cold, poor kid. If everything goes well and the dust settles on this shit, I'm going to find him in whatever hospital he ends up in and give the kid a couple of hundred grand. I figure the loveable little mouth breather's earned it.

"Rach? You okay?"

I put my arm around her. She's shaking and crying and holding onto her arm because there's a pretty nasty red raw scrape along it.

"Honey, we made it. We're okay, we're off the roof. How's your arm, let me see."

"It burns," she says.

I gently bring her arm up and kiss the wound softly. She smiles weakly at me through her tears.

"Everything's going to be alright now," I lie as we stand there and watch her bookstore become a bonfire.

By the time we reach ground level, there's a million people standing watching the remains of Rachel's dream go up in flames and the fire trucks are pumping water onto the blazing inferno that used to be my wife's bookstore. Rach holds onto me tightly, her arm wrapped around my waist and mine around her shoulder. She's trembling, a half inch away from going back into shock. She looks up and sees her beloved bookstore spitting orange flame and black smoke and she finally breaks, her body wracking and trembling with big, deep sobs. I pull her aside into the alleyway.

"Rach, I know this is hard, but we're not safe yet. We've still got to get out of here. You need to hold it in a little longer babe, you're doing great," I tell her.

"I can't…I can't do this Joe. I don't know what's happening. What are you…?"

She was going to finish her sentence and ask a different question I'm sure but she pauses as she realises she's just asked the real question; the $64,000 question – what *am* I? Her whole face changes as she finally reflects on the chaos of the last twenty minutes and what she's seen and I can't bear the way she looks at me. It's a look I've spent every day since I met her trying to avoid.

Mercifully, I spot the stolen motorcycle I arrived on exactly where I left it on the side of the road. The fire crews and the gawkers are all concentrating on the fire so we can slip away down the alleyway and join the traffic on the other side.

I lead Rach to the bike and tell her to get on the back while I start the engine.

"Whose bike is this?" she asks.

"It's mine. I had to borrow it from a friend. Come on Rach, we've got to hit the road."

With an obvious reluctance that breaks my heart clean in two, she eventually clambers on the back and wraps her arms tight around my waist.

"Where are we going, Joe?" she asks.

"We've got to get out of the city. Somewhere quiet and somewhere safe," I reply

The motorbike growls into life and we speed away down the alley. Rach's grip tightens and she shouts over the engine into my ear.

"Then will you tell me everything Joe? Everything?" she asks.

An obvious and uncomfortable pause. Then I hear myself say;

"I promise baby…everything."

27

Rach is in the shower. After a little help from Doctor mini bar, she's finally stopped shaking and crying. I know she's in there now, trying to make sense in her head of everything that she's seen today and I also know as soon as she comes out, she's going to ask me for the truth.

The truth.

What the hell would *I* know about that?

We're holed up in a hotel out in Queens. It's not particularly luxurious or anything but it'll be safe for tonight and it's out of the city. In the morning, I'll head to The Cave - we should be safe there. The security on that place is state of the art but for tonight, we're better hiding here in the hotel.

And for that, I am going to kill Stanley worse than I ever killed anyone before. I'm going to make what the Russians did to him all those years ago look like a fucking Thai massage. I know I've said I'll hang up my holsters if we get out of this in one piece but with Stanley as my last hit, I'm going to go out with a bang – literally. I'm going to conduct a symphony of pain on him. A tour de force of torture.

But that's for another time. Revenge has got to come second right now to protecting Rach. Everything's still so fresh and up in the air here that I haven't had time to come up with a better plan of action beyond hiding in this hotel.

But there's even more pressing concerns still – namely, the fact that the shower just stopped running. I figure I've got three and a half minutes drying time until she comes out of the bathroom.

Okay, so what's the line? Working for the FBI? Super spy maybe? Yeah, like a James Bond type where I'm working for the government and have never been able to reveal what I do to my loving and innocent wife for fear of placing her in danger from those enemies of our beloved United States of America.

Or I could - for once in my fucking life - be honest with her.

I could, but I'm scared. I've never been scared of anything my whole life. I can look down the barrel of a gun without breaking a sweat. I can wade into a room full of goons and swim through the bullets, no problem. I remember I got captured once and had an Italian guy literally put my balls in a vice and threaten to turn them to jelly and I told him to go fuck himself. But being honest to my wife? That scares me to death. Rach steps out of the bathroom wrapped in one of the hotel dressing gowns and drying her hair with a towel.

"You didn't get the dressing wet did you?" I ask.

"No," she answers simply. The fall on the roof scraped a good layer of skin off her arm but luckily the hotel had a first aid box so that I could bandage her arm.

I'm in a worse state than her though. Lincoln did a real number on my face – I've got a busted up nose, a real nasty cut on my temple where he fucking pistol whipped me and my ribs are pretty bruised. Plus on top of all that my ankle's swelled up all purple and blue, the size of a goddamn tennis ball. Still and all, it's not as painful as this silence.

"How's your foot?" she asks eventually.

"It's fine. The swelling will go down once I put the ice on it."

"Good," she says.

She finishes tying her hair back, goes back to the mini bar, opens a little bottle of whiskey, pours it into a glass, then opens a second bottle and pours that in too. She sits opposite me on the bed, takes a big old swig from the glass and looks at me with sad, brown eyes.

"Okay. Okay, I want the truth Joe. All of it," she says nervously.

And I decide, right then and there, that I'm going to give it to her too. I owe her that. And if it means the end of us, I can't say that I blame her and I can't say that I don't deserve it either.

So here we go.

"Honey, before I tell you what I'm going to tell you, I want you to know now - now and forever - that I love you. I loved you the first moment I met you and I love you still. That's always been the one constant in my life."

She looks like she's going to cry but she doesn't. Her eyes well up but there's a steel in them, like she's mentally prepared herself for whatever's coming and all the mushy stuff in the world isn't going to deter her from finding out the truth.

"But okay, here it is. Here's the honest truth and please; just be aware that I only kept this from you because I didn't want to hurt you," I tell her, reaching out and holding her hand.

"Joe, just … please, will you just please tell me," she says and she's scared now.

"Alright. Okay. I'm…I'm a hitman." And there they are - the three words I've always been terrified of telling her.

Her face goes blank. Of all the things she was expecting to hear, this wasn't one of them. From her reaction, she doesn't even know what a hitman *is* and why should she?

"Look honey, I'm not just the owner of a construction company. Magnum's really just a cover for what I really do. I – I'm a hitman. A hired gun. People pay me to, you know, rub guys out."

Wow, that came out *really* badly. '*Rub guys out?!*' What am I, a gangster in 1923?!

"Joe, what are you saying? Are you…" she falters, her words catching in her throat.

"Rach, please just let me finish. Let me just get it all out. I'm saying that my real job, what I really do is to make people disappear. But before you go thinking whatever you're thinking, the only people I've ever killed are the biggest scumbags in the world!"
I stand up now, pacing the room and making wild arm gestures.

"If you knew, Rach. I mean, if you *knew* what some of these people do you'd understand why I do it. Sure it's a paying job but I'd do it for free if it meant people like you got to live in a world without people like these. I mean, these are soulless, evil fucking monsters here. Gangsters who sell crack outside school gates. Paedophiles. Murderers. You think these things only ever happen to other people or in the movies but I'm surrounded every day by the shit these kinds of people rain down on the world so I do to them what they've got no problems in doing to others."

I'm rambling now and there's an urgency in my voice, like the floodgates have been opened and I can't wait to confess to my sins.

"And I know you're probably thinking about cops and that's what they do," I continue. "But the cops can't do a goddamn thing against some of these guys. They're too powerful. If the cops ever *do* get anything on them, they're out on the streets again the day after with their high priced lawyers or they'll bribe their way out. *My* way is permanent. *My* way means they get what's *really* coming to them."

There's a long silence. Rach just looks at me and I can't read her face. I can always read her but right now I haven't got a clue what she's thinking.

"I don't understand, Joe," she says eventually.

"I'm saying I'm a killer but…but I don't do it indiscriminately. I only kill people who deserve it."

"You *kill* people?!" she says. She pulls her hand away from mine and my heart breaks.

"This is what I'm trying to say, yeah. But only bad people," I tell her.

"Only bad people? Who the hell are you to decide that?" she yells.

"Honey please, don't shout. The walls in this place are pretty thin."

"I'll shout as loud as I fucking well want!" This is bad. Rach never swears but under the circumstances,

I'm lucky she isn't throwing furniture at me. She takes a huge swig from her glass.

"So let me get this straight," she says exasperatedly. "You're not *actually* a construction worker, you're a murderer. You murder people and you get paid to do it. That about right?"

"Pretty much," I answer, avoiding her eyes.

She goes quiet. The quiet's worse than the shouting. I stand there like an idiot, not knowing what to do or say. She drains her glass.

"What amount?" she asks, her eyes fixed on the carpet.

"It depends. Sometimes it'll be ten grand, others it'll be a quarter of a million dollars. It all depends on…"

"What amount, Joe!" she roars, getting to her feet and hurling her glass at the wall. She attacks me, her arms flailing as she beats against my chest. "What amount of people have you killed? Hundreds? Huh? *Thousands*?! What have you got, a monthly quota you've got to meet?"

"It's not like that, Rach," I yell, grabbing her arms and pushing them down by her side. She winces as I've grabbed accidentally her scraped arm which unbelievably makes me feel even worse. She eventually stops struggling.

"Just answer this. Is it over fifty?" she asks, her initial anger spent.

I pause.

"Yeah," I barely answer, in a low voice filled with shame. "Way."

She turns a sickly white then instantly flushes to an angry red.

"Get your fucking hands off me," she says in a low voice, dripping with anger. "Now!"

I release her and she turns her back on me, heads back to the mini bar, gets another glass and slowly pours herself another double whiskey.

"So go on. How many people *have* you killed? What's the amount of blood on your hands?"

"Don't take this the wrong way, Rach, but I – well, I guess I lost count over the years."

"Over the years? How long have you been doing this exactly?" she laughs in astonishment, like she can't believe any of this.

"I took my first paid contract when I was seventeen," I answer, knowing exactly what her reaction will be.

"Seventeen?! You've been killing people since you were a *kid*? You've been killing people since..." She stops cold as the realisation kicks in. "Oh God, you've been killing people since we met."

"Honey, look, it's not like this is the kind of thing you can slip out on a third date or anything. I can't think 'Hey, I just met a girl and she's amazing. Things are going great now so I might just tell her I'm a hitman - see how she takes it', you know? How could I have?"

"How could you not?" she replies. She looks at me and it hits me like a sledge hammer to the temple. All the hurt in the world is there in her eyes.

"All these years together, Joe. All these years - this marriage, and you've just destroyed it all. You've been lying to me every single day we've been together. I've spent every moment since we met loving you and now I find out I don't even know who you are."

"I'm still me, Rach. *I* haven't changed," I plead. "I'm still the same guy who's spent every moment since we met loving you right back. I'm still the guy that makes you breakfast in the morning and I'm still the guy you go to sleep with at night."

She stops and my breath catches in my throat hopefully. Then she turns to look at me and I can practically see the distance in her eyes.

"No you're not, Joe. You can't be that person because he doesn't exist anymore. He died about five minutes ago. Earlier, when we were on the roof, you asked me if I trusted you and I said 'always' and I meant it absolutely. Now I'll never be able to trust you again."

"You can still trust me, Rach. Okay, so I've kept a secret from you since forever – a big, dark secret that can never be covered up again. But you can still trust me. You can trust me to keep loving you and never stop loving you. That much I *can* do."

"Oh, Joe, don't you get it?" she says, and her voice is shaky with emotion. "I don't know how you became a murderer when you were still only a kid and I don't *want* to know either. All I know is that you're not a husband. Not any more. Even if I *could* forget all the lies, this wedding ring is still covered in blood. You're telling me you murder people for money and then you try and justify it to me. I don't…I'm looking at you now and you look like my husband but I don't know who you are. I don't think I've ever known."

I've had my head bowed pretty much since we started into this – I can barely make myself meet her eyes because I keep flinching away from the look I see there but now I look up desperately and right back into them.

"I'm Joe," I say. "I've always been just Joe."

I reach out and take a step towards her. She flinches away from me and what feels like a boulder splashes down in the pit of my stomach.

"Don't," she says, and she starts to cry, tears slowly welling in her eyes before running down her perfect face. "Don't. How can I let you hold me? Look at your hands," she says, grabbing my wrists and turning my hands palm upwards. "I can't let these hands wrap around me anymore. I can't let you run them through my hair or hold my hand through the park or – or touch me. They're drenched in blood, Joe. You use these hands to murder people. Every time you've touched me, you've used these same hands."

Then something strange happens to me. Something that I vaguely recall happening to me years ago when I was a kid but which hasn't happened to me for a long, long time. In fact, it's so strange that it even stops Rachel in her tracks.

"You're…you're crying," she says, as much amazed by this as she has been anything else about the last few hours. "I've never seen you cry before."

"That's because I've never hurt you before," I answer.

Her face softens. She looks like all she wants to do in the world is hold me but after an internal struggle, the hard mask drops back over her face and she turns away from me to look out of the window.
I really think I've lost her forever.

She takes a few seconds to compose herself and probably to remind herself of what a lying piece of shit I am underneath it all. In that time, I wipe my tears away and quietly promise myself I'll never cry again. Of course, that's what I said when I was eleven too.

"So where do I fit into this?" she asks eventually. "Why were those men trying to kill me at the bookstore?"

Clever girl.

I tell Rach everything. I tell her about Stanley and all about him being The Prophet. I tell her that he's been bumping guys off for weeks but now me and Danny have found him out. She snorts in disgust when I tell her Danny's in the business too and she says 'I should have known.'

I tell her all about The Lodge and how, when I went over there earlier, I saw the million dollar contract on her head and that's when I rushed over. The whole thing seems to flow so naturally from my mouth, like it's the most normal thing in the world. Like I'm Ray telling a stupid golf story or something.

"The rest, you pretty much know," I finish.

"A million dollars huh?" she says, feigning casualness. "Not bad. And what have I done to earn such a complimentary amount?"

"Nothing. Stanley's using the hit on you to keep me busy and stop me from going after him and so far it's working. He's probably also hoping that somewhere in all the heat a million dollar contract will bring, I'll maybe get taken out and then he's free to carry on killing."

"So after hiding this shit from me ever since we met, it's finally come out and *I'm* the one who's going to get killed. Thanks a lot, Joe," she says.

"Hey, one thing you *can* trust me on is that neither of us are going to die. It's not going to happen, I promise," I try to reassure her.

"And why not?" she asks, trying to sound cool but there's a huge tremble in her voice. "How many people like you are out there exactly? And suddenly killing me is worth a million dollars to them? You can't stop them all, Joe. You can't do it."

"Rach, without trying to shrug all this off, you've got no idea what I can do."

"You're right," she says. "I've got no idea of *anything* about you anymore."

She goes over to the mini bar but it's out of whiskey. There's only vodka left and she'd never normally touch the stuff but she fills her glass now.

"Honey, are you sure you need any more drink than you've had?" I ask.

"Don't call me 'honey', Joe. You don't have the right anymore," she snaps back. "And after everything that's happened in the last five hours, I'll drink as much as I damn well want."

She's already pretty well oiled by now but I can't say that I blame her.

"Look, Rach. I don't want to belittle what you're going through at the moment, but you can't afford to get so drunk that I can't get you out of here in the morning. This place is safe for tonight but we can't stay here forever. We're going to have to keep moving or we're dead."

"Oh, how convenient," she spits.

"What are you talking about, *'convenient?'*"

"You tell me my marriage is built on a lie and that my husband is a paid murderer. You come to my bookstore which I love so much, then you shoot a man in the head right in front of me. Then you throw me off the roof onto another building, nearly ripping my goddamn arm off and all because this dream, this dream of a bookstore I had, that I'd secretly dreamed of for years and had poured my heart and soul into, is burning down to the fucking ground. Then you tell me I'm worth a million dollars dead to every professional murderer in New York and to top it all off, I've got to stay with you and trust you to protect me? You must be crazy. In fact, no. I'm the crazy one. I'm getting dressed right now and going straight to the police."

"You do and you'll be dead within the hour, trust me," I tell her.

I know – 'trust me.' The irony's not lost.

She stops.

"So, what? I need to stay with you?" she asks, even though she already knows the answer.

"Yeah. Just until I can get to Stanley and clear this whole mess."

She looks away, searching for the words, then she looks back at me.

"Okay, you owe it to me to keep me from getting killed. But that's the only reason I'm still here. And you can trust *me* on this. Any other time, I would have left you. I would have walked out and never looked back for what you've done to me. I loved you from the start because I thought I'd found someone who I could trust and that I could lean on and count on and who'd be there for me all the time and who I could grow old and have kids with. I thought that was you, Joe, but you've just proved me wrong. I've never said this word to you before but I swear it from the bottom of my heart – you're a bastard and I hate you."

"And this isn't the booze talking," she goes on. "I've spent most of my life running away from one bastard or another and you, more than anyone, know that. And all this time, it turns out that you were the worst of them all. You're a bastard for what you've done to me, Joe McLean, and I hate you."

She gets up, tears running down her face, and goes towards the bedroom.

"Don't come anywhere near this room," she says finally, before slamming the door shut behind her.

The room is left cold and empty. I'm tempted to sink a few bottles myself but I need to be clear headed. I need to think of a plan of action for tomorrow, but as I plump the cushions up on the couch, pull a blanket over myself and switch the light off, all I can think about is Rachel's words.

And for only the second time in twenty years and the second time that night, lying there in the darkness of room two twelve of the Queens Hotel, I start to cry.

So much for promises.

<u>28</u>

Room service has already been by the time Rach emerges from the bedroom - there's a rack of toast and some scrambled eggs, a pot of coffee and some juice. Rach flashes me a look so frosty she might as well have a carrot for a nose.

"Can I get you a coffee?" I offer.

"I don't want you to do a single goddamn thing for me except to make this nightmare end," she says, pouring herself a black coffee.

"Slept well then?"

"Don't," she growls. "Don't try and make light of any of this and don't think a smile and a grin is going to get things back to normal here. Surely even you, in all your self confidence, can see that you've damaged things irreparably here."

"Of course I can, Rach, but please, I'm just trying to keep things calm and civil here," I protest.

"Well don't, okay? Just don't. You just concentrate on making sure I survive until the end of today," she replies.

Alright, enough of this.

"Okay Rach. Okay," I say in my best *'gimme-no-shit-even-though-you've-got-all-the-right-in-the-world-to'* voice. "I know there aren't the words for me to even begin to say I'm sorry for what I've done but this is the situation we've found ourselves in. Now you say you want to get as far away from me as you can and I understand that, I really do. But the fact is that you need to stick with me if you've got any chance of even seeing the day out and it doesn't matter what you feel about me, you're still my wife and I still love you…"

She makes like she's about to interject something here but this isn't going to turn into an argument or even a discussion – this is me laying down the reality of all this.

"…and I'm not about to let anything happen to you. But for me to be able to do that, you're going to have to shelve the anger and do exactly what I tell you, when I tell you. With some of the people who are going to come after us, if you make one wrong move or do *anything* I don't expressly tell you to do, we're both going to end up dead. So you think you can do that?"

She turns her back on me, stares at the wall and takes a long swig of coffee.

"Yeah, I can shelve my anger just long enough for you to get me out of the black nightmare you've made of my life these last eighteen or so hours," she says, her back still turned to me. "But when all this is finished and if we're still alive – and God, I can't believe I just said that – then I'll take that anger down off the shelf and use it to spend the rest of my life hating your guts."

In the course of my life I've been shot, stabbed, beaten unconscious with a crowbar and even had a psychotic Russian midget spend a weekend electrocuting my balls but nothing has ever hurt me like the words coming out of my wife's mouth right now.

I want to drop to my knees and just beg and plead for her to forgive me. I want to put a gun to my head and pull the fucking trigger. Jesus, I even feel like crying again. Instead, as a way of dealing with all this, I put on a bullshit mask of cool untouchable control and wonder to myself if I'll ever take it off again.

"You want to hate me when all this is over?" I say. "Fine. Just so long as you follow orders. And make no mistakes kiddo, they *are* orders. So here we go, order number one."

She turns around now and I ignore the look on her face that's fifty percent shock and fifty percent anger. I throw a handful of money down on the bed.

"As soon as you finish breakfast you go out, you find a beauty salon and you get your hair dyed and cut. Doesn't matter what colour. Doesn't matter what style. Just so long as any idiot with a photo of you, a gun and a dollar sign in his eyes isn't going to recognise you.

Second thing is you phone Sarah and you tell her that the stress of everything that happened yesterday and the bookstore burning down has gotten too much for you and we're getting away from it all for a week. Don't tell her where we're going if she asks but tell her that if she can handle the insurance and the cops and what not, you'll give her a twenty thousand dollar bonus in her next paycheck. Hopefully, that'll keep the cops away for a few days at least."

"Jesus, Joe, you don't ask for much do you? And what is your third wish, oh great master?" she says sarcastically.

"That you drop the attitude. But for now you can just follow order one and two."

Neither of us says anything else all through breakfast until we get into the hire car I picked up after I dumped the bike. We head into Queens and even then, the only thing she says is to sarcastically ask if I've got a preference for what new hairstyle she should go for. I tell her again to drop the attitude but I think she'll only ever be able to suppress it for now.

I eventually park across the street from the first beauty salon I see. It's not anything close to the kind of places Rachel usually goes to get her hair done and is probably about three hundred dollars cheaper but that doesn't matter just so long as she looks different to the photo of her on those fucking fliers that Stanley sent out. Man, I'd actually almost forgotten but when I think about Stanley and the last twenty four hours my blood burns and I just know that I'm going to spend a long time killing that unbelievable prick very, very slowly.

As Rach snatches the money from my hand and storms into the salon, slamming the door behind her, I head a couple of buildings down to where there's a hardware store. One of the major problems right now is that I'm light on weapons. I've got a couple of caches of weaponry hidden throughout the city but there's no way I'm heading back into New York right now and besides which, Stanley knows the location of most of them anyway. So that means I have to improvise.

Now, guns are the easiest way in the world to kill a man. You point, you pull. Take a gun away though and it's a whole different ball game. Year on year, gun crime is on the up because it's just so easy to do but if you had to swing an axe into a guy's head or look him in the eye while you choke the breath out of him, then you just watch those statistics come down. Point I'm trying to make is that if you know you can do it and you know what to look for then a hardware store is as good as an armoury.

I eventually come away from the store with two heavy duty tool bags full of knives, axes, steel bars and so on. It's not the same as having handguns, rifles and grenades but you make do. I instantly dump one of the bags 'cause it's full of screws, nails, bags of plaster and other stuff I needed to pretend to buy to throw the store clerk off the scent so it doesn't look like I'm just there to buy sharp objects, you know?

I cross over to a grocery store and pick up a couple of bags of food and drink. We're going to have to go to ground tonight and won't be going anywhere near a restaurant until this is all over so I buy a lot of food that's easy to eat – junk food mainly; chips and chocolate and like that. I drop all the bags in the trunk of the car and head back to the salon.

Now, I'm not even sure what I was expecting but it wasn't this.

As I cross over the road, Rach walks out of the salon and time slows down and she seems to walk in slow motion like in the movies where the beautiful girl leaves the bar or whatever. In all the time I've been with her, Rachel's never really changed her hair style at all. She might have gone a little shorter or a little longer now and then but essentially always the same hair cut, you know? But her once long, brown hair is now jet black and cropped short into her neck, and she looks completely different. She looks amazing.

"Rach, wow, you look…you look incredible," I stammer like a schoolkid.

She just strides right past me without even looking at me, her head held high and proud in the air.

"I'm so glad you approve, asshole. Just remember though – you'll never see me naked again," she says as she struts proudly past.

Damn, I almost forgot for a second.

By now, it's almost midday so we head into a diner for lunch. I sit us both in a booth with our backs to the wall and a clear view of the entrance. Rachel orders a chicken salad with a diet coke and I order the bacon burger with a Dr Pepper. Every attempt I make at small talk is shot down so we eat in silence. God she looks hot.

After lunch, Rach orders a coffee and I order a bowl of vanilla ice cream.

"You know, this is pretty much the last time we can do this," I say, trying again to break the silence. "As soon as we leave here we've got to 'hit the mattresses' as the Italians say."

"Oh I'm sorry, I don't speak 'gangster'. What are you talking about?" she says.

"It means that we're going to have to go into hiding. No more eating out. In fact, after today, no more *walking* about during the day time. The only way you're going to be safe is if I can hide you away somewhere secure."

"Like where, Australia?" she comments.

Great, she's a comedian now.

"I don't know just yet, we've got to let the dust settle on all this and see where we are a week or so from now. For now though, I've got somewhere safe I can keep you."

She rolls her eyes and gives a dramatic sigh of contempt. "Wonderful," she says.

The waitress drops the bill and leaves. I fish a twenty out and lay it on the plate. Rach reaches into her pocket, pulls out a credit card and puts it on top of the twenty.

"Half each. I don't want you paying for a damn thing with your blood money. And you can have this back too," she says, throwing the money I gave her earlier for the haircut down on the table.

My heart sinks.

"Rach, please tell me you didn't pay for your haircut on that card," I ask, fearful I know the answer already.

"I told you, I don't want a penny of your dirty money," she spits.

"Oh shit, it wasn't about that!" I yell back. "I needed for you to pay in cash. The second they swiped your card you sent up a digital flare to every hitman whose computer savvy doesn't start and end with a fucking Nintendo!"

God-fucking-dammit! Okay, think. So we left the beauty salon about half an hour ago. That'd easy give a handful of mouth breathers the time to come out here looking and we've been sitting here like patsies the whole time.

I head over to the window and look out onto the street but I can't see anyone. Hopefully, Rach's new disguise will hold up and if anyone sees me they'll just assume I'm here for the hit. Only thing is…ah, fuck. Coming out of the grocery store down the street from the salon and out onto the street are The Domingo Twins, a couple of spaghetti and meatball eating throwbacks who've been brought up to believe that every film starring DeNiro or Pacino is actually a fucking documentary.

Now I know they happen to have a pretty solid computer geek that works for them – his name's Michael or Michaelangelo or something, he plays cyber chess with Danny sometimes if you can believe that – which would explain how The *Dumb*ingo's managed to trace Rachel's card activity. They've probably been asking around in the salon and are just doing door to doors now in the vain hopes that the mark is stupid enough to still be hanging around…which we are.

It'll only be a matter of minutes before the twins head into this diner and spot us and all my weapons are in the trunk of the car. I'm going to need to get creative here because what the Domingo's lack in brain power they make up for in fire power and I've got Rach to consider here.

"What's happening?" she asks, appearing at my shoulder and looking nervously out onto the street. "Who's out there?"

"You see those two walking Italian stereotypes across the street there?" I ask, pointing. "Well the fat, greasy one in the bad suit on the left is Tony Domingo and the fat, greasy one in the bad suit on the right is his brother Donnie. A couple of bigger assholes you'll never meet but right now you're worth half a million dollars each to them honey, so come away from the window."

Rach sits herself back down in our booth. The colour drains from her face.

"Look, Rach? I know you don't want to hear this right now but they'd never have known where we were if you'd just done only what I told you. I can, and I'm going to, get us away from here but this is the last time I'm going to be able to tell you this. Hate my guts or not, you've got to start listening to me and you've got to start doing exactly what I say."

She nods, tears welling in her eyes.

"Okay, now I want you to stay right here in this booth. I'm going to try and get the car and bring it around so as soon as you see me pull up outside, you come running straight out and into the passenger side without stopping, got it?"

"But what if those two guys see you? Won't they try and kill you?" Rach asks.

"They'll try," I smile back.

I wait by the diner door until eventually the twins go into the dry cleaners just two stores down. I turn to look back at Rach and flash her a smile and a wink. She smiles a sad and nervous smile back at me.

I sprint across the road, straight to where the car's parked. I toy with idea of getting some of the hammers out of the trunk, heading into that dry cleaners and playing 'whack-a-mole' with the twins but decide that getting Rach clear is more important right now.

I put the key in the driver's side door, getting ready to make a break for it when suddenly I hear the unmistakeable dry click of a gun hammer being drawn back by my left ear. Fuck, I can't even *remember* the last time I let someone get the drop on me.

I turn around slowly and I'm staring right down the barrel of a .45 behind which is a face twisted in hate, his eyes burning and a shining red, fresh burn scar running up his neck.
Lincoln.

"Hey Joe," he says, grinning madly and pressing the gun to my forehead. "Where's your bitch?"

29

I think I've already mentioned that about the most important thing is to be fast. Fast thinking and even faster acting. Now I'm fast – always have been and it's gotten me out of some pretty heavy scrapes in the past – but forget what Hollywood shows you. You know how in the movie, the bad guy will be holding a gun in the good guy's back and the good guy is so fast he can spin round and kick shit out of the bad guy before he can even pull the trigger? Forget it. If you were to try that in real life with a gun pointed in your back the last thing you'd see is your spine come flying out in front of you through your stomach. Nobody's faster than the squeezing of a finger.

Which brings me to why I'm sat in the front of the car with Lincoln sat in the back seat with a gun pointed at me. I guess I'm just trying to explain away why I haven't made a daring escape just yet. Hopefully it's coming though.

"So, Joe, your fucking wife huh?" Lincoln gloats from the back seat. "And let me guess. You had no idea there'd be a contract out on her yesterday so you ran over to that fucking book store like a white knight. I bet you're her fucking hero right now, right?"

"As a matter of fact, she hates my guts," I answer calmly. "She didn't even know I was a hitman until yesterday, which is why she left me last night. I don't know where she is."

"Jesus Christ Joe, don't fucking insult me okay? All her details were put out around The Lodge by eight o'clock last night. Rachel McLean, used to be Henderson until she married your arrogant ass. Thirty two years old, ex model. Gotta say Joey, you've done okay for yourself there. Or should I say, you *did* alright because I'm going to find the bitch and kill her within the next thirty minutes. Might even rape her first, see how I'm feeling. See, I can't believe my luck. I can't believe she's so stupid that she used her card in that fucking beauty salon there across the street. What, was she just desperate to get her nails done before she went into hiding? So imagine my surprise when I zip on over to check things out, fully expecting you both to be long gone but then I see *you* getting into a car. So I'm thinking that if you're still here, she must be..."

"Ah, just fucking shoot me would you, Lincoln? Just so I don't have to hear you whine on and on like a bad Bond villain," I sigh.

"Always so cool aren't you, Joe?" he says, an edge in his voice. Good, I'm hitting a nerve with the prick now. "Strutting 'round The Lodge like you fucking own the place. Thinking you're untouchable. Make no bones about it though, I'm going to kill you any second now. I just want you to.."

"How's your neck, man?" I interrupt. "It looks pretty sore."

I look in the rear view mirror at him and his face comes pretty close to exploding, turning as red as the burn on his neck but he calms himself and the look disappears again. I was hoping to push him and force him into making a stupid move but it doesn't work. I think I'm going to die now.

"Good try Joe, good try. Ycah, okay, yeah you got me yesterday, I can admit that. Everyone always wondered which one of us would come out on top. Looks like it was you, doesn't it? Man, you left me to burn in that fucking store, I gotta hand it to you. But

God bless the FDNY, you know? Anyway, yeah, my fucking neck hurts. You got me. Good for you. Take that with you to the fucking grave."

Here it comes.

The gun moves up to the back of my skull.

Rach, I'm so sorry.

Suddenly, a gunshot sounds out and amazingly, it's not my skull that hits the window. It's the windshield of the car itself that comes smashing in. I don't know what's happened but Lincoln and I get showered in glass but I gather myself quicker than him and take full advantage. I turn in my seat and drive my fist into the middle of his face before he can react, feeling his nose split satisfyingly under my knuckles.

I dive out of the door as more shots smash into the hood. I duck behind the car and pop the trunk which gives me some cover against the shooter in front and also gives me access to my bag of tricks from the hardware store. If I'm going to enter a gun fight with a couple of hatchets and a crowbar I deserve to get my head blown off but what the hell else can I do?

It doesn't take a genius to work out that it's either Tony or Donnie out there doing the shooting but either way, fingers crossed they take out Lincoln sat in the back seat. I quickly tuck some knives and a hatchet into my belt, sneak a look around the side of the car and see one of the twins stood in the middle of the road, reloading his gun. By now, after hearing all these shots, people are coming running out of the stores onto the street, screaming and panicking. I take advantage of the confusion and bolt for the nearest building, barely making it through the door before whichever prick Domingo is out there sends some bullets my way.

The store is a little Deli and there's a handful of folks in there scared shitless that stare and scream at me as I burst through the door.

"It's okay folks, I'm a cop," I shout. "I want everybody out through the back door and I need you all to run in the opposite direction and don't stop until you see a squad car."

They don't need any more encouragement than that and they hustle out through the back kitchen. I look out into the street and both Domingo's are there now. One of them is laying down fire and pinning Lincoln in the car and the other is headed towards my Deli.

"Hey, McLean," shouts one of the pricks from outside. "Where's your wife, huh? Tell us and we'll do you quick, we promise. We can see you ain't got no guns or nothing."

Well the good thing is that neither Lincoln nor the Domingo's know Rach is in the diner but then *I* don't know if she's still sitting tight and hidden under a table or whether she's bolted out the back door with the rest of the customers. Still, my main concern right now has got to be in burying this hatchet in the head of a greasy fuck who's gotten ideas above his station. Man, this million over Rach's head seems to have sent The Lodge into overdrive – otherwise, there's no way a couple of D- listers like the twins would ever take me or Lincoln on.

Domingo fuck #1 shoots out the glass from the Deli door, trying to rattle me. If I had a gun right now this would all be over in seconds but I don't so I'm going to have to be creative. He'll be in through the door in

about ten seconds and as soon as he sees me, he'll
send a bullet right through the middle of my eyes.
Now when you throw an object like a knife (or in this
case a store bought hatchet) I don't care what the
movies show you, but unless you grew up in a fucking
circus, more often than not you're not going to hit shit.
The second I see the Domingo come through the door,
I break my cover and throw the hatchet as hard as I
can straight at his head.

Honestly? I'm not expecting to even hit him. I was
just hoping to throw him off so I could get in close,
like I did with Lincoln in the bookstore yesterday.
Instead what happens is the hatchet spins through the
air in slow motion and buries itself right into the
middle of Domingo's forehead, the impact actually
knocking him off his feet and sending him backwards.
And *that* is what's generally known as dumb fucking
luck.

His body lies twitching in the door frame and I
prise the gun out of his hand and quickly search him
for any clips but the greasy punk doesn't have any.
Typical fucking amateur, only brings one mag out to
play. Idiot. Still, I can't even explain how good it feels
to finally have a gun in my hand. Now I can finally get
into this thing.

Okay, I figure there's maybe a couple of minutes
tops before the cops show up so I've got to kill Tony
or Donnie – whichever one's left out there – and
Lincoln in the next sixty seconds, then grab Rach and
high tail it out of here by the second minute. Piece of
cake.

"Hey Donnie, what's going on over there?" a shout
comes from the street. Guess that settles which one's

lying here quivering at my feet with his face split into two halves.

I sneak a look around the door frame and see him advancing on the car with Lincoln presumably cowering behind the back seat. For all I know, Lincoln could be dead already so I'll take care of the immediate threat. I pick up Donnie's bloated greaseball body (hatchet still buried in his face) and prop him up in front of me and walk to the doorway.

"Say, Tone," I mimic, in my best greasy gangster voice. "You got any aspirin?"

Oh man, if I die in the next ten minutes it's worth it just to see the look on Tony's face as he sees his brother propped up with a nine dollar hatchet buried in his head. Priceless.

Tony roars a string of obscenities and fires blindly towards the Deli. I let go of Donnie's corpse and let it soak up the bullets. Within seconds, Tony's out of ammo too (I mean, first rule is always to go out packing plenty of spare clips, you know? Fucking amateurs.) and he charges across the street in a rage like a bull. I calmly step out onto the sidewalk, draw his brother's gun and send a single bullet in between Tony's eyes. He falls forward with the momentum and his face skids across the asphalt in a bloody red smear. So long, Domingo's.

Just Lincoln left now. I slowly advance on the smashed up car, the gun held out in front of me, not sure what to expect. I mean, it could be that Tony finished him off and he's lying dead in the back seat for all I know. I should probably get Rach and clear out of here before the cops show but I've got to make sure of Lincoln because he's going to track us down wherever we go and I'm not spending all my time looking over my shoulder. Man, I wish I had a grenade right now I could just throw in the back seat and walk away.

"Hey, Lincoln! You still alive in there or what?" I call out. I creep slowly towards the car when out of nowhere, my skull explodes in white light and thunder. I go sprawling onto the floor and the gun spins out of my hand – I can't believe I'm still conscious. It feels like my body just turned to liquid.

Before I can gather myself, I see through blurry eyes a dark shape bearing down on me. It's got to be Lincoln – he must have made it out of the car and doubled back on me, the sneaky fuck. A boot to my jaw sends my head into an ever wilder spin. He must've run out of bullets himself but as long as he's beating on me, he's not going for my gun so I curl into a ball and raise my arms to cover my face and wait for an opening.

I can just about make out Lincoln shouting something through the ringing in my ears. He doesn't let up though, raining kick after perfectly placed kick down on me. Oh man, please don't let me die being kicked to death in the fucking street by this moron. There's a break in proceedings and I try to stand but my legs decide they think I'm an asshole and give out on me. There's blood running into my eyes and I can barely see. I wipe them clear just in time to see Lincoln standing over me, swinging my own crowbar right at my head. I manage to roll left at the last minute and the swing misses my head by a whisker. I'm not going to be able to keep dodging him forever though and it's only going to be a matter of time before he takes my head off.

For the second time in the last half hour, a gunshot saves my life. Four shots sound out and three of them miss by a country mile but then I see the shock register on Lincoln's face as he notices that his right hand has just been turned into a bloody stump.

I look up expecting to see a cop, but instead I see Rachel still pointing the gun at Lincoln, her eyes streaming with tears. Her face is marble white with shock and she's still pulling the trigger even though the gun's empty.

Lincoln roars in pain and rage and aims a clumsy kick at my head. I block it easily and sweep his feet out from under him. He's in too much pain to be thinking clearly and he grabs his stump with his other hand as if that's going to bring it back. I slowly stand, pick the crowbar up off the floor and head over to where Lincoln's writhing on the ground.

I'm too tired and pissed off even to make a witty, Arnie-esque one liner. Instead, I bring the crowbar smashing down on him. He raises his arms to shield his head but all this does is turn the bones in his forearms into powder. By the time my third swing comes down, his hands aren't up any more and I smash the crowbar right into his head. His skull splits like a melon and I think he's finally dead.

But I don't stop there. I can't. The unbelievable sack of dog shit my life has suddenly turned into transforms into a well of hatred towards the broken body on the floor in front of me. I hear sirens now in the distance but still I don't stop. I just keep swinging that crowbar down and down and down and down until there's nothing left of Lincoln's head that could even be described as head anymore.

Finally, I come to. I straighten up, sweat dripping off the end of my nose and I drop the crowbar to the street with a heavy clang. Rach is still standing there in the middle of the street looking at me and I swear it's like her eyes have died.

She looks straight through me, moves like she's about to say something then doubles over and throws up all over the sidewalk.

<u>30</u>

Enough is enough. Running's *never* been my style. I'm more of a 'charge head forward, guns firing, sort things out when the dust's cleared' kind of guy. Okay, I just ran from the cops but that just makes common sense – I mean, that street looked like the set of a Romero movie when we left it. But I've been on the run since the bookstore just yesterday (which, by the way, feels like about six months ago) and I'm already sick of it.

I can't take Rach on the road like this – the last hour's proved that. We could maybe go abroad, try and hide out for a few years but who the hell wants to live a life looking over their shoulder? Besides, the food sucks in all those foreign countries.

Now I don't really have any other plan of action for getting out of this scrape other than one monumentally dumb one that's been sitting scraping the back of my skull since last night in the hotel. And that plan is –

and here's where it's brilliant in its simplicity – is that I go over to The Lodge, drive a truck through the front door, kill every single prick there who even breathes in a way that I see as threatening, ram my fist so far down Stanley's throat that I can squeeze his withered little heart into a paste then go to Disneyland.

Now I know I should probably lie low, try and draw Stanley out maybe, but my head's still screaming for me to go with the carnage plan.

And let's face it, what the hell have I got to lose? Rach hasn't so much as looked at me since we got in this car. In fact, I don't think she's even blinked yet. But there it is, she's seen me laid bare. As if it's not enough for her to have to deal with what I am she then has to see the cold reality of it up front and personal. If I'd been entertaining any idea of her maybe forgiving me over time and taking me back, I think they've just been smashed to pieces. Kinda like Lincoln's skull.

This car I hotwired is a real piece of shit. It keeps stuttering and the gears crunch with every shift but still, it was the only one left on the street that hadn't been shot to hell. A real uncomfortable silence settles in. I would put the radio on, try and relieve the tension, but I think that would seem a little blasé after what's just happened. I don't even know where I'm driving to, I'm just headed away from the street and the cops.

"Thanks," I decide to say after a five minute, silent soul search.

Rachel pauses for a while then she slowly seems to come back around to real life, like she's waking from a dream.

"Thanks for what?" she whispers.

"You saved my life back there, Rach, I mean it. Lincoln would have taken my head off for sure if you hadn't…"

"If I hadn't killed him," she interrupts.

"What?! What are you talking about?" I reply, trying to talk as normally as possible about the situation so it doesn't freak her out as much as it should. Really, I'm just glad we've broken the silence.

"I fucking killed him, Joe! I've never shot a gun in my life before! I fucking hate guns but I just shot a man and killed him!" she rages.

"In fairness, Rach, you only shot him in the hand. I'm the one who actually killed him," I add, helpfully.

"Kill him?! Joe, you smashed his head to pieces with a fucking steel bar, but I'm the one who…I'm the one who…"

She stutters, then starts crying into her hands.

"What, Rach, you're the one who what?" I ask, putting my hand gently on her shoulder.

"I'm the one who *let* you," she moans.

"Hey, hey, you didn't let me *do* anything, okay." I say softly. "You saw that he was going to kill me and you stopped him, simple as that. You never made me stand up and beat him to death. You never set him up for me. He was going to kill you right after he'd killed me so think of it as self defence, that's all."

"Oh, it's all just so simple to you isn't it, the hardened killer who can murder a man one minute then go home and lie to his wife about it the next. It's not that black and white, Joe, can't you fucking see that?" she sobs angrily.

"As a matter of fact, Rach, yes it is that black and white. A man is out to kill you, you either let him or you kill him first – there's no grey areas there. What you're doing is thinking about all this from a standpoint of morality that's been forced on you by the society we live in. But it's as old as the Bible, honey - man kills man. An eye for an eye and all that stuff. That guy back there, Lincoln, was one of the biggest pieces of shit scumbag fucking killers you'll ever meet. I just did the world a huge favour, alright?"

"Oh Joe, you just don't get it do you?" she cries. "And you never will."

"Maybe not but what I do get is that we're still alive and he's dead so in my book, that makes us the winners. And that's all life is, Rachel, is trying to keep your head above water and making sure the other guy doesn't stick his finger in your ass as he swims past you. You just get through life trying to do what's right and not hurt people."

"What?!" she screams, tears running down her face. "Are you insane? Not hurt people?! Joe, are you – seriously, I want to know - are you actually insane?! Because that's the only possible explanation for what you just said. All you *do* is hurt people! You kill them just to make money, you goddamn monster!"

I pull the car screeching over to the sidewalk, practically causing a four car pile up in the lanes behind me. They slam their horns but I ignore it and turn in my seat to look at Rachel.

"Okay," I growl, not shouting but loud enough so she knows this isn't a conversation we're having here, I just want her to shut up and listen. "Enough. You think I'm scum, I get it. Believe me, after last night, I get it. But I'm going to say this once and then I'm never going to try and justify another thing to you ever again. Okay, you remember last year? That business trip I took just after your birthday?"

"Yeah, you said you were going to Philadelphia with Gerry. But let me guess, you were lying," she says sarcastically.

"Just listen for a minute, will you?" I snap back. "No smart comments, no bullshit, just listen. Yeah, okay, I never went to Chicago. Instead I took on a contract to kill a slave trader in Romania. I know, slave traders in the Twenty First Century, it's unbelievable right? Anyway, this guy was taking girls, sometimes as young as twelve, from these poor little back water villages – I mean literally walking into people's houses and disappearing with their daughters, just taking them because he could. Then what he'd do was he'd sell them on like they were cattle. Some to work, some for prostitution and some were killed so their organs could be harvested and sold on the black market. So the families - and we're talking about fucking peasants here without two roubles to their names - these families club together and pool enough cash to be able to afford a hitman to take this guy out."

"Now I never take on European contracts," I continue. "Because, well, because it's Europe and who gives a shit? But I paid my own fare over to goddamn Romania and I gave those villagers their money back and I made that hit for free and you know why? Because I found out what this guy did to stop those young girls from trying to escape."

"He kept them all in this compound, see, and one day he caught a young girl with a baby trying to escape and get back to her family. So he gathered all the girls into the kitchen and had his guards stand over them while he taught them never to run from him. He took this young girl's four month old baby and laid it on top of the cooker and switched it on. It was one of those electric rings that takes a while to heat up, you know? So he made these girls slowly watch as the thing gets hotter and hotter until that little baby's skin started to bubble and smoke. Four months old Rach, couldn't even move itself off that cooker top. It just had to lie there and slowly burn to death."

Rach covers her mouth with her hand as tears just stream down her face.

"And you know how I know all these details? Because the baby's mother told me herself just after I lied to you, hopped on a plane to Romania, killed this black souled, evil son of a bitch slave trader and all his little soldiers and freed her and twenty two other young girls and sent them back to their families. Her name was Anna and she told me every detail of her story and never cried once and do you want to know why *that* was? She *couldn't* cry because she'd clawed her own fucking eyes out after seeing her kid burnt alive, that's why. So you go right ahead and think I'm a monster but you ask any one of those girls or their families and they'll call me a fucking hero."

"Joe, I…" she offers through her tears.

"Don't," I tell her. "Just listen. You think I'm such a bad guy and people like Janet and Ray are the normal, good guys? Well think again 'cause if it weren't for me, Ray would be dead now and Janet would be nursing one hell of a guilty conscience 'cause when Ray was having an affair with that girl from his golf club, good old Janet was willing to pay someone to *kill* good old Ray. And if anyone but me, through sheer dumb luck, would have picked up that contract then Ray'd be long gone. *I'm* the one who got those two back together and made them realise that they did actually love each other. Now who's the monster in this story? The guy who cheats on his wife, the wife who pays to have her husband killed or the guy who rescues his fucking worthless friends' marriage?"

There's a loud silence in the car. Outside, the real world carries on and normal, average people walk past carrying groceries and briefcases and bags.

"I'm not looking for forgiveness, Rach. I know I've lied to you and I know I've made you hate me. But just take the blinkers off your eyes for a second and you'll see that this is the way the world is. I love that you're innocent about the cold, hard reality of the depths and levels of suffering one human being can and will inflict on another. I've always tried to protect you from that and any dollar I've ever made, blood money or not, has gone towards keeping you safe in the illusion that this world is a nice place to live. But it's not, Rach. You can trust me on that, it's not. I could keep talking and tell you stories that would make Anna's seem like a fairy tale but I wont. Just know that, even though since the day I first met you I've lied to you, just know these things. I've never killed a woman. I've never killed a child. I've never killed anyone who I didn't think deserved to die for what they'd done. I've always loved you and I've always tried to protect you. There's two sides to me – Good Joe who you married and Bad Joe who, yeah, he kills people but Bad Joe *has* to be bad so he can do some good in this world, okay? There. End of sermon. And you'll never hear me justify myself again, I guarantee it."

She seems like she's about to say something but right now, I don't really want to listen. I've said my piece and she's seen and heard everything there is to be seen and heard about me.

"Rach, you don't need to say anything, okay?" I tell her. "I'm not expecting you to just wrap your arms around me, forgive me and say you understand. I'm sorry, more sorry than you'll ever know that I couldn't keep protecting you and that I've dragged you into this world, but I won't let you get hurt because of me. So it's time to end this."

I turn the engine on and pull the car back out into the traffic.

"Where – where are we going?" she asks.

"To Bad Joe's house."

31

"It's nice," Rachel says sarcastically, picking up a filthy and burnt shoe. "I mean, I think our house is slightly nicer but still, I like what you've done with the place."

"Funny," I reply. "Just wait'll you get inside, then we'll see what you think."

I ditched the stolen car four blocks away and we've walked all the way from there down here to the derelict buildings on the outskirts of the city. I've been looking over my shoulder the whole way but there's been no tails. When I spoke to Danny an hour ago he said there'd been no sign of any muscle coming looking for either me or Rach since the contract went out so I figure this is about the safest place to leave her while I go kill Stanley.

I pull the old panel away, scan my fingerprint and type in the code and when the doors open, Rachel's left open mouthed as this perfectly clean, brightly lit corridor extends out in front of her.

"Told you so," I turn and smile.

"My God, Joe, what is this place?" she says as she follows me in wide eyed and the doors close shut behind us.

"We call it The Cave," I answer.

"The Cave?! Oh, could you possibly sound any more like a teenage boy with that? And who's *we*?" she asks.

"Uh, I think he probably means me," Danny says as he appears at the end of the corridor. "Hi Rach, I like your new…"

Before Danny can even finish his sentence, Rach slaps him clear across his face. I mean she hits him so hard his glasses fly off and he hits the deck. He looks up at her like a puppy that's been kicked.

"Ow! Jeez, Rach, what was that for?" he whines, holding his cheek.

"You even have to ask, you slimy little prick?" Rach smoulders before turning her back on Dan and storming away. God, she looks so hot right now.

I help Danny up off the floor and I can't help but smile. "Man, she just totally laid you out with one shot," I laugh.

"Very funny," Dan says scowling. "So I take it from that she hasn't taken the news too well."

"Jesus, Dan, you blame her? Nah, she pretty much hates me right now and I think she has every right to.

If she didn't need me to protect her I think she'd be signing divorce papers as we speak."

"Man, I can't believe she found out after all this time," he says. "You always did such a good job in hiding it from her."

"I know, but what the hell could I do? As soon as that million dollar hit went out on her I raced over to the bookstore and she saw me shoot Eddie the Fish of all people right in front of her eyes. Shit, she watched me beat Lincoln to death with a crowbar about an hour and a half ago."

"Lincoln's dead?" Dan asks. "Wow, way to go Joe, he was *always* an asshole to me. Guess you settled which one of you was the toughest then, huh?" he enthuses.

"Yeah," I answer, a little preoccupied. "Listen, Dan, can you make yourself scarce for a few minutes? I'm going to find Rach."

"Sure, Joe. I'll bring some drinks through in a while," he answers. I turn and walk down the corridor after Rachel and Danny calls after me. "Hey, Joe. You got a plan to deal with all of this shit? Tell me you've got a plan," he says.

I stop and think for a second before answering.

"Kind of, Dan," I answer honestly. "Kind of."

I head into the games room and Rachel's sitting there on the couch, sobbing into her hands. Not the wracking, violent crying she's been doing before now but just a gentle weeping. I take this as a bad sign.

She looks up when she hears me come in and wipes the tears away with her hands like she's too proud to let me see her cry. I sit next to her awkwardly, wondering whether if I put my arm around her she'd try and scratch my eyes out.
I think she probably would.

"You know," she says, sniffing. "Even if I could potentially get over the truth about what you really do for a living, which I can't, and even if I could get over the fact our entire marriage and relationship has been built on a lie, which again, I can't, you know the thing that really gets me in all this is just how fucking stupid I am. I mean, you and Danny must have been laughing your asses off at me for years. Poor, stupid Rachel, too fucking dumb to realise we're both making an idiot out of her and reducing her entire life to one big, cruel joke."

"Rach, please, Jesus, I never once thought anything even remotely *like* that and neither did Dan," I protest.

"Oh bullshit, you must have. All these years I thought we had something incredible going and the whole time you were laughing behind my back. God, you must really hate me, Joe," she says.

"*Hate* you?! Are you nuts?" I tell her. "My whole life I spent wandering around like a fucking idiot looking for I didn't even know what. But then I met you and I knew what life was about. All the songs and movies that feed you this sugar coated line about love which I always assumed was just bullshit – when I met you, I finally *got* it. Every single bad love song suddenly made sense. You were, are and always have been the best thing in my life."

"Oh yeah?" she says, a cold mask slipping over her face. "If I was the best thing in your life, how come you treated me like someone you hated?"

"Hey guys, am I interrupting anything?" Dan says, as he pokes his head around the door.

"No, come in Danny, this is just perfect. I want to talk to you a second" Rach says.

"You're not going to hit me again, are you?" he asks sheepishly.

"Danny, if I was to hit you again I don't think I could ever stop. But I want you to set something straight for me so no, I'm not going to hit you," she tells him.

"Well, that's a relief," Danny says but he still sits down on the couch as far away from Rachel as he can.

"First of all," Rach says, and she's composed herself now and there's a hardness in her voice. "Have you got anything you'd like to say to me Danny?"

"Uh…" he flounders, looking to me for help but I can't offer him any. "You, ah, you want a drink?" he says.

"No I don't want a fucking drink," she snaps at him. "I want you to apologise to me. I want you to look me in the eyes and apologise to my face for lying to me since the day I first met you, you slimy little fucking worm."

"Oh God, I mean – well shit, Rach, I mean, well sure, that is that I…" Dan stutters and it's painful to watch him.

"Just fucking say it!" Rach barks.

Danny hangs his head like an eight year old who's been caught with his hand in the cookie jar. "I'm sorry," he mumbles shyly.

"Apology not accepted, Danny," she says coldly. "But at least you managed to say it. So this is where you two have been hanging out for years, planning in your infinite arrogance how you were going to set yourselves above the laws of society and play with the lives of your loved ones. I've got to say boys, it's a pretty impressive place."

"Ah, knock it off Rach, will you? Enough with the guilt trips already," I butt in. "We could spend the next month apologising to you and it wouldn't cover it. We know this so let's just move on shall we?" She flashes me a look that says she hates my guts and would happily carry this conversation on but mercifully, she lets it go. "Besides, we've got a lot more things to worry about right now."

"Right, like how we can stop Stanley," Dan says. "Hey, maybe if we make you up to be dead and photograph you then send copies to The Lodge, the million dollar contract on your head will be gone and at least then that'll give us some breathing space," he says to Rach.

"Wouldn't work," I say. "Stanley'd see through it in seconds. Besides, he'd keep coming at us – now he knows we know about him, he'll figure something else out to get at us. The contract he's put on Rach has just been the first wave, something to keep me busy so I can't get to him and tear his head off."

"Who is this guy again?" Rach asks. "He's your 'agent' and he's just flipped out and started killing people, all so he can make a profit?"

"No pun intended, I'm sure," Dan says. "But think about it. If he gets a lot more work coming in for the hitmen in his stable, then we're talking millions of dollars a year in commission. He'd dominate the entire market down at The Lodge."

"Look, whatever his motives he needs to be stopped," I interject. "He can't just keep on killing people and..."

Rach cuts across me with an over dramatic snort of derision.

"That's the most hypocritical thing I think I've ever heard," she says.

"Let it go Rach!" I snap, yelling now. "Okay? Just let it go. I know what I've done but there's more going on here right now than what you're feeling and I don't need this. I'm sitting here trying to think of ways to kill a man who's been like a father to me because he killed one of my closest friends, has tried to kill my wife and is now trying to kill me too so if I look like I'm handling things well and have got room on my plate right now for your fucking sarcasm, then you're mistaken."

Both her and Dan go quiet and avert their eyes. Rach in particular isn't used to me losing it and certainly not in talking to her like that but it's true – I'm not really in the happiest of places right now.

"Okay, fuck it, here's what we're going to do," I say eventually. "Dan, I want you to hook up some speakers and a mic to the van – as loud as you can get it. Rach, you're going to stay here with Dan where you'll be safe. Tomorrow morning, bright and early, I'm going to The Lodge with as much firepower as I can carry and I'm going to blaze a trail through that fucking place until I find Stanley."

"Then what?" Danny asks, a little dumbfounded by my master plan.

"Then I end all this and come back here to take us all out for pancakes."

Now show me a guy who works full time in a bank that says he hasn't thought at least once about trying to rob the place and I'll show you a liar. It's human nature, of course it is. So ever since I first set foot in The Lodge 'lo those many years ago, I've always thought about setting siege to the place. See, security's there's not *actually* as great as people think it is.

First off – and this is the big one – the top brass down there have got everyone so well trained not to screw around or break the house rules that they're relying on the threat of retaliation to be their biggest security. Second is the fact that The Lodge is fairly isolated and sits in the middle of the grounds. There's the long driveway out front but the south side backs out into woodlands – perfect for getting up close without being seen. Only thing is, come tomorrow, I *want* to be seen.

The other thing is that the place is filled, pretty much night and day, with …well, with (what's the collective noun for hitmen?) – a *shitload* of hitmen? And I don't know what kind of bullshit Stanley's been spreading about me but I'm pretty sure I won't exactly be flavour of the month down there tomorrow.

As well as all of the above, I'm not exactly in top shape. All the running, fighting and jumping off burning buildings I've been doing lately has taken its toll - my bruises and cuts are healing but my ankle's still a little swollen. I'd say I'm working on about 80% capacity here. Hopefully, that'll be enough.

Danny's working on the van and cobbling together some toys for tomorrow and Rachel's gone to lay down for a while. It wouldn't surprise me if she slept for a week after everything she's been through. I've put her through hell and I'm sorry I snapped at her earlier but she really wasn't helping. To be honest, I could really use a deep sleep myself right now but chance would be a fine thing.

I put myself through a gruelling hour long workout in the gymnasium. My foot needs the exercise and I really need to let off the frustrations of the last few days. In fact, once I start in on the punching bag I find that's it's really hard to stop. I feel like I could pound my fist into it all day, hoping that I can somehow punch away my problems.

After I shower, I decide to spend half an hour down at the range just to loosen myself up before I turn in but Rachel appears at the end of the corridor.

"Hey."

"Hey," she replies. "What you doing?"

"Just going to let off some steam before I turn in. You know what, why don't you come with me? I've got something I want to show you."

I walk Rachel the long way 'round to the firing range, just enjoying spending time with her (See, I'm not so naïve or overly confident that I'm unaware that tomorrow could turn out really badly and this is potentially the last time I'll ever see her). I give Rach the grand tour and even though she slips and comments once about me keeping this from her, she's still amazed by the place. I show her the gym, the games room and bar, the heated swimming pool and she remains suitably stunned. For me though, it's just really nice to be near her, you know?

"So you call this place The Cave," she says. "And the other place is called The Lodge. Can you see what I'm getting at here?"

"What, there's a lot of capital letters involved in being a hitman?" I answer.

"No – it's that you're like a teenage boy living some kind of super hero fantasy." she laughs. "I mean, *The Cave*?! This is your super secret super hero headquarters, Joe. You're living in a comic book. What have you, got a costume or something with a cape and your underoos on the outside? Have you got a special secret codename or something? I bet you do."

"You know what, you're right," I answer, faking like she's just amazed me with her insight. Really, my stomach's fluttering that we're laughing and joking together. "But it's all for Danny's benefit really. He's got such a thing for super heroes that I just go along with it to keep him happy, you know?"

"Oh bull," she smiles.

"You want to know what my super hero name is? Captain Take-No-Shit. I've got the uncanny power to block it out when people start giving me shit."

She laughs and it's the sweetest sound on earth.

"So what was it you wanted to show me then?" she says.

When we turn the corner to get to the firing range, the sight of all the guns hanging on the racks turns her cold again.

"Look, before you go all 'Chuck-Heston's-The-Devil' on me, I've brought you here for a reason," I say quickly. "Tomorrow, I'm going to do potentially the stupidest thing I've ever done and while I don't want to get teary eyed and all 'last-reel-of-the-movie' about this, there's a chance I might not come back. And I'm not saying this so you'll realise you still love me and throw yourself into my arms – I'm saying it because it's the truth. We're all three of us in a lot of danger and I want to make sure you can at least look after yourself if you need to."

"Joe, no way am I firing another gun in my life. I can't believe you're asking me to do that after what I did to that man today," she says, starting to visibly tremble.

"Rach, I'm sorry to have to do this but you've got to learn how to shoot properly. It could literally save your life. When you hit Lincoln in the hand - I'm eternally grateful for it, but you were lucky as hell with that shot. Now if anything happens to me, I've told Dan to protect you with his life but you still need to learn to defend yourself, okay?"

It's not okay, of course it's not, and her eyes tell me so. But her head and a sense of self preservation prevails and she sets aside her distaste for all this, hangs her head and mutters "What do I need to do?"

I hand her a revolver and tell her that she's to keep it with her every second of every day. I tell her to wear a shoulder holster like the cops so that she's got easy access to the gun. I show her how to load the bullets into the cylinder and she takes to it surprisingly quickly. I hand her a pair of ear guards and stand her in front of one of the alleys in the firing range. I feel like I'm corrupting her but I tell myself it's all about her survival.

The first few shots she takes, she might as well have her eyes shut and they don't even hit the paper target at the end of the firing alley. When she reloads and tries again, I tell her not to move her hand when she fires as this is throwing her aim wildly off and to not squeeze the trigger so hard. She does this on her third attempt and manages to clip the bottom edge of the paper target at least. She thinks I haven't seen it but a flash of pride appears on her face for a split second.

The lightweight nature of the revolver means that she's not going to suffer too much recoil and she'll eventually develop some level of accuracy with it. It's no good over a long distance but if someone tries to hit her from distance she's as good as dead anyway. After half an hour of constantly loading and shooting, she gets to the stage where she can at least hit the target four or five shots out of six consistently.

I'm loosening the berettas up in the alley next to her when she suddenly stops firing, takes off her ear guards and turns to me. She looks at me in a way she never has before – like she's looking at someone she just met and is weighing them up. I don't think I like it.

"I just…I just can't believe this is really you, Joe. None of this seems real. The way you were in the bookstore, the way you were in the street today. You're – I don't know, you're so, well…scary. I mean, you move so fast and you're so brutal and the way you talk. It's like you're someone else."

"I *am* someone else when I'm like that Rach, believe me. But the real me hasn't got a gun in his hand. The real me has got a glass of red wine in his hand, sitting in front of the fireplace with you."

She looks down at the floor like she wishes I hadn't just said that and I feel pretty stupid for having said it. I put my guns back on the rack and head for my room.

"Listen, it's late and tomorrow's going to be one hell of a day so I'm going to turn in. You feel free to stay down here a while and keep practising but remember; that gun goes with you everywhere from now on, deal?"

She smiles weakly.

"Deal," she says. "But in return, you've got to do me a favour, will you?"

"What's that?" I ask.

"Don't get killed tomorrow," she says solemnly.

I pause.

"Well I'm not planning on," I smile.

"No, seriously. Look, I'm not saying this because I want you to come back to me and we can get things back to how they used to be because I don't think we ever can. I'm saying it because I don't want you to die. If this Stanley is the guy who trained you, I'm worried something terrible will happen. So just…just don't die tomorrow. Deal?"

"Deal," I promise her with the warmest, most confident smile I can give her.

I'd give everything I have to be able to hold her and kiss her right now but I just have to turn my back and walk away.

I'm coming for you Stanley and I'm bringing a world of fucking pain with me.

32

"CALLING ALL DICKHEADS, CALLING ALL DICKHEADS!" blares the loudspeaker on the van. "THIS IS JOE CALLING WITH A NEWS FLASH. IN OUR BREAKING STORY, IT TURNS OUT STANLEY'S BEEN THE PROPHET ALL ALONG. THAT'S RIGHT GUYS, THE HAIRY LITTLE MIDGET'S THE ONE WHO'S BEEN BUMPING US ALL OFF. NOW IF THAT ANGERS YOU AT ALL, YOU MIGHT WANT TO PUT A BULLET IN HIS HEAD AND THROW HIS WITHERED OLD CORPSE OUT ONTO THE FRONT LAWN AND SAVE ME A JOB. *OR*, YOU COULD SEND HIM OUT AND I'LL DO IT MYSELF. EITHER WAY, IF HE'S NOT OUT HERE IN FIVE MINUTES, I'M GOING TO BURN THIS ENTIRE FUCKING PLACE DOWN TO THE GROUND. THANK YOU FOR LISTENING - CLOCK'S TICKING."

Overkill maybe? Nah, at a time like this you can't afford to be subtle.

It's just after nine thirty in the morning, the sun's out and it's a dry and crisp day. At this time, The Lodge shouldn't have too many guys there but there'll be enough to give me a real headache if they don't believe me about Stanley and decide to come out shooting.

Within forty seconds, the front doors of The Lodge open and Mikey Diaz, one of the bottom feeders, steps out onto the driveway, hoists a rocket launcher up onto his shoulder and from 250 meters away, blows my van to pieces in a beautiful orange and red fireball. I retaliate by shooting him in the balls from my vantage point in the woods 'cause I'm not actually fucking dumb enough to be sitting *in* the van. He falls to his knees, screaming in pain and holding the sticky, red smear that used to be his genitals and the doors of The Lodge quickly close shut behind him.

"*FOUR* MINUTES LEFT!" I shout from the woods. "ANYONE WHO'S NOT IN THE MOOD TO BE KILLED HAS GOT THAT LONG TO HIGH TAIL IT OUT OF HERE!"

Well I guess that's a clear message about where the guys' loyalties lie. I'll just bet that Stanley's told everyone here that he knows *I'm* really The Prophet and that I'd try something like this. Just another reason to kill him, I suppose.

But see, just because I've decided to come here all headstrong and gung ho, this isn't a kamikaze mission and I have planned *some* things at least. I drove the van up the drive via remote control while I've tucked myself away with the sniper rifle in the ground's woods and so far everything's working to plan. I left Rachel safe with Danny at The Cave and he's hooked me up with a few of his new toys and I'm armed to the teeth, ready to start world war three here so that's at least a vague plan, right?

After a couple of minutes, five cars and two motorcycles drive around from the back of The Lodge and down the driveway past the burning wreck of the van. At least they've got the smarts not to get involved in any of this. It could be that they're not willing to mix it up with anyone without getting paid for it or it could be that my rep has got them scurrying away – either way works for me.

Okay, so it seems The Lodge is backing Stanley and anyone left in there is going to be thinking that I'm The Prophet so they'll be shooting to kill which means I've got to be doing the same. No warning shots, no wingers and no leg shots – every bullet's got to be a kill shot. But ironically, that's why I want to kill Stanley in the first place, so that no more people have to die so I just hope I can get to him quick before someone makes me kill them.

Five minutes is up – it's go time.

I pull one of Danny's little remote controlled cars out of my pack, set it on the ground, pull the aerial up on the remote handset and send the thing whirring and racing across the grass towards the west wall of The Lodge. Now there's a house brick sized block of semtex strapped to the little car which is not just going to take a chunk out of the wall, it's going to pretty much do away with the wall entirely and whatever happens to be twenty feet behind it too.

But see, the beauty of the plan is that I'm not actually going to enter The Lodge from the west - I'm going to come in from the south which is where Stanley's office is located to the back of Harvey's bar. I figure he'll bolt there as soon as it all goes down. The car's in place and I sprint through the woods as fast as I can on my swollen ankle to the back of the building. My adrenaline's up and as I reach for the detonator button on the remote, I realise that I'm smiling – I'm starting to enjoy myself.

I slide the AK rifle off my back ready then press the button on the handset and the quiet Westchester morning is shattered by the sweet, sweet sound of semtex. From my vantage point, I can see the smoke and debris already taking to the air and the entire building seems to shake.

I press my advantage and send a few bursts of the AK into the big glass doors at the back. There's no returning fire but I throw a couple of grenades in just in case. With all the chaos and explosions to the west and south, anyone in the building with half a brain is either heading outside now or into the middle of The Lodge which is Harvey's bar.

I sprint into the building through the opening I've made but there's nobody in the room. Waste of grenades but you never can tell. I open the door of the trashed room and it opens onto a corridor. I see a couple of people running past the left end of the corridor but they don't see me and I decide to head right. I can make out some voices shouting in panic and a whole lot of swearing.

Even though I've been coming to The Lodge for years, there's parts of it that most of us aren't allowed and I'm in an area I've never been before. Now although there's not a great amount of security here because of the fact every freelancer knows what happens if you screw with the management (which is why I must be crazy) there's still enough guys here like Larry and Pike who are going to defend the place with their last breath. See, the 'shadowy members of the management' who run the place and rent out offices to the agents are big players – and we're talking billionaire businessmen and senators here – and they'll do anything to stop the truth about The Lodge from getting out so at any given time there's always at least twenty management employees in the house.

Which means the heat is coming.

As if on cue, Johnny the Jet (an ex-boxer and B-lister) rounds the corner and starts shouting. He gets as far as "Hey guys, he's over-" before I shoot him in the face.

From around the corner, I hear at least three people responding to Johnny's call so I flip the pin on a grenade and toss it behind me as I run the other way. I know this is all suicidal but I'm having the time of my life here – I'm cool and I'm collected and I'm still smiling.

The smile gets wiped from my face real fucking suddenly though as three bolts of white fire explode into my upper back. The force sends me off my feet and I fall sprawling forwards. Only the Kevlar body armour stops the bullets going through into my spine. Luckily, I manage to twist mid fall so at least I'm facing the shooter. I've never even seen the guy before but he doesn't even look old enough to be served in Harvey's bar. He looks all shocked like as if this is the first time he's ever shot his gun.

"Don't you move, you cocksucker," he shouts unconvincingly, pointing his gun at me. Christ, I'm not even sure this kid's balls have dropped yet. No fucking way am I getting taken out by this wet nosed punk who couldn't even go for a headshot. Besides which, who's he calling a cocksucker anyway?

"There's a grenade at your feet," I wheeze, trying to get back the breath the bullets knocked out of me.

Unbelievably, the kid looks. I mean, he actually *looks*. I raise the AK and turn both his kneecaps to powder and he falls to the floor screaming in pain. I figure I've just done him a favour anyway. Besides not killing him, he didn't really seem cut out for the hitman game.

Over the noise of the kid's wailing, a faint rustling gives someone's position away behind me. I try to get up off the floor in time but a bright, red high heel shoe kicks the gun out of my hand and I hear the click of a hammer and even I'm not fast enough to get out of this one. Her little silver pistol pointed right between my eyes, The Widow comes into view and stands over me, a leg either side of my hips.

"Hey, Widow," I smile up at her. "I gotta tell you, I can think of much worse last things to see before I die," I say, looking up her dress.

I quickly contemplate trying to sweep her legs before she can fire but she bends her knees anyway and straddles me, sitting right on my crotch. She leans right over me and presses the barrel of her gun to my temple but slowly releases the hammer and puts the gun down.

"Relax, Joe," she purrs huskily. She moves her face inches from mine and her jet black hair falls over me and I can smell an intoxicating mix of sex and spice on her. "*I'm* not going to kill you but there's plenty of guys here who will. I've never kissed a living dead man before and besides - I've wanted to do this for years," she says, then opens her full, red lips and kisses me passionately on the mouth.

Now I know I'm a married man and all and I still love Rachel despite the fact that she hates my guts but given the current climate with my marriage and the fact that The Widow might be right and I could be dead in minutes (and nearly just was) I allow the kiss to linger a little longer than it probably should. The Widow probes my mouth with her tongue and grinds herself onto my crotch and amidst the smoke, danger and screams of pain coming from ten feet away, I find myself getting a king sized fucking hard on.

She senses my tension and breaks the kiss and stands over me again, looking like a dusky and sexy angel of death. Man, I'm so turned on right now.

"Mmm," she says, licking her lips. "It was worth the wait. Look me up if you survive, big man," she says, then walks away down the corridor, hips wiggling. She casually shoots the kneecaped kid in the head as she walks past, turns, blows me a kiss, then disappears around the corner.

Wow - that might just be the weirdest thing that's ever happened to me. I hope to God I survive this, if only so I can spend the rest of my life telling that story!

I stand up and readjust li'l Joey (because a Kevlar cup and a hard on don't really go together) pick up the AK then head down towards Harvey's. Once I get there, I take a deep breath, then open the doors.

Suddenly, it's like all my fucking Christmases have come at once, I mean, really. There's five guys in the middle of the room – Georgie Deacon, Piranha Sam, Redneck Tex and two complete strangers– and they've pushed all the tables and chairs over to make a five foot barricade and they're stood behind it, guns ready, looking over the top and waiting for me.

Only problem is, the fucking barricade's facing the front doors to the bar and I've just come in through the back doors! They've all got their backs to me.

Oh God, I can't resist it.

"Behind you, assholes," I call out.

The look on their collective faces as they whip 'round is totally worth the risk. I mean, if I *am* going to die now, it's abso*lutely* been worth it just to savour those looks. Priceless. I empty everything that's left in the AK into them and it's all I can do not to laugh maniacally. Man, that's two unbelievable stories I can tell in as many minutes.

I drop the empty AK and pull out the faithful twin berettas. Just in time too as the guy everyone knows as Crazy Hal jumps up from behind the bar and just misses my head with a wild shot. I return fire but he ducks back behind the bar. I unpin three grenades and toss them over the top, almost wistfully thinking about the good times I've had here over the years in the bar that is literally going up in smoke now as shards of wood fill the room.

Everything goes quiet for a second and I enter the bar properly and head for the side door which leads to Stanley's office. In all the excitement, I'd almost forgotten why I was here in the first place. Then I remember that my agent and mentor has ruined my life and that I'm about to turn into the spirit of fucking vengeance for that and I'm suddenly filled with more excitement than when The Widow was sat on top of me.

Stanley's office used to be a stock room for Harvey's bar, which is why it's situated just off to the side. I know Stanley'll be in there, cowering behind his desk because he knows that I'll be out for blood now and he's seen me like this once before. Still, he's not stupid enough not to have rigged some sort of trap so it'd be suicide to go down there. Even so, it's like I can't stop my hand from reaching for the door handle. Before I can even turn the handle, the door suddenly explodes outwards, lifting me off my feet and sending me sprawling back into the bar, both guns spinning out of my hands. The world rotates for a minute and my face is on fire as shards of wood cut into my skin. Luckily, none of it has gone in my eyes but I can barely see anyway unless you count all the stars. The door hangs crazily on its hinges and smoke pours out of the corridor behind it. It's this waiting for the smoke to clear that gives me the few seconds I need to crawl behind the bar before I hear Stanley come out looking for a corpse. I decide to give him one as I hear his footsteps getting closer.

I grab Crazy Hal – his face littered with still smoking metal, just like mine is with wood – and throw his body out to the side. Stanley takes the opportunity to fill Hal's corpse with buckshot as I leap over the bar at him.

Only it's not Stanley – it's DeLaney. Stanley must have bought him off.

He tries to bring his shotgun around onto me but he's not quick enough and I'm already on him. We tumble to the floor together but he reacts quicker than I thought and brings the butt of his gun smashing into my cheek. He hasn't got the leverage to make it a really good swing but that, coupled with all the wood still sticking out of me, makes my head feel like it's been used like a fucking bowling ball.

I try to retaliate with an elbow to his neck but he blocks it easily as I'm just too groggy to really do any damage. I know I've got to keep close to him or I'm dead so I grab him around the waist even though this leaves my back exposed.

He takes my bait and tries to land a couple of kidney punches but all he ends up doing is punching Kevlar. I don't know much about DeLaney but I know that he's a weapons man, not really a hand to hander. He looks like he's got some oriental moves but he's not a brawler and a brawl is what I need this fight to be.

I bring the back of my head flying up and catch him sweetly on his chin. This staggers him a little but I can't press my advantage 'cause I'm still even more staggered than him. I try to bring a knee up to his balls but end up just grazing his inner thigh.

Unfortunately, this gives him a chance to pull a little flick knife from out of his belt and he jams it right into my left shoulder. The pain from this sears and burns up my arm and shoulder like hellfire.

But then he makes a mistake – instead of trying to finish me by hand while he's winning, he goes for his shotgun on the floor. I reach around the back with my good right hand, yank the knife out of my shoulder and before I can even yell in pain, I throw the knife as hard as I can and it hits DeLaney square in his throat.

He falls to the floor, clutching feebly at the knife but it's gone right through his windpipe. He flaps about almost comically as bubbles of blood burst from his mouth. He'll be dead in moments but I pick up the shotgun he's panic- strickenly scrambling for and help him on his way by shooting him double tap in the head.

Before I can even gather myself, I hear footsteps charging down the corridor from Stanley's office. I know there's no more ammo left in the shotgun so I hurl it at the doorway like a javelin, just as Stanley comes running in – and it *is* him this time.

"Die, you Motherfucker!" he bellows, the gun in his good hand blazing. With beautiful, almost precision timing, the second he appears in the frame of the door he has to duck to avoid the gun from smacking him right in the face which puts him off balance and he careens into the room, by which point I'm already almost on top of him.

He regains his footing quickly enough to try and raise his gun back at me but it's too late – I'm on him. I knock the gun out of his hand, block his feeble attempt at a punch, grab him by his throat and pin him against the bar wall, smashing most of the bottles in the process. I slap him hard across the face with all the hate I've been building up the last forty eight hours. It's a temptation just to break his neck now but I have to know why.

"Man, you're fucking pathetic," I spit. "No wonder you never took on any real threats. You're just a withered old fuck who's too scared and angry at the world to do anything else."

I slap him across the face again, not even honouring him with a punch. But instead of getting angry or pleading or anything else I imagined happening in this moment, Stanley starts to cry. Real tears come running from under his bushy, white eyebrows.

"Why?" he whispers.

"What?!" I answer, unbelievingly.

"Why did you do it?" he whimpers, unable to even look at me.

"What the fuck are you talking about?" I ask him.

"Why did you kill my fucking wife, Joe!" he rages suddenly through the tears and blood. "At least after all these fucking years, tell me that!"

Okay, I'll admit – I didn't see that one coming.

"What?! I didn't kill your wife. You're the asshole that tried to have *my* wife killed, or have you forgotten that?"

Genuine confusion slowly dawns over both of us.

"You're fucking crazy, Joe," he says. "I didn't even know you *had* a wife. You never told me anything about your personal life in all these years."

"Hey, I don't even know for sure that you've got a wife either and if you *did*, I wouldn't be able to pick her out of a goddamned line up. What the hell makes you think *I* fucking killed her anyway?" I shout back.

"Danny!" he shouts, struggling to break free. "Your little fucking tech buddy sent me an email this morning. I open it up and there's a fucking video of you shooting my beautiful Carolina as clear as day, you sick fucking bastard." He starts crying again. "Why'd you do that, Joe? Why?"

"I'm telling you, Stanley, I've never killed a woman my entire life, let alone your wife. It wasn't me, man," I answer, trying to shake some sense into him. "I got a message from Danny telling me that you were The Prophet and you'd killed Bear – he had a video of you doing it too. I came over here to confront you about it only to find that you'd put out a million dollar contract on *my* wife."

A penny slowly starts to drop for both of us. He looks me sincerely in the eyes and if he's lying, he deserves an Oscar.

"Joe," he says earnestly. "I didn't put out a hit on your wife, I swear to you. I think we've both been played."

Oh God.

Danny.

And I just left Rachel with him.

33

I thunder back the way I just came with Stanley running behind me, his stumpy little legs struggling to keep up.

"Joe, slow down," he wheezes. "I can't keep up."

"No time, man. Listen, where's your car?" I ask, leaping over the corpse of the kneeless and now faceless kid from the corridor.

"Out back in the lot but where are we going?"

Before I can answer, the human brick wall that is Pike erupts from a side door and his enormous paws wrap around my throat and he slams me into the wall before I can even think. He squeezes the air out of me and I start blacking out immediately. Stanley makes a move like he's going to attack him but Pike turns to glare at him.

"Don't move, Stanley," he grunts. "Or I'll break his neck." Pike turns to look at me. "Do you know who The Prophet is?" he asks angrily.

I barely manage to grunt 'yes' and his grip eases.

"I really should kill you, Joe," he says. "And this might cost me my job, but if I let you go you gotta promise me you'll kill The Prophet, whoever it is. Just promise me that, man 'cause I've already lost too many good friends around here."

Pike takes his enormous hands from around my throat and sets me slowly back down on the floor.

"Trust me, Pike," I answer, trying to rub some air back into my neck. "He'll be dead by the time you cxplain this away."

"Good," he says and he lets us go.

We leave Pike and run out through the south entrance and make for the parking lot out to the east side.

"Which one's yours?" I ask Stanley.

"This one," he replies, standing next to a shiny, black pickup truck. He's standing by the driver's side and is fishing the keys out of his pocket.

"Forget it, pops," I say, grabbing the keys from his hands and muscling past him into the driver's seat. "The way you drive, we'd be better off walking."

Stanley mutters and grumbles but climbs into the passenger seat anyway. I floor the pickup across the lawns, sending grass and soil tearing into the air. As we speed down the driveway and away from The Lodge, I take a look back in the rear view mirror. The building's smoking, missing a west wall and the grounds are torn to shit - I don't think I'll be welcome back here ever again.

With a curious sense of déjà vu, I floor the gas on the car, weaving in and out of the morning traffic to rush and save my wife from being killed. Stanley looks terrified next to me but knows better than to say anything about the driving.

"So why would Danny do it?" he asks eventually.

"Honestly?" I answer. "I don't have a fucking clue. When I thought it was you, I thought you were doing it to thin out the competition from other agents and that's why only pussies were killed."

"As well as being offensive, that's just about the dumbest thing I've ever heard. You really thought I'd kill guys I've known for years, just to help business pick up, you asshole?" Stanley sputters.

"Alright, okay, I'm sorry," I say, narrowly avoiding the side of a truck with a quick swerve of the wheel. "Look, I don't even know for sure it is Danny."

"Riiight," Stanley says. "That's why you're driving like a frigging maniac here. I know you don't want to hear it but your prick buddy has fucked you over. You ask me, he's been trying to get some payback from the guys because he's never been accepted at The Lodge. Shit, half the guys he killed were ones who used to laugh at him whenever he came down. It makes perfect sense."

My blood runs cold as I realise Stanley's theory does make sense when I stop and think about it. Danny hasn't been to The Lodge in years because some of the guys there would pick on him and shit – real high school stuff. He was always okay when he was with me but this one time he'd been there a few years back on his own and I remember something must have happened because he said he was never going back and he was going to work out of The Cave from then on and he has done ever since. Shit, maybe that's it. I just never even suspected it might be Dan – he's never been violent at all but at least now the stuff about bumping off the weaker ones would make sense.

"So when he thinks you're getting close to rumbling him, he sets the shit up about me being The Prophet and puts the hit on your other half to keep you occupied," Stanley continues. "Either way he's killed my wife, Joe, and he might be doing the same to yours right now so your best friend or not, I'm going to kill him."

"Hey, you're not going to do a fucking thing, okay?" I growl. "I know you think he's killed your wife and I appreciate you want blood here but until I clear all this up you're not going to touch him Stan, alright?"

He folds his arms and turns his head away like a petulant kid.

"I notice you were quick enough to come looking for *my* head when you thought it was me," he mutters under his breath. "And we'll see what happens if he *has* killed *your* wife."

Please God, let him be wrong. I can't lose my wife and best friend in the same day.

By the time we reach The Cave, Stanley's truck looks like a bumper car which he whines about until I tell him to shut the fuck up. He follows me into the dusty, disused warehouse and I ignore all his questions until we reach the entrance panel on the back wall.

As I scan my hand and the steel door slides open to reveal the corridor inside, Stanley lets out a whistle of astonishment. "Wow, pretty impressive hideout, Joe," he says. "Always did wonder what you spent all your money on."

I ignore him and bolt down the corridor towards The Nest, the games room and the room where Rachel was sleeping. I kick open the door to The Nest, my heart in my throat, but there's nobody in there. All the monitors have still been left on though and I call out but there's no answer.

My head's telling me that Danny's known Rach for years and has never even so much as spoken badly about her so would never hurt her but the events of the last few days have got my head spinning and I can't help but think the worst. My head's telling me that no way has Danny been The Prophet this whole time but there's a real bad feeling in my heart.

"Jesus, how big *is* this place?" Stanley asks. "Listen, I'll head off right, you go left and whoever finds Danny first gives a yell, okay? Let me have one of your guns too, I'm not armed."

"No way," I answer. "If you find Danny first you'll put a bullet in him and I already told you, we don't know anything for definite."

"Fuck that, Joe. What if he *is* The Prophet, he'll kill me for sure if I've got no weapon."

"Stanley, no way am I giving you a gun, man. Just come back and get me if you see anything, alright? I'll meet you back here in five minutes."

Stanley heads off down towards the Gymnasium and the storage rooms, still muttering to himself, and I sprint the other way down towards the bedrooms and the firing range. I burst through the bedroom and that's empty too but I can still smell Rach's perfume so she wasn't here too long ago.

Suddenly, I hear a gunshot and my guts turn to white. I draw my beretta and tear down towards the range, my mind racing.

The firing range is completely sound proofed so why did I just hear a shot? Why haven't they heard me calling? What the hell am I going to do if Danny has just killed Rachel?

I round the corner and see the door to the firing range is open and Danny is standing there with a colt revolver smoking in his hand.

"Drop the fucking gun, Danny!" I shout, bringing my beretta up and aiming it at his head.

Danny looks up quickly, shock registering on his face. He brings his own gun up quickly and points it back at me. Fuck. I should have taken him out as soon as he moved but I couldn't bring myself to and now we're aiming right at each other.

"Joe?" he says meekly, looking genuinely afraid. "What's going on? What the fuck are you doing?"

"Just drop your fucking gun, Danny. Now!" I yell back.

"Y-you drop yours first," he stutters. "Why are you fucking pointing yours at me anyway?"

"Where's Rachel?" I ask, fearing the answer.

"Rachel? She was just here a few minutes ago," Danny answers, his hands trembling now. "We were just having target practice. What the hell's going on, man?"

Before I can even make sense of any of this, two shots ring out from behind me and burst bloodily into Danny's chest and he falls to the floor like a puppet with its strings cut. I whip around on my heel, my gun pointed forward but I already know what I'll see. Stanley's got his one withered arm wrapped tight around Rachel's neck and the other is holding a gun to her temple. I can't see enough of Stanley to even risk a shot – he's angled Rach so she's covering the whole of him, which is exactly how he once taught me to hold a hostage. There's a nasty cut on Rachel's head that's bleeding down the side of her face and she's crying hard.

"Put the gun down, Joe!" Stanley shouts from behind Rachel.

"You fucking hurt her and you're dead," I shout back, looking for even an inch of Stanley sticking out that I could take a shot at but there isn't one.

"I don't want to hurt her Joe, really I don't, but if you don't toss your gun to my feet right now I'll turn her head into a fucking smear, believe me. You've got three seconds. One…"

I toss my gun at him before he even gets to two.

"And the other one, Joe, I'm not fucking stupid," he says. "Slowly now."

I unholster the second beretta and contemplate taking a shot but there's no way I'd hit anything other than Rachel.

"You're fucking stupid if you think I'm going to let you walk out of here alive," I say, tossing the second gun at his feet and holding my hands up in the air. Stanley slams the butt of his pistol on the back of Rachel's skull and her now limp body crumples to the floor. I instinctively move forward to try and catch her, anger and fear making my chest tight, but Stanley quickly points the gun at me and I freeze.

"Don't move, Joe. Seriously, don't make me put a bullet in you." Stanley says, cocking the hammer of the pistol.

I do as he says and stand still, my arms held up.

"What the fuck is going on, Stanley?" I ask. "I don't understand what's happening here."

"That's always been your problem, Joe," he smiles back at me. "You've always been a better fighter than a thinker. And I know you'd twist my head off in a second if you could right now but just listen for a minute and I'll tell you everything, alright? Yeah, okay, *I'm* The Prophet. And I know - it sounds like something from a bad movie doesn't it, but I wanted a mysterious sounding name for this character I was going to create."

"Character?!" I yell back at him. "What the fuck are you, insane? Wait a minute, of course you are. You just shot my best friend and now he's bleeding out in the corner and you've spent the last six months killing hitmen. Only a fucking madman would go about randomly murdering people, right?"

Stanley laughs and there's a hint of mania in there.

"Jesus, Joe, surely you of all people can see the irony in that. But there was nothing random in the guys I killed," he replies.

"No, they were all pussies, right?" I smile back, hoping to rile him like I did Lincoln. "That the pattern? You only took out the guys you could manage with that crooked leg of yours and that twisted fucking stump you call a hand?"

The smile drops from Stanley's face for just a flash but then it's back, his eyes glittering madly underneath his bushy eyebrows. Fuck, I hope Danny's not dead. I can't believe Stanley fucking suckered me in like this.

"Good try, Joe, trying to rattle your opponent. But don't forget who taught you that one, huh? And I can still use this 'twisted stump' to blow your ass away," Stanley smirks. "But you hear me out and maybe I won't have to. You're looking for a motive to all this madness? Well let me give you one. All those guys I killed as The Prophet were guys nobody was going to miss. I mean, The Priest, Frankie Slater, all those other guys? Who the hell is going to shed a tear over them? But the reason I did it in the first place, the reason I even created The Prophet, was to put the fear of God back into the community."

"Don't you get it yet, Joe?" he continues, his voice rising maniacally. "The fucking *management* paid me to do it! You know as well as I do, The Lodge has been run for generations by the leaders of this country – senators, politicians, businessmen. Shit, there's even a goddamn ex-president on the committee. And in all those years of business, The Lodge has only ever used the elite of highly trained killers. Animals, man – the best of the best. So when suddenly they look around and see fucking bottom feeders like Grey and Slater have somehow made their way onto the books, watering down the talent and making them look bad? The New York Lodge was quickly becoming the laughing stock of the franchise and there was even talk of the California chapter becoming the new head office so they figure they've got to stop the rot, which is where I come in. They paid me to trim the fucking fat, man, and *that's* why I only killed the pussies on the books. Then I came up with the whole Prophet myth which was designed to frighten any other pussies away. If they were going to leave the business on account of some boogeyman then we didn't fucking need them anyway and all we'd be left with was the hardened killers. This was all just good business."

"Good fucking business?" I snarl. I move slightly and Stanley moves the gun with me, keeping it squarely at my head. "Fuck, Stan, why not just give them a month's pay and send them home? There's gotta be easier ways of getting rid of staff. But okay, so that's why. Clearing the deck of the weak ones. Mystery solved, right? Good for the management. But why Bear, huh? Why kill Bear when he was one of the best hitmen we had?" I ask.

"Look, I liked Bear almost as much as you did," Stanley says and I nearly make a lunge for him then and there. "He was a great guy but he had to die because although he was certainly no pussy he was about to start writing a fucking expose, man! Like some of these ex-mafia types that write their fucking memoirs or some shit and reveal all the secrets of their dirty past? Well no way could the management have him doing shit like that, just no way. So I'm real sorry, Joe, but he had to go."

"No, Stanley, he didn't," I counter, and I don't think I've ever hated anyone as much as I hate Stanley right now. "You could have just fucking warned him off. You didn't have to kill him, you withered little prick!"

"Look, I'm sorry I killed him, man, I really am," he says. "Killing Bear was what set you on The Prophet's trail and I know that when you get really determined like that, nothing stops you and I just couldn't have you finding me out. Hell, the management even wanted me to kill *you* at one point but I told them I wouldn't do it."

"Oh, you want me to come over there, shake your hand and buy you a fucking beer?" I ask sarcastically. "Fuck you. You killed my friend. And for what? Money?"

"Hey, there's more going on here than just money," Stanley answers. "Why do you think nobody I represent got killed, not even you? The management told me that if I killed who I liked they'd make me a junior partner. Can you fucking imagine that? I'd be running the whole Lodge, not just working out of some back office. I've been dreaming about this for years, man."

"So why Rachel?" I ask.

"What?" Stanley says, looking confused.

"Rachel!" I roar. "My fucking wife! The woman I love more than anything in this world who you just fucking cold cocked and is lying on the floor at your feet, maybe dead. I swear, Stanley, if she's anything other than unconscious..."

346

"Relax, I didn't hit her that hard," Stanley says and I'm wondering why he hasn't just killed me yet. "But I'm sorry she got involved in this. As soon as management knew you were looking to find out who The Prophet was, they checked out your background, found out about your wife and made me put the contract out on her for two reasons. One was they thought it would keep you distracted from digging too deep and finding me out but the other reason - the more important one - is that they wanted you with no ties. And here it comes, Joey boy. They want to make you an offer, see? They know now that you're the best and they want you on an exclusive contract as their number one hitman, representing the whole of the New York chapter. They're offering you a hundred million dollars and your pick of the new contracts!"

It takes me a second to digest this shit but only a second. Stanley slowly lowers his gun and grins at me.

"Look, I'm sorry about Bear. I'm sorry that I just shot Danny. And I'm sorry about your wife, okay. But think about it – a hundred mil straight off and all you have to do is be their new strong arm and restore pride in the New York chapter. If you agree to this, you'll be set for life," he says, getting excited now.
I pause.

"That's an interesting turn of phrase," I answer. "Set for life. It's interesting you see because *that's* my life lying there on the floor. That woman represents everything that was ever good in my life and now she knows the truth about me she hates my guts and so the one thing that *truly* had me set for life – my wife and my marriage – is gone and you and your precious fucking management took that away from me. And that's why you can stick your bullshit offer and your money up your ass."

"I'm sorry to hear that, Joey, I really am," Stanley says solemnly. "You were always the closest thing I ever had to a son but I won't let you ruin things for me. And that's why you've got to die now."

Stanley raises the gun again and I know I'll never reach him before he can get a shot off but I make a try for it anyway. As he raises his arm, an ear shattering scream splits the air.

"Nooo!" she cries desperately and her scream shakes Stanley for just that split second but it's long enough for Rachel to spring up from the floor and make a grab for his gun.

Time slows as I run.

My heart stops beating.

The world stops.

In a two second span that seems like an eternity, Stanley struggles with Rachel as she wildly tries to take the gun off him. He's panicked because he can see me running towards him and as much as Rach's attack threw him off, he's too strong for her.

He pushes her away from him, lifts the gun and shoots her in the head.

Stanley lets out a squeal of panic as he tries to bring the gun round in time but it's too late – I'm on him now. I smash my fist into his face and before he can even fall backwards I grab him in my arms and snap his neck, practically tearing his head back 180 degrees.

If this was the movies, there'd be a prolonged fistfight now with both of us trading punches and kicks. But this isn't a movie. Instead, it's all over in seconds and a dreadful quiet falls over the place and I'm left standing alone.

I drop to my knees and call Rachel's name, cradling her in my arms. Her head lolls lifelessly on her neck and I rock back and forth with her, tears streaming down my face.

Then I do something I've never done before - I pray. My whole life, whenever things got bad - either when I was a kid and my old man was beating shit out of my mother and me or when I was an adult and being tortured nearly to death and guns pushed in my face – I never prayed once. Not just because I don't believe in God in the first place 'cause anyone will pray when the chips are down but I never wanted anyone's help. I've always just relied on myself to get myself out of shit but now I pray hard with everything I've got.

And maybe the big guy's listening or maybe he figures that I've saved up all my miracles over the years and can cash them all in at once but either way, Rach takes a breath and it's the most incredible sound I've ever heard. She groans in my arms and I look closer at her head. It's bleeding pretty bad but the bullet must have only grazed her skull and she's still alive. Thank God. Thank Buddah and Allah and anyone else who's listening.

"Danny?" I call out, hoping against hope that they're still listening but with fear gripping my chest in case they're not. "Sound off, man!"

From the other side of the range, I see his body stir and he rolls over on his side, letting out a moan of pain.

Two for two. I think I just turned religious.

I lift Rach up in my arms, being careful not to move her head too much and walk over to Dan. He slowly sits up, pulling his shirt over his head and there's a Kevlar vest underneath that's soaked up the two bullets to his chest.

"I've been wearing this fucking heavy ass vest ever since I first heard about The Prophet but now I'm fucking glad I..." Danny trails off as he looks up. He looks shocked when he sees Rach bleeding from a head wound but he looks even more shocked when he sees me.

"Joe," he says, stunned. "You're – you're crying. I've never seen you cry before."

"I can't lose her, man. I just can't lose her," I answer, tears still streaming down my face.

"We've got to get her to a hospital, right now," Danny grunts as he stands up.

We race down to the garage and Danny jumps into the driver's seat of an armoured truck like the one I drove to The Lodge in earlier. I move Rach gently into the passenger side and climb in after her, cradling her in my arms the whole time and I can see blood soaking into my sleeve.

Danny floors the truck, screeching through the underground garage and up the ramp out into the street, narrowly avoiding an oncoming car. He speeds in and out of traffic, making for the hospital as quick as he can.

I just keep cradling my wife and praying for one last miracle.

EPILOGUE

It's been five days and I've barely left her side.

The doctors say that she'll survive – the shot to the head was enough to splinter her skull but an inch to the other side and it would have ripped through her brain. They say the wound isn't life threatening but until she wakes up, they won't be sure of the extent of the damage.

I told the doctors Rach'd been mugged and shot and after a little chat with the cops, I was left to just haunt these hospital corridors. I've been back home once since the incident with Stanley just to grab a shower and a change of clothes but I've been staying at the hospital since. I haven't thought about any of what went on that day. I haven't thought about anything but Rachel. One thing I do know is that I've really developed a skill at crying (seems I can't fucking stop now I've started) and I've been making up for lost time with the big man because I've been praying pretty much non-stop since that morning in the firing range.

Janet and Ray have visited every day since they found out. Times like this makes you realise that as flawed as they are, they're good friends, you know? Danny's been by a couple of times too to see how Rach is doing. He's still sulking about the fact that I believed Stanley over him but he's been pretty good about it overall – it's just me who feels like shit for not believing my best friend. He's gotten rid of Stanley's body and has leaked word to everyone at The Lodge about him being The Prophet but I haven't left here yet to see what the fall out of that has been. Christ, I don't even know what day it is today. Besides, all that shit can wait until Rach is in the clear.

I tend to spend most of my days sitting by Rach's bedside either sleeping, reading the paper or mostly, just looking at her. I hold her hand and talk to her and I always saw people talking to unconscious loved ones lying in hospital beds in the movies and thought how stupid it looked but it really does help. Essentially though, what I'm feeling is guilt – overwhelming guilt.

And it's a new sensation to be honest. All these years lying to her, yeah, okay, I felt guilty about the lies and all but I was always able to justify it away in my infinite arrogance. But now that my life and my lies have come to Rachel's door and she's ended up here in hospital having been shot in the head, I'm coming to terms with what the word *'guilt'* really means.

It's evening of the fifth day and I'm down in the hospital canteen getting a coffee when one of the staff nurses comes rushing up to me and grabs my arm.

"Mr McLean," she says hurriedly. "Come quickly, it's your wife. She's awake."

I'm running by the time she's finished her sentence.

As I speed through the hospital corridors to the ward, a thought races through my head that I'm not proud of but can't stop it coming in. See, I can't help but wish that the bullet's given Rach brain damage and she's suffered memory loss and can't remember a single thing about the last week. It's ridiculous, naïve, selfish, childish and horrible but I can't help wishing it.

I throw open the doors to Rachel's room and it's the most amazing sight in the world - she's sat up in bed and a nurse is feeding her water from a glass. I dash across the room and fall to my knees by her bedside and grab her hand and kiss it and stand and kiss her and hold her in my arms.

The nurse laughs and smiles and tells me not to be too rough as Rachel's still very delicate. A team of doctors rush in and bustle me out of the way. I stand back as they spend the next twenty minutes checking Rach over, shining a light in her eyes and asking her questions and generally doing doctor-y stuff and so on. I stand in the corner of the room (suppressing those damn tears) and just stare, a big dopey grin plastered across my face.

Eventually, nearly half an hour later, the doctors give her the okay and leave. When they do, I feel like I want them to stay 'cause I'm so nervous about not knowing what comes next. There's nothing I can do though as the last one leaves, closes the door behind him and leaves the world's most awkward silence.

It's a silence that stretches between us and hangs and hovers and sits heavy in the air. Finally, Rach breaks it.

"The flowers are nice," she says weakly. I can tell this is small talk because the room looks like a florist exploded in it and 'nice' isn't a word that she'd normally use to describe a tsunami of flowers.

"Yeah, I had them delivered from that florists you love by the park," I answer awkwardly.

The silence returns, even heavier than before.

"How are you feeling?" I ask dumbly.

"I've been shot in the head, Joe, so, you know, not great," she says sarcastically. She immediately regrets it though and lowers her eyes.

Well, there goes my little amnesia fantasy.

"Look, Rach, I'm not sure what to say here," I stumble. "Stanley's dead," I say flatly.

"*You* killed him?" she asks.

"Yeah," I answer. "But I promise you, he's the last guy I'll ever kill." And when I tell her that, I mean it.

"Look, I still can't fully process everything you told me about yourself and I can't condone you being a killer, Joe. But just this once I'm glad 'cause that old guy was a fucking asshole."

I laugh out loud – can't help myself. Rach smiles weakly but it's a sad smile.

"Look, Joe, nothing's changed here. I'm still…"

I cut across her.

"Rach, you saved my life back there in The Cave," I protest, standing up and pacing the room now. "Stanley was going to shoot me and you screamed out and you threw yourself in front of the gun. You sacrificed yourself for me and you nearly died. You got shot in the head because you were trying to save my life, which is the second time you've done that by the way so you can't tell me you don't love me still."

"You're right, Joe. I do still love you," she says and her eyes well up with tears. My head goes light and my stomach fills with firecrackers.

"But I'm not *in* love with you any more," she says.

The firecrackers get replaced by cold, squirming worms.

"I've loved you since the first moment of the first day we met," she says and tears start to run down her face. "and when I thought that guy was going to kill you, I couldn't stand the thought of it and I knew I had to do something to keep from losing the man that I love. But I told you before, you're not that guy anymore. Not to me you're not. That Joe is just a memory now. But I still think you're one of the good guys. It's not just the killing stuff – I honestly believe *you* think you're fully justified in doing what you do and after that story with the girl and her baby, I'd be hard pushed to persuade you otherwise. And I believe you when you tell me you'd give it all up and never kill again. But it's the lies, Joe. I've spent every moment since we met loving and you've spent every moment lying."

"But now everything's out there, don't you see?" I plead to her. "I'm laid bare now, no more lies. You know everything there is to know, I promise."

I reach over and grab her hand in mine.

"Please, Rach, I'm begging you. I love you and there's no *me* without you. I'm more sorry than I know how to put into words about everything – the lies, the bookstore, the danger and now this. But please, I will spend every waking moment from now until the end of time making up for this and making you love me again."

I lean in close to her, breathing hard and crying myself in what's turning out to be a habit forming display of emotion. I lean in and we kiss for the first time since the day the store burned down.

But it's not a kiss of redemption and passion.

It's a kiss of goodbye.

I break away from her and stand up and I feel like being sick.

"I'm so sorry, Joe," Rach cries, her eyes full of sorrow. "I'm just so sorry."

I want to say a million things. I want to plead and beg and shout and punch and kill Stanley again and yell, but I don't. Instead, I put my hand to her cheek and wipe away her tears and softly say;

"No *I'm* sorry, Rach. More sorry than I can ever tell you. I've always loved you and I'll always miss you,"

I lean over and kiss her one last time on the forehead.

"Goodbye," I whisper softly.

I walk out of the room and close the door behind me on the one beautiful and golden thing that ever touched my life.

I wander out of the hospital in a daze, like I'm sleepwalking. I can't think straight and the cold night air hits me like a sledgehammer.

So what do I do now? She's gone – I've lost her. And it looks like I've got to start getting used to that.

So not only is my wife gone but so's one of my best friends. Plus I've had to kill my agent and surrogate father figure.

But I've still got Danny. Bless that guy, he never changes although I know I've got some serious apologising and making up to do with him.

But, you know, maybe it's time for me to become a better person. Maybe all this has been life's way of telling me I gotta go straight and stop the killing. Get a dog and a real job perhaps.

Or maybe. Maybe I should go looking for those management fuckers at The Lodge for some payback.

Who knows?